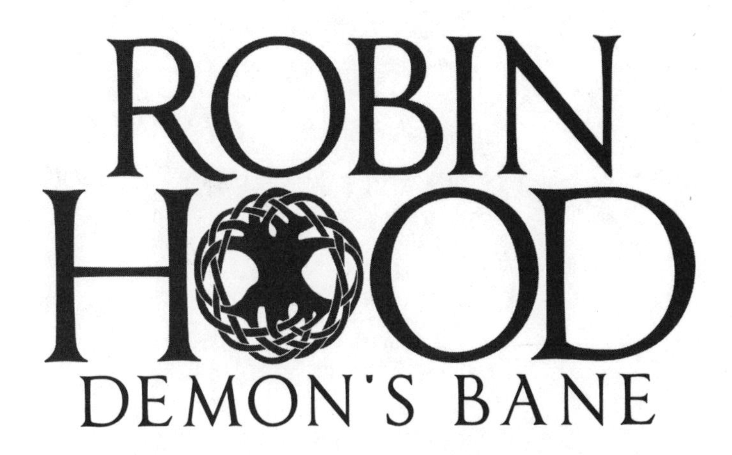

SOVEREIGN'S WAR

DEBBIE VIGUIÉ ✦ JAMES R. TUCK

TITAN BOOKS

ROBIN HOOD: DEMON'S BANE

SOVEREIGN'S WAR

Print edition ISBN: 9781783294404
Electronic edition ISBN: 9781783294411

Published by Titan Books
A division of Titan Publishing Group Ltd
144 Southwark Street, London SE1 0UP

First edition: August 2017
2 4 6 8 10 9 7 5 3 1

Visit our website: www.titanbooks.com

A CIP catalogue record for this title is available from the British Library.

Printed and bound in the United States.

To all of our readers, you truly are our band of Merry Men.
Thanks for going on this journey with us.
–DV

Dedicated to the Missus, the light in a dark Sherwood.
–JRT

PROLOGUE

The room was dark and filled with the sour iron stink of old blood and unwashed men.

He pushed himself up slowly, each hitching movement bringing a new version of pain that lit him up inside. It felt like old pain he'd lived with for years, as if it had set up home in his body. It was the deep ache of bruise and cut and scrape, not the grinding agony of a broken bone or the cold penetrating sharpness of a stab or puncture.

He'd survived worse. Of course, he'd been younger then.

Some meager light filtered into the cell allowing him to see that other men—men who'd traveled with him, been with him at war in God's Name—were now imprisoned with him. He would ask the count once his head stopped throbbing.

Damn barbarians with their damned war hammers.

He would also ask how long he'd been unconscious.

Long enough for the battle to be lost by them, to be brought wherever here was, and then locked up. From the steadiness of the ground he knew they were on land, and not sea. The living shadows that had seemed to overtake them with the ambush did not seem present, though. Only normal shadows existed in this dark and dank place.

Once his back was against the damp stone wall a voice came from nearby.

"Finally back among the living."

He blinked. Even if he hadn't recognized his friend's voice, there was no mistaking his noble features, even in the deplorable conditions they found themselves in.

"I am, Milord."

"Use my name," his friend chided.

He grunted, half from the pain, half from annoyance at the persistence.

"Richard the Lionheart," he responded, "you will always be my lord and liege above all else."

"So, I should refer to you as 'Lord Longstride,' despite the circumstances we find ourselves in?"

"Don't be ridiculous."

"Don't be ridiculous... what?"

"Don't be ridiculous... Richard."

The king's teeth gleamed in the low light. "I would never, my friend Philemon, I am the soul of propriety."

"You are very cheery for a sovereign imprisoned by a madman."

"I wouldn't consider myself a madman." The voice broke in from outside the bars of the cell. Instantly the men around them who were able rose to their feet, many of them cursing under their breath. Philemon Longstride was right there with them.

King Richard remained sitting on the ground.

The man on the other side of the bars stood in hobnailed boots of the Roman fashion, all leather straps and buckles to the knee. A heavy horsehide cape with a wide collar made of wolf fur hung over a simple square tunic of wool, held there by a thick gold chain clasp. He stood solid and built low to the ground, but with the wild ranginess of the wolf whose fur he wore. The tunic was belted with a wide strip of stiffened leather, and even in his own keep he wore an arms-length, wide-bladed sword and a short hawkbilled axe, ready at hand.

He stroked his plaited beard, fingers laden with heavy rings worn between swollen knuckles.

"You do not stand in the presence of your better?" He spoke to Richard.

"You're nobody's better, you vicious little *cur.*" Philemon lunged, reaching through the bars.

The man ducked back, twisting away so that Philemon's fingers merely scraped along his tunic. His heavy knuckled hand clamped on Philemon's wrist and he pulled, slamming Philemon's face against the bar, teeth chiming against iron. With his other hand he pulled out the hawkbilled axe, and he drove the heavy ash handle against Philemon's arm, sending him to his knees inside the cell.

"I am a cur and a mongrel, and yet you are the beasts in my pen." He shoved Philemon back, letting him stumble between men stunned by the ferocity of the maneuver. "Stick it out again and I will cut it off."

"Leave him be." King Richard spoke up.

"You do not command here. You are my prisoner, Lionheart."

"And I can tell that brings you much joy, Wulfhere."

"*King* Wulfhere."

"You are no king," Philemon spat. "A mere robber baron, and a pagan to boot!"

"You say pagan as if it is a bad thing, Christ-worshiper."

"Barbarian."

"I have carved out my holding here, and I am lord and liege in the name of my gods."

Philemon pushed up from the ground, holding his arm. "Here in the wilds where you were driven by a proper Christian king."

Wulfhere snarled, baring square teeth. "Yes, I still remember your attacks on me and mine simply because we would not bow knee to your Christ."

"I never cared whether you worshiped the One True Lord," King Richard said. "I only sought to stop your continued assaults against my people."

"You attacked me." Wulfhere lifted his chin, causing the beads in the plaits of his beard to click and clack. "That is all I care about. I shall be revenged, Lionheart."

"Then let us duel." King Richard pushed off the wall, rising to his feet. "You and I with whatever weapons you choose."

"You would face me by the river at dawn, swords in hand?"

"Gladly."

"That would answer my personal affront, if I were to leave you bleeding in the mud, but what of the blood debt you owe for my men and my property?"

"You filthy—" Philemon growled

King Richard put his hand out, stopping Longstride's rant before it started. He sighed, then spoke.

"Very well, take me out to the field, cut open my belly, and leave me for the ravens and the wolves to chew on. Whatever makes you satisfied, just let my men go free."

The men around him gasped, several crying out in protest at the suggestion their king had made. Philemon grabbed King Richard's arm. He shrugged it off, still watching their captor.

"Ah, they do not like such talk." The pagan king grinned.

"I am their king," Richard replied. "They will obey regardless of their feelings, because they are men of honor."

"And I am not?"

"You were captured many times by me—did I ever place you in a cell like this?"

"No, you put me in a room with a feather bed and a servant to bring me meals from your cook," Wulfhere spat. "Rubbing my nose in how much you have, how much you prevented me from having simply because my blood was not good enough."

"Blood does not matter unless you shed it."

"You claim that, surrounded by your nobles?" Wulfhere snarled. "You shunned me and then drove me out because I had no nobility."

"Och, Wulfhere." Richard shook his head sadly. "That was never the intent."

"To hell with your intent. I only care about your actions."

"You wished to be nobility, yet without effort. Your father

was a scoundrel and did you no favors. It fell upon you to prove you could be trusted with decisions that affect people's lives."

"You never gave me the chance. You judged me on my blood."

"It gave me pause," Richard said, "but only because a son is often like his father. You had your chance to prove it not so."

Wulfhere spat on the ground. "Petty offerings. You allow a noble's son—no matter how thin-skinned or milk-fed—more power at the start than you would ever give the son of a thief."

"And there is your problem, Wulfhere. You seek power over service. That's not the way my court runs. No one stays who seeks power. Only those who seek to serve, even imperfectly, are given a place at the table."

"Nonetheless, I carved my own from here. Now Odin has delivered you unto me, and I will have my full ransom for you."

"Be reasonable, and John should pay it without fuss."

Wulfhere's smile pulled his face crooked. "Ah, much is different since you crossed the sea to kill pagans, Richard. You are in for a rude awakening." He turned to leave.

"What news, you bastard?" Philemon demanded.

The pagan king ignored him and rounded the corner in a swirl of horsehide cloak and rough laughter. Longstride stood a moment more, staring, waiting, but the mongrel was gone.

"That went well, I think," he said. Philemon flopped onto the ground and regretted it instantly as new pain shot up his spine.

"Well enough." Richard shrugged. "But our fate may not depend upon the man who holds us captive."

"What does *that* mean?"

"Lawrence is not among us."

"Lawrence with the..."

"Yes, him."

"Where did he go?"

Richard waved his hand to indicate a vague outside.

"That is slim hope," Longstride said dubiously.

"Hope is still hope." Richard leaned back and closed his eyes. "And that can change everything."

PRISONS AND PRISONERS

CHAPTER ONE

The Hood was dead. Everyone knew it. His head had been placed on a pike for all to see. Though none dared lay flowers at the foot of it, the people all mourned Will Scarlett in their hearts. What fragile hope had remained in their bosoms was snatched away.

So was Prince John Lackland, brother to King Richard, and in the week since his death the man who had been his servant ruled in his stead. The Sheriff's reign was far more cruel. His dog soldiers scoured the countryside for any with even the tiniest spark of fire left in them and snuffed it out. Those who could had fled to Sherwood Forest, where they huddled together, seeking out others like them, trying to forage and survive.

The newcomers were easy to spot. They were the ones who jumped at every sighing in the trees and stared fearfully all around them. It wasn't the Sheriff and his demons that they feared here, but rather the legends of the ghosts that inhabited the forest.

Still, ghosts and legends seemed the lesser evil when compared to the darkness raging without. So, they watched the trees with fearful eyes and stayed because they had nowhere else to go.

* * *

Friar Tuck prayed, yet the words tasted like ashes in his mouth. Will and Cardinal Francis were both dead. Robin gone since the battle with the Sheriff and, for all they knew, dead, as well. His dear friend Alan-a-Dale, the last bard, had been muted, his tongue torn out of his mouth. Now Alan haunted the woods like a ghost. Only he and Marian were left of the original conspirators.

Little had been seen of Lady Marian since the slaughter. With nothing to do about Robin's absence she had refused to mourn and focused on the fate of her maidservant, Chastity. There had been no word what had happened to the girl.

Friar Tuck assumed the worst.

It was easier that way.

Tuck had taken to doing the only thing he could, holding services—such as they were—for the dead. There were no bodies for them to bury, so it was a purely symbolic act, though he believed it was an important one. That morning alone he had performed a service for Little John, and another for Lenore.

So many gone…

He was too worn out for anymore tears. The ones he'd shed had long ago dried up. There had been too much death, too much loss. He ventured into the forest, not far enough to lose the camp but just far enough that he could feel that he was alone. Sitting on a dead log, staring at nothing, he wondered when God would avenge His fallen.

There was a light step, and he twisted around in alarm.

Marian stood there, wearing a plain brown cloak fashioned from a tattered monk's habit to protect her from the chill in the air. She wore the slender torc around her throat, made of a bright gold and woven of dozens of thin strands that twisted around one another, mimicking the pattern of ancient knotwork, ending in the form of birds. Dark hair spilled from the cowl in a tangle that hung, unbrushed and possibly unwashed, across her chest. Marian was much changed these last few days. The winter's privation of their camp had carved away any of her castle-living softness. She was slender and hard like bone, her skin taking on the milkiness of the snow, gleaming against the darker tone of her somber clothing, as though she glowed with a light inside.

Her eyes moved, her sight roving among the bare branches overhead, never setting in one place, not looking at him when she spoke.

"Fear not," she told him, her voice soft. "Good shall prevail."

Had grief driven her mad?

"You're insane," he said, the words rushing out of him, bitterness twisting them.

She cocked her head to the side, regarding him as though he were strange to her. In that moment she seemed... less than human, like she wasn't of the world anymore. The hair on the back of his neck stood on end.

"You despair, you who should know better," she reprimanded him.

Anger surged through him. He was a man of God. Who did she think she was to lecture him on faith and hope?

"And you should give a damn about those who've died!" he snapped. It was true. She hadn't been at the funerals. She'd been here, in the forest, giving into her own madness.

"We will prevail," she said, her voice hardening. "The losses are... unfortunate... but they were to be expected."

"Unfortunate?" he shouted at her. It was so much more than that. It was terrible, overwhelming, unthinkable. Something dark moved inside of him.

All of this was so hard.

So much to take in, to carry, to hold. A shudder passed through him and suddenly she reached out, and before he could shy away from her touch, she put her hand on his head. Warmth seemed to pass into him and he had the unnerving sensation that she was ministering to him, reaching down and touching his soul and trying to bring healing and restoration. It was disorienting.

"God has blessed you, my lady," he said, the words wrung from him. He felt ashamed of his own weakness. He closed his eyes and heaved a ragged sigh as he realized that there were tears yet to come.

"We are not alone. You will see," she said softly. "This war belongs to all men. They will rise and fight when they are called upon."

"There is no war," he said bitterly. "Only ashes and death and refugees."

"We fought together."

"We tried," he said. "We failed."

"The time was not at hand."

Mystified, he opened his eyes and looked up at her. When first he saw her he thought the glow might have been a trick of his eyes. He realized now that it was real, and more intense than it had seemed. He had to squint as he looked at her.

"Has God made you one of His own angels?" he asked, marveling.

"No," she answered, "but He has shown me our victory. I stand confident in it." She smiled faintly at him, then fell silent, and he was content to just sit, letting her words sink in. He had felt so alone since his brothers had been burned, and Cardinal Francis killed. Inside he had been broken, and yet now…

He was not alone.

Tuck thought of Much and Old Soldier and several of the others. They might not be brothers of the cloth, but they were brothers in arms, in spirit, and he would not trade them for anything. That realization drove him to his feet.

They needed him even more than he needed them. He started toward the camp, then turned back.

"My lady," he said, "if there is anything you can do for Alan, *anything* to bring him back to us…" He started to choke up. The bard was… *special* to him, one of his oldest and dearest friends. Though he lived, it felt as if Tuck had lost him, too.

"I will tend to him," Marian said, inclining her head.

"Thank you," he whispered before turning and scurrying back to the clearing.

* * *

Marian turned away after Friar Tuck had left. Her heart ached for him, but he was strong. He would carry on. Moments of doubt, those were what plagued him, and they were easily enough countered. There were others who were not so easily ministered to.

Something had broken in Alan-a-Dale, far beyond his physical injuries, and she wasn't sure that she or any power on earth could fix it. There was more to it than the loss of his tongue, terrible as that had been. Something had broken in his spirit.

He might have to be put aside.

She moved through the forest and after a moment Champion came to walk beside her, the fox's paws making not a sound as they trod on the dead leaves underfoot. In the past weeks he had become so much more than just a pet. He was her friend, her constant companion—and, when need be, her guardian.

Marian's breath was visible in the morning's cold. She stretched out her hands and let her fingertips brush against trees as they passed them. Each one was alive, though struggling. Each had its own pain, its own battle. She could feel it, read their stories in the rough bark that caressed her skin. Sherwood Forest had claimed her as one of its own, and she didn't quite understand what that meant.

The fey could not hide from her anymore, nor did many of them even try. The druid blood in her veins called out to those of like kind. It was through that shared connection that she could find Alan-a-Dale, a bard of the old ways, whenever she chose now. As it was he was less than a mile from the camp, sitting with his back to a tree, his fingers strumming his harp so softly that she saw him before she could hear the music he was making. Music? The sound he tortured out of his instrument had no melody. It was a jangle and a crash of notes torn from strings, the ancient wood almost screaming through them. It was discordant and it actually hurt when it hit her ears. The notes reached deep inside of her and pulled forth an anger she had buried as deep as she could.

He glanced up as she stopped in front of him. It was as though the young man with the rakish charm had aged a decade. His face was lined with care, his brow furrowed.

"You've lost your tongue, not your ears," she chided. "Surely that sound hurts you as it does me."

He shrugged and strummed his fingers against the strings again. She crouched down and grabbed his hand, stilling it against the ancient wood, then shook her head sharply. He sighed and gave her a short nod, agreeing to cease. She released him and stood back. Champion circled her twice then went to sit next to the bard, to stare intently into the man's face.

"Even the fox knows there is more wrong than should be," she said.

With a roll of his eyes Alan reached into a pouch and pulled forth some parchment and a small piece of charcoal. She waited. Some ideas were too complex for him to try and express with gestures.

He handed her the parchment, the words were ghost lines, white on cream.

I failed.

"You did." She gave it back to him. "We all did. We are still alive, though. Uncle Richard once told me that the mark of a great man is that when he is in the right, he keeps trying no matter how many times he fails."

Alan scribbled on the parchment and then handed it back.

So many died.

She nodded. "And more could have died. More did die from the pox, and if we do nothing but sit here communing with the trees and feeling sorry for ourselves, then *everyone* will die."

She handed back the parchment. A minute later Alan returned it.

Robin. Without him all is lost.

She looked at Alan, weighing what to tell him in that moment.

Could this broken thing seated before her be trusted? If she guessed wrong, what would be the consequence? Before she could decide, however, she heard the sudden flutter of wings and looked up just as a bird descended onto her shoulder. It chirped at Marian and for a fleeting moment she could see what it saw, feel what it felt.

She turned back to Alan.

"Get up. We must go. A stranger has entered the forest."

As much as Alan didn't want to move, even he knew better than to defy Marian when she looked and sounded like that. His mind may have been a fog of pain and sorrow over his state and the way of the world he now occupied, but he still had the habits of a bard to observe. He'd watched her of late.

Disregarding her tone and words could wind him up with her hauling him to his feet.

Or drawing a blade and putting it to his throat.

He scrambled to his feet and followed her and the fox back toward the camp. As they walked he reached out to the forest, trying to feel what fresh threat might be awaiting them.

The forest wasn't speaking to him, though. Neither were the fey that had once whispered in his ear while he slept. He had failed the forest, his calling, everything. And everyone.

There was a reason bards didn't get involved, a reason they put down no roots nor took families. They had to be free to wander the land, speaking truth as they saw it. That was the responsibility handed down through the centuries from the first bard to Alan—and now he was going to be the last.

Francis had been right about Marian. She moved as though she was one with the forest in every way, and instinctively his focus fell upon her. Before he realized what was happening the harp was back in his hands and he was strumming a melody. It was as though the notes themselves were forming words that he could hear, as if the music alone was telling her story without need of his voice. It was pure, reacting on him on a deep level, stirring his emotions, pulling forth and demanding of him more than any song ever had.

He felt himself giving his life force to the song, to give it breath, weight, a life of its own. The agony of the creation was exquisite, and he was nearly overcome by the time they arrived at the edge of the clearing. He heard voices, some muted and fearful, others loud and angry. Marian stood for a moment, foot raised before stepping forth out of the woods. He understood and froze with her.

At last she stepped forward, and he let his breath out.

The Queen of Sherwood meets her subjects.

All of them, including Alan himself, were beneath her. It wasn't an accident of birth but a truer form of nobility that sprang from the soul. For just a moment he felt a flare of hope deep inside.

Perhaps we don't need Robin.

He followed her into the clearing, and his fingers found the strings of his harp and played music that would let everyone know that she had arrived, that she would save them, that all would be well.

Because maybe it would be—and even if it wasn't, even if the Sheriff of Nottingham and all his dog soldiers rounded them up tomorrow and put them to the blade, they still needed to die believing.

He ended with a flourish.

Logs had been set up in the center of the clearing, around a cook fire, and several people clustered around the flames to ward off the chill. There were perhaps seventy people there, and as she stepped into sight they fell silent, leaving whatever they were doing to crowd around. He saw despair and sorrow in their eyes. Yet there was something else, too—a determination flickered across their features as they stared at Marian.

They need her just now, he mused. *Someone they will live for. Someone they will die for.* He could help with that. Music carried emotion by itself. It didn't require his voice. As he played,

Friar Tuck pushed his way forward.

"What's wrong?" he asked, voice tense.

"There's a stranger in the forest," Marian said.

A refugee in a ratty cloak toward the back of the crowd turned, moving away, Alan noticed. Moving toward the trees. Alan took a half-step to follow when Marian spoke to the crowd again, even though it felt as if she addressed him.

"Be at peace," she said. "All is well. Stay by my side."

He froze, unsure... and he did not like the feeling. The others murmured and glanced uneasily at one another. A few reached for weapons.

"I do not think he means us harm," she continued. "Much will escort him here so that we might see this stranger for ourselves."

Friar Tuck jerked slightly. Alan, too, was uneasy at the thought of bringing a stranger to the encampment. Marian laid a hand on the holy man's arm.

"We all were strangers here, not so very long ago."

Tuck nodded, but a frown remained on his face.

"Alright, you heard milady," Old Soldier snapped, and he pointed. "Guards, to your positions." Though he was not a particularly large man, his bearing demanded obedience. Just like that everyone scattered, moving to take cover or take watch or just take up a weapon. Some hid, while others simply found a place to wait. Alan looked again for the tattered refugee, but he had gone.

Most likely hiding.

Friar Tuck moved in closer as the rest left, and there was relief in his old friend's eyes. Alan gave him a small smile and nodded. Marian was right. There wasn't time to indulge their own sorrows. They needed to work together, if any of them expected to see another sunrise.

"How long until they're here?" Tuck asked.

"Not long," Marian said. "Half an hour. Less."

Abruptly there was a moaning in the trees, and Alan felt a ripple run up his spine. Marian cocked her head as though she was listening. Seemingly satisfied, she nodded her head. There was excitement building in her eyes.

She thinks help is coming, he realized.

He just hoped she was right.

Marian moved to one of the logs and sat down. Instead of facing the center, though, she faced outward, toward the path by which Much would enter. After a moment's hesitation Alan went to sit beside her.

He strummed quietly, meaning not to disturb but rather to help her soothe and organize her thoughts. He watched as Friar Tuck moved around the camp, checking on everyone, taking his role as spiritual father very seriously, as he should. Alan couldn't imagine how much his friend must be missing Francis, who had been a spiritual father to everyone.

Muted conversations sprang up here and there, but then several minutes passed and everyone grew still. It was as if a collective breath was being held.

At last there was rustling in the brush. He let his hand fall idle, waiting to see what song he might be called upon to play next. There was some movement, and then Much stepped into the clearing. The lad seemed to have grown since Alan last saw him. He seemed bigger, taller. He no longer had the air of an overgrown child to him but that of a man. What had happened had changed them all, but Much now walked with a confidence few men could ever summon. Alan smiled. The miller's son was all grown up and no one would ever look down on him again.

Another figure appeared a few steps behind Much, and all eyes fixed on him. The man was tall, thin, and wore a black cloak wrapped tightly around himself with the hood up as though to obscure his face.

There was the creak of bows, and Alan knew that half a dozen arrows were already trained on their visitor, just waiting for him to make a false move. Death would come swift and sure. Just so long as it didn't come prematurely. The bard's fingers hovered over the strings, waiting, daring not break the tension with even a single note, lest it cause deadly repercussions.

Much strode up to Marian and then knelt.

"Milady."

"Rise, Much," she said, her voice strong and clear. "Who have you brought to us?"

"One who has traveled far, milady, and endured much," the stranger said.

"Show yourself that we may be the judge of that," Marian said, lifting her chin slightly. She looked and sounded every inch the queen. The stranger bowed.

"As you wish, milady," he said. He pulled free his cloak and dropped it on the ground to reveal a red cross emblazoned on a dirty and torn tunic. He was a knight, one who had gone with Richard to fight in the Holy Land.

Marian rose abruptly. "What news can you tell me of King Richard? Has he received word of what is happening here? Is he returning to help?"

The knight looked at her and then dropped his eyes. "He has received no word, milady, and he cannot help. Indeed, I am here seeking aid in his name."

Marian glanced swiftly at Friar Tuck then turned back to the knight. "What aid does my uncle require?"

"As much as you can give. He's been captured by a pagan king who is in league with his brother, Prince John."

CHAPTER TWO

Marian struggled to keep her face from showing dismay. These people needed her to be strong, yet she stared at the man in front of her. He was painfully gaunt, cheeks hollowed out and lips blue from the cold. She felt as if she should recognize him, know his name, but she also had a feeling he was much changed from when she last would have seen him.

"Tell me everything," she said.

The gaunt knight rubbed his face, his hand coming away oily. He opened his mouth and shut it again.

"Are you ill?" Friar Tuck asked.

The knight waved the question off with a weak gesture, his face turned to the ground. He swayed once then dropped to his knees, folding in on himself and slumping to the ground. Much moved to grab him by the shoulders and only caught his tunic, which tore slightly.

"He is unconscious," the miller's son said.

Marian flicked her eyes to Much. "Please see that he is well taken care of. Fetch me the moment he awakens." Much dipped his head and took hold of the knight's arm, lifting him up into his arms as if the grown man were a child. The knight didn't move as the younger man carried him away. Watching the man's face as they went, she remembered him.

He was a king's man.

He's broken, Marian realized, *but I need answers from him.* Yet, he had made it this far. There was hope for him. *And perhaps for Richard.*

She rose and signaled Friar Tuck and Alan-a-Dale to walk with her. They kept two paces behind as she entered the forest. Once there she felt she could breathe easier, think more clearly. The fear eased its hold on her mind, though not entirely. She did not go far, just enough distance to gain them privacy. At last she stopped and turned.

The friar was sweating. "Milady, I am so sorry," he said.

"This is an unexpected blow," she admitted, "but we cannot give in to fear." *I cannot give in to fear,* she told herself. "We must determine what we're going to do about it."

"Do?" Friar Tuck's forehead wrinkled up. "What could we possibly do about it?"

"If this knight's tale rings true, we will send men to rescue Richard," she said.

Tuck's eyes nearly bugged out of his head. He leaned his considerable girth back against a tree and stared at her as if she was an insane child.

"Marian, what few men we could spare, they'd never pass through England alive. And even if by the grace of God they managed to escape the Sheriff's clutches, they would face the same dangers Richard faced—the same enemy who managed to imprison him. What hope could they have for surviving, much less freeing him? We don't even know where he is held, much less if this is some ploy by the Sheriff to lure us from the safety of Sherwood"

She flicked her eyes to Alan. He stood, face thoughtful. She raised an eyebrow, but he made no move to share his thoughts.

"You saw that knight," she persisted. "It was Sir Lawrence—I remember now. You heard what he said. The man who has Richard is in league with John. This knight came to us without a letter—no demand for ransom. He escaped and made it back to England and then found us despite the Sheriff and his iron fist.

If he can make it to us, then surely a small group can retrace his steps."

"Every messenger you've sent has failed to return, milady," Tuck protested. "We can now be certain that they were captured, perhaps killed."

"Because they were messengers, not warriors," she said firmly. "That is what we should have sent in the first place."

"I mean no disrespect. I know he's your uncle—"

"He's more than just my uncle," she said, cutting him off. "He's England's only hope for survival. He is the rightful king. With John dead, Henry is going to try and claim the throne. The Sheriff might even support him. Nottingham's only claim to nobility is the bastard child he got out of Lady Longstride."

Both men looked slightly taken aback, but she pushed on. "We can't have a demon or his willing bedfellow on the throne of England. All this strife won't be going unnoticed outside our borders, either. France has been waiting for an excuse like this, to seek to conquer us."

"As much as I hate to say it, war with France right now might be a good thing." Friar Tuck licked his lips. "Let them contend with the Sheriff while we regroup."

"We don't have the luxury of waiting. Remember what the Cardinal told us. If England falls, this evil will spread and overcome the world. No, this battle has to be fought here, and it has to be fought by us."

Alan nodded fiercely.

"You agree with me?" she asked.

He nodded again.

She looked back at Friar Tuck and placed a hand on his arm. "If we can rescue Richard, we will have an army behind us."

"If his army has not already been slaughtered."

She stared at him intently. "If they have, then we can alert Rome," she conceded. "Tell them what has happened here." At that a spark of hope flared in her friend's eyes. She knew how alone he felt, cut off from the church.

"This is a war that is being fought on two fronts," she continued, "and we need all our allies with us. If the Pope called, France would have no choice but to work with us, rather than war against us."

Again Alan nodded. Friar Tuck looked as though he was about to give in when suddenly he stiffened, almost pushing off the tree. He blinked at her.

"You said 'if we can rescue Richard,'" he said tersely. "You wouldn't be thinking of going yourself, would you?"

She shook her head firmly. "As much as I wish to, my place is here. The people need me. I do have one or two in mind, though."

Tuck glanced uneasily at Alan. "Surely not—"

She held up a hand. "Do not worry my friend, I need Alan by my side," she said with a slight smile. "You, as well. No, what I will propose is an entirely... different course than our enemies might expect." At that she frowned, and uncertainty flickered across her mind.

"I'm afraid you're going to need more than just us."

"Yes," she said, unable to contain a wave of sorrow that rolled over her. "What I really need is something I no longer have."

"What is that?"

"Someone on the inside, someone who could tell us what the Sheriff is planning right now."

Glynna Longstride was nothing if not a doting mother. The Sheriff had to grant her that as he watched her nursing their child.

He was surprised she had survived giving birth to his spawn. As he watched her now, though, he realized he shouldn't have been. She was strong, strong in a way that most humans could never dream. Ten minutes after the child had been born, she'd been up on her feet, placing it in his arms, murmuring how beautiful the creature was.

He doubted any other human would call it beautiful.

It looked human, but *wrong*, as if mixed right, but in the

last moment someone took a finger and stirred, upsetting the formula. The eyes were too big, the inside corners nearly touching at a bladed nasal bridge. The cheekbones were too sharp, pulled up and back toward the ears that lay pinned against the skull.

Its mouth stayed slightly open, too-full lips unable to fully close over a triple row of teeth. Its skin was the pale of spoiled cream and shiny, as if made of wax. The hair on its head was black as coal and lay in wet swirls around its temples and crown, spilling down the back of a neck too short to look right.

In his eyes, it was the most wondrous creature he'd ever beheld, and he found himself desiring Glynna all the more for having given it to him. A baby had never been in the plan, but he realized now it should have been. There were so many more possibilities open to him now.

"What is it, my love?" she asked, looking up at him.

"Richard's cousin Henry has amassed an army," he said. "He's readying to move against us, to try and take the throne."

"Then we shall pluck out his eyes and feed them to our son," she said fiercely.

"That is certainly a very entertaining possibility," he acknowledged. "Let us entertain some others at the moment, though."

"You want to make an alliance with him?" she asked. "What could he possibly have that we would ever need?"

"At the moment, if reports are true, a very large force of men."

"You could sweep them away with a wave of your hand."

"Yes, but I also could use them to sweep across Europe. None could hope to oppose me."

"Even if Henry were interested in making a deal," she said, "what if he turns out to be as short-sighted as John?"

"Then I will deal with him as I did with John."

His pets slunk into the room, darker than the darkest shadows. They raced up his legs and wrapped themselves around his neck, black fur stroking his cheeks. They had been on the hunt and he could smell the human blood on their breath. They were very efficiently dispatching his enemies. At least, those outside the forest.

He sighed. He could send Henry's army where he couldn't send his own. Sherwood Forest needed to be emptied of those who would stand against him. His spellcasters were still working on breeching the forest's defenses, yet he couldn't wait for them to arrive at the solution. As much as it pained him, an alliance with Henry would be expedient.

For the moment at least.

Big things were happening. Much could tell.

The arrival of the knight had brought a great deal of excitement. Almost everyone at the camp had come up to ask him about the man and find out what Much knew, how he'd found him, and more. He guessed this is what it felt like to be important, a great man people looked up to for leadership.

While it made him proud, it also made him anxious.

Everyone kept asking him for his opinion. Was King Richard dead? What was Lady Marian going to do? Was there a way to leave England safely? He didn't have any answers, and so he felt as if he was letting people down.

Lady Marian, Friar Tuck, and the bard went into the forest together and they had not yet returned. He wished they would. Everyone should be asking *them* questions, not him. Still, he knew better than to go and disturb them. They'd come back when they were ready.

"How are you holding up, lad?" Old Soldier moved over to him and clapped a hand on his shoulder.

"I'm alright," he told the old man.

The truth was he was a bit in awe of Old Soldier. He'd seen the man in battle now, and it was impossible not to be. In the day-to-day, Old Soldier was always sure of himself and what he was doing. When fighting, he was a hundred times more so. It made Much wonder why the man had ever given up being a soldier. He could have gone off on the crusade with King Richard.

Maybe if he had the king wouldn't have been captured.

Much looked around the clearing. A lot of the men who were there and alive owed that to Old Soldier's actions in the last couple of weeks. When he thought about that he was glad that Old Soldier hadn't gone with King Richard. It made him feel guilty, but he was glad nonetheless.

"How are you?" Much asked. Little John and Old Soldier had been like brothers. If Much missed the fallen giant, he could only imagine how Old Soldier was feeling.

"Been worse," the older man grunted enigmatically.

Much nodded. "Me, too," he said, although truthfully he couldn't remember ever being worse. There had been so much loss, so much tragedy. He still grieved the murder of his parents, the loss of his friends, and the death of his hero, Robin. It was a lot to take in. Too much. Maybe that was why he felt more than a little numb, and fuzzy headed, like he was sick somehow. He just kept going, though, trying to help as much as he could. He knew there were people hurting worse than him.

"Your father would be proud of the man you've become," Old Soldier told him.

Much dropped his head. "Thank you," he muttered. "I'm just doing what I can."

"And that's the mark of a man. You've done well, son."

Much nodded, and the two of them stood there for a moment, neither moving, neither speaking, each somehow knowing they needed the other.

"There's something else weighing on you," Old Soldier observed after a minute.

Much frowned. "The trees at the edge of Sherwood. They're dying."

"This early winter is taking its toll on the forest same as everything else."

Much shook his head. "It's not like that. There's something wrong with them. They look sick. Some of them have turned gray with black spots, and others look like they're rotting."

Old Soldier scowled. "It's bad enough the Sheriff visits death and disease on the people, but to touch the forest..." He trailed off. Much understood. Sherwood was eternal, not like them. The fact that evil was harming it scared him. Much wondered how long it would be before evil reached all the way to their camp. He tried not to think those thoughts, but they would come unbidden, often at night. He wondered if Old Soldier had the same kind of bad dreams that he did.

Then there was movement just inside the tree line that caught their attention. Old Soldier's hand went to his sword. When Marian, Friar Tuck, and Alan stepped into the clearing he let it drop.

"I think our lady has made up her mind," Old Soldier muttered softly. "About something."

Much nodded. He could feel it, too. She always glided across the ground with grace and authority. Now, though, there was something new. She moved faster and had a look of determination about her. Friar Tuck didn't look happy, however, which made Much nervous.

Marian moved to sit on the felled log. She gathered herself before sitting down.

"She makes that log look a throne," Much said, giving voice to how he felt.

"It is a throne. It's *her* throne," Old Soldier said. "Best not ever forget that. Now, look lively, she wants to see us."

It was true. Friar Tuck signaled them to draw near, and they hastened to comply. As they did so, Much noticed a couple of others drawing close, including a tattered refugee, and the knight he had left in the care of the people who had taken to medic duties for the camp. The knight must have eaten, and he'd donned warmer clothes borrowed from someone. He was still gaunt and pale, but he was on his feet and no longer looked as though he had one foot in the grave.

The small group clustered together around Marian, looking to her for wisdom, her guidance. She took a moment and looked at each of them before she spoke.

"We find ourselves again in extraordinary circumstances," she began. "We need the king's men, and we need King Richard himself to help us in this fray. However, it seems they are more in need of our help than we are of theirs. Therefore, a small group of men will be sent to liberate the king and his soldiers, with the intention of bringing them home."

"I will go back, milady," the knight said, "and to show others the way. However, the distance is substantial. Several days' journey at a hard pace on horseback, longer if we travel surreptitiously—and we *will* have to travel as such. The journey will be treacherous."

"Sir Lawrence, I'd expect nothing less from you." She smiled at him. "Your arrival here speaks of your honor and loyalty to the sovereignty of England. We thank you for your service. I will assign men of matching valor to accompany you."

He nodded and took a slight step back, as though making room for others to step forward. As he did, Lady Marian turned and pinned Much with her gaze. He twitched and found himself stumbling forward as though she had compelled him to do so.

"Much, Old Soldier," she said. "I'd like you both to accompany Sir Lawrence."

"Me?" Much found himself asking her wonderingly. He had never dreamed to leave the area, let alone the country. The thought of traveling so far, and in service to Marian and the king, was at once exciting and overwhelming.

"Yes," she replied. "You have the ability to see without being seen, and you are courageous and loyal. Old Soldier has tactical skill and can help plan the escape."

"Thank you, milady," Much said.

Old Soldier simply bowed.

Sir Lawrence spoke up. "You do not understand what we will face."

"Then speak, man," Old Soldier said.

Lawrence took a deep breath, facing Marian again. "They are held by Wulfhere."

"Wulfhere Skullsplit?"

Lawrence nodded.

"The man is no real threat," someone called from the crowd. "Richard put him down handily the last time he tried anything."

"And yet King Richard and my fellow soldiers are all held within his keep, under lock and key if they haven't been killed." Lawrence spat over his shoulder. To Marian he said, "I tell you he is more powerful now. His men and he have fashioned themselves as Vikings of old, and they fight ferociously. They actually attacked us at sea. And… no, never mind."

"What is it?" Marian asked.

"Milady, we should have been victorious over Wulfhere and his men, even with the ambush." He shook his head. "It was as if they fought with more strength than men should have. And there was this darkness, it blinded us. So many were caught unaware, lost…"

Marian nodded.

Lawrence cleared his throat. "Three is hardly enough to counter an army."

She turned to look at him. "But these two are each worth an army. I'm sure you've heard and seen a great deal since you returned." Sir Lawrence nodded, but Marian continued as if he hadn't. "The remaining nobles are dead, or in thrall to evil. We will find no help from them. The people have been starved, tortured, and driven from their homes. Very few have the strength to survive such a journey.

"I know the importance of this mission," she said. "That is why I have given you two of my best fighters. What you will lack in numbers, you will make up for in the quality of your allies."

Much felt himself swell with pride. The knight glowered, however, and Much had the urge to punch him for disrespecting her. Before he could, however, the refugee in the tattered clothes stepped forward, pushing through the crowd to stand next to Lawrence. Marian looked at him and he nodded. She turned back to Lawrence.

"I have one more I can send with you," she said. "He is much needed here, but if he chooses to go and rescue the king, then I must respect his wishes."

Sir Lawrence stared incredulously. "This beggar? You can't be serious?"

"I'd have a care, Sir Lawrence, if I were you. Looks can be deceiving, particularly in these troubled times." She glanced at the man in the tattered cloak and hood. "Isn't that right?"

"It is, my lady," the man said, straightening and shrugging off the ragged cloak like a shed skin.

Much gasped with shock and delight.

Robin Longstride had returned.

CHAPTER THREE

There were gasps from all around, and Robin's name being repeated over and over. It had been Marian's idea, to let people think he was dead while he healed. Some had painted him as a hero, even a savior. It did not sit well with him and so he had been convinced to shuffle around when in camp, to hide his face and simply be left alone. He was still injured, but he couldn't afford to hide and lick his wounds any longer.

He hated the thought of leaving her, but knew that she was right—freeing King Richard and bringing him home was essential, if they were to prevail. If he could bring some of the king's soldiers with them, all the better.

"Robin of Longstride?" Lawrence asked.

"Yes." There was so much more he wanted to say. He wanted to ask about his father, but there would be time for that later. Instead, Robin looked the knight over. "We should leave as soon as we can. As soon as you are able, Sir Lawrence," he said. "Will you be prepared to do so in the morning, after you've had a chance to rest?"

The truth was the man probably needed a fortnight before he would be ready, but time was a luxury they couldn't afford. As it was, waiting even that long was dangerous. Lawrence nodded gamely, and at Marian's direction he was led off to one of the makeshift shelters.

That loosed the dam, and everyone swarmed around Robin—some crying, others laughing, all wanting to touch him and see for themselves that he was real and alive. He smiled and tried his best to bear up. These were his people, and they needed the reassurance. He glanced at Marian, who smiled wistfully at him. She knew he wasn't fully healed, but she also knew that without him the mission to save Richard would fail.

He turned back as Much gave him an unexpected hug, his thick arms gripping like a vice. Robin winced but didn't say anything. The lad had lost so much.

After a time things quieted down, and the day turned to dusk. Marian wasn't sure where Robin had got to, but she suspected he had slipped off into the woods. She didn't blame him. He had an impossible task ahead of him, and he needed to be able to ready himself for it. She'd already instructed Friar Tuck to help Old Soldier pack whatever he thought they would need for the journey.

Marian sat on the log close to the fire trying to gather her thoughts. She looked up as she heard a soft rustling sound. Jansa, the cook from the castle, stood there looking anxious. Marian smiled at the woman, hoping to ease whatever anxiety she was feeling.

"Jansa, come, sit here next to me," she said, patting the log next to her. Jansa hesitated a moment and then sat down on the barren ground in front of her. Marian wanted to urge the woman up onto the log, but decided it might cause her unneeded anxiety.

A moment of sorrow washed over her. Richard had warned her of the need to keep distance from those who saw him as their leader, lest his authority be undermined. She'd never truly understood before now, and she suddenly realized how desperately lonely her uncle must have been—must always be.

With Chastity there hadn't been any such barriers, because they had been friends since childhood. She held back tears as she thought about her friend and sent a brief prayer heavenward. She shook herself slightly and turned her gaze down to meet Jansa's.

"How are you faring?" she asked. "And how is your daughter, Esther?"

"Well, milady, better than we could have asked for," Jansa said. She wrinkled her nose suddenly. "Although we'd be a mite better if that oaf, Thomas, wasn't cooking. He always burns the meat and has no knowledge of how to make a proper stew. It's not fit for man nor beast to eat."

Marian stared at her in surprise. They were all living in the middle of the forest, in the worst conditions most of them could have imagined, and yet Jansa was concerned about the quality of the food. Then she smiled as she realized she shouldn't be so surprised. Jansa was a cook, and a very good one, raised in the castle by her grandmother who had been a cook before her. Here in the middle of the forest, she was probably at her wits' end. Perhaps feeling more than a little lost and useless.

"You know, I would take it as a great personal favor if you wouldn't mind assuming the cooking duties," Marian said. "Of course, this is all very primitive here, and I wouldn't want to impose."

"I would be honored, milady." Jansa beamed from ear to ear.

"Excellent. Then it is decided. I will find other work for Thomas."

"Don't get me wrong, milady, he's a decent man. He's just a horrible cook. I offered to help, but he so wants to be useful."

"Now that you mention it, I had noticed," Marian admitted, and it was true. But she hadn't had the luxury of caring about something so trivial. However, improved food would likely help the morale of them all. "Can you remind me which one is Thomas?" she asked, slightly embarrassed.

"The short, fair-headed man with the large hands," Jansa said. "He's a woodworker."

"Is he?" Marian said. "Well, then, I can definitely find other, better uses of his time."

"I'd appreciate it, milady. Like I said, he so wants to be useful."

"And he shall be." Marian barely managed to suppress a

smile. It was what they all sought these days. "After all, we have plenty of wood around us to work, and the whole camp will be grateful to have you as cook. Is there anything I can have one of the men fetch you, that would be helpful?"

"Whatever vegetables can be found would be appreciated, milady, but otherwise I have what I need. We left the castle in a hurry, but I brought some seasonings."

"How on earth did you manage to do that?" Marian asked, unable to contain her surprise.

Jansa smiled. "We had been packed and ready to go for weeks. I figured when you left, so would we."

Marian wished she could embrace the other woman. Instead, she just gave her a smile.

"Thank you."

"Thank you, milady," Jansa replied. "Now, I think there might be something I can do for you."

Again Marian had to suppress a smile.

"What is it?" she asked.

"I know one or two in the castle who are still loyal to your uncle, and to you. I figure if I send word in the right way, I might be able to find out about your maid."

"Chastity?" Marian asked, her breath catching slightly.

"Yes."

Marian balled up her skirt in her fists, trying to control her response. "I'd very dearly love to know what has happened to her, but I wouldn't want to risk any lives," she said. "Chastity wouldn't want that either."

"Just tell me that you want to know."

"I want to know," Marian said.

Jansa nodded. "Then I will find out. And now, with your permission, milady, I'm going to go tell Thomas that I'll be doing the cooking from now on."

"Best to have him come speak with me," Marian said. "I'll break it to him gently."

"Yes, milady," Jansa said. She stood with some difficulty,

started off, then turned back. "I was very sorry about Will Scarlett. He was a rogue, but he was a good man."

"Yes, he was," Marian said. *More than most anyone knows.*

Jansa nodded then headed on her way.

Marian sat back, struggling with her emotions. Everyone had lost someone, and the odds were great that more would be lost before it was all over. She felt selfish wishing for Chastity's safety, but couldn't help it. She reached down and stroked Champion's head. He sat up and leaned into the affection, a rumble of satisfaction coming from his chest. She was grateful more and more every day for the fox's presence. It helped steady her, keep her calm.

She remembered what her uncle had told her He wanted to spare her from the burden of leadership. As it turned out that decision had been out of both of their hands. At that thought she stood abruptly. Champion stood with her, ears forward, alert. She needed to walk a bit. The forest called to her and she moved quickly toward it.

Once inside the tree line she closed her eyes for a moment and breathed in the scents all around her. The crisp air filled with the sharp tang of the evergreens, a trace of wood smoke brought to the forest by her people, and, underneath it all, the rich, heady aroma of loam, the forest replenishing itself with decay and death to bring forth life. It was the very essence of magic.

She began to walk slowly, placing each foot with purpose, feeling the life of the forest around her. Every instinct told her to open her eyes so that she could see where she was going, but whatever it was that had been growing inside her since she and Robin journeyed to the heart of Sherwood, urged her to trust.

Trust the forest.

Trust herself.

Trust the magic inside her.

She kept walking, making slight adjustments when she felt the urge to do so. She wasn't sure how far she walked or how long, but the longer she walked the more alive she felt. She could hear, no, *feel*, the creatures that were alive in the forest. She could hear the creak of the branches in the cold. The padding of Champion's paws beside her seemed to grow louder and louder even though her mind told her the fox moved through the forest with a predator's silence.

Her senses took in the smell of the trees and the frost and the earth. She could detect the scent of Champion's fur and the musk of other animals from time to time. There was something more, though, and she finally decided it must be the faint smell of death as the premature winter took its toll on all in the forest.

She stopped at last and tilted her head back, lifting her face toward the sky. She was one with nature, just another creature inside the vast forest. Her hopes, dreams, fears began to fade away until there was just her, the fox...

And a man.

She opened her eyes swiftly. Robin was standing about ten feet from her, watching her closely.

"You walked all this way with your eyes shut," he said.

"Yes," she said. "The forest, it speaks to me now. That's the only way I can describe it."

He reached out a hand and brushed it against a tree trunk. "It has always spoken to me. Though lately it has made itself even clearer."

She watched as his fingers stroked the bark of the tree and she shivered as she realized that she envied it. Watching him she could no longer feel the bite of the cold. Warmth seemed to be spreading through her. He felt *elemental* to her, part of the forest itself.

His hand fell to his side and he walked slowly forward. Her heart began to beat faster. The way he cocked his head to the side she had the uncanny feeling that he could hear it. He stopped when he was barely an arm's length away. His eyes seemed to pierce her, and she stood, rooted to the ground.

"Your ancestors knew that the forest was alive, knew the creatures who dwelt here," he said.

"I believe they were your ancestors, too," she answered. The way he was looking at her sent heat to her cheeks. She should look away, Marian knew, but she couldn't.

No! It wasn't that she couldn't look away. She didn't *want* to look away. She wanted to *never* look away.

"Marian, I don't want to leave you," he said, voice thick and husky.

"I don't want you to leave either," she said, having to clear her throat to get the words out. He reached out and touched her cheek. She leaned into it and a sigh of longing escaped her.

"It is strange to me, how we can want something we've never had," he said, sliding his hand behind her head. "Want it so much that we might die without the having of it."

"It is part of nature, part of who we are," she whispered. She reached out and put her hand on his chest. She could feel his heart now. It was beating fast, keeping time with hers. That was as it should be. They were alone. Two of God's creatures in their forest home. All the artifice of society was gone, and for the first time in a very long time what she wanted was clear, simple, without artifice.

And right in front of her.

She put her hands on either side of his face and pulled it down to her. She kissed his lips. He was hesitant at first, and then she felt the moment when he gave himself over. She could taste the longing on his lips, and it mirrored that which was growing inside of her.

After what seemed an eternity he pulled away.

"Marian, what do you want from me?" he asked.

"I want you to come back to me," she whispered.

"I'll try."

"More than that," she said. "Promise."

"You know I can't promise," he said.

"But I need you to," she answered, feeling as if her heart might break.

"Ask me anything," Robin said, "but I can't make a vow to you that I'm not sure I can keep." He wanted her, almost as much as she wanted him. She knew it, and for just a moment she let it all play out in her mind—a life with him, a home... children.

"I want you to give me a child," the words slipped out before she could stop them.

He jerked as though she had struck him.

"Marian, you don't know what you're saying." He stared at her like he thought she had lost her mind.

"I know exactly what I'm saying," she countered. It was true. "I want to be yours and you to be mine. I don't want to wait for you to come back. You might die. I might die. Why put off what we both want?"

He stared at her, his face flushing.

"It's not proper."

She wanted to laugh. Nothing that had happened was proper, or civilized, or *right*. Still, she had a feeling she could stand there and reason and argue until she was blue in the face. So she kissed him again. Wrapped her arms around his waist and pressed close to him. She couldn't help but think of when they had danced at King Richard's party, and the fire that she'd felt in his arms.

Robin stepped back, pulling out of her arms.

"Marian, I can't do this," he said. "You're a princess, and if Richard falls, you must be queen. You need someone who can match you. I will follow you. I will serve you. I will worship you, but I can't be a stumbling block."

"Retreating from the field of battle?" she challenged.

"Yes," he said, taking a deep breath.

"Then you're a coward," she said. The words rang through the air between them. They were harsh, but she did not regret them. He looked desperate, like a trapped animal. She expected him to respond to the insult with anger. Instead, he just shook his head.

"Then I'm a coward," he said, turning to walk away.

"No!"

"But you called me one," he said over his shoulder. "Perhaps rightly so."

"I meant, no, you cannot leave," she said firmly. "I did not give you permission."

He stopped and she could tell that every muscle in his body was taut. He spoke without turning.

"If I can rescue the king and bring him home," he said. "If we can defeat the Sheriff. Then, perhaps I will ask King Richard for your hand in marriage. Perhaps I will be worthy of doing so."

"All we have been through and you still think yourself not worthy," she shook her head. "Do you not love me?"

He turned, looking pained. "Of course I love you. I have loved you for so very, very long."

"Do you not desire me?"

He balled his hands into fists at his side.

"Any man would desire you."

"But do you?"

"Yes," he murmured so that she could barely hear him. She took a deep breath, feeling on more solid footing.

"Do you know how many men have asked Richard for my hand in marriage?"

Robin flushed deeper. "My father said every lord had offered up himself or his son."

"Do you know why my uncle rejected every offer?"

Robin shook his head.

"He wanted me to have a say in the matter. He thought it was important."

Robin stared at her. "So, he brought all those offers to you?"

"He did."

"Why did you reject each suitor?"

"Oh, Robin… silly boy." She shook her head again. "Because they weren't you."

CHAPTER FOUR

"What are you saying?"

"I'm saying that when your father proposed Robert, as my husband," Marian replied, "I should have been bold enough to tell my uncle to suggest you instead. I have regretted not doing so every day since."

Robin moved so that he was standing again in front of her. He stared into her eyes, searching them, trying to understand what she was telling him.

"Why?"

"Because I love you." She smiled up at him. "I want you. I *choose* you."

At that he wrapped his arms around her. Instead of kissing her, though, he buried his face in her neck. His whole body shuddered. A few moments later he let go of her, dropped down onto one knee, and addressed Champion.

"Go get Friar Tuck," he whispered to the fox.

Champion turned and started running back toward the clearing.

"You *can* talk to animals," Marian breathed.

"Only those that wish to listen," he said. Robin was shaking like a leaf from head to toe. He wanted to move, to take her hand, touch her in some way. He was afraid that if he did, though, it would somehow break the spell they were both under.

* * *

Just when he could stand it no more he heard the sound of someone hurrying through the forest toward them, moving with great difficulty and much muttering. He smiled, and a minute later the fat friar came into sight, being shepherded by the fox that was nipping at his heels and tugging at his robe.

As Friar Tuck stumbled to a stop next to them, he wheezed with exertion. Still Champion grabbed at his robe.

"You dragged me here," the monk roared. "You can stop now!" When the fox stopped, he looked up at Robin and Marian. "What's the emergency?" he asked, eyes wide with fear.

Robin's mouth had gone completely dry.

"We want you to marry us," Marian said in a level voice. "Right now."

A look of consternation settled on Tuck's face. "You can't be serious."

"Oh, but we are," Marian said, putting more force into her words. "We want you to marry us in the eyes of God."

"Here? In the cold?" he said. "But, your uncle—"

"Marry us or we'll get Alan to do it." Marian tilted her chin up, eyes hard as stone. "According to the old ways."

"Now hold on a minute there." Friar Tuck turned bright red. "He can't get you married good and proper in the eyes of God and the church. And I never said I wouldn't. You just have to give a fellow a chance to catch his breath."

Robin found his voice. He reached out and put a hand on Friar Tuck's shoulder.

"We don't mean to startle you. We just want to be wed before we are parted again."

Friar Tuck nodded slowly, and a smile lit up his face. "The truth is I've prayed for this day," he confided. "It's just not how I expected it to happen."

"Nor did I," Robin said with a wink. The friar laughed and slapped him on the back so hard he almost knocked him over.

"Very good, then," he said, having regained his composure. "You know, though, there's a lot of fine folk back in the clearing who'd love to celebrate with you. When you think about it, everyone could use something to celebrate about now."

"While I appreciate that," Marian said, "we'd like the ceremony to be private." She gave him a meaningful look. "Just us."

"Are you planning on keeping your marriage a secret?"

"Only until morning," Marian said, blushing. "We'd prefer to be undisturbed until then."

"Ah, I see."

A long moment passed with no words.

Champion gave a short bark.

"You are sure?" Friar Tuck asked them.

"Absolutely," Robin and Marian spoke in perfect unity.

"Well, then, let's get on with it." He positioned himself between them. "Take each other's hands."

Robin reached out and took Marian's hands in his own. Their breaths steamed out, but he realized he didn't feel the cold as he used to. Nor did Marian, it seemed. As the friar talked he tried to listen, but he found himself lost in her eyes. He managed to answer when called on, and listened in awe when she answered, but the words all seemed to run together.

"I said, you may kiss the bride," Friar Tuck said, and Robin with a start realized the man was repeating himself. He leaned down and kissed Marian, his lips touching hers gently. When he would have pulled away, however, she wrapped her arms around his neck and drew him closer until their bodies were pressed together.

"Come on, Champion," Tuck said wryly. "We are clearly no longer needed here." Still Marian held the embrace, until a long moment after they were alone.

"I thought they'd never leave," Marian whispered against his lips. Then she grabbed hold of his tunic and began to pull it over his head, and he felt a fierce surge of joy. Marian was his and he was hers. Whatever the future held, nothing could take this moment from them. He picked her up and spun her around as he kissed her, there in the forest with only the trees to see.

Friar Tuck hurried back to the clearing, eager to leave the young couple to themselves. The fox trotted beside him, although he kept glancing over his shoulder. Tuck couldn't help but feel happy that Marian and Robin had finally realized they were meant to be together and had done something about it.

He was, however, deeply sorry that both Will and Cardinal Francis hadn't lived to see it. He was pretty sure neither man would have been surprised. Indeed, Will had been vocal—at least to him—in his hope that the two of them might finally realize they were in love with each other.

That they have...

He lifted his eyes heavenward and hoped his friends were both smiling down. Imagining them doing so was some slight comfort. He made it back to the camp finally and looked around, bursting with the need to tell someone what had just happened. Not surprisingly, his eyes fell on Alan. He knew that Marian and Robin wanted privacy until the morning, and he could trust the bard to do nothing that would disturb them.

Alan was sitting on a log, thoughtfully strumming his harp as he stared off into the distance with intense concentration. Tuck made haste to go and sit by his friend and forced himself to wait until the bard had ceased playing.

It felt like he sat there forever before the harp fell silent. Alan shook himself slightly and with the motion seemed to come back from somewhere. He looked surprised to find Tuck sitting next to him, then he smiled gently.

Where did he go, Tuck wondered, *while he was playing.* He very much wanted to know.

When Tuck didn't speak, the bard raised an eyebrow. Tuck glanced around to make sure no one was nearby then he leaned in close and whispered.

"I just married Robin and Marian."

A look of surprise, then instant delight, sprang across Alan's face and his fingers teased forth a happy chord from the strings they were touching. He turned and glanced toward the woods, as if expecting to see the happy couple emerge.

"They wanted to be left alone tonight," Tuck explained. "They plan to share the news with everyone in the morning."

Alan nodded his understanding, and a mischievous grin lit up his face. He made a kissing motion and touched his fingertips to his lips.

Tuck nodded. "I would imagine. Robin is a lot of things, but I don't think he's stupid."

Alan laughed. It was odd to hear, sound came out but it was almost like a bray, just one note without a tongue to form others. Even if it didn't sound like it had before, it was still good to hear, and a moment later Tuck found himself joining in, slapping his friend's knee. They had been surrounded by so much death, it was a tremendous relief to celebrate life in any way.

The next morning, the people gathered round the two of them, all pressing close, some reaching out to pat their arms and shoulders in congratulations. Robin and Marian stayed close together, never more than an arm's length apart, no matter how many of their people pressed in.

Someone took up a bawdy wedding song, one found normally in a tavern among fellows deep in their cups, rather than on a bright cold morning in the forest. Nevertheless, the crowd joined in and sang along, becoming especially boisterous in the chorus. Alan strummed his harp and Friar Tuck began a clapping rhythm.

Despite the raucous—nearly scandalous—nature of the lyrics neither of the newlyweds blushed. Robin took Marian in his arms and whirled her around, showing her off to the people who revered her dignity and honor and royalty, but found themselves connecting with her as a woman for the first time. Though separate, she was one of them.

In that moment they became more than symbols and myth.

They became real.

"I still cannot believe it," Much said, a smile on his face.

"Those two have been in that dance for a long time, son," Old Soldier replied. "Longer than you've been living." The creases in his face were deeper with a grin of his own.

"I'm happy for them."

"And sad as well."

"How did you know?"

Old Soldier looked deep at Much, into the marrow of him.

"If you had a woman like Marian, you'd never leave her, even to save the king."

The moment it was spoken, Much knew it to be true—knew it so deep and pure in himself that it felt like an arrow shot into his heart. He found himself nodding, but when he spoke his words weren't bitter.

"If I had a love like that, I wouldn't leave her to save Christ Himself."

Marian's head spun with the joy of the moment. Here in the forest of which she now felt a part, in the arms of the man she loved, her *husband*, and enveloped in the joy of people she cared about...

It was as perfect a moment as could be.

She should have known it could not last.

They came around the main campfire and found themselves face to face with Sir Lawrence. He stood, watching them somberly, dressed in a dark gray wool tunic over leather pants tucked into sturdy boots. A dark cloak hung on his narrow shoulders, not concealing the long sword strapped to his side.

"Sorry to interrupt your... celebration?" he said. At the

sight of him, all fell silent, their joy dashed by the sour look of recrimination on Lawrence's face.

Robin straightened. "We've had little to celebrate of late," he said. "We will not apologize for it." Lawrence looked at him for a long moment before bowing his head slightly.

"As you wish."

Robin studied the man through narrowed eyes, looking for even a trace of sarcasm or a sneer. Even a glimmer of it, and he would ride that man to the ground and put his knife against the pulsing vein in his throat.

He found none, just a resignation and a weariness that was far too familiar. So he turned to Marian, speaking low for her ears, even though the cold crisp air would carry his words to the people near them.

"I love you," he said earnestly. "Now I must gather my weapons and go do my queen's bidding."

"But what if she has changed her mind about sending you?" Marian's eyes were dry but the slightest tremble was in her voice.

"She hasn't." He smiled a wry smile. "She weighed her decision carefully. Despite last night's events, she is not prone to whimsy and never known to recant."

"She sounds like a hardarse."

Now Robin's eyes took on a twinkle, despite the sorrow at leaving her. He moved his mouth closer to her ear, close enough that even the winter air wouldn't take his words.

"Not hard, milady, but definitely firm."

He pulled his head back in time to catch the blush that painted her cheeks. Her hand was iron on the back of his neck as she pulled him in and kissed him with a fierceness that took his breath and made his knees weak. Then Marian pulled back, eyes wet like hard flint in a riverbed, and spoke through clenched teeth.

"You return to me, Robin of Longstride," she said, "or I will destroy the earth to find you."

"Yes, milady."

CHAPTER FIVE

"Are you sure?"

The Sheriff turned and reached out. His fingers, encased in the hard black gauntlet, ran down her cheek—not gently, she never wanted that from him, but precisely hard enough to feel yet not hard enough to bruise. It made her throat tighten.

"He could not hide from me if he were to consider betrayal. He is performing the task he has been assigned and will be here in a moment." Glynna nodded, trusting even with the knot of worry in her chest that made her heart thrum weirdly behind her breastbone. She'd had it since the moment she let her child go.

The Sheriff turned back to the altar, lighting the candles with a touch of his finger. Glynna moved beside him, watching. The candles were thick pillars of wax taken from bees that had been fed on red clover and nightshade, the honeycomb pattern showing through their sides as they were lit. The wicks were the braided hair of hanged men, and each time flame leapt from the Sheriff's touch she caught a whiff of their acrid smoke.

Glynna had been married to Philemon in this chapel, in a ceremony of light and laughter, overseen by the Cardinal when he'd been a younger man. When he'd still been alive. Now the room had been desecrated. The crucifix behind her had been turned upside down, the head of the corpus sawn off and discarded to the left where it lay looking up at its former body with wide anguished eyes. The wood of the altar had been darkened by the spilled blood of sacrifice and divination left to dry and stain it permanently.

To the right sat a jar of noxious yellow fluid—a mixture of urine and phlegm from the Sheriff's stable of wizards and sorcerers, some of it hers—with a handful of the back molars of Saint Germaine, the relic that had been encased inside the altar.

So much blasphemy.

It thrilled what was left of her soul. She'd always been drawn to the darker path, the shadow side of the Old Ways, the Moon Road and spilled blood on stone, but since Nottingham had opened her eyes, opened *her*, it felt as if she had found her true nature. The old her had passed away and become new in his light. She was a wineskin filled with his dark wine.

In his other hand her love held the iron torc that bestowed kingship. After they had killed the little prince he had put it around his own neck. He had warned her that he could only wear it briefly and true enough within an hour's time it had begun to burn him until he had to remove it. He had told her that their child would be just human enough to wear the torc.

Our child will be king. A savage spark of pride raced through her. He would bring the whole world to his feet.

The last candle sparked to life and the air in the room took on a charge, shadows growing from the corners of the ceiling despite the added flame light. The Sheriff reached for her and drew her close. She shivered at his touch and thrilled when he spoke the one word.

"Anon."

The tall twin doors of the chapel opened in unison and a humming chant crept into the sanctuary, vibrating in the atmosphere as the wizards, sorcerers, and necromancers filed in in twin rows, more than a dozen in all, stepping into the pews when they reached the front of the church. Their chanting stayed, a sonorous buzz of consonants and vowels and other sounds that were never truly meant for the human throat. It wasn't a language they chanted but a phonetic song of magical intent, at once a summoning and a saining.

Through the open doors swept a tall, angular man, his head shaved poorly with patches of dark stubble here and there among scrapes and cuts, as if he'd performed the task while drunk or during a seizure. The Mad Monk strode forward with long deliberate strides, his ash—covered robe flowing behind him. He was naked underneath, his anatomy spare and sparse, cut to the bone by privation so that it was apparent his joints did not work as they should, rotating in contortionist ways that made the viewer's own joints ache.

In his spade-like, swollen-knuckled hands he carried their child.

He bowed to her and the Sheriff once he arrived at the altar and gently placed the offspring onto the bloodstained wood. The child rolled, looking up at her with a sharp intelligence that she supposed would frighten any sane person.

Symbols traced in dark paint covered every inch of the child's skin, the candlelight gleaming over them. The squiggles and marks ran together in her eyesight, wavering with sorcerous potential.

The Mad Monk spoke. "It has been done as you have required, Master."

The Sheriff smiled. "Then let us consecrate our firstborn to the Dark Lord Of All."

It was the happiest day she'd had since giving birth.

"You have to relax and lean into it, son."

Much held tightly to the reins of the horse under him, legs locked tight on the crude saddle. He eyed his traveling companions with jealousy at their ease on the backs of the hell beasts they all rode. They swayed with each clop of hoof on the frozen ground, yet he jolted with each step of his mount, bouncing stiffly in the saddle. His entire body hurt in places he didn't even know he had.

"I'm not used to horses," he said to Old Soldier.

"Have you ever ridden before?"

"No."

"I can tell." The older man pulled close and reached out for the reins. "So can your horse. You're making it nervous."

"I know how he feels." Much looked down at the ground that seemed so far away.

"She." Robin trotted up. "Your horse is a female."

"I've never been good with those either."

The laugh that burst out of Robin was so sudden and sharp that Much's horse jumped underneath him.

"Your time with that will come. Never fear."

"Do you three not realize how serious this all is?" Sir Lawrence hissed. He pulled the reins of his horse, slowing enough that they were in line as close as the horses would allow.

Much turned red. "I'm sorry—"

"Don't apologize," Robin cut him off. He shifted in his saddle, turning to the thin, dour knight. "You will find us deadly serious when the time comes."

Lawrence merely grunted.

"What is your issue?" Old Soldier asked.

The man's face twisted into a snarl. "My *issue* is that after all I went through to escape capture, I am sent back with an arthritic old man, a stripling who cannot ride a horse, and a fool who laughs and dances because he has no idea what danger is."

Much's vision went red.

All he could see was the shape of the man mocking Robin and Old Soldier, the two men he respected more than anyone in the world. Everything fell away—his anxiety over riding, his fear at being off the ground—all of it narrowed to just the shape of Sir Lawrence in a field of crimson.

He moved, not thinking, just moving, working from the animal base of his brain, pulling his legs up and getting them under him on the wide back of the mare. He launched himself from horseback, issuing a strangled war cry.

There was no time to react. One second Robin was opening his mouth to answer Lawrence's accusation, the next Much dove into the man, tackling him off the horse he rode and driving him to the ground. They landed in the frozen mud, both their mounts rearing and spinning away.

"Grab the horses, we need them!" he yelled to Old Soldier. "I'll handle this."

The older man wheeled and moved after the two animals as Robin slid off his horse. Much sat on Sir Lawrence's chest, pinning the man down. The young man's fist was back behind his head, ready to fall like swift sure lightning and strike the other man in the face. Already the skin over Lawrence's eyebrow had split and bled freely.

Robin slung the bow off his shoulders, letting it slide in his palm until he had the stout yew wood by the notch where the string was anchored. He lunged and hooked Much's hand with the other end of it, jerking it against the lad's elbow and pulling him off the fallen knight. Much tumbled back toward him, and Robin reached out and pulled the young man up by the heavy shoulder seam of his rough wool tunic.

"Easy, now, easy." Robin kept his voice low and deep, like he would to soothe a spooked animal. Much flailed for a second and then calmed as his back was pressed against Robin's chest.

Lawrence was up, sword out in his hand, and his face twisted in rage. He took a step toward them, knuckles white on the hilt, intent raw on his face. Suddenly he was stopped short by the edge of the dagger Old Soldier pressed against his throat, the old man reaching from behind, arm up and locked tight under Lawrence's own.

"Easy, now, easy." Old Soldier echoed Robin's words in Lawrence's ears. The knight stopped cold, not moving even a fraction of an inch lest the keen blade part the skin and allow his blood to spurt free, to steam in the winter air.

Much shuddered in Robin's grip. Robin felt him come back to himself, so he let him go and the young man stepped shakily away.

Robin cocked an eyebrow toward the knight.

"Seems you may have misjudged your words."

Lawrence nodded, just a fraction. A trickle of blood sprang against the blade at his throat.

"We are not fools, children, or doddering old men," Robin continued calmly. "We are men born of war. Underestimate us at your peril." He slung the bow back over his shoulder as Old Soldier lowered his dagger and stepped away.

"Do not make the same mistake twice," Robin concluded.

"I will be sure of..." Lawrence broke off with a groan, folding in at the waist. He leaned forward, swaying on his feet and holding his side. His skin sheeted with sweat and went waxy. Instantly Old Soldier grabbed the man's elbow to steady him, keep him from dropping to the ground. The motion pulled Lawrence's hand from his side, revealing a spreading red stain.

"You're wounded," Robin said.

"Aye," Lawrence replied through gritted teeth as he was eased to the ground. "I am. It will pass." Nevertheless, Old Soldier pulled at his tunic. Lawrence pushed his hands and Old Soldier clipped him lightly on the cheek.

"Sit still and let me have a look."

Lawrence stopped fighting and leaned back.

The tunic lifted to reveal a raw, ragged puncture a few inches above Lawrence's hipbone. The wound seeped with watery blood, the heavy scab on it broken.

Much loomed beside Robin. "Did I do that?"

Robin shook his head. "It's an old wound."

"It was received in my escape," Lawrence said as Old Soldier assessed the injury.

"Go fetch the wound kit from the leather knap on my mount," the older man instructed. Much moved off, assuming the order was for him.

"It will be fine," Lawrence insisted, his breathing calmer. "I crossed the wilds and then England, interrogated the villagers, and then found you people in Sherwood—all with this wound. I will make it the rest of the way."

"Don't make me clip you again, son."

"You won't out stubborn Old Soldier," Robin said, "and no one knows more about dealing with a swordthrust than he."

"Got two of them myself," Old Soldier said.

"Let him dress your wound, and we can get a few more miles out of you," Robin added. Lawrence lay back as Much returned with the kit.

CHAPTER SIX

Friar Tuck pondered Thomas as the two of them stood talking in hushed tones with Marian. The young man was tall and stood ramrod straight. He looked as fit now as he had the first day Tuck had laid eyes on him. Fitter even. The privation of the forest, cold air, and sleeping underneath the sky seemed to agree with him. His eyes were bright, his breathing deep and regular, and he moved with an ease that the friar found himself envying.

What he didn't envy was Thomas's cooking skills which, as it turned out, were non-existent. It had been with a great deal of relief that Tuck had discovered that Jansa would be taking over those duties. Already he found himself far more comfortable and less irksome, thanks to the improved quality of the food.

Salt was a blessing for which he truly thanked the Lord.

He did wonder, though, why Marian had asked to speak with them both privately. When he had inquired whether or not she wished to keep counsel with Alan, as well, she had responded that the bard needed to build his strength, and they should let him rest for a while.

Friar Tuck wasn't sure that Alan needed rest so much as a good, swift kick in the seat of his pants. Still, he was trying to be patient. He knew what the bard had lost and was probably one of the few who understood just how much of an atrocity that had been. At least he had begun playing something that resembled music again, instead of the discordant screeching it had been. He assumed they had Marian to thank for that change.

Marian looked at Thomas and him with a very grave expression. For just a moment he panicked, thinking that perhaps Jansa had taken sick and she was reinstating Thomas as cook. He told himself that was ridiculous, though, since he'd seen Jansa a short time earlier, and she'd looked the picture of health.

"What may I do for you, Lady Marian?" Thomas asked, his face pinched and anxious.

Maybe he's worried, too, Tuck mused, *that she's going to ask him to start cooking again.*

"I understand that you are a wood worker," Marian began. Instantly Tuck could feel relief steal through him, and one look at Thomas's face let him know the other man was experiencing the same.

"I am," Thomas admitted.

"Excellent. I have use of your skills."

"What is it you want me to build, milady?" Thomas asked, sounding a bit anxious.

"Tools of war," she said.

Thomas frowned. "I've already helped make arrows and bows and cudgels. Several of us have been working to make as many of those as we can."

Marian shook her head. "I appreciate the effort and we will need them, but I'm thinking bigger."

"How much bigger?"

Marian stared at him intently. "Have you ever heard of a trebuchet?"

Thomas frowned. "For a trebuchet to cause real damage, it would require forty-five men to work the ropes. We just don't have the numbers."

Marian smiled. "Perhaps we could get that down to just a handful of men."

"How?" Thomas asked.

"I've heard stories about modifications instituted by King Philip of France, a couple of years ago. I think we can take advantage of his design work."

"You've 'heard stories'?" The skepticism lay raw on the man's face. It made Friar Tuck want to slap it. Marian's eyes narrowed and her tone went waspish.

"I am the niece of Richard the Lionheart," she said, "raised by his own hand from a child. Do you assume he only taught me to cross-stitch?"

"N-no, milady." Thomas went pale.

"I am well-versed in the vagaries of modern combat."

"My a-apologies," he said. "I did not think clearly."

"Forgiven."

"Just tell me how, milady, and I will do everything I can to make it."

"Excellent," Marian said, unfolding a piece of parchment and handing it across. Friar Tuck stared over his shoulder at the drawing on the page. There were diagrams he didn't quite understand, but Thomas began to nod his head, slowly at first, then quickly. Finally he looked up at Marian, and there was a light in his eyes that hadn't been there before.

"I think we can make this work, milady," he said.

"Excellent," she responded. "We will need every advantage we can conceive and create."

"It's quite ingenious."

"I am sure a man of your skill can improve upon my crude designs."

Thomas's mouth opened, then closed, unsure of what to say. Marian left him like that for a moment before breaking into a grin and reaching out a reassuring hand and touching his arm.

"It is well, Thomas. I am only jesting."

Thomas wiped his forehead.

"You're thinking of laying siege to the castle?" Tuck asked incredulously.

"I'm not 'thinking' of it. I *will* lay siege to it," Marian said firmly. "The Sheriff's demon soldiers have tried time and again to enter the woods. They can't as yet. Sooner or later, though, the Sheriff will find a way to flush us out of here, and then we will all die. Our only hope is that we reach out and flush him first."

Friar Tuck didn't know what to say, so he just stood there gawking at her. He couldn't even bring himself to look around the clearing, because he knew it would only remind him of just how hopelessly they were outnumbered. A few dozen able-bodied men and women from the seventy that had come to the forest, to stand against the Sheriff, the king's guard, and the Sheriff's dog soldiers...

"Will you be wanting other siege weapons, too?" Thomas asked.

"Yes, but these new trebuchets are our first priority," Marian said.

"We're going to need wagons and horses to transport some of these things when we're ready to move them," Thomas said.

"Leave that to me," Marian answered matter-of-factly. "For now, take whatever men you need and begin working on this design."

"Yes," Thomas said, bowing before scurrying away.

"You would destroy the castle?" Tuck asked. "The throne room?"

Marian shook her head. "The throne room isn't a single place. It is wherever the rightful king holds court, be it grand or humble. The castle itself has already been destroyed in my eyes, forever tainted by the evil of the Sheriff and all his puppets. Losing it is a small price to pay if we have a chance to defeat evil."

"But how?" Tuck asked, his own frustration and despair welling up in him. "The Sheriff is inhuman. Arrows can't kill him."

"Then we'll just have to find something that does," Marian said thoughtfully. She turned abruptly and walked off toward the forest. Tuck thought about calling out to her, but realized it was probably just best to let her go do whatever she was of a mind to do.

He clenched his fists at his side, trying to push down his own fear and frustration. Marian was smart. Cardinal Francis had said that she was the key to everything. Tuck had to believe his friend knew what he was talking about. So he took a deep breath. The Lord worked in mysterious ways, and he had to trust that He was at work here.

A short distance away, Alan watched the exchange between Marian, Tuck, and young Thomas. When the wood worker left the other two he began making the rounds of the men in camp, starting with those who were skilled at making things with their hands. Marian had given him a piece of parchment and—most likely—instructions for making something.

If he had to guess he'd say it was a weapon.

Marian was the next to walk off, and she walked straight into the forest with a determined stride. That left the good friar, who looked worse off than he had at the beginning of the conversation. Anxiety stood out in every line of his old friend's body, and he could sympathize.

Alan was wearier than he had ever been in his life, but he dared not show it. He had to be strong for Friar Tuck and the others. Each man was at or near his breaking point. The weeks of fear and uncertainty, the cold, the rationed food, had worn them down until they seemed like ghosts of their former selves, pantomiming the motions of living without really doing so.

He sat down on a log near the fire and unfastened his harp. His fingers found the familiar strings and began teasing out a melody, one that started low and slow and then began to build. He sought to build the fire and strength within the sluggish bodies and hearts around him. After a moment the boy Haylan came to sit beside him.

Word had reached them even here in the forest that Haylan's mother had died a few weeks back. Alan had known it was coming, but being right brought no joy—just greater sorrow for the life he could not save. Haylan's older brother, Audric, had reacted with rage and grief. Haylan, though, had turned inward, keeping more and more to himself.

Alan's heart ached for the boy and it hurt even more that he couldn't speak words of comfort to him. So he played his harp and gradually he forgot about the rest of the men, women, and children at the camp as his eyes focused in on the young face next to him.

The music stirred something deep inside his young companion. It rippled over his face, wildly different emotions chasing one after the other, none staying for more than a few seconds. The boy was an orphan, and because of his father's death, one without skills. It would be hard for him to make his way in the world, if he survived.

There was spirit there, though, living just below the surface. The boy had fire in him. He also had the kind of determination that would be needed to rebuild when this was all over.

If any of us lives to see that, Alan thought with a sigh. He was so wrapped up in his own thoughts that he almost missed the soft sounds coming from Haylan. Startled, he turned his full attention to the boy. Haylan's face was scrunched up in concentration and words came slipping out of him. They were words of hope and victory, and the voice that sang them was clear and unwavering, even if it was soft.

The sound cut right through Alan and pulled at his soul.

He blinked at the boy in surprise. Haylan had the Gift.

Sudden tears filled Alan's eyes as he realized he might not be the last of his kind after all. He nodded encouragement to the boy, who responded by singing louder. Soon his voice rang out like a bell. Out of the corners of his eyes Alan watched as one by one, everyone in the camp stopped to listen. In the silence that fell around them Haylan's voice gained more power until it filled the clearing. He sang of war and loss and victory and hope. The words just seemed to tumble out of him, a silver stream so vibrant and alive.

Alan cast a quick look to Friar Tuck, who stood staring slack-jawed. Alan smiled. His old friend was not easily impressed, and it only confirmed his own estimation of the boy's gifts, his raw talent.

After a moment Alan let his fingers fall from the strings of his harp so that the boy's voice alone filled the clearing. It was as though he could feel the mighty forest holding its breath as it, too, listened to the song, and the boy who sang of things well beyond his years.

When at last Haylan came to a stop Alan reached out and embraced him, letting his tears flow freely. He was in awe of the miracle he had just watched, and the sure knowledge that the song of the old ways would live on beyond him in this boy.

"I couldn't help it," the boy whispered.

"Nor should you have tried to," Friar Tuck said, moving up beside them and resting a hand on the boy's shoulder. "God has given you a mighty gift and presented you with the finest of teachers." There was raw emotion in the man's voice. Suddenly, for just a moment it was so clear. The world was falling apart. Evil was threatening to overrun them. Yet despite the machinations of the devil and all his allies, life would go on.

"Alan will teach you everything he knows," Tuck continued. "He shall be father and mentor to you now."

Alan released the boy and smiled at him in what he hoped was an encouraging way. His fingers found his harp strings again and he began to play. He would be the child's instrument and the child would be his voice, and together they would be mighty and all of England would hear their song.

Tuck had been shocked by what Marian suggested. It couldn't be helped, though. The castle was expendable. As, in truth, were all of them. It was possible none would survive the coming battle, but the sacrifice would be worth it if England could be saved.

That was yet another reason she'd had Friar Tuck marry her and Robin before he left. Every step she took in Sherwood, she couldn't help but think about him. So many emotions pulsed through her. Love, sorrow, fear, desire, and, above all, hope that he would come back to her safely.

As she walked farther into the forest she paused frequently to make sure that no one was following her. She couldn't afford to have her secret discovered. Each time she stopped, though, she felt only the forest around her and the animals that called it home. There were no humans and even the fey seemed absent, for which she was grateful. Not all of them were to be trusted. It wasn't that they would choose evil over good. It was just that they thought differently than men and it made them unpredictable.

Even to her.

Even though she wore the torc taken from the heart of the forest. The second torc, the one belonging to Robin, had been stolen. Last she'd seen it Prince John had taken it, so she had to assume it was in the Sheriff's possession now. She grit her teeth in anger at the very thought. She didn't know what he could do with it, but she knew that they needed to get it back.

She paused one last time before finally reaching her tree. It stood, tall and majestic even though it had died long before. There was a hollow in its base and it was there that she had hidden the book entrusted to her by the Cardinal.

When they had used it to obtain the two torcs, it had gone blank except for the incantation on the last page. When the torcs had been taken, the writing had returned. She hadn't had a chance to read it all yet, but knew she must. She hoped against hope it would give a clue as to how the Sheriff could be defeated. If it didn't...well...

She just prayed that it did, for all their sakes.

CHAPTER SEVEN

Philemon Longstride had grown used to the iron tang of blood in his mouth, though it seemed a bit stronger than on other nights.

The guards flung him into the cell. His bloody knees landed on the hard ground. He refused to give the bastards the satisfaction of hearing him cry out in pain, then took a moment to gather himself. He breathed in the fetid smell of the dungeon and breathed out the pain that seared through him. The guards closed and locked the cell behind him and went on their way without saying a word.

The fat of soft living had melted off him the last few months, leaving behind only muscle and iron. His wife, Glynna, would have appreciated it. She'd always been drawn to strength and appreciated masculinity. He closed his eyes for just a moment and let himself imagine his homecoming. Her running into his arms, the girls hugging his legs, Robert embracing him, and Robin...

Robin staring at him with that same disapproving stare he always did.

He sighed and opened his eyes. He and his youngest son had always been opposites. So much so that there had been a time when he wondered if Robin was even his son. Stuck here in this cage, though, those differences didn't seem to matter as much. He just hoped that when he made it home, Robin and he could learn to understand each other. That was, as long as Robin hadn't let the place go to hell in his absence.

"You risk too much, Philemon." The voice came out of the darkness and he dragged himself to his feet. "You should not antagonize the guards like you do," King Richard continued, his voice weary.

"Ah, but every time I'm out of this cage I learn something new," Longstride replied. "A bit more about the layout of this place, news, gossip."

"Truly I should have made you a spymaster instead of Robert," Richard said, a note of humor in his voice.

"Yes, but then he'd be here, and you know I'm a better conversationalist," Philemon said. He kept his tone light, even though his stomach clenched at the mention of Robert. He hadn't been able to shake the growing conviction that his son was dead. He didn't know *how* he knew, but he felt it, deep down. Every night as he fell asleep he begged God to not let it be true, and every morning he awoke more convinced that it was.

Richard chuckled. "You know I always enjoy our little talks. I'm quite convinced they're the only thing keeping us both sane at this point."

Philemon believed that to be true as well. Since their capture at the hands of that thieving shitsack Wulfhere, many of the men with them had lost themselves to sorrow. One had taken the short road out at the end of his own belt.

Sir Lawrence had escaped capture, hopefully fleeing back to England to seek help. A handful of the other nobles had died from some strange sickness, one going insane before he did so. Philemon would hear the echoes of that man's screaming for the rest of his life. Worse than the screaming, though, had been the hallucinations. The man had been convinced that England had fallen to the dark one, and that devils had claimed the land as their own. He shuddered just remembering the rantings.

He had been on the verge of killing the man himself just to make it stop.

One by one they had been reduced, taken away, until only he, Richard, and four others were left. What had become of the men serving under them was anyone's guess.

"So, what did you learn on this little expedition tonight?"

Philemon grunted. "Something about the plan has changed."

"What do you mean?" Richard asked sharply.

"Wulfhere is no longer in communication with your brother John."

Richard sat up straighter. "With whom is he communicating?"

"The Sheriff—at least, that's what I heard." His eyes had finally readjusted to the dark enough that he could see Richard frowning.

"The man who came with John?"

"That's my best guess," Philemon admitted.

"I wonder why?"

"I wish I knew."

"I'm not sure if this improves our situation or not."

"Nor am I, but for some reason I doubt it does."

"I feel the same, my friend."

The king fell into a thoughtful silence. Philemon turned to the bars of the cell and began testing them again, as he did every night, looking for a weakness. One of these days he hoped to be able to bring something back with him which they could use to saw through them.

After a few minutes had passed Richard broke the silence. "Come, sit down and let's talk for a while. I need to hear someone's thoughts other than my own."

Philemon gave up on the bars and went to sit by his king. Despite years of friendship, the circumstances in which they found themselves had led to more familiarity with his sovereign than either of them could have expected. Still, he imagined that when they were free of this wretched place, things would return to normal.

"Why did you turn down Robert when I suggested him as a suitor for your niece?" he asked, the words tumbling out of him before he could stop them.

"You know why."

"I don't care to speculate, sire."

"And yet clearly you must have, else you wouldn't ask."

"I'm just trying to pass the time," Philemon said carefully.

Richard sighed. "I want Marian to choose for herself. It's sentimental and frivolous, but I want to see her happy, and not married off to someone for convenience sake."

"Has she chosen someone?" he asked.

"She has not—at least, not that I'm aware of. Though at the banquet, before we set sail, she favored your younger son with all her dances."

"Yes, I think Robin is quite taken with her," Philemon admitted. "Then again, he'd be a fool not to be." He sighed, remembering his command to his son to try and secure Marian's affections, and Robin's refusal to be bartered like an animal. He would never learn to be a leader, or to play the games needed to gain and keep power. It was time to accept that about Robin, and stop trying to make him into something he wasn't.

"I like Robin."

"Sire?"

"He's a bit hotheaded, could use a healthy dose of prudence," Richard said. "He speaks his mind, though. Does what he thinks is right and he doesn't stray from it. That's why I let him poach deer."

"You know about that?" Philemon asked. "I strove to curtail the activity, but he is as hardheaded as I am."

"Of course I knew," Richard said with a chuckle. "I know as well that whatever he kills in the forest goes onto the plates of the hungry. If you stop and think about it, there are a great many who are dependent on him to provide." The king's voice reflected kindness.

"Maybe he takes more things seriously than I give him credit for," Philemon said grudgingly.

"I don't envy you the business of raising that one. Marian was headstrong enough."

Philemon chuckled even though it laid a fresh layer of pain

across his ribs. "Not unlike others of the royal family."

"I have been told there are similarities."

"I'm sure she'll grow to be a fine woman."

"She will." Richard paused. "She has, and I promised myself that when I returned I'd have a serious conversation with her about her responsibilities."

"I tried to have that conversation with Robin before I left."

"How did it go?"

"Not well. If I don't make it back, I'm pretty sure he'll be dancing on my grave."

"Don't speak like that!"

Philemon shrugged. "The truth is liberating—but, I'll try again when... *if* I get home." There were heavy footsteps coming down the stairs and he stood again, gingerly, wondering what their captors had in mind now. A few seconds later four guards stopped in front of their cell.

"Come," one growled. "Lord Wulfhere wants to see you."

"Which one of us?" Philemon asked.

"Both."

Wulfhere's keep wasn't as large as Richard's castle—not as sprawling nor as spread out, for the hilly land around it would not allow such construction—but it was not small. The rooms of it were stacked, using the rough-hewn rocks it was built from to make a considerable fortress. Some parts, like the dungeons, were carved into the crag itself, the rocky soil serving as impenetrable walls. Neither Philemon nor Richard knew what the outside appeared as. Philemon had been unconscious, and Richard under a rough burlap hood when they'd been interred.

Now they were walking up a lot of stairs.

At first there was a series of switchbacks within a narrow shaft. The walls were the hard-packed soil held back with timbers that had been dried and oiled and smelled like a grave. At the top, the stairs became a simple slope of flat stone that widened with each step. Above them they could hear the sound of people, the murmur of conversation and the clatter of cutlery on board.

Their eyes adjusted quickly as they stepped to the threshold of the underground. Ahead of them was a scene from the Norse days of old.

The middle of the keep had been fashioned into a long hall with a table down the center. Each side was lined with Wulfhere's men, all of them hunched over wooden platters of food that they shoveled into their mouths. A few engaged in conversation, but mostly they ate as if it would be their last meal. Children, women, and some men whose stature did not lend itself to soldiering, all bustled to and fro, carrying meat on spits, pitchers of drink, and bowls of steaming dishes.

The air hung thick with smoke coming from a long trough of coals, a brazier that stretched along most of the left wall, radiating enough heat to make the hall comfortable, nearly stifling if it weren't for the drafts of winter air that slid between stone and neath the door. It served two purposes, heat and cooking, with great hunks of meat turning on spits above.

The scent of cooked meat clenched Philemon's empty stomach so hard it almost dropped him to his knees.

"Stay strong," Richard said out the side of his mouth, and over the growl of his own empty stomach. The guard pushed them forward into the room.

"My guests!" a voice bellowed from the other end of the table. They looked over the heads of the men seated there—men who now stared at them with open hostility—and found a raised dais with a stout throne covered in animal skins. On it sat Wulfhere.

"Bring them forward."

The guard pushed them again and they began walking through the room. Despite the privation Richard strode like the king he was, spine straight, shoulders back, chin pointing directly ahead. His eyes moved neither left nor right, focused on his destination.

Philemon slipped into the role of his king's guard and spy, taking the time to assess their enemy. Yes, they were outnumbered, yes, they were escorted by an armed guard, but their hands were free.

They call them chances because they are unpredictable.

The men along the tables had a hardness and a wariness to them. Every one bore at least a single visible scar, most had several. Their hair hung shaggy around their shoulders, most sported ragged beards as well. There were tattoos, the dark sooty ink marks spilling from many sleeves and collars. These men had embraced the barbarian lifestyle demonstrated by their king. One man with the lean build of a predator had lost a hand somewhere, and the end of his forearm was a knotted mass of dark scar tissue. Philemon made note of him in particular. Anyone with only one hand who still held a place at this table of brigands was a dangerous man indeed.

Finally they stood before the throne of Wulfhere.

He sat above them. His left hand stroked the wide head of some mongrelized mastiff cur, the dog a stack of muscle with a chest as broad as a man's and a square jaw made for cracking bones. It stared at them both with bored eyes.

"Do you not kneel?" Wulfhere asked.

"I do not," Richard answered, before Philemon could spew the answer that clawed at the back of his teeth.

"Still think you are better than I." It was an accusation.

"Where are my men?"

"Kneel."

"If I do, you will tell me of my men?"

"If I wish to," Wulfhere sneered.

"Then no."

"No? Are your men not worth kneeling before me?"

"Is that your word? I kneel and my men are set free?"

"You have no bargaining power."

"You wish to humiliate me, and yet I will not be debased."

"I could order my men to *make* you kneel."

At Wulfhere's words the guards behind them tensed, raising their weapons. Philemon lowered himself just slightly, choosing which guard to attack first, which one from whom he might be able to wrest a weapon in the shortest amount of time.

"You could have your men kill me," Richard responded. "You can torture me, bury me in shite up to my chin, drag me through your streets by my intestines, but at no point of any of that will I have *chosen* to kneel before you. That knowledge will be like rats in your guts, eating away at the soft bits of you, and I will have won even in my death."

"You are just a man."

"I am a king."

"So am I!" Wulfhere roared, coming to his feet with his axe out and ready. The mastiff jumped to its feet as well, a long, low growl rumbling from its wide chest. The men behind them began to bang on the table, knives in hand, and to howl, their throated cries rolling along the stone walls of the hall. Wulfhere waved his axe, encouraging the display.

Richard stood impassively as the ruckus subsided. Philemon admired his calm, collected demeanor. Once the hall quieted to a murmur and Wulfhere stood on the edge of his dais looking down at them both, with his axe in hand, he spoke.

"You have men who would kill at your command?" Richard asked.

"Every one of them."

The men howled again.

"They would die in your place?"

"They would go to Valhalla this moment for me."

The howls were there, but Philemon swore they were less.

Richard waited until the hall fell silent once more, until the only sounds were the crackle and hiss of the meat dripping on its spits and the breathing of the people, before he spoke.

"Would you do the same for them?"

Philemon stumbled, his foot turning on a rock.

"Keep moving, you old fool," the guard growled.

Philemon lurched forward. He only had two guards now, but his hands were tied and a rag had been wrapped over his eyes in a crude blindfold. He could still see under its edge, but only enough to see that they walked over grass. The northern wind cut through his dirty tunic, cold and sharp as a stiletto.

"Keep up with that 'old fool' talk," he said, "and I will gut you like a fish when I am free."

"You're just as stubborn as your king," the same guard said. "*Old fool.*"

He heard someone spit, and something wet hit his cheek. Philemon clenched his teeth on the rage that boiled inside him.

After Richard's question, which left the entire hall silent, Wulfhere had ordered that Richard be taken back to the cell, and Philemon be "put with the rest of the nobles."

"Be strong, my friend," Richard said as they were parted. "I will pray for you."

He'd take the prayers, but he'd prefer a sword, preferably the one that had been taken from him. He continued walking, using the uneven ground to help hide the fact that he was working his wrists against the rope. The skin burned, raw and abraded, but, whether from his efforts or the blood his new wounds seeped, his bonds were just a bit looser. His shoulders were tense, waiting on one of the guards walking behind him to see what he was doing.

Thank Jesu they tied my hands in the front.

"Wulfhere is a king." A different voice.

Must be the other one.

"He's a thief," Philemon said.

"All kings are thieves."

"Not mine."

"Him, too. He stole Lord Wulfhere's birthright."

Philemon stopped and turned. "I know your lord. He is not nobility."

"Nobility is not blood."

Philemon reached up, moving slowly, and pushed the blindfold off his eyes. Neither guard moved to stop him. He shook it free from his head.

"True," he said, sizing them up. "I have known some of noble blood who were worse scoundrels than your lord." The men were young—as young as Robin—and he knew with the certainty of age that even unarmed, they would be able to defeat him.

If it were a fair fight.

One of the guards, the one who was built like a cistern, had his sword out. *He's the one been poking me in the back*. The other, thin as a piece of hemp, had slid his sword belt around so the weapon hung under his cloak. It made walking easier, especially over rough terrain, but it made drawing the sword much slower.

Philemon struggled to stay calm.

This felt like a chance.

"I bet you are a scoundrel, noble," the thin guard said. "Probably as vicious as a rabid weasel, and twice as hungry."

Thick leaned forward, poking Philemon's chest with the point of the sword.

"What's the most you've stolen, old fool?"

"Your mother's maidenhood, you bastard."

Thick sputtered, face blazing red and a vein popping out on the side of his temple. His rage exploded in a string of curses.

Philemon swung his hands up, driving the thick knot of his bonds against the sword edge. He hissed as the sharp point scraped up over his breastbone, slicing the skin over his sternum—not deep, but enough to feel. He jerked his hands back, feeling the rope part as it slid up the sword, and kicked out, driving his foot into the knee of Thick. He felt it fold under his boot and the guard dropped with a grunt. Philemon had to jerk back quickly to avoid the sword's edge.

Thin tried to pull his sword but his cloak tangled the hilt.

Hands free, Philemon stepped in, seizing Thick's wrist and driving his knee into the man's jaw. Thick's fingers went limp and jerky and Philemon snatched the sword from them. He spun, slashing Thin across the stomach just as the man got his sword pulled. Thin dropped, intestines spilling from the long wound that yawned from hipbone to hipbone. He opened his mouth to cry out, and Philemon drove the sword's point into his mouth.

Thin died in a gurgle.

Thick struggled to sit up, face white from the pain of his dislocated knee. Philemon stood over him.

"Young fool," he said, and he slit the guard's throat.

Two swords and two cloaks later, Philemon made his escape.

CHAPTER EIGHT

Much knew he should be afraid, but all he had felt since leaving the camp was pride and excitement. He still marveled that Lady Marian had chosen him for such an important mission and reveled in the knowledge that Robin was alive.

When Sir Lawrence spoke to him now, it was as one man to another, and Old Soldier continued to teach him even more about fighting. Truly God was on their side and they must all be invincible.

The only thing that dampened his enthusiasm was how frequently they had to stop. Though he tried to hide it, Sir Lawrence was in poor health. The rest of them could tell, though, and Robin allowed for longer and more frequent pauses than he would have otherwise.

Much felt bad for attacking the man earlier.

The delays made him nervous, because he knew his king was in captivity, and his friends back home were in great danger, as well. Whenever they stopped it was as though he could feel the seconds of their lives slipping away. From the anguished look on Robin's face, he suspected his hero felt the same.

"Don't let your mind wander," Old Soldier said as he rapped the back of Much's knuckles with the flat of his sword. Without meaning to, Much dropped the sword he'd been holding and felt himself flush with embarrassment as he scrambled to pick it up.

"What's wrong with you this evening?"

Much hunched his shoulders. "Lord Longstride looks worried."

Old Soldier laughed dismissively. "He's not worried—he's just anxious to see the missus again. One day you'll understand, when you have a lady love of your own."

Much's eyes drifted over to Sir Lawrence who was already asleep, curled up on the ground inside his cloak. Old Soldier followed Much's gaze and then turned back with a grim look.

"We need him," the older man said. "He knows how to reach the king. We can't let him die before we get there." Old Soldier's words chilled Much a little, particularly the "let him die" part. Maybe that was what was so unsettling. Old Soldier had bandaged his wound and declared it no real danger. Yet Sir Lawrence looked like a man who was dying, even though as far as Much could tell there was nothing wrong with him beyond exhaustion.

"There are two ways a man dies," Old Soldier said softly, as though reading Much's mind.

"Two?" Much asked.

Old Soldier nodded. "He dies when his body is brutalized beyond repair, organs are ruptured, that sort of thing."

"And the other way a man dies?"

"When he *believes* he is going to," Old Soldier said. "I've seen men on the battlefield keep fighting and live to celebrate the victory after being stabbed a dozen times, even in the chest and the gut. I've seen others fall over dead from a single wound to the shoulder. They gave up in their hearts and their minds. They believed they were going to die, and so they did."

"Do you think Sir Lawrence believes he's going to die?" Much asked.

"Yes."

"And that's what's wrong with him?"

Old Soldier nodded.

"Then why hasn't he died yet?"

"Because his sense of duty to his king is still driving him forward. But mark my words, no sooner do we free Richard, than Sir Lawrence will die." At those words Much felt a chill snake its way up his spine. He was suddenly intensely grateful that Sir Lawrence was a stranger to him. Otherwise he might have wished them not to free the king, so that he might go on living.

"I know, son, it's tough," the old man said. "'Tis one of the brutalities of war. The human spirit can endure much, but every man has his breaking point. I've lived long enough to know that to be true."

"Even you?" Much asked hesitantly.

"Even me," Old Soldier said grimly. Much felt something in his chest tighten. His emotions must have shown on his face, for Old Soldier suddenly grinned and clapped him on the back. "Don't worry, though. We're nowhere near it. Yours either. We have steel in us, you and I, and we will be standing when all the rest are dust."

Much couldn't help but smile back.

Glynna awoke from a nightmare of her previous life and lay still for a moment in the dark, shivering, as she drove the images back into the shadows. She reached out for her love and she found him. He rarely slept, but he had taken to staying through much of the night with her.

"What is it?" he asked. The sound of his voice washed over her, dark, beautiful, and helped chase away the lingering vestiges of the dream that had so disturbed her.

"I had a nightmare," she confessed.

"What about?" he purred. He turned to her and brought a pale hand up to caress her cheek.

"About my... about the time before I knew you," she said, not wanting to confess that there had been anyone in her life before, even though he well knew there had.

His hand froze. "What about it?" he asked intently.

"Images, memories."

"Tell me," he said. His voice, usually seductive or amused when speaking to her, had turned cold. Glynna found herself wishing she hadn't brought it up. She didn't like it when he on rare occasion treated her like all the other pitiful, mewling people. He should never use that tone of voice with her. It made her chest tight in a painful way, as though his love was something she could lose.

Then again, hadn't Philemon Longstride lost hers?

She hesitated, turning that thought around in her mind. Glynna had felt many things for her husband, pride and lust being chief among those. She couldn't say, though, that she ever truly loved him. Not like she loved the darkness made flesh that lay beside her, still touching her cheek with an icy hand.

"We were back at the manor, years ago, before it was burned," she began. "Philemon had been gone a fortnight, traveling with the king. He was supposed to be away for a couple of months. My oldest girl was just a babe. Robert had taken on some of his father's responsibilities, even though he was so young. He worked the fields, went to check on the families who lived on our land. One day, he didn't come home for supper. I started to worry. I sent messengers. He wasn't in the fields. No one had seen him all day."

She could remember the terror she had felt when it all happened. The nightmare had brought that back to her. Now, though, she felt strangely disconnected from it, as though looking at someone else's life.

"Robert had wanted to go with his father, but Philemon told him no, that he had to protect the Longstride lands. I was beside myself. I thought for sure that something had happened to him. I didn't know what I would say to his father when he returned. I couldn't sleep all night.

"Then, the next morning, I left the house, determined to search for Robert myself. No sooner had I stepped out the door when I saw his younger brother. He was walking hand-in-hand with Philemon, who had come home early. He was going to lecture me on letting Robin run wild in the woods, as if anyone could stop him. He stopped, though, and got this funny look on his face when he asked me where Robert was. As if somehow he knew that something... had happened to..."

She trailed off. She could feel her love's icy fingers brush against her throat.

"And what did you tell him?" he breathed in her ear.

"I told him that the lad had run off, no doubt with some wench who had managed to turn his head. After all, he was the one that abandoned me. He was the one who deserved the blame."

"And had he?"

"No. He'd made a visit far away, and his horse took lame on the journey home. He walked the beast until night fell, then finished the journey that morning. He arrived home not half an hour after Philemon did. His father forgave him, of course."

"There's more to your nightmare than just that old memory."

"Yes," she acknowledged. "That was what I told Philemon all those years ago. In my nightmare, however, I told him something different."

"What did you tell him?"

"I told him Robert was dead."

Her love's fingers tightened around her throat. "You dreamed that your husband came home, led by Robin, and you told him that Robert was dead?" He sat up abruptly.

"Yes," she said, finding it hard to catch her breath.

"Are you sure this is not prophecy?" he growled.

"I am not unfamiliar with portents and visions."

"Do you know where Robert is now?" he demanded.

She nodded slowly. "In his grave."

"How do you know this?" he asked.

"The little princess told me."

She could see his eyes burning, glowing in the darkness, and it sent a thrill through her.

"Did she tell you who put him there?"

"You did, my love."

Silence greeted her declaration. He let go of her and sat on the edge of the bed. She sat up and put her chin on his shoulder.

"What is wrong?" she urged.

"Your dream has more weight than you've given it."

"What do you mean?"

"I think that Richard may yet be rescued," he said, "and that your wretched husband and son will have something to do with it."

"Then we will kill them," she answered quickly. "Just as we killed the little prince who was so much bother."

"Of course we will. Thanks to you, my love, we will be ready."

The Sheriff watched his assorted sorcerers and spellcasters as they whispered among themselves. Five minutes watching told him all he needed to know. They still did not have a spell that would breach Sherwood. The ancient forest was proving a more formidable barrier than even he had anticipated.

No matter, though, for soon Henry would arrive and the Sheriff could command his troops—send them into the woods to find the outlaws. Most of them were refugees, weak from hunger and abuse, not hardened criminals or seasoned soldiers. They would not be deep in the forest.

There was a great deal of agitation among those who had gathered. They knew they were failing him. Their numbers were dwindling, and they were growing desperate. Even the Mad Monk, who always liked to appear in control, was agitated. He hadn't been quite right since Glynna had killed the necromancer he cared about. If the grief and uncertainty helped him focus, all the better. If not... well, there were numerous uses that could be made of a sacrifice.

He switched his attention to the leprous Scotsman who appeared to be flaking off parts of himself at a faster than usual rate. It was within his power to heal the man, but he had a deep belief that it might affect his ability to do magic. Indeed, the

Scotsman seemed to revel in his own diseased state.

Then the leper's apprentice—a young, very thin boy—pulled the Sheriff's attention more. Something was changing in him. He was becoming darker, thinking more. He watched the youth watch the others, as someone who began to understand that power belonged to those who took it. That led to the question of when and how he planned on taking it.

"It's *not* impossible," the gnarled old witch Sera said to the Scotsman. "Impossible's just small-minded thinking, while the universe is vast. I've been to the edge of the forest. It's not immune to us." She held out her hand and he could see that she was grasping a dead twig that was gray and black. "The Forest can be breached. It can be killed. You just don't know how to do it effectively."

"Alright, then how would *you* do it?" the leper demanded.

"Key the lock," she said. "We need to persuade one of the fey to divulge to us the origin of the magic that protects the forest."

"The fey are long dead," someone else scoffed. "None has been seen for generations."

"That's not true. I saw one as a child," the witch said, lifting her chin.

"That was a hundred years ago, Sera," the Mad Monk growled. She glared at him, clearly wishing him dead on the spot. The Sheriff thought about obliging her, just to scare the rest, but decided against it. He stepped out of the shadows cloaking him, and even the Mad Monk jumped at his sudden appearance. He looked around the room, pinning each person there with his eyes.

"The fey do exist," he said. "As their power fades, the land is more easily corrupted. Catching one is the difficult part. Who here thinks themselves capable of such a task?"

"I will try, my lord," the apprentice spoke up.

Ah…

"What is your name?"

"Ean."

"Alright, Ean," the Sheriff said. "Bring me a fey within a fortnight, or your prayers will not be granted."

"My prayers?"

"If you fail me, you will pray that I kill you, child," he said. "Do you understand me?"

"I do." Ean gulped. "My lord?"

"Yes?"

"If I accomplish the task, will there be a reward?"

The Sheriff chuckled. "If greed is your motivator, then yes, you will be rewarded." He glared down at the boy. "So there are two roads you may walk on. Do you understand?"

"Perfectly, my lord," the boy said, fear flickering in his eyes, yet steadfast in his resolve. The Scotsman started to protest, but quickly fell silent when the Sheriff turned to glare at him. Then he took in the entire assemblage.

"The rest of you have two weeks to figure out what to do with the creature, once Ean brings him here. Two weeks to live—that might be all any of you have. I suggest you use the time wisely. Oh, and I'll be moving you to new… quarters." He snapped his fingers and a dozen soldiers rushed into the room. His magic users were becoming skittish. He couldn't risk them bolting before the job was done.

"My lord, where are you sending us?" Sera asked, voice quavering.

"Don't worry, it's dark and damp," he sneered. "You should feel right at home." He turned on his heel and walked out, enjoying the smell of fear that filled the air.

CHAPTER NINE

If Chastity wasn't in hell, then she had to be in the next closest thing. She was in a dungeon somewhere, in near-total darkness. She vaguely remembered being tied up, put in a sack, and thrown in a wagon. She had been in the dungeon ever since. She had been beaten severely and had no idea why the prince hadn't had her killed outright. Not after Will confessed to being the Hood and died in her arms.

A tear slid down her cheek as she thought of him. She didn't even know if his sacrifice had saved the others. She prayed that it had, though she was under no delusions that anyone was coming to rescue her. Even if they thought she was alive, odds were good they would never find her.

Since arriving in the dungeon, she'd only seen one man—the one who brought her moldy bread and refilled a bucket of water near her every day. She had assumed the prince was waiting to question her about Will's allies or was planning on making a spectacle of her with a public execution.

Or worse, to use her as leverage against Marian.

The very thought made her shudder. Her lady was her friend and her better, and she would follow her to the ends of the earth. She would even gladly die for her. What if Marian was tempted to try to get her back?

Something had changed, though. It had been seven days since the man with the bread had last appeared. This left her convinced that, for whatever reason, he was *never* coming back. Which meant she was going to die alone in this dark, godforsaken place, and no one would know what had become of her.

Her muscles cramped painfully and she gritted her teeth. The water in the bucket had run out three days earlier, and the thirst was far worse than the hunger.

"I refuse to die here in the dark like an animal," she said, forcing herself to say the words out loud, to make them real. The sound of her voice in the silence startled her. It was weak and cracked, hardly resembling her own even though she knew it must be.

This reinforced her resolve.

She was starving and parched. Her body was bruised and battered. Her hands were shackled together, a single chain running between the manacles clamped around each wrist. Another chain anchored the first one to a ring buried deep in the wall. She had tested both chains, link by link, trying to find a weakness. There was none. As for the ring, no doubt it would still be wedged deep in the stone centuries from now, when the rest of the building had collapsed.

A rat ran over her foot and she kicked, sending it flying with a high-pitched squeal. She hated the nasty things and every time one touched her it made her skin crawl.

Slowly she began to test the chains again, only to realize that she was even weaker than she had been the day before. It was as if she could feel her life slipping away from her. At this point even the moldy bread would seem a feast, and the dirty water would be more delicious than wine.

I shouldn't have kicked the rat. I should have caught it and eaten it.

She had to get out of there. She leaned her head back against the stone wall and prayed for the strength to escape.

Chastity had lost weight since her imprisonment, and the cold of the dungeon seeped deep into her bones. Then she noticed something new. The manacles were looser on her wrists than they had been. She began to try and work the left one loose. The cold metal bit into her flesh as she strained to get it off.

She couldn't do it. Her hand was too big.

Dislocate your thumb.

The voice whispered in her head. It was not her own. She hesitated. Was it an angel trying to help her, or a devil trying to trick her?

She took a deep breath, realizing she was going to have to take a chance. Folding her thumb inside her palm, she laid it against the stone. The fear of pain made the back of her neck prickly and hot. Gritting her teeth she leaned as hard as she could. There was immense pressure and a sharp pain and the joint slipped out of itself in a red blast of hurt that made her vision go white.

Choking down the scream she wanted to let loose, she fell back. It took her a long moment to ease enough that the pain went dull and throbby in her hand. Then she grasped the manacle... and was able to pull it off. She put the thumb back into place but the burning pain remained. Still, she had one hand free. Hope swelled within her as she grasped her right thumb and wrenched.

This one hurt even worse, but as the manacles clattered to the ground she gave a hoarse shout of victory. It quickly turned to a grunt of anguish as she tried to get her thumb back into its natural position. Even once she did, it felt odd, but there was no time to worry about it as she headed toward where the door had to be.

The bottoms of her feet scraped painfully against the ground as she moved forward, hands in front of her. The darkness was oppressive, but it was not absolute. She was the only prisoner in the dungeon. If there was anyone else there, they'd been dead before she arrived. The door would probably be barred, but since she had been chained to the wall, the man who had brought her food might have grown careless.

After a few moments of groping, she reached the wall, then slid her hands along the rough stones until they encountered wood. There was no handle. Whispering a prayer, she put all her weight against the door. To her relief it started to move.

Then it stopped, open only a few inches—just enough for a breeze to come in. She breathed deep, hoping to inhale fresh, clean air. Instead a putrid smell assailed her and she doubled over, coughing uncontrollably.

Forcing herself to breathe through her mouth, she willed herself not to smell the stench that wafted through the narrow opening. The door wasn't barred, but there was something blocking it, keeping her from opening it all the way. As much as she didn't want to find the source of the odor, she needed to get the door open and leave the dungeon if she hoped to survive.

So she straightened up and leaned her shoulder into the barrier, then began shoving with everything she had. It slowly gave an inch. Then another. She gritted her teeth again and tried not to cry out in pain and frustration. Finally the opening was big enough, and she managed to squeeze through, further tearing her already filthy, ragged dress in the process.

On the other side of the door there was more light, let in by a narrow slit in the wall, and she found what had been blocking the way. The man who had brought her the food and water was on the ground, dead. She gaped at him for a moment in horror. The body was rotting, maggots feeding on it. She couldn't tell at a glance what had killed him, and that terrified her.

Turning, she saw a set of stairs leading up, and she was halfway to the top before she managed to slow herself down, her panicked mind urging caution at the last moment. There was no door at the top and she crept up the last few steps, straining her ears to discover if she could hear anything. Reason told her that if there were others present, they surely would have noticed the missing man and come down to try and find him.

She couldn't hear anything.

Still, she flattened herself against the wall as she ascended the last few feet, then peered around the edge of the wall and into an empty corridor. The torches on the wall had burned out, but light shone from another narrow slit window at the far end. The place felt empty. It was more than that, though, deeper somehow. It felt... abandoned. She crept into the hallway and headed for the window, anxious to try and figure out where she was.

The window was narrow, the kind that archers usually used on walls or towers. She was relatively certain, though, that she wasn't on one of the higher floors. Glancing out, she saw that the building was set on a rise with the ground sloping steeply away. She could see Sherwood Forest—at least, she assumed it was Sherwood. The sun was near the horizon, and the light was starting to fade. It would soon be night.

Turning, she made her way back down the corridor, heading for the far end. Walking more swiftly now, more convinced with each step that there was no one but her. After a couple of turns she finally found the main hall, and from there it was easy to find the kitchen.

The room was as empty as the rest of the building. She lit a torch and then she found a bucket of water and eagerly drank some down, the liquid soaking into her parched throat. When she'd had enough she turned and surveyed the rest of the room.

There, on one of the counters, was a massive tray of what looked like a few dozen tarts. Stomach rumbling, she moved to stand over the tray. One tart had a bite taken out of it. She picked it up and sniffed, wondering what was in it. There was a sickish sweet smell about it. She put it down and picked up an uneaten one, ready to pop it into her mouth.

She froze, though, staring at the partially eaten tart, and her thoughts flashed to her captor, dead outside the dungeon. What killed him? There had been no obvious signs of blood around the body.

He must have bitten into it.

She dropped her tart back onto the tray and wiped her hand

on her dress. Why so many tarts for an empty castle? Who were they for?

Was it possible that the food was poisoned, and that eating the tart had killed him? It seemed crazy. Then she noticed that the way the tarts were laid out, another one seemed to be missing. There were a few crumbs where it would have been.

More crumbs lay on the counter, and she traced them. They led behind a large pot in one corner. She pulled it out, and then jumped back. The body of a dead rat was there, most of a tart next to him as though it had fallen from his mouth.

Her eyes flashed back to the tray of tarts and she found herself counting them. Someone had made these tarts with the intention of killing a large group of people. They were meant to be taken elsewhere, but where? No one else was present. Where had they gone?

Suddenly it struck her.

Sweets.

The noble children who had been kidnapped—the ones whose location she and Marian had been unable to discover. Chastity gasped as she realized that the Prince must have intended to kill them, tricking them with the little sweets. The tarts had been delivered to the castle, but hadn't made it past the kitchen.

The man outside the dungeon ate one and it killed him before he could give them to the children, Chastity realized. She had no idea what the poison was, or whether John or the Sheriff had seen to it. What she did know was that the children hadn't been in the dungeon with her. If they were being kept in this castle, that meant they had to be locked in one of the towers.

She picked up a small lantern, lit the candle inside, and moved out the door with a mission in mind. Making her way as swiftly as she could back into the main hall, she found the staircase there and ascended it. If the children were prisoners here, too, then like her they'd have been several days without food and water.

On the upper floor she found another narrow staircase that led, most likely, to a tower. She took the steps as fast as she could, her own muscles quivering in anguish. Abruptly she regretted leaving the kitchen without bringing the bucket of water with her. If she found the children, they would be in desperate need of it. Perhaps even more than she had been.

Her heart was racing and she was panting by the time she made it to the top of the stairs. There was a small landing and a heavy door with a heavy bolt securing it. She slid back the bolt, pulled it open, and stepped inside. Then she gasped.

Littered across the floor like a bunch of discarded ragdolls were the missing children.

CHAPTER TEN

All the horror of the past few months washed over Chastity as she stared at the bodies of the children. Tears welled in her eyes. If she'd only known they were here. If she'd only been able to escape sooner.

If only we had not been captured by that evil bastard.

If only King Richard hadn't abandoned us to this.

She heard a small groaning sound and one of the figures began to move. She dropped down next to a young boy who blinked up at her. There was fear in his eyes. His lips moved as though he was trying to speak, but only another groan came out.

"You're going to be okay," she said, her voice shaking with relief that her initial impression had been wrong. "I'm going to go get you some water. I will be right back, I promise." She tried to put reassurance into her voice. Standing up, she ran back down to the kitchen as fast as she could, grabbed the bucket of water and a dipper, and hurried back, careful to not slosh any of the life-giving liquid. By the time she made it back into the tower the boy had sat up. Around him, others were starting to stir, and she felt a surge of hope.

With a shaking hand she held the dipper of water while the boy drank from it, slowly at first, and then more eagerly. She made soothing noises the entire time. Her eyes kept darting around the room. Finally a girl struggled to a sitting position nearby. Her cheeks were smudged nearly black with dirt except for where tears had left streaks down them.

"I'll give you some more in a few minutes," she promised the boy when she took the dipper from him. He nodded and she moved over to the girl and gave her some water to drink. After several long sips the girl looked at her with big eyes.

"Are you an angel?" she whispered hoarsely.

"No, just a girl like you. But I promise you, I'm going to get you out of here. Everything's going to be okay now," Chastity said as calmly as she could. Yet as she moved on to help the next child sit up and drink some water, she could feel the fear rising in her. Every minute that passed there was a risk that someone would come to the castle, to check and make sure that they were all dead, as had clearly been intended.

Everything in her screamed at her to hurry, to move the children before it was too late. Looking around, though, she wasn't sure any of them were up to walking down the stairs, let alone fleeing the castle. Several of them were emaciated, and a couple were shaking uncontrollably—whether from fatigue, dehydration, or terror she couldn't tell.

"It's going to be okay, I'm here to rescue you all," she said, raising her voice enough that everyone could hear her.

"Not all," the girl with the tear-streaked cheeks said softly. She pointed to three different children, two boys and a girl. Chastity's heart felt like it was breaking as she realized that those three children were already dead. How long had the children been living there with the dead bodies among them? She tried to push the thought from her mind as she moved on to the next child and helped him drink some water.

She didn't want to look at the bodies, but it was as though she had no choice. She was almost compelled to look, to see the ravages of deprivation on the tiny bodies, the frozen faces, the lifeless eyes. Shuddering, she nearly spilled some water and forced herself back to the task at hand.

All the other children could still end up that way if she didn't do her best to prevent it. She had to think fast, move quickly. The panic welled up in her again, but she fought it down. She was hungry and that wasn't helping. The fatigue, pain, and lack of food were starting to take their toll. She was shaking more now, and it was getting harder and harder to steady the ladle of water. She had to find them some food.

A hand suddenly closed around hers, and she looked up from where she knelt. The first boy who had awakened was staring at her solemnly.

"Let me help," he said. "I think you need to rest a minute."

"I'm fine," she said.

"Don't lie to me," he whispered, so soft she was sure only she had heard him.

"Okay," she said, nodding slowly. She sat back and watched as he helped one of the younger boys drink.

"Do you know where we are?" she asked him.

"I recognized the hall. I was here once with my father. This is Lord Locksley's home. I don't know where he is, though," the boy said, frowning at the last.

Lord Locksley was dead, but she didn't want to burden the children with that knowledge. At least now she knew where they were. It wasn't as much help as she would have liked, though, since she wasn't entirely sure which direction to go when they left the castle, other than straight into the forest.

That really was the best choice. The forest held dangers, but none of them compared to the Sheriff and his demons. She took a deep breath.

"We're going to get out of here soon," she said.

The boy looked up at her. There was fear in his eyes, but hope as well. She was pretty certain she wasn't the rescue he and the others had been praying for. The Lord worked in mysterious ways, though, and she knew He had led her up the stairs to find the children.

"They are all very weak," he said. She noted that he didn't

include himself in that statement. Standing up, she moved toward the door.

"I'm going to go find some food," she said. "That will help build their strength. In the meantime, make sure everyone has enough to drink, including you. I will bring more water as well."

"Okay," he said, although he looked a little more fearful.

She took a torch from the wall and lit it with the candle in the lantern. She would light the rest on her way back down the stairs and in the hall so they could see to leave.

"I promise, I *will* be back," she said, praying it was a promise she would be able to keep. He nodded and she turned, heading back toward the kitchen as quickly as she was able and lighting the torches along the way. The only thing she'd noticed there was the tray of poisoned tarts. She couldn't help but wonder if anything else she might uncover would be poisoned as well.

Once in the kitchen she found the larder. To her relief she discovered some jars of jams and some salt pork. Carrying as much of the food as she could out to the great hall, she set it on the table. She threw away the poisoned tarts so none might accidentally find and eat them. Then she filled another bucket of water from the well, and returned to the tower.

The boy who was helping the others looked up, relief clear in his eyes. All the children were sitting up now, and their eyes were starting to look clearer than they had earlier.

"There's food downstairs in the hall," she said to him. "Do you think they are capable of walking down the stairs to get it?"

"Food?" the one girl asked, pulling herself painfully to her feet.

Chastity nodded. "Yes, in the hall. Can you walk down the stairs?"

"Yes," the girl said, even though she swayed slightly on her feet. "I can make it, even if I have to crawl."

"Good," Chastity said, trying to sound strong and encouraging instead of sorrowful at the child's state. "After everyone eats something, we'll leave here."

"Can we go home?" a young boy asked, and several voices

suddenly spoke up, echoing the question. They were all hoarse and thready, but the eagerness and longing were unmistakable.

"Soon," she promised, not having the heart to tell them the truth. Some of them didn't have homes to which they could return. Families either. She turned away suddenly lest they read the anguish on her face. These children had already been through so much, and for some of them the worst was yet to come.

"Let's get downstairs so we can eat and get out of here," she said, still looking away.

The girl walked past her on unsteady feet. Once she reached the stairs she put a hand against the wall and began to descend, carefully taking each step. Another boy and a little girl who looked to be a relative, a cousin perhaps, walked past, clutching each other's hands.

"Be careful," Chastity advised. "Go slow."

One by one the other children began to shuffle past her. When they stopped coming only the boy with the water and two other youngsters were left.

"I don't think they can walk," the boy said solemnly.

"What's your name?" she asked.

"Bartholomew."

"My name is Chastity, Bartholomew," she said. "How are you doing?"

"I'm fine," he said, though his eyes gave the lie to his words.

"I can carry them down, one at a time," Chastity said. "I'll take the first one. Will you wait here with the other one until I come back?" she asked, not wanting to leave any of the children alone, especially not in a room with the dead.

He nodded.

"Okay."

She bent over a boy who seemed to be all arms and legs, though they were painfully thin. "Can you put your arms around my neck and hold on?" she asked.

The boy nodded faintly and lifted his arms. His grip was tenuous and she realized she couldn't rely on him to hold on.

Gritting her teeth she picked him up and put him on her hip, trying to let part of her frame carry his weight, since her arms were still weak and her hands still throbbing in agony from the damage she had done to her thumbs.

She walked slowly, taking the steps carefully. The boy's body flopped loosely and kept trying to fall backward. It was all she could do to keep holding onto him and not lose her footing. By the time she made it down to the great hall she was shaking and drenched in sweat. She managed to lower the boy down onto a bench and he flopped over against the table with a little cry.

At least the table was holding him up.

The other children were already eating. The little girl who had gone down the stairs first looked up and flushed slightly as though she'd been caught doing something wrong.

"We already prayed over the food."

Chastity nodded and forced herself to smile. "You did good. Keep eating and make sure everyone eats something."

The girl nodded and got up and carried some of the pork over to the boy Chastity had just carried down the stairs. She wasn't sure he was even going to be able to feed himself, and her mind was already racing ahead, wondering how they would manage to carry two children out of there and all the way into the forest.

She wondered if there were any horses in the stable. If there were, though, they too might be suffering from dehydration. She squeezed her eyes closed in a quick prayer that God would lead the way.

"I'll return with the other two," she told the girl before heading back to the main staircase. What seemed like an eternity later she barely managed to drag her own body up the last few stairs to the tower. The one boy stood quickly and he picked up the water bucket that was still partially full. She bent down and spoke to the other child. The girl, though, wasn't even able to lift her arms to put them around Chastity's neck.

Picking the child up, she held her close. Her arms were shaking with the exertion and terror filled her that she might drop the child on the way down.

"Can I help?" the boy asked.

"Walk beside me, and help me balance if I start to fall." She hated to put the burden on the boy, but she was terrified of what might happen if she lost her footing. As it was, she could tell that her bare feet were beginning to bleed. The stones beneath her were becoming slick, and she cursed the day that her mother had forced her to start wearing slippers as a child.

She'd been happy being barefoot, and when she was little she could walk on anything and it never hurt. Her mother had told her, though, that if she was going to be a lady's lady, she had to wear proper things, shoes being chief among those. In the years that followed her feet had become as soft as a royal's.

True to his word Bartholomew hovered right next to her, his hand lightly touching her back as though trying to offer her support. She could tell that he wished he could carry the girl down, but was wise enough to realize he didn't have the strength. He would grow up to be a fine man, compassionate, level-headed.

If he ever got the chance to grow up.

She gritted her teeth as they made it down the last of the narrow tower steps. She wished she could set the girl down for a moment, but knew that if she did she'd never be able to pick her up again. They finally made it to the main staircase and she readjusted her grip before putting her foot down on the top stair.

She grunted as she lowered her body down, step by step. Everything was hurting, throbbing. A muscle in her back seized and started to spasm. She cried out, and her grip on the girl loosened for a moment.

Bartholomew reached out quickly and put his hands under the child, lifting her slightly and holding her while Chastity tried to force her own body back into submission.

"I can take her," Bartholomew said, his terrified voice belying his brave assertion.

"No, save your strength for later," Chastity panted.

She considered sitting on the stairs and trying to scoot herself and the child down, but realized that might produce an even greater strain. So she forced her foot down to the next step, grunting again as it took her weight. Slowly, painfully, they made their way down each torturous step. Her eyes stung but no tears came. Muscles in her cheeks started to twitch. Her right calf cramped hard and she paused, teetering on the edge of a stair.

"God help me," she breathed.

The cramp eased, she was able to step down. Three stairs left.

Two.

One.

She reached the ground and a sob was wrenched from her. She shuffled slowly to the table and then placed the girl onto the bench. The child fell sideways but remained there. Chastity's legs gave way and she crashed down onto the bench beside her.

Small hands of the boy on her other side reached out and pushed the girl up to a sitting position. Bartholomew sat down at the table, eyes enormous as he eyed the food. He reached out, grabbed a piece of the salt pork, and then bit into it eagerly.

Chastity reached out toward the food, but her hands were shaking so hard she could barely grasp a bit of pork for herself. Suddenly the girl who had been overseeing the distribution of the food was beside her. She put a piece of the pork into Chastity's mouth. It was tough and salty, but she couldn't remember ever tasting something so delicious in her life.

Bartholomew had set the pail of water on the table, and the other children began to take turns drinking. The saltiness of the pork was probably a good thing, making them want more water.

She slowly looked up and down the table. They were all starving, but they were all chewing slowly. It was all they could manage at that point. She couldn't help but wonder once more how on earth she was going to get herself all the way into Sherwood, let alone take them with her.

She finished chewing the piece of pork she'd been working on and reached to take another. Her hand froze as a sick feeling suddenly twisted in the pit of her stomach.

"What's wrong?" Bartholomew asked, staring intently at her.

She didn't know. It was as though she could sense something she couldn't quite hear or see. She struggled to put it into words. All she could hear, though, was a sudden screaming inside her own head. Bile flooded her mouth and she broke out into a cold sweat.

Before she could say anything she heard a deep creaking sound that came from the entrance to the building. Her heart nearly stopped as she realized their time was up. Someone had just opened the front door of the castle.

THE WILDERNESS HOURS

CHAPTER ELEVEN

Robin began to think that volunteering to lead the quest to free King Richard had been a very bad idea. It wasn't just what lay ahead of them—the dangers they'd face, the impossibility of the task, the prospect of seeing his father and having to tell him about his mother and his siblings.

It was also the anguish of knowing what... *who*... he'd left behind.

All those people living in the forest were his responsibility. He hadn't asked them to be there, or for them to need him, but somehow it had happened anyway. He had never intended to be lord of the manor. Instead, somehow, he'd become the lord of the forest, with even more awesome and terrifying responsibilities at his door.

As he tried to fall asleep his mind drifted from one face to the other. Friar Tuck. Alan-a-Dale. Esther. He knew all their names. Knew their stories, and the better he knew them, the more terrified he became that he'd lose them. Like Cardinal Francis. Little John. His pompous, arrogant, noble cousin, Will.

And just when those faces began to haunt him so much that he'd break out into a cold sweat and squeeze his eyes tight shut, thoughts of Marian would save him.

Marian.

His wife.

He still wasn't sure exactly how that had happened. He'd admired her, been infatuated with her since they were children. He remembered the first time he'd laid eyes on her. It was shortly after her parents had been killed and she'd come to live with her uncle, the king. Robin's family had been invited—along with the other nobles—to a Twelfth Night feast. She had been greeting everyone as they entered, wearing a blood red dress, her hair shining in the torchlight. Her smile had been light, carefree, but there had been a sorrow, a darkness in her eyes that seemed to reach out to him. It had touched the hard, lonely spot in his heart. Suddenly he had been very aware of the one thing that was lacking in his life.

Love.

His father didn't love him. At least, not like he loved Robert. His mother despised him, he'd always known that. Robert was too busy pleasing both of them to care much about a little brother who didn't share any of the same interests.

That was why he went to the woods. It was the one place he didn't feel alone. The birds and beasts didn't shun him. Many even seemed to welcome him as one of their own. At least, that was how it had always felt to a lonely boy.

Then he'd felt that surge of connection with a little girl who had just lost her family. Despite standing there in all her finery, surrounded by servants and greeting everyone with an ease and grace that were admirable, she was just as alone as he was.

Now neither of them was alone. They had each other, and they always would.

As long as we both shall live.

Each night that thought brought his sentimental musings back to a dark turn. He became afraid of being killed on this quest and leaving her alone. He was even more afraid, though, that he would return to find her dead. He knew in his soul he couldn't bear that. He couldn't have won her heart and hand, just to lose her.

The pain of that prospect was sharper than any knife, and he sucked in his breath as he tried to wrestle his thoughts under control. Why couldn't he just dwell on the happy thoughts, the memories of their moments together, the dreams of their moments to come? Some inner demon instead drove him to imagine the destruction of all that.

He didn't deserve her—Robin knew that with all of his soul. Perhaps that was why he was afraid that she would be taken from him.

Old Soldier was up, standing watch. Robin was supposed to be resting, but sleep didn't come easy, especially when he wasn't in the sanctuary that was Sherwood. Every new night sound and smell made him uneasy.

The older man shifted his weight, getting ready to end his time on watch. He was a marvel of endurance and determination. Robin hoped he would be as steadfast and strong when he reached that age.

The older man moved, walking over whisper soft then crouching down and touching Robin on the shoulder.

"Your turn, my lord."

"I told you to call me Robin," he said as he sat up.

Old Soldier raised an eyebrow. "And I told you to get some sleep. Looks like neither of us is good at doing what he's told."

Robin actually chuckled at that. "You are right about that, my friend."

"I'm right about a lot of things," the old man replied. "One day you're going to get that through your thick skull."

Robin's grin widened. Old Soldier insisted on standing on ceremony, referring to Robin as Lord, deferring to his decisions, but he wasn't at all afraid to speak his mind to him. The contradictions in his nature were part of what made him so interesting.

"Tell you what, you get some sleep, or I'll suggest to King Richard that he give you a title when this is all over," Robin said.

Old Soldier snorted derisively. "What good would a title be to someone like me? I'd hate being a lord."

"Exactly," Robin said with a wink.

Old Soldier muttered under his breath, but he laid down and covered himself with a blanket. Robin turned and walked several feet away. Before he reached his sentry station he could hear Old Soldier snoring. Whether it was real or faked for his benefit, he wasn't sure.

The smile slowly faded from his face as he contemplated the darkness around them. They'd built no fire that would draw attention to their presence, and the night was bitter cold. Robin didn't mind, though. Noise carried farther in cold air. If there was any threat out there, he should know about it long before it reached them.

Not that it would matter. They were four men in a land turned hostile by the Sheriff's men on the hunt, with limited weapons and no good way to defend themselves. He rolled his shoulders, loosening them up a bit as the muscles stiffened in the cold. It was a fool's errand they were on, and it would likely be the death of them all.

Sherwood felt anxious. That was the only way Marian could describe it. Since Robin left she had spent time every day by herself in the woods. The trees whispered to her, the animals communed with her. There was a growing sense of unease, though, that had become almost palpable. Something was coming. She just wished she knew what it was.

It was night and shadows lay dense and thick underneath the trees. The forest was always dark, but night brought its own kind of darkness, thick and mysterious. She had grown to love night more than day, though. Everything felt achingly alive, just as she felt when she was in Robin's arms.

She sighed. With each day that passed she missed her husband more. Her mouth tugged up at the corners as she considered how their relationship had changed. She couldn't help but wonder what her uncle would say when he found out the news.

Then the most subtle of sounds reached her, the crunch of ground beneath a hoof. She turned. There, standing close enough that she could see him clearly, was a majestic stag the likes of which she'd never seen. He was huge, his crown of antlers almost as big as the rest of him. He was watching her, studying her. She could feel the intelligence in his gaze.

A guardian of the forest.

Slowly he inclined his noble head as though acknowledging her as an equal. No, it was more than that. As kin. He was accepting her as part of the forest, a keeper of its secrets. A guardian.

She dipped her head back. They stood for a moment, listening together to the sounds of the night. He could feel the anxiety, too. It was there in his stance. The silence stretched between them until she felt she must speak. That was the curse of being a human, she mused—the pressure to vocalize, to give words to things which shouldn't need naming. She held her tongue, though.

Finally the great stag turned and disappeared back into the shadows from whence he'd come. She let out her breath, only then realizing she had been holding it. More and more she understood Robin's connection to the mighty forest. It was becoming a part of her, and she of it. Soon she'd be one of the wild things, cut off from the society that demanded her to be otherwise.

She blinked and shook her head. Forced herself to turn and trudge back toward the camp. She didn't want to go, but the others worried when she was not there. Those who knew her worried for her safety. Those who didn't worried for their own. Either way, leadership had its burdens. The more keenly she felt it the more she thought that Robin had been right to run from it. That choice was a luxury they no longer had, though.

As she walked she prayed again for his safety and the others. She also prayed for her uncle and all the men who'd gone with him, particularly Robin's father. The rest of his family was lost to him, but she hoped there might yet be a bond between him and his father. Now that the rest were gone, how could there not be? If they had shared nothing in common before now, they would at least share their loss and grief. It was a shaky start to a relationship, but it was more than Robin and his father had ever had.

A sudden aching nearly overwhelmed her as she thought of her own parents, lost so many years before. She wished they could have lived to see her married, to meet Robin. She sighed. Odds were they wouldn't have approved. Then again, she didn't know that for sure. So there was no harm in pretending that they would have loved him and embraced him as their own.

"Hurry home, Robin," she whispered, willing her words to be carried on the breeze to wherever he was.

Marian was almost to the camp when she heard music dancing in the air. It seemed to shimmer around her, magical, uplifting. Her spirit responded and she gave voice to words she didn't understand as she found herself singing softly. Once the compulsion would have frightened her. Now she just accepted it as a gift.

Alan was playing again. It was good. It helped him, and all the rest. He had taken young Haylan under his tutelage, and that was good, too. It gave them both something to do, something to think about other than what they had lost.

When she stepped into the clearing she wasn't greeted by those who had been keeping watch for her return. It surprised her a little, and she walked toward the fire where she could see bodies huddled together.

They're listening to the music.

It was true. They were transfixed by it, and as she moved closer she could see many of them swaying gently. She finally spotted Alan and was surprised to see that he wasn't the one playing. She shifted to the side so she could look between two men sitting across the fire from them. Haylan was playing Alan's harp.

The boy's eyes were closed and he had a look of rapture on his face. He was pouring his heart and soul into the music. She could feel it, and it seemed the others could, as well. Alan could certainly tell. He had a huge smile on his face and he was beaming with pride. On his other side Friar Tuck sat, clearly entranced. Occasionally he slapped his knee.

The young musician ended with a flourish.

"That was very good," Marian said encouragingly. "You are a swift learner."

Several of the men jerked, clearly startled by her sudden appearance and she winced slightly, sorry to have ripped them from the dream that Haylan had woven for them.

"Thank you," Haylan said solemnly. He was taking his new vocation quite seriously, as well he should. The job of a bard was important, particularly in dark days such as those in which they were living.

Haylan handed the harp back to Alan, and the spell lingering around the camp was broken.

"Play us a jaunty tune we can dance to," Jansa said. Alan dipped his head and let his fingers dance lightly over the strings of the harp. Then he began a lively song. In a flash the woman was up on her feet with a laugh and a blush. She locked her eyes on Thomas and the man was at her side in an instant. He took her hand and led her in a dance that was more exuberant than graceful. After a moment a few others joined in.

Marian laughed and clapped her hands in time to the rhythm. It looked as if Jansa was a lot happier with Thomas now that he wasn't the one in charge of the food. Marian was a bit surprised, but then realized she shouldn't be. Conflict often bred romance. She wished the couple well and hoped that they would have a long and happy life ahead of them.

A wind whistled suddenly through the clearing, lifting her hair with an icy hand. Only she seemed to notice it, and a shiver crawled down her spine. She turned, surveying the perimeter, wishing that she hadn't been staring toward the fire. Struggling as her eyes adapted again to the dark, she took a few steps away from the others.

Something moved at the edge of the clearing. She could swear it. Taking another step, she saw movement again. She turned and glanced back toward the others, but all of them were preoccupied with the music and the dancing. And with a sinking feeling she realized that she'd seen no sentries on guard when she returned to the clearing.

The enemy could surround us, and we wouldn't know.

Marian strode quickly toward the edge of the clearing, eyes flicking back and forth as she tried to discern what had been moving at the tree line. Her mouth had gone dry and her palms were beginning to sweat. The wind returned, and this time there was an audible sigh as it lifted her hair and caressed the back of her neck.

She gasped and spun, but there was nothing there.

Dark thoughts crowded her mind. Chief among them was the fear that the Sheriff had finally found a way to breach the magic that kept him out of the forest. If he had, then they were all about to die. She should sound the alarm, but it felt as though an icy hand had wrapped around her throat, squeezing until she couldn't breathe.

Again something moved at the edge of the woods. This time it was only a few feet away. Marian stared in horror as out of the darkness a gray, skeletal arm reached out for her.

CHAPTER TWELVE

Chastity pushed up off the bench, heart in her throat. The enemy was coming for them and they were all dead if they didn't do something quickly. She grabbed a knife that they'd been using to cut the pork.

"Stay here," she said as she headed toward the door.

Bartholomew caught up to her. "What can I do?" he asked.

"We need to get them into Sherwood. If I can't lead them, you'll have to. Do you understand?" she asked.

"Yes."

"Good. Move everyone to the kitchen, as quickly and as quietly as possible. You can get outside from there. Watch and be careful. Don't let anyone see you."

"And you?"

"If I can, I'll be there in a few minutes," she said. "If I'm not, then go without me."

"Okay." He nodded, turned, and headed back to the table. She could hear him whispering to the others. She made it out of the great hall and shut the doors behind her. She paused then, listening, trying to determine how many had come for them.

"—idiot never sent word that it was done," she heard a man's voice say.

"So we have to ride out here. The Sheriff should have sent one of his demons," a second voice groused.

"Quiet, fool."

"There's none to hear me complaining," the second man said. He hiccupped. It sounded as if he had been drinking, which was good for her.

"Look, we've gotten lucky so far. Let his... men... do the really nasty work. We keep our heads down we'll get through this and maybe even get some money out of it."

"What money?"

"Well, this was all Locksley's, right? I'm guessing there's some jewels, gold, something here we could just help ourselves to."

"Won't some of his men still be here?"

"I heard they all scattered once he was killed. That only leaves the old man guarding the brats. He should have left days ago and gone back to the Sheriff."

"Maybe he's smarter than us," the other one slurred.

Chastity glided forward. The men were coming closer. She could hear footsteps now. It seemed like there was just the two of them. She prayed that was true.

"You drunk?" the other demanded.

"I've been drunk since the monastery. Hadn't you noticed?"

Chastity felt rage flash through her. These two had been part of the attack on the monastery. All those innocent monks killed. She took a deep breath and then stepped out into the dark entrance area where they were standing. She did a hasty curtsy.

"I'm sorry, my master didn't know you were coming or I would have greeted you sooner," she said, rushing toward them as though flustered. They jumped at the sight of someone rushing out of the gloom.

"Your master?" the sober one said. "Oh, the bloke who's been here taking care of the brats."

"Aren't you a pretty one," the drunk one said, his eyes roving over her.

She was within reach of them when the sober one said. "How come your dress is all—"

Before he could finish his sentence she kneed him in the groin. He bent over with a gasp. She pivoted and slashed the drunk one across the throat with the knife. Blood spilled out and he collapsed in a pool of it as she turned and did the same to his friend. She jumped back as his body hit the floor and stood there a moment, panting as the two twitched and spilled their life's blood.

Her heart was pounding.

She waited a moment and then went to the front doors. She pushed one open and stepped outside. There, in the courtyard, were two horses saddled and ready to go. She sobbed in relief before turning and hurrying back inside.

She found the children in the kitchen, wide-eyed, frightened, but clearly ready to go. Some of them were supporting the two who couldn't walk, so they were all together. Bartholomew broke out into a huge smile when he saw her.

"Okay, let's go. We're going out the front," Chastity told them.

The Sheriff had only left a single man to guard the children and her. Then again, she had been chained in the dungeon and the children were too weak and frightened to put up a fight. If he had been scheduled to report back, though, the Sheriff might well decide to send more men, beyond the two she'd killed. The urge to hurry clawed at the back of her mind.

She quickly checked the stables and was disappointed to find neither horse nor wagon that they could use. They'd have to make do with what they had. She made it back to the children and the two horses.

She went to pick up the one boy. Bartholomew and two other boys hastily picked up the girl and made to carry her together. She nodded approval and they all made their way as quickly as possible back toward the courtyard. There were some murmurs of fear when they walked around the bodies of the two soldiers, but no one hesitated.

Once outside she eyed the children. There were twenty-six of them, all nobles, so the older ones at least should know how to ride. Clearly each horse needed to carry two children—one of the ones who couldn't walk, and another who could hold them in the saddle.

Curse the ones who took the wagons.

She pushed the thought from her mind. There was no wagon. They would make do with the horses they had. Time pressed against her.

"Bartholomew, get up on this horse here," she said, indicating the one nearest her. The three boys hastily set the girl on the ground. Bartholomew then walked over. It clearly took most of the strength he had at that point, but he was able to mount the horse by himself. Once he had done so, she handed up the boy and helped position him. Then she returned to the kitchen and gathered the food they had found, filling some skins with water. Outside she loaded them into the saddlebags, where she was relieved to find some additional provisions.

"Now, I'll lead the horses," she said. "You just need to keep him in the saddle. Can you do that?"

Bartholomew nodded.

Chastity turned and surveyed the others. "Who can ride the other horse and hold her on?" she asked, as she gestured to the girl who couldn't walk.

"I can," one of the taller boys said, stepping forward. She nodded and helped him mount the horse, then picked up the girl and settled her in front.

"Hold onto her tight. Her strength is completely gone."

"I will," the boy said earnestly. Chastity gathered up the reins for both horses.

"Alright, let's go," she told the others.

She went slow so the other children could keep up. When they passed out of the castle forecourt and she looked down the hill to the forest she began to breathe a little easier. There were no riders on the road, and they would be angling away from it anyway. The moon was up and shining brightly so that she could see for quite a distance. The forest lay in front of them, a dark mass in the night, more foreboding even than in the daytime.

"Just keep going. We'll be safe soon," she called out, hoping to keep the children's spirits up. She knew that many were afraid of the forest, and she hoped none of them panicked when they got to it.

"If you need to ride for a while, milady," Bartholomew said, "I can walk the horses." She realized she was limping and turned to glance at him.

"I'll be fine, thank you. And you can call me Chastity."

"Whatever you say, milady."

She couldn't help but smile. She was a servant in a tattered, bloodstained dress, but apparently in his eyes she was so much more because she had come to their rescue. It made her feel a little funny. She wondered if Marian ever felt odd when people looked up to her and expected things from her. *Probably not.* Marian had been born to nobility, raised with duty and responsibility.

When they were well clear of the castle Chastity paused. All of the children who were walking were breathing hard and starting to stumble more frequently.

"Let's rest for a few minutes," she said.

Half the kids sat down, and the other half fell down. She bit her lip and turned to look back at the road. It was still empty, but she couldn't escape that sick feeling that she would see riders on it at any minute. They weren't safe, and inside her mind she was screaming at herself to keep moving.

Yet while she was in bad shape, the children were so much worse off from their long captivity. One boy clutched his ankle, grimacing in obvious pain. A girl shook like a leaf, her breathing so shallow and rapid that Chastity was afraid she was going to faint. She had to give them a few minutes, otherwise they'd start dropping before they made it to the forest.

She looked again toward Sherwood. The forest loomed against the night sky, a deep black against indigo. Near but not close.

At the rate they were traveling it would take them an hour or more just to make it there.

She thought about the two dead soldiers, and her unease increased. Where had they come from? Was it somewhere close by? If so, their absence would be noted sooner, rather than later.

She turned to Bartholomew. "Are you able to guide the horse to the forest?"

He nodded, but he still had the limp boy in front of him.

"Help me get him down," she said. Together they got the boy into her arms and she set him down on the ground.

"Okay, two of you are going to ride with Bartholomew just into the forest, you'll dismount, and he'll bring the horse back. Who will be able to dismount with his help?" she asked.

"I can." It was the girl who had been the first out of the tower.

"Me, too," another girl piped up. Chastity swiftly helped them both up until one was seated in front of Bartholomew, and the other behind him.

"Hold onto each other tight. As soon as you get inside the tree line, girls, dismount and wait for us there. Bartholomew, bring the horse back as swiftly as you can. Do you understand?"

He nodded.

"Good," she said. "Be careful." Bartholomew urged the horse forward at a trot while Chastity turned to the other rider.

"How about you?"

He nodded. "I can take two to the woods with me."

"Good."

With his help Chastity got the girl down off the horse and onto the ground. She and the boy would go last because Chastity would have to help get them on and off the horses.

Two children stepped forward and she helped get them up. The effort left her muscles strained and she was gasping for air. Pain began to shoot through her temples and it felt like it exploded behind her eyes. She closed them briefly.

"Go." She heard the horse moving off and tried to get the pain under control—or at least push it to the side. She could hear moaning behind her after a few moments, and she opened her eyes to see the little girl start to convulse. Chastity stared in horror, but the other children just moved slightly away without showing much emotion.

"That's been happening off and on for a long time," one girl told her in a resigned voice.

"What do we do?" Chastity asked.

"Just wait," the girl said. "It will stop."

Chastity balled her hands into fists at her side and bit back the curses that wanted to pour out of her mouth. John and the Sheriff had done this. They had to pay.

After a moment she sank down onto the ground next to the little girl.

"It's going to be okay," she said, hoping the child could hear her. She kept saying that over and over, trying to convince herself of it more than anything. At last the convulsions stopped, and the little girl appeared to fall asleep. Chastity breathed a silent prayer over her then stood up and looked toward the forest. Bartholomew was out of sight and the second rider had his horse halfway to the tree line.

Her anxiety began to mount again. Until they were all in the forest they were exposed. She turned and counted the children. There were twenty now. That meant five more trips for the horses. She glanced again at the road, feeling as though spiders were crawling across her skin.

She wanted to urge the children to walk a little more, cut the distance between them and the trees. There were two among them now who would need to be carried, though, and she could only handle one. As though reading her mind one of the boys stepped forward.

"If you want us to keep walking, we can carry her," he said, pointing to himself and two others.

"You're sure you have the strength?" she asked.

"Yes," he said with a bit of bluster.

"Okay, let's go," she said as she reached down to pick up the boy. She put him on her hip as she'd done when carrying him down the stairs. Unfortunately his arms gripped her neck no tighter than they had then. She started across the ground, her bloody feet feeling like they were on fire. The children staggered to their feet. She wasn't sure how she was going to get them all the way to the camp. That was a problem for later. Getting them into the safety of the woods was all she could think about right now.

She saw Bartholomew and his horse emerge from the woods and begin cantering back. She was grateful for the haste but concerned that in his weakened condition Bartholomew might not be able to keep control of the beast at that speed.

Hush yourself. He can, because he must.

The gap closed between them swiftly and finally he pulled the horse up in front of them just as the other boy and his horse disappeared into the trees. Chastity put down the boy she was carrying and helped two more children mount the animal.

Once they were secure Bartholomew turned the horse's head and sent him back at a swift walk toward the forest. She leaned down to pick up the boy, wrapped her arms around him and lifted. She was able to pull him an inch off the ground before dropping him, causing her to cry out in frustration.

"Pick me up," the little boy muttered. "Please."

"I can't," she said.

He looked up at her with fear-filled eyes.

"Here comes Jacob," one of the girls said, pointing. Chastity turned and saw the second boy and horse emerging from the woods. He urged the horse into a trot as he headed for them.

We're not gaining enough ground.

"How many of you think you can make it all the way to the forest walking?" she asked.

Six of them stepped forward.

"Okay, I want you to start walking straight there. You'll meet up with the children that Bartholomew and Jacob are dropping off. Get inside the trees, and no matter what happens don't leave them once you're there. Do you understand me?"

All six nodded.

"Good. Now go, as fast as you can."

The two oldest began to jog wearily forward, clearly taking her words to heart. The other four began walking. She watched them for a moment. It was slow, painful progress, but at least they were on their way. That left twelve still with her.

Twelve they had to transport by horse.

A couple minutes later Jacob pulled up in front of her, his face was pale and he swayed uneasily in the saddle. She put a hand on his arm.

"Are you alright?"

"Yes," he said, his voice raspy. He wasn't, but neither was he about to admit that. She admired him for it, but was worried for his safety and that of the others.

She put two children up on the horse with him and then looked him in the eyes. "Go slow. We still have a lot to do, and I need you to be able to continue," she said. He nodded and then headed off, letting the horse walk at its regular pace instead of pushing it to go faster.

Ten to go.

Ten who couldn't make the walk.

Ten sitting there with her, waiting to be caught. She kept eyeing the road, praying no one would come down it. She could feel the fear in the children around her. She knew she should say something to reassure them but couldn't find the words. She was having a hard enough time keeping from screaming at them all that they needed to run as fast as they could.

Bartholomew emerged from the forest again. He cantered the horse back and soon was on his way again with two more children.

Eight left.

Minutes later he caught up with Jacob just at the edge of the trees, and the two disappeared into the blackness. Endless seconds ticked by that then dragged into minutes. The foremost children on foot had made it almost a third of the way to the forest. Those walking were considerably farther behind.

Finally both horses emerged from the trees, but only one had a rider. She jerked at the realization and stared fixedly until she could determine that Bartholomew was leading the second horse. They both came on at a slow trot.

"Jacob fell off trying to get the other two down. I told him to stay," the boy explained. "When he argued with me I said we could get three of the others on instead of two if he did."

It was smart thinking but looking at the remaining eight she was hard pressed to figure out which of them had the strength to guide the horse. Bartholomew followed her gaze.

"I can lead the horse back. All they'd have to do is hold on." She nodded, then helped two children up onto his horse and three onto the other one.

"Everyone hang on. You'll go slow, but you must stay on the horse until you get to the trees."

They started the perilous journey back, Bartholomew allowing the horses to walk at a snail's pace. That left three with her. One more trip and they'd all be safe. She turned to glance at the road and froze.

A dozen riders had appeared and even as she watched they changed course, heading directly for her.

She didn't know where she found the strength, but she reached down and wrapped an arm each around the two weakest children. The third stared at her, eyes wide.

"Run!" Chastity cried.

CHAPTER THIRTEEN

There was something wrong. Wulfhere's castle should be far enough away that they wouldn't have to worry about guards or patrols. By Lawrence's reckoning, they were still half a day from their goal. Though nothing noticeable had changed, Robin had learned long ago to trust his instincts over his senses. He unslung his bow from his shoulders and pulled an arrow from his quiver. He notched it but kept it lowered.

Before he heard a sound he smelled blood on the breeze. He tensed. If it was a wounded animal, it would be unpredictable and twice as dangerous.

If it was a man...

He eased the bow up higher, getting ready.

A moment later he heard a shuffling noise. He raised the bow up all the way. It sounded more like the shambling steps of a man than an animal. There was a thud, followed by cursing.

In a voice he recognized.

Blinking in shock he quickly lowered the bow. "I am a friend to the King of the Britons," he called out softly. "Do I recognize the voice of Philemon, Lord of Longstride?"

There was a pause and then a gruff response. "Aye."

"Step closer, that I might see you and greet you in the name of our Lord Christ," Robin said, throat tightening up a bit. Behind him he heard the others stir from sleeping. Moments later Old Soldier came to stand behind him.

"I recognize that voice," he whispered.

Robin nodded. The entire time he had been wondering if his father was alive or dead. To know that he was alive filled Robin with relief so great that it took him by surprise.

"And who are you?" Philemon asked as they could hear him walking closer.

Robin opened his mouth to speak, but found that he couldn't. Old Soldier pushed past him.

"They call me Old Soldier," he said, his voice gruff.

There was a shout of joy and suddenly he could make out his father, coming toward them. Robin stepped backward and returned the arrow to his quiver. He watched as his father and Old Soldier embraced. At last the men pulled apart and he was surprised to see the tears streaking down Philemon's cheeks.

"I had feared never to see home, or anyone from it ever again," Philemon said. He peered around Old Soldier, squinting in the darkness. "Who do you have with you?"

"Sir Lawrence showed us the way."

"Lawrence, you made it back to England?" Philemon said. "Thank Christ you did."

"I'm relieved to see you alive," Sir Lawrence said.

"It's a miracle, I'll tell you that much. The bastards will think I'm dead until they discover the bodies of the two men I killed in my escape. I hid them, so hopefully that gained me some time."

"How badly are you hurt?" Robin asked quietly.

Philemon froze and turned his head. He took a step forward, pushing away the others.

"Robin?" he asked.

"Yes, father."

A moment later his father threw his arms around him and buried his head in Robin's neck. He stood for a moment, surprised, then brought his arms up and hugged his father back. Gently, at first, then fiercely.

"I thought I'd never see you again," Philemon said.

"As did I," Robin admitted. His father finally stepped back but kept hold of his shoulders.

"You look different to me."

"A lot of things have changed," Robin said, still struggling to find the words. "But you haven't told us yet how badly you're hurt."

"I've lived with worse."

"We need to get your wounds taken care of, so we can make ready to rescue the king," Old Soldier said. At that, Philemon acquiesced.

"A few stab wounds, none of them much more than a prick. They hurt like the devil, though."

"Sit down and I'll patch you up."

With a grunt, Philemon sat down on one of the blankets. He glanced at Much, clearly trying to place him.

"Father, this is Much, the miller's son," Robin said.

Philemon nodded. "Glad to have you with us." He looked back at Robin in surprise. "Where is everyone else?"

Robin shook his head. "This is all that could come."

"What? They denied the call to come to their king's aid?" Philemon roared in anger. "Traitors!" He continued on, cursing until Robin crouched down next to him and shook his head.

"As I said, a lot has changed." He glanced uneasily at Old Soldier, who gave him a nod. Now was not the time to mince words.

"England's overrun by demons spawned from hell," he said. "John was a sorcerer. The man he brought, the Sheriff, is no man at all but a creature raised from hell who is now trying to cover the land in darkness."

"What are the lords doing about it?"

"Many are dead, killed outright before they even knew what was happening. The others were forced into pledging fealty to John. They swore blood oaths that had some sort of dark magic to them. It's turned them to mindless creatures."

"And you?" Philemon asked.

Robin took a deep breath. "I'm helping with the rebellion, all who can and will stand up to them."

Old Soldier snorted. "He's being too modest. Robin is the leader. He shelters all who come to him within Sherwood. The ancient magic of the forest has been keeping the demons at bay—they can't cross its borders. At least, not yet."

"If that's true, why come at all?" Philemon asked. "Why leave?"

"Frankly, we need Richard, you, and whoever is left to come help us take back England. Every messenger we've sent has been intercepted and murdered. Ships were burned at the harbor. We have been in desperate need of aid, with no way to get it. Cardinal Francis, before they killed him, couldn't even get word to Rome."

"The cardinal is dead?" Philemon whispered. He shuddered.

Robin nodded. "Yes, and the monks at the monastery were all murdered. Only Friar Tuck escaped. They set a plague loose on the people. It took a third of the population before we found a cure."

"Lord Robin battled the fey for it," Old Soldier said proudly.

Philemon gave his son a strange look, then sighed wearily.

"I suppose I shouldn't be surprised to learn that they exist, too," he muttered. "I guess there's no harm now in telling you that the crusade we're on—it's not about just fighting men."

"You were bound for the holy land to fight demons," Robin said.

"Yes," his father replied. "The darkness. It's been long prophesied, and now it's here. I think, though, that we were mislead as to where it was going to first show its face."

"Perhaps," Robin said. "Or perhaps King Richard's crusade forced it to come first to England."

Old Soldier helped Philemon remove his tunic and shirt, and then started cleaning out the wounds. Robin was relieved to see that while they were numerous, they didn't appear to be too deep.

"How many knights and soldiers are still alive?" Robin asked.

"I don't know," his father admitted. "Most were captured,

rather than killed. What has happened since then, I'm not sure." He sounded as tired and frustrated as Robin felt. "This plague, you said it took a third of the people before you were able to find the cure."

Robin nodded.

"Your sisters?"

"Dead," Robin said, unable to keep the pain and the bitterness out of his voice. Grief twisted his father's features. He would have given anything not to be the bearer of such news, but there was nothing that could be done. He cleared his throat. "It's worse than that, father."

"How can it be worse?"

"Robert... the Sheriff murdered him. I didn't even know that Richard had sent him back until I found him on the road—he was dying. I'm so sorry."

A cry of anguish tore from Philemon and he buried his face in his hands. Old Soldier kept working quietly on a knife wound in his back. At long last Robin's father looked up.

"The dead, who else?"

"Many." Robin licked his lips. "Little John gave his life to save mine, in the battle where Prince John was killed."

"The prince is dead?"

"Yes, but the Sheriff and his demons still hold the people captive. We've had word that Henry is coming, perhaps to join him."

Philemon cursed roundly. Then he took a shuddering breath.

"Anyone else?"

"Will," Robin said, barely able to say his cousin's name without breaking down.

"The plague?" Philemon asked roughly.

"No, killed in battle."

Philemon looked surprised. "I never took him for the fighting type."

"And yet he fought more bravely than any man I have ever known," Robin said, tears burning his eyes.

"So much gone. So much changed."

Robin hesitated. The manor was gone. He himself had burned it. They could speak about that later, though, if they both survived. He knew he needed to tell him about his mother, what she had done.

As if reading his thoughts Philemon asked, "And your mother?"

Robin cleared his throat. "She lives, but she has betrayed us all."

"What do you mean?" his father asked, looking up to meet his eyes.

"Father, I..."

"Tell me the truth," Philemon growled. "Don't hold back."

"She has become the consort of the Sheriff."

"What! Does she not know that he is a demon?"

Robin blinked at his father, surprised that the man didn't seem shocked that she had been unfaithful. Only with whom.

"She knows," he said. "I believe that's what drew her to him in the first place. She has given birth to his... child."

At that Philemon roared in rage and leaped to his feet. Much and Sir Lawrence both stumbled backward. Old Soldier stood calmly and gripped his shoulder. He glanced at Robin.

"Yes, it is true that she has betrayed you," Old Soldier said, then he tried to soften the blow. "We cannot be certain that she's not under some enchantment, even though she seems to have her wits about her."

Slowly the elder Longstride sank back down to the ground. He sat silent then for nearly an hour while Old Soldier cleaned and tended to his wounds. Feeling worse than useless, Robin returned to sentry duty. Eventually Much and Sir Lawrence went back to their blankets, though he wasn't sure if they actually slept or just pretended to.

After Old Soldier had cleaned him and given Philemon something to eat, he came to speak with Robin.

"You father will be fine as long as the wounds have a chance to heal. He's a strong man."

"He always has been," Robin muttered.

"His heart will heal, too, in time. He's lucky that he still has you."

Robin rolled his eyes. "I'm not sure that's the word he would use. I was always his least favorite."

"I don't think that's true." Old Soldier shook his head. "Men usually don't waste so much time and energy on their least favorite of anything. I think he saw greatness in you and didn't know how to bring it out. Regardless, as you said, a lot has changed."

Robin sighed. "It doesn't matter now. What matters is rescuing the king and what's left of his army, and returning to England before the Sheriff can unleash fresh horrors."

"If he hasn't already."

Marian followed the creature into the forest. It spoke not a word to her, just beckoned, then slipped through the trees like some kind of mist—half substantial, half ethereal—taking her in a direction she was sure she'd never been. Although her initial response had been one of fright, that had melted away into curiosity.

The creature was one of the fey and it was old. Though terrifyingly thin, it had a hint of flesh and skin on its bones. Why it had come for her or where it was taking her remained a mystery, but she felt in her gut that she had to go. They walked what seemed like a couple of miles and then it stopped in a spot where the trees grew up in a circle. "Fairy rings," that's what she'd heard her mother call such places when she was little, although Marian herself had never seen one.

The creature led her to the center of the circle and indicated that she should stay there. It moved to the ring of trees and passed each, one by one, touching it. When it had completed the circle she realized with a start that all the trees had begun to glow.

As had the torc around her neck.

Suddenly creatures appeared from everywhere. There were more fey than she'd ever known existed, let alone seen. They were all sizes, shapes, and colors. Some rode in on the backs of animals, others seemed to fall from the trees above, while still more seemed to rise from the earth below. They all formed a circle, standing shoulder to shoulder between each of the glowing trees. They didn't greet each other or speak, but simply stared at her, the intensity of their gaze building until she could feel it as a pressure on her skin.

Marian turned in a small circle, trying not to reveal her deep unease. The torc continued to glow and its presence offered her a strange sort of comfort. Still, something extraordinary was happening here, and she couldn't shake the feeling that everything hinged on what occurred next.

When the last fey arrived the air grew still. Even the birds stopped singing in the canopy above. The gray skeletal creature drifted back toward her, the only creature actually inside the circle with her. It opened its cavernous jaws and a voice rolled out of it like fog.

"Lady of the Forest, you have sheltered strangers in the forest," it said. "You have allowed sickness to breed outside of its borders, and you have not stopped this unnatural winter. Tell us now why we should not kill you and reclaim that which you took."

Marian stared at him in horror as his words sank in. She looked around the circle again. Some of the eyes that met hers were curious, others downright hostile. Then it hit her. They had brought her here to defend her actions, to explain herself. And if they didn't like what she had to say…

They would kill her where she stood.

CHAPTER FOURTEEN

Alan was a bard of the old ways. Sitting next to Haylan and playing the harp while the boy sang gave him a deep sense of joy and peace. He would not be the last bard after all. Tonight, though, wasn't so much about teaching the boy as it was about keeping the others distracted.

Those around him gave themselves over to the music.

"It's a wonderful night," he heard Jansa say.

"I'm sure even the ghost and other spirits are dancing with us," Thomas said with a laugh as he spun her around.

Slowly the people who were living here were losing their fear of the forest and the other beings that dwelt there. Had they known more about the fey they would not have dropped their guard so easily. Still, Alan forced himself to keep smiling.

He had seen the fey come for Marian.

Something of great import was happening. The air around him was charged and it felt as though all of Sherwood held its breath. Whatever Marian was being called to do, it was meant for her alone. All he could do was wait, keep others from noticing her absence, and watch for her return.

Turning his attention to the people around him, he tried to attune himself to their moods, their needs. Besides being a truth teller and a news bringer, a bard was also a healer, offering the salve people needed to transcend the pain of their lives.

When Jansa had asked him to play something they could dance to it had confirmed his suspicions that she had been falling in love with Thomas. He was happy to play the tune that helped bring them closer together. It could be a hard, cold world, and people needed to seize joy when they could.

Particularly in these dark days. For some it might well be their last chance to do so.

Those were grim thoughts, however, and as much as he needed to distract others, he too needed a distraction, a respite from the horrors he had endured, and those yet to come. So he watched Jansa dancing with Thomas and the joy on her face warmed him and lifted his spirits. His fingers moved faster over the strings of the harp. Friar Tuck hopped about with the child Esther, both trying to keep time with the music and failing miserably—because the song wasn't for them.

He'd play a song for each of them, even if it took half the night.

Marian touched the torc around her throat and felt warmth thrumming through it. Its power filled her until she couldn't help but wonder if her eyes were glowing, like the trees.

Then, slowly, she heard the whispers. No creature was speaking, and yet she could hear their thoughts as clearly as if they were.

Interloper.

Intruder.

Filthy human.

It wasn't anything she could have anticipated, and with each new voice the cacophony grew and her heart tightened in her breast.

All they do is take and destroy.

She's no different.

She's not chosen.

The noise became almost deafening in her head... and then, amidst it all, she heard one voice that said something very different.

She is the one, if only they would see it.

Turning slowly, she saw the fey girl from the river she and Robin had needed to cross. The one who hated laziness.

The one who left me Champion.

"You're right. I am the one." She squared her shoulders and faced the girl. "I am she who was prophesied of old. I am willing to hear advice. I weigh the evidence I have. I listen to my instincts." She parroted back the things the fey girl had told her when Marian had passed the river test. Before she could finish, though, she heard the girl again in her mind.

They will only respect blood. Theirs and yours.

Marian took a deep breath. "And I am flexible enough—"

She spun, yanking free the knife she kept in her bodice. She slashed the gray skeletal fey across his hand before he could move. Pale fluid like liquid silver bubbled up from the wound. Then, before he could move, she slashed open her own hand.

"—to change course quickly," she finished as she grasped his hand with hers. Their blood mingled. "I am blood of your blood. I come from you. I return to you. I am one of you, and you are one with me," she said, praying this was what the fey girl had been trying to tell her.

The thin gray creature shuddered so hard she thought he was going to fly apart. He opened his mouth, wheezed, and a puff of smoke was all that came out.

I've killed him, Marian thought.

She tried to pull her hand away from his, but he closed skeletal fingers around hers and held on. Then she felt tingling where their skin was touching.

Then something seemed to ripple across the surface of him—an image almost, like a reflection in a pond that was disturbed by a pebble. It started with the hand she held and spread up his arm and then over the rest of him. When the ripples slowed there was something different about him, new. His color changed from dead gray to a rich, vibrant brown shot through with streaks of green. She stared slack-jawed as the colors deepened, and he seemed to grow more substantial, the wispiness leaving his form as he grew taller and wider until he towered over her by a couple of feet. His new color made him look like a tree. Marian blinked, not sure what to do.

"You are worthy," the girl from the river said. "You are the chosen one."

"What happened?" Marian asked.

"You have already been to the heart of Sherwood." The girl indicated the creature next to Marian. "This is what you might call its soul. It has been sick, dying, poisoned by the evil of the land until it became the thing you saw earlier, a ghost of itself neither living nor dead. With your blood, your life force, you have restored it." The fey girl looked around at the others in the circle. "Proving for once and for all that you are indeed the one who was foretold. We will help you save the lives of the people who dwell within the forest and without."

Marian felt hope flare to life in her heart. She took a step toward the girl.

"You'll help us fight?"

"Yes."

The voice was low, rumbling, and emanated from the newly restored spirit beside her.

"Yes," the other fey standing in the circle chorused. Relief and gratitude surged through her.

"Thank you," she whispered.

"Thank you," the girl responded. "You have come to save us all. Even if it means losing everything."

"What do you mean, losing everything?" she asked. Marian felt the flame inside suddenly go cold. Her mind instantly went to Robin. But the girl shook her head.

"Now is not the time for questions."

"She is right." A blue boy spoke up. "Not now. Not this night."

"Why?" she asked.

"Because you must go before it is too late," the spirit beside her said.

"Go where?"

"You will know when you are there," the girl said, slipping back into her maddeningly cryptic ways, "but do not forget to take your defenses."

Before she could respond everything began to change again. One by one the fey returned whence they came until she was once again alone with the spirit.

"Come now, quickly," he said.

She had trusted him this far. She had to continue and prayed that whatever was waiting for her, she had the strength to face it.

Terror pulsed through Chastity as she stumbled as fast as she could toward the treeline. She tried to run, but with a child in each arm and her body battered, all she could manage was a limping shamble. As it was, her heart was about to burst from her chest.

Upon hearing her cry, Bartholomew pushed the horses to a fast trot. She saw him glance fearfully back at her and at the oncoming riders, as if trying to calculate whether he was going to make it to the forest before they caught him. Two of the three youngsters on the horse he was leading bounced painfully in the saddles. If they were struggling to stay on the horse at a trot, they'd never make it if he pushed the horses to a gallop.

She didn't know if they would make it and had to focus on trying to save the two children she carried. Chastity was struggling so hard to breathe that she couldn't shout anymore orders. He'd have to make the choice himself.

The other girl stumbled along just a few feet in front of her. She was one who hadn't thought she could walk to the woods, and it looked as if she might collapse at any moment. The two children who had been jogging ahead began to run in earnest, terror giving them unexpected speed and strength. The four that had been walking were trying to run, as well.

They're going to die, she thought in despair, *and so are we.*

Part of her wanted to drop the two children and race forward, where she might help the others who had a better chance of making it to the woods. Yet even though her hands were slipping, and they were dead weights, she couldn't bring herself to do it. She cursed herself for being a sentimental idiot.

Stumbling, she nearly fell on the uneven ground, and a sob escaped her. She regained her footing and glanced toward the road. The riders had cut the distance between them in half. They were angling toward the two horses. At the rate they were moving they would capture Bartholomew and the children with him. The only two who even stood a chance were the children who were running, since they were the closest to their goal.

Only half the children were safe inside Sherwood. Even so, her heart began to fill with despair. With no one to take care of them, they might die even in the protection of the trees.

Just drop them.

Save who you can.

Save yourself.

The voice that echoed in her head wasn't the same one that had come to her in the dungeon. This voice was hard, insistent, and there was something seductive about it. Despite that, she tightened her grip, determined to fight on to her last breath. She thought of Will and how he'd sacrificed himself. Though his wound had been fatal, he'd done what he could to buy time for the others.

Buy time.

She stopped in her tracks. The children slid out of her nearly paralyzed hands and fell limply to the ground. Freed from the extra weight she felt dizzy light for a moment. Then, she picked up her tattered skirts, turned, and ran straight toward the riders.

As she ran she began to scream. It was unlikely the riders could hear her over the pounding of their horses' hooves, but it helped give her strength and courage. She raced toward them as fast as she could, ignoring the searing pain in her feet. Images of Will flashed through her mind. She'd be with him once more.

That filled her with an even fiercer determination. Soon her battle would be ended.

"Will!" she began shouting his name. She would fight in his place. She would do what he would have done. She could save the children. Surely at least the ones on horseback.

The pain in her body seemed to stop, and suddenly she felt as if she was running even faster. *A final gift from God.* He would help her to save the innocents.

One of the men turned his head. He saw her. He must have shouted to the others because they all turned to look at her. She waved her arms in the air and probably looked like a lunatic, but she didn't care. Whatever it took to keep their focus on her, and not the children.

Two of the riders broke from the other four and headed toward her. Chastity's heart sank. She had hoped to distract them all. With only two coming her way, though, she had failed. The others would kill the children.

Still she ran forward, because she didn't know what else to do. Tucked in her bodice she had the knife she had used to kill the two soldiers. She pulled it free now and held it in her right hand, determined to fight with her last breath. Maybe if she did it would be enough to distract the others and bring them back.

The two horses closed the gap quickly. She would try to unseat the riders. If they were on the ground, she'd have more of a fighting chance. Then she began to stumble, and she realized that what strength she had left was fading fast. The rider nearest her unsheathed a long, wicked sword.

He held it aloft, to try to cut her down with it. She had to be more clever than him, though. Her mind was slowing down, going fuzzy even as she tried to think about how she could get the upper hand.

They were nearly to her.

She stumbled again, then staggered, swaying slightly as the riders came just feet away. Then, her legs gave out completely, and she fell face down in the grass. The ground shook as the horses rushed by her. Wind whistled over her, and she waited for the blow that would kill her.

Then suddenly she realized that she couldn't hear the thundering of the horses any longer. She turned her head and pushed herself up to her hands and knees. The riders had passed her. The horses stood, fifteen feet away, their riders motionless in the saddles. She shoved the hair out of her face and stared.

Suddenly the two men tumbled from their saddles and hit the ground. Their horses screamed in fear and lunged sideways before running off.

There, sitting astride one of the horses the children had been riding, a cloaked figure sat with an arrow notched in his bow. Her eyes flew toward the forest. She could see the children still running. There was no sign of Bartholomew and the other horse.

The horses of the other four riders milled about in confusion. Near them she could see dark forms on the ground. She turned back to the man in front of her, who lowered his bow. Her mind tried to process what was happening. Had God sent them an angel, a rescuer?

The cloaked figure returned the arrow to its sheath, slung the bow over his left shoulder, dismounted, and began walking toward her.

"Robin?" Chastity called out, her voice shaking.

"Not quite," the figure said before pushing back the hood back.

Chastity gaped in shock.

Marian, her lady, stared down at her anxiously.

"Are you alright?" Marian asked.

Chastity nodded fiercely. "No, milady, but praise Jesu I will be now."

CHAPTER FIFTEEN

It was Much's turn on watch and he stood it proudly. The trust that Lord Robin and Old Soldier placed in him meant more to him than anything. He always took the early morning watch, which was darker than sin and twice as nasty. It was quiet, though. The creatures of the night usually had started to settle down. He also got the joy of watching the first light of dawn fight back against the darkness. He imagined that was what they were doing, and it gave him a thrill.

He wished his parents could have lived to know the great deeds he had accomplished, and the responsibilities that had been entrusted to him. He believed, though, that up in heaven they had to be smiling down on him and telling him what a good lad he was, that he was making them proud.

It had been a rough night. After the appearance of Lord Longstride, it had taken effort for any of them to get back to sleep. Well, all except Sir Lawrence. The knight had drifted off right away, his snores faint—fainter even than they had been the night before. That worried Much, and he knew the truth of it.

Sir Lawrence was dying. Much personally suspected that the man had been holding out just to get them to the place where the king was being held captive. Now that Lord Longstride had arrived and could do that, though, Much wondered if Sir

Lawrence might just decide to die in his sleep.

As light began to streak the sky he felt a hand descend on his shoulder. He prided himself on not jumping, even though Lord Robin had once again managed to sneak up on him.

"I don't think you slept," Much observed.

"I always said, the ears of a fox," Lord Robin said kindly.

Much smiled.

They stood together for a couple of minutes, watching the sunrise. At last they heard Old Soldier moving around and turned away. He joined them and handed each of them some hard cheese, some salted deer meat, and some bread. It had been the same food every morning since they left Sherwood, but it satisfied.

Much ate his while standing, like Robin did. Old Soldier squatted while he ate. As they were finishing Lord Longstride stirred and sat up with a shout. He looked around wildly for a moment, his hands raised as if to fight and then his shoulders slumped.

"Nightmare," he muttered before heaving himself to his feet and moving off a ways to do his business.

Old Soldier nodded sagely. "He'll be having those for a while."

Robin was busy surveying the landscape. His father had shouted loud enough to wake the dead, which made it all the more concerning that Sir Lawrence still slept. If it weren't for the tiny whisper of sound coming from him as he breathed in and out, Much would have thought for sure he was finally gone.

Robin debated inwardly what to do about Sir Lawrence. With his father's arrival they no longer needed the man as a guide. It might behoove them to leave him here with food and water, so that he could rest up for the journey back. Deep in his gut, though, he knew there was no journey back for the man. He sighed. This was one of the aspects of leadership that he hated the most. Deciding who lived, who died, and, sometimes, how they died.

He hated putting others in harm's way.

His father came back and took the food proffered by Old Soldier, giving a grunt of gratitude. He made a happy sound as he bit into the meat.

"Venison," he said, turning to eye Robin. "From Sherwood, no doubt."

Robin shrugged. "The forest provides for its own."

The old man squinted at him. "How many you got living there now?"

"Round about seventy, with more coming each day," Old Soldier said. Robin was grateful that he was able to supply a number. The truth was, he had never bothered to stop and count.

"Seventy men?" his father asked in surprise.

"Men, women, and children," Robin corrected.

"You've got women and children living in the woods... like animals?" his father said, the familiar disapproving tone cropping up.

"Yes, *living*," Robin replied, locking his jaw. "Which they wouldn't be doing if they'd stayed where they were." His father stared at him for several seconds, then nodded before taking another bite of the meat.

"Some of those are as good fighters as the men," Old Soldier said, pride in his voice.

"I don't doubt it," Lord Longstride said, sounding suddenly weary. "I just wish it didn't have to come to that."

"They've got a right to fight for their lives, their families, their country same as anyone else, the way I see it," Robin said.

Old Soldier snorted. "And good luck trying to stop them."

Robin gave a short laugh. "Especially Marian."

"The lady Marian?" His father blinked. "You've dragged her into all of this?"

"Queen Marian," Much spoke up with sudden reverence.

"Queen?"

"She traveled to the heart of Sherwood, and sovereignty of the land was granted to her by the forest guardians," Robin said. "And I didn't drag her into all this. Truth is, she dragged me," he admitted, warming as he thought of her.

His father chewed contemplatively for a moment, then swallowed.

"Anything else I should know?" he asked sarcastically.

Robin smirked. "Well, you should be proud of me. I finally did one thing you told me to."

"Oh, and what's that?"

"I think it's safe to say I got Marian to pledge herself to me," Robin said with a chuckle.

Much and Old Soldier laughed as well.

"Oh, what makes you so certain she has?" his father asked gruffly.

"Well, I think she made it pretty clear when she insisted that Friar Tuck marry us before I left to free the king." He was rewarded by the look of complete and utter shock on his father's face.

"You're married?"

"Yes, father, I am," he said, unable to hold back the grin that spread across his face.

"To the lady Marian?"

"The same."

His father lurched forward...

...and threw his arms around Robin. "By thunder, you finally *did* do something I told you to do." His grip was tight, and when he pulled away, his face was beaming with pride as he slapped Robin on the back with one of his large hands.

"Congratulations, my boy!"

Robin managed to stand his ground under the onslaught, but barely.

"Thanks," he said, enjoying his father's enthusiasm with a hint of confusion. It was nice, as was the feeling of warmth radiating through him.

"Did you get a child on her yet?"

"We'd only been married a handful of hours when we left," he said. "I did my best, though," he added, his cheeks burning. His father roared with approval and slapped him on the back again.

"Then we need to move fast. You've got someone waiting at home for you, and we wouldn't want her waiting too long," he said with a wink.

"I must admit I'm eager to be back myself."

His father laughed again and Robin braced himself.

"What's all the commotion?" Sir Lawrence asked groggily as he slowly sat up.

"My boy's a *man*," Philemon said. "A married one at that."

Lawrence nodded tiredly. "The lady seemed quite pleased about it, as well."

"I knew she liked you," the elder Longstride said, pride rolling off of him. "No lady gives every dance to just one suitor unless she's making a statement."

"You were right," Robin said. He was still grinning.

"Of course I was," Philemon said. "Now, let's get this over with so I can congratulate my daughter-in-law in person."

Robin was amazed at how the news had lifted his father's spirits. He was grateful, as well. After the devastating news he'd had to give him the night before, it was nice to be the bearer of welcome tidings.

"How far from here is the king being held?" Robin asked.

"Fifteen miles, give or take," Philemon said, his expression serious again. Robin glanced at Sir Lawrence, who nodded.

"I knew we were getting close."

"Yes, you've done very well," he said gently.

"Where's he being held?" Old Soldier asked.

"Dungeons below the castle. I was there, too, until I made too much of a nuisance of myself," Philemon said.

"And what of the soldiers?"

"Last I saw they were being herded into cages outside, like they were some kind of animals waiting to be slaughtered," Philemon said, anger filling his voice. He spat on the ground. "A pox on Wulfhere."

"Are they expecting any kind of rescue attempt?" Old Soldier asked.

"No. In fact, as I understand it, that mangy bastard is in league with the scoundrel John. Or, rather, was. Can't say I'm sorry to hear that the bastard is dead. He's been communicating with the Sheriff of late."

"How are they communicating?" Robin asked.

"By messenger, I believe."

"What is it, Lord Robin?" Old Soldier asked.

"I'm thinking I pass myself off as an envoy from the Sheriff. That will get us access to the castle. From there we can study the lay of the land and figure out how best to proceed."

"He's a cunning one," Philemon said. "He wouldn't have lived this long without being so, curse his black heart. It will be hard to fool him."

"Then we'll have to be even more cunning," Robin replied. He turned to Much and gave the young man a wink. "Like a fox."

Friar Tuck was worried. It was dawn and there had been no sign of Marian. He didn't think anyone else had noticed, but he had, and he was starting to become truly concerned.

It wasn't unusual of late for her to disappear in the woods for hours, and he respected her time spent there contemplating, planning, and communing with the forest and its denizens. This, though, was unprecedented. She'd never failed to sleep at the camp.

The worst part was, if she was in trouble, he had no idea how to help her. He had no idea which direction she would have gone or what dangers she might have encountered. Next to Robin she was the one who knew the most about this area of the woods, given the time she'd spent exploring it.

He was going to have to ask Alan's help.

Discretely, though, so as not to raise the alarm. The last thing they needed was everyone panicking over the disappearance of their queen, as many had taken to addressing her.

It had been a night of revelry, the first for many in a long, long time. The way Jansa and Thomas had looked at each other, he wouldn't be surprised if he ended up performing another wedding ceremony soon. He was glad for them, but it was hard to feel any sense of joy or hope under the circumstances.

At last Alan approached, looking as if he hadn't slept at all. Tuck led him away from the others so that he could speak without being overheard.

"Marian did not return last night," he said gruffly, struggling to keep his voice low. Alan nodded slowly, but didn't show the surprise that Tuck had expected. The monk narrowed his eyes as he studied his friend's face.

"What do you know?"

Alan looked as if he was about to shrug. Tuck glared at him and, with a sigh, Alan pulled some parchment out of his bag. Tuck stood, waiting, and once again cursed their enemies. Before Alan could write, however, there was a noise in the woods.

A deer darted past, as if running from something. Friar Tuck stiffened, wondering if the devil's own had finally found a way to breech the forest and attack them in their sanctuary. Alan shoved the parchment and chalk back into his bag. They locked eyes for a moment, and the friar could see his own fears mirrored in his friend's eyes.

It couldn't just be Marian. The deer didn't run from her.

No, this was something, some*one* new.

His mouth went dry even as he prepared to raise the alarm. He half turned, ready to run over and wake up all the others, tell them to prepare to fight for their lives. Just then, Alan laid a restraining hand on his arm and shook his head.

"Have you gone mad?" Friar Tuck hissed.

Then there was a lot more noise—including the snort of a horse. It sounded as if an entire army was tromping through the woods, headed their way. Friar Tuck tensed, wishing he'd kept a weapon on him, like Old Soldier had urged them all to do. Suddenly the brush in front of them parted, and a small boy staggered into the clearing.

Painfully thin, he was covered from head to toe in filth, and his hair was long and ragged. His clothes were torn and hanging off him. However, Tuck realized, they were clothes that only a noble child would wear. He blinked in shock as another child came from the bushes, plowing into the first and tripping over him.

Behind him the camp stirred to life. He could hear the noise and the confusion as everyone called out to their neighbor, wondering what was happening. Friar Tuck just stared, slowly becoming aware that they were witnessing a miracle.

Even more children staggered out of the brush and the trees, only to collapse on the grass in the clearing. Then, finally, Marian came on foot, leading two horses. Behind her two boys and a young woman led six others. They all pushed their way into the clearing.

The people there surged forward, the fear on their faces changing to a look of concern and wonder. Marian was radiant, her skin practically glowing in the early morning light. She surrendered the reins to a young man who used to be a stable boy. He led the animals away, and the others leading horses followed after him. With a surge of relief Tuck recognized Marian's servant girl Chastity as one of them. He said a prayer of thanksgiving.

Marian smiled. "We have much to discuss," she said, "but first we must tend to these children. They are the noble children, held captive by the enemy to manipulate their families. Chastity has found them and set them free."

Cheers went up around the clearing. Tears stung Friar Tuck's eyes as peasants raced forward and laid hold of the tiny newcomers who clung to them as if they were their own parents. Then he shook his head slowly. Some of the children's parents were dead, victims of the pox and John's immeasurable cruelty. Many of the men and women who embraced them had lost children themselves to the same evil.

Here, perhaps, a measure of healing could begin.

He turned back to Marian, his emotions working powerfully.

He had so many questions, so many thoughts to share. She smiled at him wanly, and he suddenly noticed that she had gone terribly pale.

Before he could say a word, she collapsed in front of him.

CHAPTER SIXTEEN

The Sheriff stood on the rise as the sun came up. Most days he hated the cursed thing, preferring the darkness. That was his domain, and he relished it.

This morning, though, he permitted himself a small smile as the sun glistened off the masts of a dozen ships sailing into the harbor. Henry had arrived with his army—an army of humans that should have no trouble entering Sherwood and burning it to the ground. And then, well, then he would convert them—turn them into *his* kind of soldiers—and with them he would swarm across Europe, swiftly spreading his kingdom far and wide.

The flagship held Henry, pretender to the throne. It took all of the Sheriff's self-control to keep from burning it with the little royal aboard. Yet it would be far easier to control the men if they knew Henry was working with him. Eventually, however, the prince would lose his value, and he could be cast aside at leisure.

This time maybe he'd even take his time and enjoy it. Glynna would like that. He smiled as he thought about how creative she could be when she wanted to inflict pain. She kept surprising him.

As the first ship made dock he strode down the hill. It was time to greet the prince, welcome him to Nottingham, and make sure he was very clear on who was actually in charge.

* * *

Despite her own exhaustion Chastity was quick to hurry back to Marian's side as soon as she saw her lady collapse. Terror flooded her as she wondered if somehow her lady had sustained an injury while at the hands of the soldiers.

By the time she reached her, however, Marian was already awake and getting to her feet with the help of Alan and Friar Tuck.

"It's fine," Marian insisted, smiling. "I haven't eaten in a while, nor slept. I'm just a bit worn out from all the activity last night." Her face was pale, though—too pale, and it worried Chastity. She bit her lip and didn't say anything in front of the others. She helped Marian to the tent where she could rest undisturbed and then went to get some food to take to her.

When Jansa saw her, she threw her arms around Chastity and the two women wept for a moment over all that had been lost and their relief at seeing each other again. Then Chastity made her way back to Marian and urged her lady to eat. Marian picked at the food, eating a little, but leaving most.

"You should eat, too," she urged. "You're going to collapse soon yourself."

"I'll get something later," she said, even though her stomach growled embarrassingly. Marian closed a hand over hers.

"I'll only eat if you do."

With a frown Chastity sat down next to her and pulled a hunk of meat off the plate. She bit into it, and the flavor seemed to explode in her mouth. It overwhelmed her, she went dizzy, and tears stung her eyes.

"See, isn't that better?" Marian asked gently.

Chastity looked at her. "There's something different about you."

"I have a feeling there's much that is different about both of us," Marian said, her smile slipping slightly. "I am so terribly sorry for what happened to you, and to Will."

Chastity's chest tightened at the thought of him.

"Thank you," she said, pushing down the grief. She ate some more of the meat. Now that she was sitting, and the immediate danger was past, the exhaustion began catching up to her. Her arm felt like it was a tree branch as she struggled to lift it in order to keep eating.

"So, what is different for you?" she asked Marian, wanting to hear about her lady's adventures rather than dwell on her own misfortunes.

"Let's see," Marian began. "The fey pledged to battle for us, when the time comes."

"What?"

Marian nodded with a smile. "Last night, they took me to a secret meeting. I had to justify... everything and convince them to help. That's where I was when they warned me that you needed help."

"Remind me to thank them for that."

Marian nodded again. "I haven't had the chance to tell Friar Tuck or Alan about any of that yet."

"I imagine it will keep a couple of hours until you've eaten and rested."

"I imagine you're right, though they will be relieved to hear it."

Chastity frowned.

"What is it?"

"I thought when you came to rescue us that you were Robin, and just now you didn't mention needing to tell him. Has something happened to him?" she asked, praying that it hadn't.

Marian hesitated. "Robin is... away."

"Away? Where?"

Marian gave her a wan smile. "Sir Lawrence came here and gave us the news that King Richard and his men had been captured by a barbarian king who was in league with John."

Chastity gaped at the news.

"Surely he hasn't killed the king?"

"Not to the best of our knowledge. Sir Lawrence escaped to tell us what had happened. He went back with a couple of others to try and free Richard."

"Robin's leading them, isn't he?"

Marian nodded and Chastity's heart broke for her friend. She grabbed her hand.

"I'm sure Robin will be safe and he will return with the king."

"I hope so. I pray so," Marian said, her voice gentle.

"He will, you'll see." Chastity began eating again. "So, clearly quite a lot has happened. Anything else I should know about?"

"Just one thing, I guess," Marian said, her cheeks suddenly turning bright red.

"What?" Chastity asked, cocking an eyebrow.

"Before he left, Friar Tuck married Robin and me."

Chastity almost spat out her food in shock.

"You... you're married?"

"Yes."

"You married *Robin*?"

"Yes, I did."

Chastity dropped the plate and threw her arms around her closest friend. "Princess, that's the best news I've ever heard!" she cried.

"Thank you," Marian said, hugging her back. "I thought you'd approve."

"Approve? Yes, yes, and yes!" Chastity pulled away, her heart overflowing. "How did he ask you?"

"I asked him," Marian said with a smirk. "Well, more like told him."

Chastity laughed at that. Somehow it didn't surprise her.

Marian began to laugh as well.

"He was so surprised!" Marian said.

Chastity laughed harder.

"I'm not sure he knew what was happening!"

They both convulsed with laughter now, wild and uncontrolled. It felt so good. They hadn't laughed together so hard since they were children.

"I bet the look on his face was priceless," Chastity said.

"You should have seen him! I told him I was having him, whether we were married or not."

"You didn't!"

"I did! He just sputtered."

"Scandalous!" Chastity's sides hurt so badly she clutched at them, bruised and sore as they were, and she bent over gasping for breath. "So much for refined and ladylike," she said when she could.

"Well, you know, sometimes men just don't know how to say what they want."

"It's a good thing you don't have that problem."

"No, I don't." Marian beamed as though she was lit up from the inside.

"Was it... everything you had hoped for?" The words came tumbling out of her. She flushed. "I'm sorry, I shouldn't have asked that."

Marian put a hand on her arm. "It was more than I'd hoped for," she said.

Chastity nodded, for a single moment feeling as if she was living vicariously through her friend.

"It's not anything like I ever imagined my wedding night, though," Marian continued. "We were alone in the forest when Friar Tuck married us. Then, he left, and we were alone with just the trees and the woodland creatures. Robin was so shy at first, so reserved—worried, I think."

"Yes?"

Marian nodded. "Then I literally ripped his shirt off him, and that put an end to that."

They both dissolved into laughter again.

"Welcome," Glynna said from her seat in what had been Richard's study. The top of her gown lay around her waist, one breast covered by her suckling offspring, the other bare without shame. "My lord shall be with you momentarily."

King Henry kept his eyes on her, staring unabashedly. His entourage moved behind him. The bodyguards kept themselves alert but the rest of his retinue were unaccustomed to such an open display and as such chattered furiously. Henry snapped his fingers, the harsh noise silencing his staff.

He smiled. "Forgive them. They are not used to such... *openness*."

"Even in France? I thought every woman there was a whore."

"No, that would be the men."

"Ah." She shifted the child to the other breast, leaving the first exposed and gleaming.

"And what is your name, you exquisite creature?"

"That is quite the inquiry." Glynna tilted her head. "I was Lady Longstride, but she is no more. Hmmmm, perhaps I am Lady Nottingham." She shook her head, thick honey tresses shaking like liquid gold, a few thick strands stuck to her wet breast, splaying around it like spider web.

"You do not know your own name?"

"A name tells the nature, and my nature has changed so much since I was named."

"I do not know what that means."

"It means she has become a queen of ancient and has no name that fits as such." The voice of the Sheriff came from the shadows. All of the shadows. He appeared, stepping into the room seemingly from nowhere.

"And who might you be?" Henry asked, hand upon the hilt of his sword.

"Don't do that," the Sheriff snapped.

Henry moved his hand from his sword.

"Don't make him angry," Glynna pouted.

"I was called here by Prince John," Henry said. "Why am I being subjected to this... interrogation?"

"You were called by me," the Sheriff said.

"Who are you?"

"I am the Sheriff of Nottingham, and I am here to reward you for your service, Henry."

"I am a king. A sheriff can offer me nothing."

"I warned you," Glynna said, putting the child on her shoulder to burp. The Sheriff did not raise his voice, did not yell nor scream, he simply spoke in a low, even tone.

"Leave us."

One by one all of Henry's retinue froze, turned, and marched out of the door, the last one pulling it closed behind them.

Henry crossed himself.

"Do not do that again," the Sheriff said, "or I will turn you into Henry the Cripple."

"I see the sword on your side, but harming me will be no easy task."

The Sheriff smiled. "Challenge accepted." Then he was in front of Henry, even though the man had not seen him move. Henry's mouth opened to speak, and the Sheriff rammed his hand into it.

Fire.

Pain.

He was stretched, so stretched, the muscles across his chest failing, until he hung only by tendons. Fire burned, banked deep in muscle fiber.

He uttered an incoherent gurgle, but remained immobile.

The manacles on his wrists and ankles were so imbedded into his skin that it felt as if they were a part of him. But mostly it was the fire. It gnawed at his flesh, taking him all the way to bone and marrow.

Relentless, cruel fire.

He could not scream.

Could not pass out.

Only suffer.

Henry came back with a jerk, feeling his face held in the hand of the Sheriff. The dark man pulled it so close to his own that Henry thought they were about to kiss. The breath that issued forth was sickly-sweet, the breath of a carrion eater.

"You are mine, at any moment I choose to have you."

And Henry knew it was true.

* * *

It was nighttime when Chastity awoke. She must have slept through the day. Marian was gone, and the camp was quiet around her. She picked up a piece of meat left on the plate and chewed on it as she got up. Every muscle ached, but she reminded herself that it meant she was alive.

Outside the night was quiet and crisp. The moon was high in the sky. All around there were people sleeping, some huddled inside tents, others on blankets in little clusters. She walked carefully through them. Just the act of walking a short distance caused her to be short of breath. She looked for the children and found a few clustered together, but the rest seemed to be spread throughout the camp.

It was at the edge of the woods that she finally found Marian. Her lady was sitting on a log speaking with Friar Tuck and Alan. She stopped when Chastity came up to them.

"What is it?" she asked, wrapping her arms around her.

"I'm telling them about my trip into the woods last night, and the pledge of the fey," Marian said. She took a deep breath. "I'm afraid the time we will need them might be coming sooner than we expected."

A chill danced up Chastity's spine. "Why?"

"We've had word that Henry has arrived with his army."

"Is he here to battle the Sheriff?" Chastity asked, hoping for just a moment.

Marian shook her head. "No, we believe he is here to join their forces. This will more than double the size of the army the Sheriff has at his disposal."

"Maybe someone can get to Henry," Chastity suggested. "Explain to him what's really happening here."

"I don't think that will work," Friar Tuck said. "The Sheriff isn't exactly trying to hide what he is anymore. I think if Henry didn't know yesterday who he was dealing with, then he knows today. And a friend saw them breaking bread together in the castle."

"A friend," Chastity said, blinking. "I thought those loyal to us came with Jansa?"

"There are one or two who stayed behind. They couldn't get out when everyone else did. It might be lucky for us that they couldn't," Tuck said. Alan nodded agreement.

Instantly Chastity started thinking of all the servants in the castle, wondering who was loyal enough to the king and the lady Marian, that they would still spy for them. She didn't know, and that scared her. She just hoped this spy really was loyal to the king, and that no harm would befall them as it had so many others.

After the death of Will, treachery was first on the list of things she expected from others.

"We also have an answer to something else that has been troubling us," Friar Tuck said, his voice heavy.

"What?"

"When John was killed, it did not break the spell binding all those who had signed their names in blood," he answered. "They are still walking around as men in a trance."

"Which means that even if we could get word to them that their children have been rescued, we can expect no help from them," Marian said. "I'm not even sure they would comprehend what we were talking about."

Chastity heaved a sigh. "Three of the children died in that tower."

Marian nodded. "Bartholomew told me that another one named Rory was left behind when they were moved there. We should assume that he's dead, as well."

"So, we saved the children, but that's all we managed to do," Chastity muttered.

"Don't belittle that," Marian said while the two men nodded. "It is still a great thing."

"We could contact their mothers, their other relatives," Chastity said. "See if any of them would be willing to fight."

"Friar Tuck is going to see what it would take to accomplish that... how many of them are even still alive, after the pox and everything else that has occurred."

"Surely there will be a few of them still alive and willing to do something—particularly if they know their children are alive."

"The Sheriff's men didn't take all the children. One from each family," Marian said. "We can verify that in the morning when we talk to the ones you brought here. So the families might still have something to lose."

Chastity folded her arms across her chest. "At least we have a bargaining chip we didn't have before."

"Yes," Marian agreed, rubbing her temples. "I'm just trying to figure out the best way to use it."

"There's more bothering you than that," Chastity said. "You said we might have to fight sooner than anticipated."

Friar Tuck cleared his throat.

"The soldiers under Henry's command are human. Unlike the Sheriff and his demons, they are not spellbound, nor any type of magical construct. They could enter this forest."

"They could find us," Chastity realized.

Marian nodded.

Alan made a quick series of gestures that Chastity didn't quite follow.

"Alan's right," Marian said. "They might not even bother trying to find us. They might try to burn us out."

"They wouldn't dare," she hissed. Yet a sick feeling twisted in the pit of her stomach.

"I think we both know they would. The question is, how can we stop them?"

"By giving them another target," Chastity suggested.

Marian looked up sharply. "Another target? What?"

Chastity took a deep breath. "Don't you think it's time to resurrect the Hood?"

CHAPTER SEVENTEEN

Most of the newcomers, including Chastity, slept through a great deal of the next three days. Marian wished fervently that she'd been able to do so, as well. Instead, she became busy planning how to use the Hood to move their enemies *away* from Sherwood.

It would be tricky, but she was fairly certain she, Alan, and Friar Tuck had found a solution. Even so, she worried and prayed for Robin and his small band. As if that wasn't enough, another concern occupied her in the early mornings—one she could not avoid.

Marian had her eyes squeezed together tightly as she leaned over the fallen tree. She had been vomiting for what seemed like forever, and she remained as still as possible, praying that it was finally over. She felt a paw tapping her ankle. Champion was worried about her.

He wasn't the only one.

She could feel unease rippling through the forest around her as the creatures took notice of her state. She wished there was something she could do to reassure them, but at the moment it was all she could do to reassure herself.

Champion pawed at her more urgently. At once she realized there was someone in the woods. Even through the waves of illness she could feel it, even if she was helpless to do anything about it. She kept her head down and continued to pray. After a while she heard the rustling of leaves behind her.

She sensed no evil so she waited, believing that whoever disturbed her meant her no ill will.

"My lady?" a woman's voice asked at last, hesitant and full of concern. It was Jansa, the cook. Slowly Marian opened her eyes and turned her head just enough that she could see the other woman. Jansa stood there, eyes wide, clutching some sort of dried leaves.

"My Esther told me you were sick," she said. "This is the third morning in a row."

"Yes," Marian said, barely able to get the word out.

"I brought this to help—it's mint," Jansa said, bending down to hand her the crushed leaves. "You can smell them and eat one if you like."

Marian took a couple of the leaves and pressed them to her nose. She breathed in the scent for several seconds before finally putting one in her mouth and chewing it. It seemed to work as slowly the urge to vomit began to dissipate. When it had gone altogether, Marian got to her feet.

"Thank you," she said, feeling a surge of gratitude for the other woman. "How did you know?"

Jansa shrugged. "It helped me when I was with child, so I was sure it would help you."

Marian blinked at her. "But I'm not with child."

Jansa's eyebrows shot up in a look of surprise. "I beg your pardon, milady, but I'm fairly certain you are. It's been four weeks since you took Lord Robin to husband."

Marian blushed at the memory. Her hand touched her stomach briefly. Could it be true? She had yearned for this in her heart, but the thought that it might actually be so was overwhelming.

"I beg your pardon, milady, but this is a joyful thing," Jansa said earnestly.

Marian smiled. "Please, keep this between us until I know... until I am certain."

Jansa nodded and relief surged through her. The last thing she needed was wild speculation about what this could mean to England. Her hand involuntarily touched the torc around her throat.

"I'm sure he'll be back," Jansa said reassuringly. "That man has more lives than a cat."

"He does at that," Marian agreed. "Thank you again for the mint."

"It was no bother."

Marian was also deeply grateful that Jansa had taken over the cooking duties. Mealtimes had become a lot cheerier for it. At the moment, though, the thought of food made her stomach clench, so there would be no breakfast for her. It was just as well. That left more for the others.

Jansa lingered. "Is there anything else I can do for you, milady?"

Marian shook her head. The truth was, though, she wasn't willing to rejoin the others just yet. She wanted to make sure her stomach remained settled. She didn't really want to be alone, though, either. She'd had too much time alone with her thoughts lately.

"Actually, come to think of it, there is something you can do for me," she said.

"Milady?" Jansa asked.

"You can tell me when it is we'll be celebrating your taking Thomas to husband?"

Jansa flushed red, which made Marian smile.

"My lady, I don't know what—"

Marian raised her hand. "The whole camp knows that you're sweet on each other."

"I... truth be told, my lady, I don't know who we'd ask for permission."

Marian blinked in surprise and then a swell of pity rose in her. She had forgotten that even peasants needed permission to marry, often from their lord. She had been certain that Richard would have approved, so she hadn't thought twice about marrying Robin. There would be no higher authority to authorize their union.

"I would be honored to give my blessing to your union."

Jansa's eyes went wide with excitement. "My lady, you would do that for us?"

"Of course," Marian said. Truth be told it would be the happiest duty she had yet to perform. "Name the day."

Jansa licked her lips. "I'll have to speak with Thomas, but, if it's alright with you, I'm thinking today is a fine day to get married."

Marian actually laughed, understanding entirely.

"I agree, it is a *fine* day to get married."

Jansa curtsied then hurried off, so excited that she forgot to formally take her leave. Cautiously Marian stood up. Her stomach definitely felt settled, so it was time to return to camp before she scared Friar Tuck, who'd been marking her comings and goings with a watchful eye.

She found him keeping counsel with Alan-a-Dale, an expected sight these days. In a little while Alan would start his morning lesson with Haylan. Strange how even living in a makeshift camp in the middle of the forest, they could start to fall into predictable routines.

Haylan's older brother Audric had become friends with Bartholomew. It was an unlikely duo, but they were united in their need to exact revenge on those who had hurt them. The two were deep in discussion over something, and she had the sudden feeling that it would be good to learn exactly what they were busy planning. It might be necessary to redirect their efforts, instead of standing back and letting nature take its course.

She moved to join the bard and the friar and they both welcomed her with fleeting smiles. Involuntarily she touched her stomach, wondering if either of them suspected what Jansa had sussed out. She forced herself to smile and drop her hand to her side.

"There's a tax shipment that the Hood can grab," Friar Tuck said.

"Since the Sheriff still believes him dead there will be few guards."

Marian nodded. "Enough that the three of us can handle it?"

The two men exchanged glances.

"Enough that Alan and I can handle it," Tuck said.

"We started this together, and we're continuing it together," Marian said firmly. "Besides, neither of you is nearly as good with a bow as I am. We need to keep up using one if we want people to believe this is the same Hood."

Both men looked as if they were on the point of arguing with her, but she held up a hand.

"If we cannot successfully pull this off, then it's only a matter of days at most before they come for us. We need to put every effort into making this a spectacular robbery, and into leading them to think the Hood has found a new hideout... far away from here."

Alan nodded and glanced at Friar Tuck, who sighed.

"We think we've found a place," he said. "We think we can convince them the Hood is hiding out in a series of caves. If we do this right, they could spend weeks searching and never find a thing."

"Why would the Sheriff believe for even a second that the Hood had abandoned the safety of Sherwood?" Marian asked.

"It would be a longshot, for certain. We would have to leave at least one soldier alive and with the strong impression that the Hood no longer found safety in the forest, perhaps because of the arrival of Henry's army. We could even mention the fey or the ghosts, playing up on the fears the soldiers already have about them. We need to try something to pull their attention away from this place."

"Okay, we'll try," Marian said. "So, this tax shipment, when do we take it?"

"Tonight while they camp on the road. It's coming from a distance and they'll have to camp tonight, several miles from the castle. It won't be in the forest, though."

"All the better, since we need them to disassociate the Hood from the forest, at least as long as there are human soldiers on their side. We should go early, figure out the best way to attack before they arrive."

"We've already prepared for that, my lady. We leave in an hour."

"Good. I'll be ready."

Sometimes Robin had good ideas and sometimes he had terrible ideas. What had seemed like a good idea earlier now seemed terrible. They had taken a couple of days to scout and to acquire some things they would need for his plan to work.

He had managed to locate the soldiers who had left England with King Richard. They were still alive and indeed being held in some sort of animal pens a stone's throw from the castle. Since his father would be recognized, it would fall to him and Old Soldier to free them. If they did it right, then they could unlock the pens before the guards could call an alert. Then hopefully the sheer numbers of English crusaders would overwhelm them.

The barbarian king's army was smaller than Richard's and surprise would this time be on their side. Hopefully that would be enough so long as Wulfhere did not have time to cast any dark spells like he had the night he captured them all. If he did, numbers or no, then the likelihood of success would be incredibly slim.

The hardest part would be getting Richard out of the dungeons, and then out of the castle. That job was left to Much. It had been decided that Sir Lawrence would remain close to the road to act as lookout in case unexpected reinforcements arrived. The knight offered no resistance.

Old Soldier parted company with them for a while, intent on finding food to feed the army once it was freed. In the last two days of travel, Robin tried to teach Much everything he could so that the miller's son would pass as his manservant. The boy was nothing if not an eager learner. He listened, asked good questions, and got most things right the first time. Then they managed to acquire some clothing that—to the layman's eyes—would make Robin look a proper lord and Much a proper servant. Robin had no doubt that Will would have scoffed at what he was now wearing, but they hoped a barbarian like Wulfhere wouldn't know the difference.

On two of the grandest horses they could steal they traveled along the open road. Robin rode with his spine straight, putting as much swagger and arrogance as he could into his bearing. Before they parted his father remarked that he didn't know if he was proud or disgusted by the final result. Robin knew how he felt.

Approaching the castle just after noon, they rode at a steady trot. The greatest failing in Much's disguise was that he could not sit his horse well. Robin was just grateful that the young man wasn't falling off. He reminded himself that there were plenty of servants who only traveled with their master by coach and would have looked just as ridiculous astride.

The sentries at the front of the castle watched them come up the road and remained in place—which was good. When they reached the gate Robin pulled his horse to a halt. With a little more difficulty Much managed to do the same. Robin rolled his eyes as though disgusted by the display.

"I am Lord Locksley, here on behalf of the Sheriff, ruler of England. I bear important messages for your king," he said.

The two sentries looked at each other.

"Today, if you please," Robin said. "We have traveled far on these godforsaken roads, and I am in need of a proper meal and a bath," he continued, putting to his voice an imperious edge of impatience that would have made the real Locksley proud.

The sentries looked at each other again.

"Do either of you speak English?" Robin demanded, letting his frustration show. When neither man spoke he dismounted. Walking up to the closest sentry, he slapped the man as hard as he could. "Take me to your king," he said, clipping each word.

Hastily the other sentry drew his sword. Robin turned and gave him a disdainful glare. The man clearly weighed his options, turned, and shouted inside. The gate began to rise.

"That's more like it," Robin said as he remounted his steed. When the gate had risen high enough he urged his horse forward. Its shoulder slammed into the one sentry, sending him spinning away. Robin didn't even look. Much rode beside him. As they passed under the giant steel teeth he fought the urge to look up.

They rode into the courtyard and he heard the gate lower back into place behind them. A groomsman ran up. Refusing to let any concern show on his face, he threw his reins to the man and dismounted. Much managed to do the same, slipping and floundering a bit, but not actually falling off—a small miracle. He scurried to keep up with Robin's long stride as they moved toward the imposing doors that would lead into the castle proper.

They swung open and without hesitation Robin strode through.

The doors slammed shut again behind him. He stood for a moment as his eyes adjusted to the sudden gloom. Though there were torches burning everywhere, they did little to push back shadows that seemed to writhe and slither over each other as though alive.

He steeled himself. He had seen such and worse in the castle occupied by John and the Sheriff. Locksley wouldn't have cared about such things—at least, not the version of Locksley that Robin was playing. Instead he looked around, trying to get his bearings, mapping what he could see so that when the time came they could make their escape quickly.

He steadfastly refused to give into the fear that was clawing at the back of his mind, or listen to the whispers that echoed in the dark around them. Because if he did then he'd have to acknowledge the truth of their situation. They were in the belly of the beast, and they were almost certainly never going to find their way out.

CHAPTER EIGHTEEN

Despite the cold late-evening bite of the winter wind, Alan was sweating profusely. He hadn't worn the cloak of the Hood in weeks, and in his heart he'd hoped never to have to wear it again. He, Tuck, and the lady Marian waited for the tax shipment. It was just the three of them—a bard, a friar, and a woman, against armed guards.

He keenly felt the absence of both Will and Robin.

Each of them had taken position in a tree to better keep out of sight and harm's way until they were ready to spring their trap. It had been far easier for Friar Tuck to climb this time than it had that first tree, so long ago. He wished he could put it down to the monk gaining muscle and agility. Truly, though, his friend was losing weight.

Friar Tuck had always been possessed of a mighty girth, about which Alan himself had teased him mercilessly in the past. Seeing it dwindle, though, filled him with sorrow. It was evidence of the harsh conditions, the deprivation that had been thrust upon them all. It was as though Friar Tuck's waistline symbolized the state of England, and judging from its current state, the country was wasting away.

His thoughts shifted to the lady Marian, and Alan frowned deeply. He suspected that she was with child. That alone should have been enough for her to stay behind. Yet they were living in desperate times and he feared things were only going to grow worse.

He just hoped the three of them survived this fight.

There were supposed to be six guards traveling with the shipment, so they were outnumbered two to one. Still, they could be grateful. Before the Hood had "died," the numbers would have been much greater.

He couldn't help but feel as if they had failed. The uprising of the people had yet to materialize. Of those who were fit enough to resist, most were too terrified to join them in the fight against the Sheriff and his demons. With Henry and his soldiers added to the mix, whatever hope they'd had of winning seemed to have disappeared.

Alan and the cardinal had crafted such great schemes. This was their folly. It had already destroyed the cardinal and all but destroyed him.

His fingers involuntarily reached for his harp, as they often did in times of distress. When they didn't connect with it he felt a momentary flare of panic, until he remembered leaving it behind in the camp. He couldn't risk losing it tonight—it had been given to him by his mentor when he was a boy. In some ways its absence pained him more than the loss of his tongue.

At least this separation was only temporary.

The sky began to darken as the sun sunk lower on the horizon. Clouds began filling the sky, a warning that they were likely to be without a moon to guide them. At least it couldn't help their enemies either.

Straining his ears, he listened for the sound of an approaching caravan. They had it on good authority that the tax collectors would be stopping here for the night, one of the more frequently used rest points on the road. He was half surprised no one had put an inn there yet, as it would make an extremely convenient location for travelers.

From where he was positioned he could see neither Tuck nor Marian. Alan wondered if their concern was growing along with his. Dark thoughts crowded his mind and he tensed, glancing all around as far as he could. Anxiety bubbled within him, and it felt like spiders were beginning to crawl all over his skin. He prayed there was nothing wrong—that he was just experiencing his own paranoia, which had been heightened since his capture.

His breathing came in short, shallow gasps which made his chest ache. The cold air caused his throat to tighten, and he felt as though he couldn't breathe, as if there literally wasn't enough air.

It wasn't true, he knew it, but the fear of it was in his mind now. It brought along all of its nasty, unpleasant friends, including anger.

They shouldn't be here, he thought fiercely. The three of them were needlessly risking their lives, and for what? To buy a couple of days for the camp in Sherwood before it was taken and burned? They'd be better off scattering now, taking their chances. Maybe some of them would make it.

He thought of Ireland and the people there who had welcomed him so generously when he had been there, retrieving the cursed book. Perhaps he could find a tiny boat, one that the Sheriff and his minions hadn't burned. He and Haylan could escape and live among the green hills and friendly people—him playing, Haylan singing, and both of them drinking enough to forget about England.

He called up a memory, an image of one of the little towns as it sparkled under the morning sun, the lushness of the green around it giving it a look of perpetual spring. Suddenly, though, a dark cloud intruded on his thoughts, casting a shadow over the town. He tried to fight it back, tried to reclaim the memory as it was and not give in to the twisted vision.

Darkness covered the sky and the green grass dried in an instant, withering and turning brown and brittle. Something seemed to crash over the town itself, like a giant wave of the ocean. He saw cottages blown to pieces, the town center destroyed as rock and stone flew apart, scattering to the four corners of the earth.

People ran outside, screaming in terror. He watched the cobbler's daughter fall to her knees, her fingers were digging into her own cheeks, scratching as she screamed. Blood bubbled up beneath her nails and poured down as she continued to claw and peel away her own skin.

Finally she collapsed on the ground, a bloody red mass that moved no more.

A young lad Haylan's age ran from the church, and the moment he stepped foot outside a black fist seemed to spiral out of the sky and strike him to the ground. His clothes caught fire and he lay there, screaming and thrashing back and forth, unable to put them out., Moments later he stopped screaming and his blackened body seemed to curl in on itself before turning to ash.

There were cries and screams as the people tried to escape their houses. One by one those cries were cut short as the darkness claimed each of them. There was nothing he could do, no sound he could utter. He could only watch in a horror that threatened to consume every last shred of sanity.

A grunt escaped him, a vague tremor of the vocal chords he still possessed, rendered less than useless by the loss of his tongue. He squeezed his eyes shut but the vision remained. So he forced them back open, willing himself to see instead the English countryside with the campsite below and trees all around.

But the vision wouldn't let go. He heard noises, voices, and couldn't tell where they were coming from. He could swear he heard someone shout his name. Something brushed his leg, and he kicked out hard. Smoke filled the sky, and he breathed some of it in. It began to choke him. He clawed at his throat, whimpering and gasping all at the same time. The waves of sooty air parted for a brief moment to show him the complete and utter destruction of it all.

The village was gone.

So all will come to pass. The voice seemed to echo inside him.

Something bit his leg. He twisted hard, and then suddenly he was falling. His hands clawed at only air, and a branch slapped him hard across the cheek. He could smell horses and sweat and blood filling the air. Then he crashed onto something hard with a cry of anguish as pain exploded through him with a fiery surge.

Marian stared in horror as Alan fell screaming from the tree in which he'd been perched and landed on his back on top of the team of horses pulling the wagon laden with the taxes.

The beasts shrieked as if the devil himself had fallen upon them. They reared and plunged and then bolted down the road, spilling men and dragging the wagon with them. Below her Marian heard screams and shouts as the soldiers and the driver tried to figure out what was happening.

There were ten soldiers, plus the driver, instead of the six she'd been told there would be. Four of them had been riding horses, and each took off in a different direction, scattering men as they did. Three of them took off after the horses, and she let her notched arrow fly, dropping the man in the lead. One of the others plowed into him and they fell, then a third tripped over them as they hit the ground. He landed with screams of terror that caused the hair on the back of her neck to raise straight up. The two living men thrashed around on the ground as each strove to get away from the dead man.

She turned her attention back to the seven men beneath her. She shot off two arrows and killed two more soldiers in the span of time it took Friar Tuck to fire an arrow and kill a third. The rest scattered, looking for shelter as they shouted to each other, trying to figure out where the attack was coming from.

One man tripped and the arrow she had fired at his chest instead went straight through his throat. He fell with blood spraying outward. It coated the driver, who fell to the ground as though he were the one who had been struck. She swiveled in the tree, careful not to lose her balance, and found another target. He fell without a sound.

Suddenly there was a roar. She turned back.

Friar Tuck had jumped or fallen out of the tree. He landed on his feet, the cloak wrapped around him. Holding a sword aloft, he shouted something unintelligible. The remaining men turned and ran.

And just like that, it was over.

Marian watched from the tree as Tuck went and knocked the driver unconscious, then the two men who had fallen with the first man she'd killed. That done, he started after the wagon.

Marian shook her head. He was worried about Alan and it was making him reckless. She slung her bow around her shoulders and carefully climbed down from the tree. Once on the ground she headed away from the road to retrieve their horses—including two extras brought to carry the gold. Her heart was still pounding from the fight.

The plan had been to attack the men after they had already made camp for the night and were asleep. She had no idea what had happened to Alan, and while it had worked out, it had been sloppy, dangerous.

Reaching their horses she discovered that one of the soldiers' beasts had come to a stop nearby. She mounted her animal, gathered up the reins for the rest, and moved them out at a brisk walk, following the ruts in the ground left by the careening wagon.

Minutes later she found it, tipped on its side, its rear axle broken and the chest containing the gold lying on the road. Friar Tuck was busy trying to extricate Alan from the two horses, for they had become tangled in the traces. He drew his sword and began hacking away at the leather straps.

Marian winced as one of the horses screamed and lashed out with its front legs, barely missing Alan in the process. She held back, trying to keep the horses with her from becoming hysterical, as well.

"Stand still, for the love of all that's holy!" Friar Tuck roared as he hacked away at another section of harness. Suddenly part of it fell to the ground and one of the terrified horses jumped straight up in the air. It landed and began to buck. The harness slid off, the animal broke free, and it lit out down the road, still jumping and twisting every few feet.

The other animal seemed to start to calm slightly. It stomped its feet and whinnied restlessly, but let Friar Tuck cut him and Alan free of the whole mess. At last the friar pulled Alan free of the wreckage, then half-carried, half-dragged him to the side of the road before setting him down. He turned back to the horse who was eyeing him, eyes rolling. To Marian's surprise he actually managed to calm the horse down enough to lead him out of the wreckage, as well. He kept hold of the beast's bridle with his fist and led him off the road.

"Well, that couldn't have gone worse," he said with a grunt as he came to a stop.

Alan sat up slowly.

"At least we're all alive," Marian said. They had gotten lucky that the soldiers had all been flesh-and-blood men, and that none of the Sheriff's demons had been among them. It was proof that their enemy had believed the Hood was dead, and that the taxes would be safe.

Now he knew otherwise.

Friar Tuck bobbed his head. "What do we do about the gold?"

"If it's loose, we've got a problem. If some of it is bagged, we can pack it out of here on the horses," Marian said.

Friar Tuck let loose of the horse, and to her mild surprise the animal stayed where it was, tired and frightened but not enough so to run off. The holy man went back to the chest, and moments later had it open. The gold inside was in bags—heavy by the looks of it when he hefted one. Still, they could transport those on the horses.

She glanced uneasily back down the road. They needed to move quickly before any of the soldiers got up the courage to try and come after them. The horses were still skittish, though she was doing her best to calm them.

"Alan, are you alright?" she asked.

The bard nodded slowly. She wanted to ask him what had happened, but they didn't have the time. They'd have to discuss it later.

"Good. Are you able to travel?" To her relief he nodded again. "Can you help Friar Tuck load some of the gold bags on the horses?"

Alan stood up and walked stiffly over to the chest. Friar Tuck touched him briefly on the shoulder. They began to unload the sacks.

In all the chaos Friar Tuck had not been able to make mention of abandoning Sherwood as they had planned. Marian debated briefly whether or not to give up on the idea of trying to use the caves as a diversion but ultimately decided that they had to try. Now that the Hood had reappeared it was going to make the Sheriff all the more intent on sending Henry's men into the forest. If they could create even a little doubt as to the Hood's current whereabouts, it would be helpful.

It took them twenty minutes to secure the bags onto the two extra horses. Then Friar Tuck and Alan mounted slowly and they started out, quick to head toward the caves as agreed upon. They left tracks subtle enough that they wouldn't be obvious, but which a sharp-eyed hunter would spot. She just hoped that someone did so. If no one bothered to follow the tracks they were leaving, then this whole thing had been for naught.

There was a sudden sick twisting in her stomach as she realized that, realistically, they would have to do this at least once or twice more.

And that next time, the Sheriff's demons would be ready for them.

CHAPTER NINETEEN

Philemon was still reeling. The loss of his children weighed heavy on his heart and he worked to hold back the grief. The betrayal of his wife, while not entirely unexpected, was still a struggle to understand. He'd finally given up. Ever since she'd started dabbling with magic Glynna had been a changed person, a moon woman, darker than the girl of light and sunshine he'd married.

He'd tried to stop her, but clearly he had failed. Then again, if he was honest with himself, she hadn't been right since the birth of Robin, when she'd claimed the child she had just birthed couldn't possibly be hers.

There had been a time he had wondered if the boy was *his*, but there was no denying that Glynna was the mother. He'd never heard of a woman, though, rejecting her own offspring with such vehemence. It had shocked and grieved him. He had to admit, though, that her hatred of Robin had somehow tainted the way he'd treated his son.

There'd always been a sense of disappointment with Robin—that he wasn't like his older brother, or even his sisters. If they made it out of this alive, Philemon would spend a lifetime trying to make up for that.

If Robin would have it.

The change in Robin was profound. When Philemon had left England with King Richard, Robin had looked a boy to him. Now he was most certainly a man. Strong, both of body and mind, and with a resilience to him that Robert had never shown.

The horrors Old Soldier had recounted had further cemented his respect for his youngest son. All those times he had criticized Robin for spending hours in Sherwood, he now thanked God for. Had it not been for Robin's familiarity with the forest, so many of their people might have died—or worse.

Most surprising to him was the revelation that Robin had married the Lady Marian. Philemon hadn't been blind—he had seen Robin's feelings for her ever since they were young. He hadn't suspected until the night of King Richard's announcement, though, that Marian in any way reciprocated them. Had he known, he would have suggested Robin as a match for her. How might that have changed everything, had he done it a year ago?

Well, in the end neither he nor the king had had any say in it. It had been his observation that when a man and a woman loved each other, nothing could keep them apart, not for long at any rate. It hadn't with him and Glynna.

Glynna. He still couldn't understand it.

Old Soldier walked beside him, the two of them slipping quietly through the dark. They weren't far from where the English crusaders were being held by the pagan thief's men. Last he had seen them, most had been alive. He prayed that was still the case. It sounded as if they'd need all their forces, if they hoped to retake England from the demon who now desecrated the throne.

Assuming they managed that, there'd be the question of setting back out for Jerusalem. Other kings were heeding the pope's call to go and fight. If only his holiness could have realized that evil would make its first stand in England...

Old Soldier reached out and touched his arm, and Philemon came to a halt. The man was older than him—by how much he couldn't guess—but he'd take Old Soldier over half a dozen young men any day. He knew things about battle, strategy, that you only learned by hard, bitter experience. Even Philemon was willing to defer to him.

Once they stopped moving Philemon heard the sound of footsteps. There was a guard ahead. The man was pacing. Old Soldier moved to the right and Philemon went with him, giving the sentry a wide berth. What he really wanted to do was kill the man, painfully and with relish. They had agreed, though, that they needed to wait until two hours before dawn. They needed to give Robin a chance to maneuver inside the castle.

They shifted course again, and suddenly the stench of squalor and death assaulted his nostrils, the odor powerful enough that he nearly started to gag. They had to be just downwind of the prisoners. He pressed his sleeve against his nose and mouth, grateful that he had been able to acquire a new shirt since having escaped the castle. He tried to breathe only through his mouth, but it was difficult. His eyes began to water as he struggled to keep from coughing or retching.

A glance at Old Soldier revealed twisted features that proved he, too, was struggling with trying to breathe in the fetid air. Nevertheless they began to maneuver closer. The silver lining was that they were unlikely to encounter any guards over here. No one with any choice whatsoever would be where they walked.

Robin would have given just about anything to be outside rescuing the soldiers, instead of standing in the castle's throne room staring at the man who had been in league with John and now with the Sheriff.

The pagan king was shorter than Robin expected. Not small though, no—he was possessed with an almost bestial vitality that sang through him as he stood. He was dressed like a barbarian of old, a Norseman come over the waves to plunder and pillage, thick beard and wild hair. He even wore an iron hammer on a leather thong around his neck, and a thick gold arm ring fashioned like a dragon eating its own tail.

Perhaps most surprising was that he carried himself with even more arrogance than John had—something Robin wouldn't have thought possible. The man moved slowly, not because he was lazy, but because he knew that by making people wait he exercised even more power over them. He reveled in the fear and uncertainty of those around him, and it made Robin sick. His fingers began to twitch, and he realized that he was a hair's breadth away from trying to put an arrow through the man's heart.

But monsters who danced for the devil could be hard to kill. He couldn't risk trying and failing, not before he'd been able to free King Richard. Next to him Much shifted from foot to foot. Robin could feel his unease and silently willed him to calm down.

The king studied the parchment that Robin had brought, something that was ostensibly from the Sheriff, but was in fact a letter composed by Robin and his father. Finally he glanced up from it.

"So, the Sheriff has brought his people to heel, has he?"

Robin cleared his throat and reminded himself to answer with arrogance in kind.

"Milord has won the loyalty and adoration of his subjects," he said. Then he added, "Any who might have felt otherwise no longer have their heads."

"We are pleased to hear it, Lord Locksley," the king said.

Robin forced himself to smile. That's what the real Locksley would have done. The man had been many things, but his name was helping Robin now, and he was grateful for that.

"So, he is ready for the next part of our plan," Wulfhere mused.

"That is my understanding," Robin said, continuing to leer. He thought of Will and all those weeks spent kissing up to John. He wondered how his cousin had managed it for so long. He found it painful, just for a few minutes. Still, the thought of Will gave him strength, and he forced his smile even bigger.

"Milord has asked that I bring back your response quickly," Robin said, "and that I report on the state that John's brother is in." He said the last part as though it was distasteful to even admit that John had a brother. In a way, it was.

"Of course," Wulfhere said. "You can be on your way in the morning, but tonight you will be my guest for dinner and a little... entertainment." That sent a chill up Robin's spine, at the mention of entertainment. He was sure that whatever this barbarian had in mind, it would be an abomination. He thought of some of the entertainments John had provided and feared that whatever was in store that evening might be infinitely worse.

He forced himself to smile again.

"You would honor me," he said, bowing his head.

"Excellent. My steward will show you to your rooms where you can get freshened up," the king said. "I'll see you in an hour."

Robin bowed and so did Much. They then turned and followed the steward from the room. As he showed them to a bedchamber Robin kept his eyes moving, taking in every detail of the halls they passed through. There were fewer servants walking the halls than there were at King Richard's castle, even after John had occupied it. With any luck that also meant fewer spies, although he couldn't put it past the king to have demon helpers. He and Much weren't going to be able to let their guards down for even a minute.

Alan was deeply shaken from the vision and his fall out of the tree. Nothing about the ambush had gone as planned, and they were all very lucky to have escaped with their lives.

He tried to clear his mind. Always he'd had more control over his own thoughts than other men, able to organize them, study them objectively, and come to rational conclusions. His memories were sacrosanct and crystal clear, which was a blessing as a bard and a curse as a man.

He couldn't deny, though, that something had crawled its way inside his mind to show him the destruction of that village. It was probably the same something that had bitten him in the leg, causing him to lose his balance and fall. What had seemed like a long, tortuous vision must have occurred in an instant.

While Marian and Friar Tuck made haste planting the gold in the network of caves, he rested outside. Rolling his pant leg up, he found the bite mark left by the demon—for that had to be what it was. The wound was red and swelling quickly. It also itched worse than being scratched by a cat. He was going to need to put a poultice on it to stop the swelling and draw the poison out. The plants he needed for that were in Sherwood, though, so he'd just have to grit his teeth and bear it until they could get back there.

He prayed that their ruse worked, and it fooled the Sheriff into thinking that the Hood had changed his lair. He had his doubts, but they were clinging to straws these days, doing what they could to survive until help might arrive.

Two thirds of the tax money would remain here in the caves. It needed to look as if this was where the outlaw was hiding his loot before it could be redistributed. He had suggested that they also needed to bring some food and weapons, if they wanted to make the caves seem like a believable hideout. They would do so on their next trip. He thought it a mistake to wait but understood the difficulty they would have had in bringing those things with them this time.

Everything about this plan was difficult. Will had sacrificed himself to distract the Sheriff and the Prince from trying to find the Hood. Now they *needed* the Hood to distract the Sheriff from his plans to invade Sherwood. It was all a mess.

Marian and Friar Tuck reemerged from the caves looking satisfied. The three of them got back on their horses and, carefully obscuring their tracks, began their journey back to Sherwood. Alan resisted the urge to scratch at the bite. After all, it would only make it worse.

At the appointed hour Robin and Much made their way downstairs. They'd both done what they could to steel themselves against whatever horrors might await them at the king's table.

Robin could feel the time growing short. They needed to free King Richard before his father and Old Soldier set free the soldiers.

When he entered the banquet hall, he was surprised to notice that the table was set for a far smaller number than he would have anticipated. A steward appeared the moment they stepped through the doors, and he led Robin to a seat toward the head of the table. Much moved to take his place where servants would eat.

"It looks like a more intimate gathering," Robin said.

The steward nodded but didn't respond. Robin realized he hadn't actually heard the man say a word yet. It was possible he was mute. It was even more possible that he'd learned that keeping his mouth shut was safer, when serving a king such as Wulfhere.

Taking his seat, Robin wondered how long they'd have to wait before the king arrived. As it was it was only a minute or two. He rose to his feet as the king entered, accompanied by two guards, and then sat again after the man had taken his place at the head of the table.

Robin glanced across to where there was an empty seat facing him. It seemed in poor taste to show up later than the king. Wulfhere seemed jovial, however, if it could be called that.

"Before we bring out the food, I thought we should welcome our other guest this evening," he said, a wolfish smile in place. All at once Robin's skin felt like it was beginning to crawl. He wondered if, like John, the king had a pet demon that he liked to keep around.

"And who would that be?" he asked, struggling to keep his tone light.

"Actually, I think you will find this rather amusing. It's one of your own countrymen—someone who seemed most eager to see you again when I told him you were here."

Robin's blood ran cold. Had a messenger from the Sheriff beaten him here, with news of John's death? Or if it were someone from England who knew Locksley, they would instantly expose him as an imposter. Despite his fears, he kept his composure.

"How unexpected," he said simply.

Then he glanced down the table toward Much, who had to have heard. The young man's face had gone completely white, and he had his hands clenched on the table. Robin was armed with only a sword and a dagger. Much had a dagger hidden inside his tunic. The table had dishes but no cutlery, nothing that could be used to attack. If they had to fight their way out, they'd be woefully overmatched.

Robin turned back to the king.

"So, who is this... admirer?" he asked, leaning again on the arrogance of the role. King Wulfhere laughed as if Robin had just made a great joke.

"I'm not so sure that he's an admirer, at least not these days," he said enthusiastically. "He *did* have an awful lot to say about you, though, and I could tell that perhaps he has a score to settle."

Robin began to sweat, despite the cold and damp of the room. Had Wulfhere already decided that he was an imposter? If so, his cunning ruse would come to an end in a spectacular fashion. He glanced quickly around the room again, looking for guards and servants. Again, there were fewer than he would have expected.

Taking a deep breath, he surreptitiously wrapped his hand around the handle of his dagger. Maybe he could throw it and kill whoever the newcomer was before he could say a word. He might be able to justify it as part of the "score" that needed to be settled. It was a long shot, but it was all he had.

"I look forward to seeing him," Robin said, baring his teeth in an effort to smile. Then he heard a door open behind him and he stiffened, knowing he needed to be standing if he had any chance of fighting his way out of this. He stood, swiveled, and began to pull out the dagger.

The blade was nearly free when he froze.

Standing there, surrounded by guards, chained, filthy but every bit the lion he had always been, was King Richard.

CHAPTER TWENTY

Robin stared in shock. He had never dreamed King Wulfhere would do such a thing. Richard stared at him, as well, but kept all emotion from his face.

"Richard, what a surprise to see you again," Robin forced himself to say, sneering to the best of his ability. "I trust you've been enjoying your stay here."

King Richard hesitated for a moment and Robin held his breath.

"I've known you to be a lot of things, Locksley," Richard growled, "but I had to see for myself that you had turned traitor."

It took all of Robin's control not to drop in relief when Richard called him that. He could read the curiosity in the man's eyes, but it was guarded. He couldn't be sure what Robin intended, but he was giving him the benefit of the doubt. For that Robin was immeasurably grateful.

Pushing back his chair, he strode up to Richard, eyeing him carefully.

The king looked tired, but aside from the filth he seemed uninjured—at least on the surface. Richard flexed his muscles slightly, rattling the manacles that bound him as he did so. It was a sign of strength, letting Robin know that he was ready to fight and to use the very chains that bound him as weapons, if necessary.

There were six guards in the room. Four of them were guarding Richard. Aside from those there were the steward, two other servants, and King Wulfhere—who could not be discounted. The man was no wisp of a thronesitter. The door behind Richard was still open, and Robin could see stairs descending downward to what had to be the dungeon.

Robin gripped his knife tighter as he realized in a flash of insight that they were never going to have a better opportunity. He had no idea what Wulfhere was planning to do next, but instinctively he felt that if he waited to find out, either he or Richard or both of them would end up dead.

"I have a message from England's true king," Robin said.

"What does that ungrateful whelp have to say for himself?" Richard growled, clearly not having to fake the anger that boiled in his voice. Robin turned his head slightly and snapped his fingers in Much's direction.

"Oh, I'm not talking about John. Much, you remember the message the Sheriff gave me?"

"Yes, sire..." Much hastily scrambled to his feet.

"Good." With Much free of the table, they had a fighting chance, even if it was a fool's chance. Robin turned back, yanked out his dagger, and lunged forward as though he were going to kill Richard. At the last moment he twisted, slashing the dagger across the throat of one of the guards.

With a roar Richard grabbed the heads of two more and slammed them together, crushing their temples with the manacles around his wrists. Robin stabbed the fourth guard before the man could get a weapon free, hooking him deep in the side, under his ribs where all men are soft. He turned and threw the dagger into the chest of the guard on the other side of the room, while Much threw his companion into a wall.

The two servants went skittering through the doors, whether to save their own skins or to get reinforcements Robin didn't know. Either way they were out of time.

"To the dungeon!" Robin shouted. Much nodded, produced

his dagger, and rushed past Robin toward the stairs.

"Wait!" Richard roared. "There's no one left down there; it's a trap!"

"Then where are the other nobles?" Robin asked.

Something was wrong. Old Soldier could feel it. It was that itch at the base of his left shoulder blade, the one he always got when there was something his brain hadn't figured out yet.

The smell of death and blood permeated the air. It would have been expected on the field of battle, but not at a prison. It was too fresh for that. He stopped in his tracks and turned to caution Lord Longstride. It was too late, though. Longstride tripped over something in the dark and went down with a heavy thud. At least he didn't cry out.

Cautiously Old Soldier moved over to him. Longstride had tripped over a decapitated body. As he crouched down he could see that there was another one just a foot away. Then he saw a third, then a fourth.

He helped Lord Longstride back to his feet, then the two men backed away carefully. When they had put some distance between them and the bodies Longstride cupped his hand around Old Soldier's ear and whispered.

"The other lords, he's killed them."

"I don't know where they are, but they're not down there," King Richard shouted. Robin frowned. It didn't seem likely the castle had other places to hold prisoners. Perhaps they had been put outside with the soldiers. But why?

There was a sudden high-pitched whistle, and then soldiers burst out of the dungeon, weapons held high. Robin drew his own sword and did his best to back toward the door that would lead them to freedom. Much and King Richard kept pace with him.

"I need my sword," King Richard said.

"Grab one off a dead guard," Robin said. Then there was no more time for words as the wave of soldiers crashed against them. Out of the corner of his eye he saw Richard retrieve a blade from one of the fallen guards. With his hands shackled together he would have a hard time wielding it, but at the moment there was nothing to be done.

Next to him Much was hacking away with his knife at whomever came within arm's reach of him. For his own part, Robin was coming to an even greater appreciation of the master smith who had made his sword so long ago. He thrust and cut and the sword seemed to sing as he moved faster and faster.

While the bodies of the soldiers kept hitting the ground, Robin and his companions kept moving steadily backward, blades flashing in the torchlight. King Richard, manacled as he was, was still more than a match for the soldiers who faced him.

"Robin!" the king shouted.

"Yes?"

"Keep fighting."

He wondered what on earth Richard thought he was going to do. Before he could say anything, though, the king turned and ran toward a door at the far end of the hall as fast as he could.

Robin was stunned. He shook his head, trying to rid it of the roiling thoughts and emotions that threatened to distract and consume him. He redoubled his efforts. His shoulder began to ache from the speed with which he was whipping the sword and from the jarring impacts as it collided with steel and bone.

Much cried out in pain and Robin's guts twisted inside him as he realized the young man had to have been struck. He moved back faster and Much joined him. Their enemies surged as though thinking that they had gained an advantage.

He was sweating profusely, and his hand slipped for a moment on the hilt of his sword. A soldier got in under his guard and slashed him across the thigh. Robin hissed, keeping in a shout of pain. He wished he knew how many soldiers were left, but all he could see were those immediately in front of him. He put his sword through the throat of the one who had cut him and then shook the body off his blade and onto the ground.

He heard Much grunt again and he winced, praying that the wounds he was receiving were superficial. The miller's son hadn't survived so much in the last few months, just to die in this godforsaken place.

"Richard, we need you!" Robin roared.

He had no idea where his sovereign had gone, but he hoped King Richard could hear him and would return to help them before it was too late. He risked a glance to the far side of the room, but didn't see his king. He didn't see the pagan king, either.

He frowned as he turned back and stabbed another soldier. A feeling crept into his mind then—though he couldn't identify it.

I hope Richard knows what he's doing.

His foot slipped and he half fell. A sword whistled through the air right where his head had been. He thrust his blade up into the stomach of the man in front of him, then scrambled out of the way as the body fell forward. Robin made it to his feet just in time to fend off a simultaneous attack by two different men. One of them got in a blow which sliced across his cheek. He could feel the skin part and the blood start to spill down to his chin.

When he had felled both men he glanced up and realized that there were only a few soldiers left. Hope flared brightly for a moment. He lunged forward, intent on ending this so he could find King Richard and the three of them could escape.

The sense of unease grew.

Much fell and Robin spun, his sword slashing the throat of the man who was about to bring his sword down on the miller's son. The soldier fell half on top of the young man, but Robin didn't have time to stop and help Much up.

Feeling like a man possessed, he faced off against the remaining guards. The sword seemed to take on a life of its own as he slashed and stabbed his way through them. He had never felt so at one with a blade before. It was almost as if he could hear it singing, crying out for more blood to appease its insatiable appetite.

Then, suddenly, it was over.

Robin stood, panting and dripping sweat and blood onto the floor as he surveyed the sea of the dead. He looked for only a moment, though, to be sure none were about to rise up and come after him. Then he turned and pushed the dead man off of Much. Reaching down, he helped the young man to stand. Much's face was pale except for where it was streaked with blood.

"Are you alright?" Robin asked.

Much nodded, but didn't say anything.

"We need to find King Richard," Robin said, glancing toward the door at the far side of the room. He willed the king to appear there. Richard knew where they were, and it would be easier for him to return than for them to have to go and find him. Robin wondered, too, about the pagan king. If Richard had gone after him, he could be in serious trouble. It had been *very* difficult to kill Prince John. He could only imagine what it would take to kill this despot.

"Something's wrong," Much whispered.

Robin felt it, too. It had been growing in his mind the last few minutes and had had nothing to do with the battle they were fighting. He took a step forward, and suddenly he heard screaming in his mind, as though something was trying to keep him from taking another step.

He glanced again at the fallen bodies of the soldiers. Most had been wearing helms of some sort. He wondered if any among them were demons that would rise again shortly, as did the Sheriff's fiends.

"We can't leave the King," Robin said out loud, as much for his own benefit as for Much's. "He's the reason we've come all this way."

Behind him Much made a whimpering sound that made Robin's hair stand on end. He had known the lad a long time, and Much had a heart of oak. He was not frightened easily, if at all.

"We have to go now," Much whispered, his voice half-strangled. Robin spun on his heel, but only made it a couple of steps before he realized what was happening. Torches were going out around the room, plunging parts of it into darkness.

He stared in fascinated horror at a torch close by. Something thick and dark oozed *up* the wall toward it. It reached the torch, ran up along its sides, and then snuffed its flame completely. The liquid blackness didn't stop there, but kept going, sliding up the wall.

Robin turned and saw that the stuff was covering the door that led to the front of the castle, as well. He shuddered at the thought of touching the door and coming into contact with whatever the substance was that was inexorably coating the walls.

"What is it?" Much asked, the fear heavy in his voice.

It was too thick to be some sort of ink, and too substantial to be a shadow—even a demonic one. Robin glanced around and saw that the remaining torches were also threatened. The ooze had only just begun its ascent on the far wall. He blinked, wondering why it was happening faster, the closer it was to them.

A sudden, terrible suspicion occurred and he turned his eyes back down to the floor. The soldiers still lay on the floor, blood pooling around them. Only the blood didn't remain there. It ran in streams and rivulets away from the bodies. The liquid that was climbing the walls of the room—sealing off their escape and extinguishing all the light—was blood.

CHAPTER TWENTY-ONE

They needed to get out of there. Robin raced to the door, where the blood was still oozing, flowing upward like a slow-moving tide.

Everything in him revolted at the idea of touching it, yet he stretched out his hand. He needed to open the door so they could get out of the room, flee the castle, and rejoin his father and Old Soldier outside in the cool, fresh air.

He reached for the door but the closer his hand got the harder it shook, becoming impossible to control. It was as if the limb had taken on a life of its own and was fighting him to keep from having to touch the liquid.

It's just blood, he told himself fiercely.

That wasn't true, though. Blood didn't behave like this, it didn't flow up walls. It had been enchanted somehow, and that terrified him. He tried to will his hand to reach the last couple of inches, to touch the blood-covered door. An image flashed through his mind of the liquid turning and flowing up his arm until it coated him, sliding up his face, choking him to death before it even blinded him.

His stomach lurched and before he realized it he was on his knees vomiting. There was blood on the floor, as well, which was staining his clothes as it flowed around him and beneath him, striving to get to the wall.

It's not flowing up my body. After he'd emptied the contents of his stomach he struggled back to his feet. He tried once more to reach out, and again his hand fought him. With a scream of frustration he gave up and spun toward the far wall.

The blackness was crawling up over the last two torches. They sputtered, flickered.

Then they went out.

There was no rational reason for the pagan king to have executed the nobles. No reason at all.

Except...

Philemon spun toward Old Soldier.

"It's a trap," he gasped. "They knew we were coming."

Suddenly something hit him from behind and threw him to the ground. He landed, his head right next to the severed one of Lord Montjoy, who had been his friend since childhood. Philemon was godfather to his son, Rory.

Through the sudden grief he could feel pain as someone pummeled his ribs. Old Soldier was fighting someone, he realized, just steps away. The ring of steel on steel cut through the air. If the whole army hadn't known before that they were there, they did now.

Philemon heaved himself up and threw off the man who had knocked him down. His opponent tried to scramble away, but Longstride flipped him and grabbed hold of his legs. He twisted and was rewarded with a scream when the man's leg bent forward and then broke.

Leaping to his feet, Philemon stomped on the man's neck, crushing his windpipe. Then he drew his sword and spun just as two more attackers appeared from out of the darkness. What he would have given to have his own sword right then, and not one scavenged from a dead man. Still, it was weighted nicely, and he was able to twist and twirl it through the air with a great deal of speed and force. The flat edge of the blade rang against the metal helm of one of his attackers. Though no blood was drawn the man fell, grabbing at his head.

Philemon stooped under a blade thrust by another soldier. He grabbed the sword of the fallen man and stood up, bringing them both to bear. The second soldier took one look, spun, and started running. With a curse Philemon yanked a dagger free of his belt and sent it spinning through the air. It sunk in the other man's back up to the hilt so there was no sense in trying to retrieve it.

He turned just as Old Soldier felled the man he was fighting.

"Robin," Philemon gasped.

"Leave him to fight his way out," the old man said brusquely. "We've got problems aplenty out here." He nodded in the direction of the holding pen and Philemon saw the glint of more steel in the darkness.

"They've been waiting for us," he said bitterly.

"It seems as though," Old Soldier said. "Just wish I knew how they knew to expect us." Philemon moved so they were back-to-back.

"I don't know," he grunted. "All I know is where they're going."

"Tell them to spit in the devil's eye when they get to hell," Old Soldier said.

"And here I was going to tell the ones I killed to kiss his arse."

"If we can get through to the holding pens, we might be able to release our men."

"If they're still alive," Philemon said grimly. Out of the corner of his eye he saw Old Soldier raise his sword high.

"If..."

Robin stood, sword raised and heart pounding in darkness that was so complete, so absolute, that it was like nothing he'd experienced before. This had to be what it was like to be blind. His eyes strained, but there wasn't a hint of light. It began to hurt, and more than that it was unnerving.

He forced himself to take a deep breath and closed his eyes so that they were no longer straining. Even through his eyelids the blackness was oppressive, but not unbearable. He could hear frightened breathing close by.

"Much, close your eyes," he said. "It will help."

The young man was silent for a few seconds. Robin listened as his breathing slowed.

"Thank you," Much said.

"How injured are you?"

"I'm not sure."

He was probably in shock. Once it wore off, things could change quickly. Robin stood there, trying to decide what they should do. He knew that if he attempted again to open the door it would be just as futile as it had been earlier. For whatever reason, his body wouldn't allow him to touch the blood.

As his breathing and heartbeat came under control he focused on his hearing, trying to discover if there was anything else alive in the room with them. He could hear Much breathing still, and the slow, raspy breath of a soldier who was dying in the darkness. Then he heard something else.

Just a whisper at first.

He strained, trying to make it out. It came again. Was it a footfall? No. That didn't seem quite right. It sounded again, echoing lightly this time. Again the hair on the back of Robin's neck stood on end.

Suddenly the sound came again, loud—so loud it filled the chamber and hurt his ears. It was all around him, roaring, triumphant, diabolical.

Laughing.

When they passed into the forest Marian heaved a sigh of relief. Even though Sherwood itself was threatened, she couldn't help but feel safe in its embrace. She glanced at her companions.

Friar Tuck looked tired. She was afraid for a moment that he might fall off his horse, but the friar held on doggedly. Riding next to him was Alan. In the bard's eyes she saw both relief and pain as they passed beneath the trees. He had sustained some sort of injury, but he hadn't shared what it was. When they got to camp she'd make sure that he was examined thoroughly. He would have to be treated quickly. They couldn't afford to have anyone sick or injured.

A short time later they made camp. A few months ago they wouldn't have had the horses with them, for fear they might make a sound that would reveal the location of the refugees. It had been weeks, though, since any dared to enter the forest. Legends about it being haunted had only grown stronger with the rumors of the Hood's death.

Dismounting, she handed the reins of her horse to one of the men who used to work in the stables. Friar Tuck practically fell out of his saddle, but Alan sat as though frozen, his jaw clenched in pain.

"Alan, can you make it down?" Marian asked.

Slowly he nodded. A second man came up and held the bridle while the bard attempted to dismount. When his foot touched the ground he crumpled with a deep groan. His horse jumped sideways. Fortunately the man holding him knew what he was doing and was quickly able to maneuver the animal away from the fallen man.

Marian knelt. "Tell me what's wrong... I mean... Show us where you are injured," she said, having to remind herself yet again that the bard's days of speaking were over. He reached down and hissed in pain as he slowly pulled up his pant leg. Marian recoiled as she saw the ugly red bite marks in flesh that was already swollen.

"Something bit you?"

He nodded, but it didn't look like any bite mark she had ever seen.

"Was it a demon?" she asked, hoping she was wrong.

Alan nodded and grimaced. She looked up at Friar Tuck.

"I don't know how to treat it," she told him.

The holy man knelt down next to her and studied Alan's leg carefully. "It looks as though there's poison in it," he said after a few moments. Alan nodded fiercely. He pulled a knife off his belt and made as though to cut open the infected skin. Friar Tuck grabbed his hand, staying the action.

"You want us to lance it and drain the poison?"

Alan nodded again. Desperation was starting to creep into his eyes, and it only served to punctuate the fear that was already there.

A trio of boys lingered near, watching with wide eyes. Friar Tuck barked orders at them to get the cook. They scurried off, and a minute later Jansa ran up.

"I need to make a poultice," Friar Tuck began. He rattled off a list of ingredients and she nodded.

"I can put that together," she said when he was done.

"Do it quickly, and bring me some bandages and hot water."

"Hot water I can manage. Clean bandages will be harder."

"Do what you can," Friar Tuck urged before turning his attention back to Alan. Marian clenched her fists at her side, wishing they had even a drop of the healing elixir that had cured the pox. Alas, that was all gone.

"Will it be alright?" she asked, wishing she wasn't asking in Alan's presence, but needing to know the answer.

"I don't know," Friar Tuck admitted. It looked as if it nearly killed him to do so. She met Alan's eyes. The fear she saw there hurt her. He shook his head slightly and then shrugged his shoulders.

"Is there some sort of ritual that needs to be done?"

"Probably, confound it all," Tuck said, his face turning bright red. "Where's a Cardinal when you need one?" He wiped a sleeve across his forehead. "I need to think. There should be something. Casting out demons, counteracting their effects. Curse it all! What is taking that woman so long?" he roared at the last.

Marian put a hand on his arm, trying to offer him what little reassurance she could. She took a deep breath, willing her own heart to stop its frantic beating. It felt like a caged bird in her chest. She'd lost too many friends, and the thought of losing

Alan—especially to something like this—was unbearable.

"Is there anything I can do?"

Friar Tuck bowed his head, and she couldn't tell if he was considering his answer or praying. Either way she waited until he finally lifted it again. He turned to look at her and there were tears of frustration glistening in his eyes.

"Jansa can assist me," he said, shaking his head. "You should go get some rest."

She was about to open her mouth to argue with him, but her stomach chose that moment to start roiling. Maybe she *should* rest, she thought. At the very least, the thought of going somewhere and closing her eyes for a few minutes sounded very appealing.

Marian needed to check in with Chastity, too. Her friend was holding up remarkably well, given all she had gone through, but Marian needed to see her, speak with her, just to reassure both of them.

Slowly she moved toward the tent in which she slept, *when* she slept. The boys who had brought Jansa were talking anxiously and making gestures toward Alan. She realized that while she recognized Audric and Bartholomew, the third one was unknown to her.

He was pale and painfully thin, with jutting collarbones. His eyes darted everywhere as though they couldn't be commanded to settle on any one thing. He licked his lips incessantly, looking like a wild, frightened creature ready to bolt at a moment's notice.

"Audric, who is this?" Marian asked sharply.

"He's from a village that the Sheriff's men burned," Audric replied. "He heard there were those sympathetic to the Hood, living in Sherwood. He had nowhere else to go and he wants to fight the Sheriff bad. So he came into the woods hoping to find someone. One of the scouts found him."

Marian turned and scrutinized the newcomer carefully.

"What's your name?" she asked.

The boy looked at her with great, round eyes.

"Ean," he whispered.

CHAPTER TWENTY-TWO

The table had been set with the finest silver, and they dined in an open balcony set high upon one of the castle towers. Large steel baskets held miniature bonfires at each cardinal direction, the flames crackling up as high as a man's chin. The night air was cold but still, and so the heat cast by the fires warmed them like a spring afternoon.

Henry pulled apart the roasted bird on the platter, fingers glistening in the bright, buttery light. Glynna, sitting across from him, cut her meat with a tiny knife consisting of a wrought stem and a razor-edged triangle about the length of her knuckle. It looked and performed quite like a chirurgeon's scalpel. She ate in small bites, chewing thoroughly to keep the disgust off her face as Henry's beard shone brighter with grease. He noticed, but he didn't care.

The Sheriff drank some dark concoction from a large goblet.

"This is nice." Henry waved a bone in front of himself. "Squab gets a bit cool on the trip all the way up here, but it is tasty."

"We will give your regards to the chef," Glynna said.

Henry's eyebrow went up. "You speak to the kitchen staff?"

"No," Glynna replied, cutting another strip of meat, "but since you liked their meal we will not have them killed today."

Henry studied her for signs of humor. He found none as she

put food in her mouth and chewed while looking at him the way a cat looks at their own shadow.

A knock came from behind them.

"Enter," the Sheriff called out.

The door swung open to reveal a soldier. His uniform was filthy, covered in dirt and dried blood. He stumbled in, nearly going to the ground as he drew near. He made it to the table before dropping, the bones of his knees thunking hollowly on the stone beside the Sheriff's chair.

The Sheriff swung his hand out, letting it drape before the soldier. The man leaned down and pressed his lips to the back of the milk pale fingers. The Sheriff nodded, accepting tribute. He pulled his hand away and spoke.

"What has happened?"

The soldier's mouth opened, and his throat moved, but all that came out was a rattling hiss.

"What was that?" Glynna asked, taking a drink from her wineglass. The soldier closed his mouth and swallowed, jaw working to create even a bit of moisture.

"A drink please," he croaked out.

"Give your report, or I will throw you off the balcony," the Sheriff said.

The soldier nodded, swallowing several more times. Finally, he managed a whisper.

"The gold has been stolen."

"Who would dare!" Glynna cried.

"The Hood," the man rasped. "He is back. I saw him with my own eyes."

"The Hood?" Henry asked.

"A low thief who travels around the forest, stealing my gold," the Sheriff said. "I killed him months ago. You passed his head on a spike, on the road that brought you here."

Henry studiously refrained from observing that there were many heads sitting atop lances along the road to the castle.

"The Hood is dead," the Sheriff said with finality.

"He is not," the soldier answered. The Sheriff glared at him and he went limp, face falling to the stone floor with the same force his knees had. From there his voice was muffled. "I am sorry to bear ill tidings, my lord, but he attacked us and took the taxes."

The Sheriff leaned forward, taking Glynna's dainty knife from her dainty hand. He speared a morsel on its point, placed it into his mouth, and began chewing it. Pulling it from between his teeth he leaned slightly away from the soldier, letting his hand fall.

The hand holding Glynna's knife.

The soldier tried again to apologize when the Sheriff drew the tiny blade, just big enough to nick an artery, across the man's throat. Blood sprayed in a wide fan that washed the Sheriff's dark armor, running in streams and rivulets off its shiny slick surface. The dead man slumped and then slid sideways as if he were a puppet whose strings had been severed. The Sheriff handed the delicate knife back to his love and turned to Henry.

"Finish your chicken," he said. "Gather your men, and go into the forest. Find and fetch me the head of this rebellion."

Henry turned his attention back to his plate.

Alan waited for his friend to cut him open. His entire leg felt like it was on fire. He began to scratch at it, and once he started it only got worse. He scratched faster and harder until blood bubbled up in a dozen places. Tears welled in his eyes and began to fall.

He gouged at his own skin with his fingernails, starting to tear out hunks of it as the agonizing fire grew and the itching consumed him, unlike anything he'd ever felt before. What passed for a scream was wrenched from him, and he began to thrash on the ground.

God, take the itching and the pain, he begged in a fit of agony. *Or take me.*

Tuck and Jansa came running up. They hit the ground next to him and grabbed his hands, trying to pull them away from his bloody skin. He fought back. They had no idea how terrible it was. The scratching brought fresh pain, but also a momentary sense of relief. He knew the itching came back double, but he was beyond being able to control himself.

He who had always been entirely in control of his mind and body.

Alan had never been drunk, because that was to lose control. He had never allowed himself to fall in love because that was to lose himself. When John had taken his tongue he'd never lost his pride, his dignity. His mind had remained clear and wholly his during the torture.

But this... this agony sent his mind skittering out of control. Logic, reason didn't matter. In his mind he screamed prayers to any deity who would listen—desperate, nonsensical words filling his mind. Nor would his body obey his commands. He wasn't himself anymore. He was slipping away. Every painful moment was part of the larger tapestry of chaos that reigned supreme within him.

He was...

He was...

I can't even remember my own name.

His hand flashed out and he grabbed at the knife that Friar Tuck held in his left hand. If only he could get the blade, he could plunge it into his own breast and end this torment.

"Hold him!"

The friar bellowed to someone, though Alan didn't know or care who. Hands—at least he thought they were hands—grabbed him, pushing him down on his back on the ground. Someone knelt on his shoulder. Someone else straightened his leg.

He screamed more, a choking, incoherent sound.

Just kill me!

Just kill me!

He wept because they could not hear him. Then, he saw the knife in the big man's hands. It lifted into the air and then came plunging down. For a moment pain worse than anything he had ever dreamed could exist flashed through him… and then all was darkness.

Friar Tuck sobbed for his friend, for the agony he was in. He sobbed because he was afraid he wouldn't be able to help. He sobbed because he couldn't remember the stupid words to any blessing or prayer that might bring healing to the man who had gone deathly still beneath his knife.

So he did all that he could. He cut into the swollen flesh. Black and green and yellow liquid exploded outward, spraying him and Jansa. The stench of rotten meat filled the air.

Dear Lord in heaven, how did the wound become infected so quickly?

Resolutely he continued, trying to cut out all the infection. Tears stung his eyes and clouded his vision. He couldn't wipe them away because his sleeves were covered with his friend's blood and the poison that was raging within him.

"I've never seen this," Jansa said, her voice shaking with horror.

"A demon bit him," Tuck gritted, unable to keep the grief and fear from his voice.

"Dear heavens. How far has the poison spread?"

"I don't know."

"You might need to take the leg." It was one of the men who had been a friend to Little John.

"I can't," Tuck wailed. "It would kill him." The same thought had already come to him.

"It *might* kill him," Jansa said. "The poison will definitely kill him, if you can't get it all."

"No, I can't," Tuck said doggedly. He hadn't the skill. He hadn't the courage. "I don't know how to do it and save him. I won't." He was babbling and he knew it.

Jansa laid a hand on his shoulder. "We'll get out everything we can then, and put on the poultice. We'll pray and we'll find some other way."

He nodded. There had to be another way. But even as he told himself that, he couldn't get the horrible feeling out of his heart and his soul.

No matter what he did or didn't do, Alan was going to die.

CHAPTER TWENTY-THREE

Much was afraid, but he trusted Lord Robin. Lord Robin would figure out a way to get them out of there. That's what he kept repeating over and over in his mind, to try and block out the laughter.

The laughter seemed to be coming from all around them. That shouldn't be possible, Much thought, but then again blood shouldn't be able to climb walls, and yet somehow it had done just that. Lord Longstride had warned them that the king of the castle was in league with the devil. Clearly he was right. Not that Much had ever doubted him in the first place.

"At the back of the room, there was a doorway but the door wasn't shut," Robin said.

"I remember seeing that," Much said.

"That's where we have to go. We can't touch the blood on the walls, but without a door we should be able to walk right through."

It sounded like a good plan. Much wondered where the doorway led, and he hoped that they could find King Richard by going that way. Really he just wanted out of the room that they were in very, very badly.

"How do we find our way there?" Much asked.

"Carefully," Robin said, his voice grim. "I can navigate fairly well in the dark."

Much wasn't about to argue with him. If Lord Robin said he could, then he could. A moment later a hand descended on Much's shoulder, and he jumped.

"It's me," Robin said.

Together they started walking, slowly. Much trusted Lord Robin to lead the way. They would go a few feet, pause, and then walk a few more. Much wasn't sure, but he thought they had made it about halfway down the hall when all of a sudden the laughter stopped.

Lord Robin came to a halt.

The silence was as thick as the darkness.

"Why did it stop?" Much asked in a whisper.

"I don't know, but I don't like it," Robin said.

Much tensed. He tightened his grip on the knife he'd used for most of the fight, knowing he should have picked up a sword from one of the guards. Old Soldier had made sure he could fight with a sword, although he was better with the knife. If more of the enemy was coming for them, though, they wouldn't be able to see them to fight.

They won't be able to see us either, Much realized. It was some comfort, but what if the king had demon soldiers that they hadn't run into yet? Could those see in the dark?

A shiver crawled its way up his spine and shook him hard.

"Are you okay?" Robin asked.

"Yes," Much hastened to reassure him. He didn't want Lord Robin to know that he was scared of what might be waiting for them.

"Let's keep going," Robin said. They took a couple of steps, when suddenly Much felt like something was standing on his other side. Pain knifed through his arm as though he'd been scratched by something. He swore.

"What's wrong?" Robin asked.

"Something scratched me," Much said, hating that his voice was shaking a bit.

"What?"

"I don't know. I felt like there was someone or something

next to me, and then the scratch."

"Is there something next to you still?" Robin asked tensely.

"I can't feel anything."

"Tell me if there's anything else."

"I will," Much promised.

Slowly they started walking again.

Robin was sweating, and it was taking a lot of effort not to swear with every step. That wouldn't help calm either of them down, though, and calm was desperately needed.

Something had scratched Much in the darkness. Robin had a terrible feeling that something had been a demon. Walking through the dark, feeling that there were hostile eyes watching them, reminded him of the night he'd tried to assassinate John in his bedchamber.

This darkness was alive, writhing around them. As much as he tried to ignore it, to focus on their destination, he couldn't. Every time he stepped forward he had the sensation of something backing up just a couple more inches to keep him from running into it.

They were being taunted, toyed with.

That feeling was growing stronger with every passing moment. He'd hoped briefly that the cessation of the laughter had been a good sign. Now, though, he feared it was just the beginning of something diabolical.

His senses felt as if they were on fire, and he was starting to get overwhelmed. He couldn't keep his mind off the things slithering in the dark, just beyond reach. They would be coming for Much and him soon. The question that remained was how to fight them.

He wondered again where the doorway would lead them—if and when they reached it. He prayed that once they were out of this room there would be light again, and they'd be able to find their way out of the castle.

If they could do all that and find King Richard, too, then they'd be unstoppable. Of course, at the moment all of it seemed highly unlikely. Robin prayed that his father and Old Soldier were faring better outside.

The bodies began to pile up. Between the soldiers they'd killed and the corpses of the slain nobles, it was getting hard to find places to step where he wouldn't be walking on bodies or tripping over heads.

"How many more, can you tell?" he asked.

"No," Old Soldier said with a grunt as he pulled his blade free of another opponent. "But let's assume a couple hundred. That way, if it's less, we can be pleasantly surprised."

"I'd forgotten what an optimist you are," Philemon said sarcastically. "We need to set our soldiers free, and we can't do that from here."

"We also need to survive, and here we have the advantage. We've figured out where to step."

"Mostly," Philemon said as he felt his heel come down on what was probably a hand. There was no time to readjust his footing as another attacker came charging at him. The man's sword whizzed past his ear and he cursed before slashing his attacker across the throat.

A sudden thought occurred to him.

They didn't even know if their countrymen were here and being held alive. After all, the nobles had been slaughtered. If the fighting men weren't alive, then he and Old Soldier needed to flee. If they were alive, and close by, they needed to know help was on its way, and that they should fight with whatever they had in them. The enemy already knew exactly where he and Old Soldier were, so he had nothing to lose...

"Good Christian men of England," he bellowed at the top of his lungs. "I am Philemon Longstride! Can you hear me?"

A voice rang through the darkness, and his heart leapt.

"Aye, Lord Longstride, we hear you!" It was a familiar voice, but he couldn't place the man to whom it belonged. "We are here!"

"We are fighting to free you," he called back. "Do what you can, and we will reach you shortly."

A cheer rose up and he was heartened to realize all the voices came from nearby.

"Awfully optimistic, aren't you," Old Soldier muttered. "Still, that's one question answered."

"Now, to get them," Philemon said.

"And just how do you plan to do that?"

"Simple," Philemon answered. "We attack." Saying that, he lunged forward, sword hacking left and right as he ran through the enemies who stood against him. So startled were they that he gained ground quickly. Behind him he heard Old Soldier curse as he started after him.

He killed some of the enemy soldiers, others he knocked to the side with his charge. Out of the darkness he could see a fence of some sort, looming up just ahead. That had to be where they were holding their men.

"We are almost to you!" he shouted.

"Hurry!" the familiar voice called back.

He reached the fence, grabbed it, and looked through to see men lying on the ground in masses. His heart stuttered. He wondered where the ones who were cheering had been.

"Where are you!" he bellowed.

"Right here, Lord Longstride!"

He turned his head to the side and his blood ran cold as he realized he was staring into the face of a traitor.

Robin could feel the darkness shifting, moving around them. It was alive. He forced himself to keep his eyes closed, knowing there was still nothing he'd be able to see and the attempt to make out anything would pull attention away from his other senses. The result could be deadly.

Something brushed past him and it caused him to jerk. In turn Much jumped, as well. He wanted to stop moving, but their only hope of survival was getting out of this room. He forced himself to keep going as steadily as he could.

He stepped on something that slithered beneath his boot and he quickly kicked it to the side. Then he paused for a second and could hear Much starting to mutter under his breath. It took a moment for him to realize the young man was praying.

"Much, keep praying," Robin said softly, "but do it silently. I need to hear what's around us."

Much stopped speaking, and silence once again descended. In it Robin's ears were straining nearly as much as his eyes had been earlier. Whatever was in the room with them was moving without making any noise. As they began to move forward he wished that they were also silent, but each footfall sounded as if it was made by a giant.

At least he knew they were headed the right way. The one time they'd drifted too close to the wall his foot had refused to move forward until he adjusted direction. By his calculation they had probably walked almost two thirds of the length of the room. They just needed to stay focused and keep moving.

A sudden whispering broke the silence, and he was about to reprimand Much when he realized it wasn't the miller's son. The sound came from all around them, sometimes near, sometimes far. He couldn't make out the words, but the menace behind them was clear.

He heard something directly in front of him and he slashed at the space with his sword. It was empty, nothing was there. Suddenly, something wet and hot licked the back of his neck. He spun with a shout, nearly toppling Much in the process. Again he swung his sword and again he connected with nothing.

Standing still for a moment, limbs trembling, he tried to calm his mind. Whatever was there didn't want them to leave the room. It tried to distract and confuse him. Very deliberately he turned to one side.

"Are you all right?" he asked Much as he put a hand back on his shoulder.

"Yes," Much whispered, his voice shaking.

"We need to keep walking. Whatever we hear, or feel, or *think* we feel, we have to ignore it. Do you understand?"

"Yes." But the young man sounded doubtful.

He turned again and began to walk forward. The whispers intensified. Something brushed Robin's arm but he ignored it. All that mattered was getting out. Something else swiped at his calf, causing a sting of pain. He gritted his teeth and kept moving. Something tugged on his ear and it took all his will not to shout and start swatting at it.

It's not there, he told himself. *You've tried attacking it with your sword, twice, and there was nothing there. Just keep going. It wants you to stop, wants you to lose focus and become trapped in here.*

He forced one foot in front of the other, keeping his hand clamped tight on Much's shoulder. The two of them were going to make it out of this together. They just had to keep walking.

He stepped again on something that slithered and again kicked it to the side, but without missing a stride this time. An invisible hand yanked his hair. The whispers grew louder and he knew they had almost made it. Then, suddenly, from behind him in the darkness, back where he had been licked, he heard something that made his blood run cold.

"Lord Robin, why haven't we started walking yet?" Much asked.

CHAPTER TWENTY-FOUR

Robin stood, frozen to the spot, his hand still on what he had thought was Much's shoulder. His mouth had gone completely dry as he struggled to decide which was the real Much—the shoulder he was touching, or the voice behind him in the darkness.

"Much," he whispered, "can you hear me?"

There was no sound from whatever was standing next to him.

"Much!" he called loudly. "Where are you?"

"Standing here, waiting to walk. You said we were going to walk and not stop for anything. We haven't started yet, though. Why is your voice coming from so far away?"

"Much, is my hand on your shoulder?"

"Yes, Lord Robin."

He wanted to thrust his sword into whatever was standing next to him, but even through the haze of terror in his mind he reminded himself that he couldn't be sure which was real and which was the trick.

If Much was standing next to him, why didn't he speak? Was it because something was keeping him from doing it? Every instinct told him that the real miller's son was the one behind him. He'd taken his hand off the man's shoulder when the thing had licked his neck. It was possible that when he reached out again, that this thing had been there instead.

Sweat poured off him as he tried to determine what to do. Whatever he decided, he had to do it quickly. He twisted and kicked out. If it was Much, he would stagger and cry out under the onslaught. His boot connected with something solid, but it didn't give.

With an oath he let go of the thing he'd been holding and swung his sword around. It sang through the air but connected with nothing. Whatever it was, it had moved or become immaterial again.

"Much, I need you to walk toward the sound of my voice," he said, trying to keep his voice calm.

There was a pause and then Much spoke up.

"I can't, you're holding me back."

"Much, I'm not the one holding your shoulder," he said.

Much gave a shout of panic and Robin heard the sound of a fist hitting something. Much shouted again and there was a mighty thud as of someone or something hitting the floor.

"Much?"

Silence fell.

"Much!"

He strained his ears and heard a grunting sound as of someone struggling with a heavy burden. Then a scream of agony ripped through the room.

"Much!" Robin shouted, lurching toward the sound. Something yanked the back of his shirt, and his feet slid from under him. He landed on his back and rolled, regaining his feet in a moment. He spun in a circle, trying to determine where the attack would come from next.

Nothing.

No, not nothing. There was something.

Breathing.

Something in the darkness was breathing. No, it was more than that, it was as though the darkness itself was breathing.

"Much!"

There was no answer and his stomach lurched. He couldn't lose him. Not now. Not like this. He moved forward again and then stopped after two steps as he realized he was now completely turned around and lost in the dark. He had no idea which direction he was facing. He didn't know where Much was, let alone the door through which they hoped to escape.

They were trapped.

Philemon stared in horror at Sir Lawrence, who was standing a couple of feet away, dozens of the enemy soldiers at his back. It had been his voice calling out.

"Lawrence! What are you doing?"

"The only thing I can do," Lawrence said. "Survive."

"I don't understand," Philemon said.

"They broke him," Old Soldier said from behind.

"But, you escaped, you went for help..."

"That never happened. I was captured but separated, and King Wulfhere... showed me the error of my ways."

"How can you say that, man?" Philemon roared.

"Did Richard tell you what we're up against?" Lawrence said sharply. "What we're really being asked to fight?"

"He's our king. All he needed to tell me was that we needed to fight."

"Well, some of us would have liked to have known the truth before we pledged ourselves to a crusade that's doomed to failure. Fighting against men, that's one thing. Fighting demons? I didn't sign up for that."

"You signed up to fight the forces of the Devil himself."

"That was before I knew the Devil was real!" Lawrence's teeth ground around his words.

"If he is real, then so is—"

"Shut up," the knight demanded. "That isn't true. If God exists, then He is a coward or a bastard. The Devil has been there in every bad deed, every death I've dealt. Every time I have followed a noble's order he has arrived."

"Blasphemy!"

"Only to the loser of the conflict. You cannot win."

"Without treachery like yours we could."

"Ha!" Lawrence responded. "You have no idea the treachery—but not true treachery. I have not betrayed my true dark lord."

"You're Wulfhere's man now."

"Aye."

"He will use you and spit you out, son."

"Not after my service. I went to Sherwood as I was ordered, and found these fools. And I brought their best back to be taken hostage, as well."

"Coward!" Philemon hissed as he leaped forward. He thrust with his sword, but one of the soldiers standing by Lawrence blocked his blade, sending it flying from his hand. Lawrence began to laugh.

Standing next to the fence, Old Soldier watched closely. He believed that he and Lord Longstride still had a chance of making it out of this alive. He also believed that the opportunity would present itself once and only once, and that they had to be ready to take it when it did.

Lawrence was busy bragging. The man appeared different to him. The pallor of his skin that had seemed an omen of death instead reminded him of what he'd been told happened to the nobles who signed blood oaths to John the usurper.

But I saw his wound, he thought. *I dressed it.* If dark magic was afoot, however, then he could have been deceived.

He glanced again at the pen full of men. They appeared to be dead. Surely if they had just been asleep the noise of the battle would have roused them. He squinted his eyes. The man closest to him was breathing, the slight rise and fall of his chest a giveaway.

Then, very slowly, he saw the man's hand move, one finger at a time. Then the hand slid under the fence rail and tapped him three times on his right boot.

He blinked in surprise. When he had served in the king's guard as a young man, the triple tap had been the way they would wake each other when it was time for guard duty, or something important was happening. More importantly, it was also a way of waking a sleeping comrade without letting his superiors know the man had fallen asleep. As he had once explained to a young recruit the three taps literally said *"Are You Awake?"*

Old Soldier carefully tapped his toe three times on the ground to indicate that he understood. The man slowly moved his hand and this time he pointed.

Carefully, slowly, Old Soldier turned his head slightly until he could just make out what the man was indicating. There, about a foot behind him, was the gate to the pen. Hope surged through him. He slowly swiveled his head back, trying to pay attention to what Lord Longstride was saying.

He needed to warn the lord before he acted, so the man would be prepared. He could think of no way to do it without drawing attention. The only shot he had was a long one. There was no reason the lord should understand the significance of the triple tap, but perhaps just making contact would be enough.

Old Soldier's blade was out and held low. As it was the point was just to the left of Lord Longstride's shin. Very carefully he moved it and tapped his lord three times on the leg.

The noble kept talking, but he moved his head slightly and cocked it as though listening. He knew something was about to happen. That was as good as they could manage at this point. Old Soldier slowly moved his hand behind him until he felt the gate. It was closed with a chain. His fingers touched the metal and then kept going, searching out a weak spot.

Finally he found it. The fence looked to have been newly reinforced, but the gate was old and the wood was rotting in one section. That's what his questing fingers told him.

With his left hand he gripped his sword tighter. His was a broadsword, good for the kind of battles where your enemies surrounded you tight. You could swing the sword and take out a number of them if you had the strength and the balance.

He was tired. The battle had taken its toll on him, but he had enough strength in him for one great feat that would change the tide of everything. He just had to make sure it went off as planned.

"Your king is as good as dead," Lawrence taunted.

"Our king!" Lord Longstride roared, jumping forward to punch Lawrence right in the mouth.

As he did Old Soldier took a step backward, pivoted, swung the broadsword up and over his head, and then brought it down on the rotted part of the gate. The wood shattered beneath the force of his blow and splinters went flying. He jumped back as the men inside rose with a roar and rushed the opening. They shoved their way out. The first ones dove at the men behind Lawrence, wresting weapons away from them as the second wave scrambled to pick up swords that already littered the battlefield.

Lord Longstride grabbed Lawrence and ran him through. The coward bled black poison onto the blade.

"Drop the sword!" Old Soldier bellowed.

Lord Longstride heard and did, just managing to sidestep as Lawrence crashed to the ground. Old Soldier grabbed a sword off a body and tossed it to his lord. All around them the battle raged. Cocky, well-rested, and well-fed soldiers against a ragged army of half-starved men. It was going to be brutal and bloody, but he was counting on the outcome.

Robin stood, panting and exhausted. He had been searching and he couldn't find Much. He kept expecting to trip over the man's body at any second, but he hadn't. He kept calling, but the young man wasn't answering.

A sudden groaning caught his ear and he stopped.

"Much, is that you?"

"Yes, Lord Robin."

"Are you hurt?"

"Yes."

That word drove a new bolt of fear through Robin's heart. Much never admitted when he was injured. For him to say that, the injury had to be grave indeed.

"Can you walk?"

"I'm not sure," Much replied. "I'll try."

"That's okay, just keep talking and I'll come to you," Robin said, starting to walk in the direction of his voice.

"It's okay." Much coughed. "Go, save King Richard."

"I'm not leaving here without you, so do as I say," Robin said, putting authority into his voice.

"Yes, my lord." The voice was weaker.

"Tell me a story, Much."

"A story? What kind of story?"

"A good one, with a happy ending, those are always the best," Robin said, heart in his throat. He paused, waiting for Much to speak again.

"I don't know many of those," Much said.

"Surely you must know one at least," Robin pressed.

"There's the story of you and Queen Marian."

"Yes, let me hear you tell that one," Robin said.

"But you already know it," Much said. The young man wasn't thinking straight. He didn't understand why Robin needed him to keep talking.

"But I want to hear it, hear how it's told. It makes me feel better," Robin said. "Please, Much, just tell me the story," he begged.

Much coughed again. "How should I start?"

"Once upon a time. All the best ones start that way, don't you think?" Robin asked, fighting back tears. He could hear the way Much was coughing. It sounded wet, as if he might be coughing up blood.

"Yes, I guess so," Much said. "Once upon a time there was this beautiful princess, and her name was..." He drifted off. Robin was getting close to him, but he still needed the sound to help.

"What was her name, Much?"

"What? Oh, her name was the Lady Marian." His voice was weaker still. He was fading.

"And what did she look like, Much?" Robin pressed.

"She was the most beautiful woman who ever lived. She had a smile that could make you feel warm like the sun was shining on you."

Robin cursed under his breath as he tried to find the young man. He was close. He could still hear whispering all around him in the room, but he forced himself only to hear Much's voice.

"And did she smile at you, Much?" he asked.

"Oh, yes, she smiled at many people. Mostly, though, she smiled at this one man."

"That man must have been very, very lucky," Robin said, slowing down. He should be almost on top of the boy.

"Oh yes, very lucky," Much slurred.

Robin bent down and felt rough cloth beneath his fingers. He sat down on the floor and found Much's face. He touched the boy's cheek with his hand. It was cold and wet with something thick and sticky.

"The luckiest man in the world," Robin said, struggling to get the words out.

"I... can't... remember... the rest," Much said.

"Then I'll tell you. This man was lucky not just because the fair Marian smiled upon him but also because he had friends who were the most loyal and the most true."

"Everyone... needs friends," Much whispered.

"Yes, and one of the dearest friends the man had was the son of a miller, who was strong and tall and had the noblest heart of any man he'd ever met." He found and held Much's hands. The boy was slipping away from him, he could feel it. Any moment now and he would be gone.

"And he was very sorry that he ever got his friend into trouble," Robin said, unable to stop the tears.

"It's okay," Much whispered.

Listening as the breathing grew ragged and thin, Robin knew that it wasn't.

SACRIFICES

CHAPTER TWENTY-FIVE

Robin felt it the moment Much passed. It was as if part of himself was ripped away.

Sitting there in the darkness, he wept for a moment before forcing himself to his feet with a shout of rage and grief that could not be contained. Of all those he had lost, somehow this hurt the most. He didn't know why, but it was as though the sum total of all who had died weighed upon him in that moment.

The cost had been too great.

No more.

With gritted teeth, he turned and moved forward, feeling for the sensation when he got too close to a wall. Once he did, he turned to his right and started working down the room…

Marian sat up abruptly, her heart pounding wildly in her chest. She had been just about to drift to sleep when she could have sworn she heard Robin cry out in anguish.

Chastity stooped and entered the tent, her forehead crinkled with worry.

"Are you all right, my lady?"

"Chastity, we're not in the castle, we're out in the wilderness and I don't care who overhears. Call me Marian, like you did when we were little."

Chastity bobbed her head. "It's hard getting used to."

"I know."

"What is it? You shouted."

"Did I?" Marian asked, rubbing her head. "I was having... I don't know, I wasn't quite asleep so it wasn't a nightmare."

Chastity sat down. "Was it a vision?" she asked, her eyes widening.

"I'm not sure I'd call it that either. It felt more like something that was happening now, but not here."

"Was it something to do with Robin?"

Marian nodded, suddenly unable to speak.

"I'm sure he's fine."

Marian didn't say anything. She felt in her heart that Robin lived. She also felt that something was deeply wrong. Whatever was happening to him, it was certainly not fine. She couldn't burden Chastity with that knowledge, though. Her friend had already been through too much to carry Marian's worries and burdens as well.

"How is Alan?" she asked and then winced inwardly. So much for not adding to her burden. Then again, it wasn't as if she could hide the bard's condition. Chastity hesitated a moment and then dropped her eyes.

"He lives... for now."

"For now?" Marian asked, fear knifing through her.

"The wound was terrible. Unlike anything any of us has ever seen." Chastity took a deep breath. "It's said he was bitten by a demon."

"He was," Marian said. "What more can be done for him?"

"Friar Tuck is praying, and there are several praying with him, including Esther."

"I should join them," Marian said, moving to stand up.

Chastity frowned. "You'd probably do him... all of them... a lot more good if you rested instead. Not that your prayers aren't powerful, it's just... there are many who can pray, but only one who can lead. We can't afford for you to become ill from exhaustion."

Marian understood what Chastity was trying to say. When her friends were suffering, though, she had to do *something*. She put a hand on her friend's shoulder.

"Thank you... for everything," she said, because she couldn't think of anything else to say. Chastity nodded and tears welled in her eyes. Impulsively Marian reached out to embrace her. The young woman buried her head in Marian's shoulder and began to sob. So she sat there and held her friend while she cried, and as she did Marian prayed for Alan and for Chastity and for all of them.

Friar Tuck was in agony as he prayed, at times breaking down in broken sobs. Several were praying with him, including the girl, Esther. Sometimes they prayed quietly, sometimes he tried to pray out loud. When he did and could not continue she would pick up with her gentle voice and quiet strength.

He had done all he could in the physical realm. Now he was doing all he could in the spiritual. He was praying with a fervor he hadn't known since the pox had swept the land. He felt light-headed, then feverish despite the cold of the air around him. He begged with God. Tried to bargain and even made childish threats. Throughout it all he could not stop weeping.

It had been bad enough that Alan lost his tongue. Now he might well lose his life. Tuck hadn't been able to amputate the leg. He should have. He knew that. He just didn't have it in him to do it, and there was no one else with the skill or the courage to do it for him. If Alan died, it was his fault. So he prayed and would continue to pray until Alan was on the mend.

Or with the dead.

Philemon was tired, but the battle still raged around them. He kept glancing over at Old Soldier. Every time his arm grew so weary it wanted to drop the sword he was wielding, he would tell himself the same thing.

I won't stop fighting until he does.

And he knew, deep in his gut, that Old Soldier would never stop fighting. So, together they would battle until it was done.

His thoughts strayed again to Robin, and he offered up tiny prayers that his son was alive and that he would see him again soon. To be parted now would be more than he could bear. When his thoughts weren't on his son, they were with his king.

He had to keep telling himself that King Richard couldn't be one of the beheaded bodies they had discovered earlier. The king was too valuable a prisoner to have been so summarily dispatched. Philemon hoped that inside the castle Robin had found Richard and that the two were together, fighting their way out of there, and would join them soon. Every time he thought of that he redoubled his efforts, wanting to make sure that when they arrived the fighting here was done and they could make for England as fast as horses and ships could take them.

Another enemy soldier died on his blade and he shook the body to the ground. Beside him another English soldier fell and he felt the loss, the grief, as if the man were one of his own. He turned and killed the soldier who had ended his countryman.

"God save the King!" Old Soldier roared.

English voices rose in response.

"God save the King!"

The chorus served to spur them on, despite their fatigue.

"Long live the Lionheart!" Philemon bellowed. He glanced to the sky. He had no idea how long the battle had been raging or when dawn might be coming. He wasn't sure if it would show them more horrors, but he hoped it would drive at least some of the darkness back.

"We are winning," Old Soldier shouted to him.

Whether or not he believed it or was just trying to bring relief and reassurance Philemon didn't know. Either way he was grateful, because he felt his spirit lift just hearing the words.

"We'll have them all slain before King Richard can join the party," he said.

"The King might thank you for that. Then again, he might wish you left a couple alive for him," Old Soldier grunted. But Philemon was worried that the king might be fighting more than his share inside the castle.

"I'll gladly let him yell at me for a fortnight."

He'd welcome Richard and Robin yelling at him for a lifetime, if it meant they both made it out of the castle alive.

"Robin's going to be just fine," Old Soldier said. "He's a cunning fighter," he added as he bested another man. "I never saw his match with the bow and arrow, and he's not bad with a sword either."

"I hope so, since a sword is what he has."

"It will be more than enough, you'll see," Old Soldier said, grunting as he blocked the blade of a particularly large opponent who had arms the size of tree trunks.

"Need any help with Goliath there?" Philemon asked.

"Nah, you know what they say."

"What's that?"

In response Old Soldier dropped to the ground and swung his sword, which sliced clean through the giant's knee. The man screamed in agony as he toppled backward.

"The bigger they are, the harder they fall?" Philemon offered.

"If you need a leg up, cut them off at the knees." Old Soldier wiped gore off his face with the back of his sleeve.

Philemon shook his head and turned back just in time to face a soldier who was charging him. He got his sword up to block at the last possible second and cursed himself for not paying close enough attention to what was happening around him. This wasn't over, and he needed to remember that or it would be his son doing the mourning.

Robin became convinced that he was going in the right direction because the whispers grew louder, more incessant. He could almost hear what they were saying, but he didn't try, instead working to block them out. Something brushed against him and he lashed out, but did not turn his body.

Every step forward was harder and harder to make, as though he were walking through a snowdrift. He had to push his foot forward each time. He realized in anguish that his progress had been slowed to a crawl. His feet were mired, though there was nothing actually holding them—at least, nothing that he could see or feel.

"Get away from me!" he shouted. The words sounded muffled, as though he were listening to someone speaking from far away, behind a closed door. Nor was there an echo. It was as if what he said was held captive.

Which meant no one would hear him, no matter how loudly he screamed. If King Richard still lived and made it back, they might spend days within a couple of feet of each other and never know it. The thought brought new panic.

His father and Old Soldier would be fighting their way through the enemy soon, if they weren't already. They were counting on him to get the king out of the castle. Yet he wasn't even going to get *himself* out.

The darkness became even more solid. He started to feel fingers plucking at his clothes. He shouted the first couple of times and then gave up. He tried swatting the air, but there was nothing there. Whatever was there could touch him, but he couldn't touch it.

Lifting his right foot he tried to push it forward, but couldn't. He strained with all his might until his muscles were quivering.

At last with a gasp he managed to get his foot down in exactly the same place it had been when he picked it up. He stood, trapped as though in quagmire. Something punched him in the stomach and he doubled over, fighting to keep his balance. Robin knew that if he went down it would all be over.

Something kicked him in the back of his right knee. Even as it buckled he frantically threw his weight onto his left leg. He overshifted, though, and nearly fell straight to the left. His arms flailed wildly.

God help me!

There was no way out.

"You're going to die," a voice cackled just behind him.

Robin shouted and tried to twist, swinging his sword up. There was nothing there. He twisted back around. Despair roiled within him. The voice was right. He was going to die here.

Suddenly, a blinding white light flooded the far end of the room. Robin could see it even through his closed eyelids. He opened his eyes and yelped in pain at the brightness after so much darkness. There was something in the center of it. He squinted. He must be dead and an angel was come to take him.

Then it moved, and he realized that he knew the stride, the stride of a man who was confident in his own rightness, assured of everything he did. King Richard ran toward him, sword held aloft.

The blinding white light came from the weapon.

CHAPTER TWENTY-SIX

"Sire!" Robin shouted. The king looked to be twenty feet away. As Richard held the sword high, Robin heard the darkness around him.

It screamed in pain and terror.

"Back to hell with all of you!" Richard roared.

The darkness ran from him and the light from the sword began to fill the room. Robin struggled to move his feet. Whatever had hold of them was losing its grip as the king approached. Richard had a large sack slung over his shoulder. Setting it down, he reached into it with his free hand and pulled out a short sword.

"Catch!" he shouted, throwing the blade to Robin. The sword spun in the air and Robin was able to snatch the hilt without slicing his hand open on the blade. As soon as he grasped it the weapon blazed forward with light just as blinding as that which came from the king's sword.

He slashed downward, seemingly through thin air, but heard more screaming. Whatever had hold of his feet let go, and the darkness retreated back to the corners of the room. Thus freed, he raced across the room, slashing with the weapon until there was only light shining throughout the chamber.

In the light he could clearly see Much's body, and it tore at him. He turned away, looking back to King Richard who stood, hair fanned out around him like a mane. The lionheart had never looked fiercer.

"You and the boy killed them all?" he asked, gesturing to the fallen soldiers.

"Yes," Robin said, barely finding his voice.

"When did the darkness kill him?" he asked, gesturing to Much as he strode forward.

Robin shook his head. "Five minutes, half an hour, I don't know. Time didn't pass in the normal way."

Richard strode over to Much's body. He stared down at him for a second.

"Brave lad," he said.

"As brave as I've ever known."

Richard dropped to one knee. "God Almighty, if it be Your Will, we ask that you return this warrior to us," he prayed. He lifted his sword and placed it on Much's shoulder as though knighting him.

Robin stared in wonder.

Suddenly light seemed to shoot out of the body, and before his eyes he saw the wounds on the body heal and disappear. King Richard lifted the sword and stood up.

"Rise, Much," he said, his voice full of authority.

The young man's eyelids flickered and then opened. He sat up abruptly and then, hesitantly, as though unsure of himself, climbed to his feet. He gathered his balance, rose to his full height, and stood there, blinking in the light.

"I heard you calling me, sire," Much said to Richard, his voice shaky but recognizable. "You did, didn't you?"

"I did," Richard said. "It wasn't time for you to leave us yet."

Much nodded as though he understood. Then he turned and looked at Robin and his eyes lit up.

"You're alright!"

"I am," Robin said hoarsely. He walked forward and grabbed Much's shoulder, desperately needing to convince himself that what he was seeing was real and not some illusion. "And so are you." He flicked his eyes to King Richard. "How?"

Richard hefted the sword. "These were a gift from His Holiness, brought from the heart of Rome. The blood of martyrs and saints has infused them. They have been blessed and had magic worked into them. They can drive back the darkness, when ordinary steel can't. If we act quickly enough, they can also restore what evil has taken." He looked at the miller's son. "A few more minutes, and he would have been beyond our reach."

"They can restore?" Robin asked hopefully as he stared at the blade he was holding.

"Only what has been taken unnaturally," the king replied. Robin nodded, then he glanced around.

"We need to leave," he said. "Did you find the pagan king? Is he still a threat?"

Richard hesitated. "Wulfhere is still here. I lost him when he fled from the room. In searching I found these and knew we would need them when we made it back to England."

"We can't worry about him at the moment," Robin said. "We have men outside working to free your army—my father, Old Soldier, and Sir Lawrence. We must move quickly to help them."

"My army?" Richard said. "They are still alive?

"I think so, but if we don't go now and help, they might be dead before the first light of dawn."

Richard nodded. "Lead the way."

Robin turned and moved swiftly toward the main doors. The blood had disappeared from them, and from the walls. Where it had gone he didn't know. When he reached out he braced himself, just in case some spell still remained. His hand touched wood, though, and with relief he threw the doors open.

Holding the sword aloft he hurried out.

Father, we're coming, he thought. *Hold on.*

* * *

If he had been tired before, now Philemon was exhausted—he could barely move his arm. His sword felt like it weighed more than his entire body.

Old Soldier had switched hands and had been fighting with his sword in his left hand for ten minutes or so. That lent him new vigor, and Philemon envied him the ability. He had never learned to fight with both hands, though, so he didn't dare try.

All around him the night seemed to be growing darker. At first he thought it was his imagination, but he quickly realized that it was not. It might have meant the dawn was coming soon, but he feared that the darkness was more unnatural than natural. All he could do was pray that it was a sign of the new day, and not an omen of their doom.

They followed the clash of battle outside the castle, coming over a small ridge to find men standing on a mass of corpses outside a shabby pen of mud. The swords lit the scene, and it took Robin only a moment to spot his father and Old Soldier, both covered in bloody grime. They crouched back-to-back, surrounded by enemies who looked younger, stronger, and fresher than they. Scattered here and there other soldiers fought, in pairs and in groups, ragged Englishmen against outlaw barbarians.

Robin charged down the ridge toward the men trying to kill his father and his friend. He didn't shout or unleash a war cry, but ran with the short sword in his fist, living up to his surname as his legs devoured the distance.

Plowing into the back of one of Wulfhere's soldiers, he drove him off his feet to tumble headlong. Old Soldier didn't miss a beat, swiping his notched blade across the base of the man's neck. The sword was too ragged to cut so crushed the skin and flesh and bone. The corpse fell with its helm skewing almost completely around.

Robin spun, slashing out with the sword, feeling it thud against the bodies of the men directly to his left and right. The soldier on the left folded around his wound, dropping to his knees as his own blood spilled between his fingers. The one on the right had a bracer of boiled leather around his middle that ate the slash, saving his intestines from being spilled.

He leaned back, moving away, as Robin twisted on his forward foot and drove the sword with his weight behind a straight thrust. The soldier looked surprised another blow came so quickly. Surprised all the way to the red mud in which he fell.

The fury claimed Robin, riding him. It weighed on his back, making him feel wild and out of control. He jerked his eyes around, searching for another opponent, when he was pulled short by the blast of a trumpet.

On the ridge stood Wulfhere. As everyone turned toward, him he tossed the hunting horn away.

"Enough of this," he bellowed

To Robin's left, King Richard spoke up, "Then surrender."

"I will have your head roasting on my brazier."

"Is that a challenge to combat, Wulfhere?"

The robber king looked at the men he had remaining. They stared at him with cold judgment and Robin understood that his position was held by strength of arm alone. Wulfhere could not refuse an open challenge on the field of battle. If he did, his own men would fall upon him like wolves on a carcass.

"We fight as we are," he growled.

"I win my freedom and the freedom of all under my protection," Richard said—but it wasn't the pagan king who replied. A hulking man holding a fearsome war hammer, its head and shaft matted with gore, stepped forward.

"Aye," he said. If Wulfhere fell, this man would become the new warlord.

The pagan king spoke again. "And I win the skin of you and everyone under your protection."

"Not our lives?"

"I will leave you your life," Wulfhere said. "Mayhap you will be strong enough to hold on to it without your skin."

Richard sighed. It was the best deal he would receive.

"My oath."

"And mine." Wulfhere filled his hands with axe and sword. Without another word, the two combatants rushed each other as their men formed a circle and roared out encouragement.

Sparks fell into Richard's eyes, knocked from the edge of the holy sword. He grunted at the impact, the axe blow shuddering pain from his wrist to his armpit.

He was going to die at Wulfhere's hand.

The pagan king was fierce, stoutly muscled and driven with a feral cunning that lent itself to combat. Richard kicked out, driving his foot into Wulfhere's hip—not enough to hurt him, but enough to drive them apart so he could catch his breath. The time in captivity had lessened him. The battle had taken the rest of his strength.

The respite lasted only a moment. Wulfhere lunged again, this time swinging up the wide, short sword he favored. Richard danced, striking down with the holy blade to drive away his enemy's weapon. Wulfhere fought for more than his position as leader—he was fighting for his life. It was powerful motivation.

Richard fought for *all* their lives.

His foot slipped on a rock.

Wulfhere was there, windmilling the axe and sword in a web of mutilation and death. Richard scrambled back, using every bit of hard-won skill to survive. Behind him, through the chants of the men around him, came a familiar voice. A voice he had heard as a boy, speaking to his father—and then to him as if he *were* his father.

"Be yourself," Old Soldier said.

The words rattled in his skull.

Be yourself.

Wulfhere swung the axe, almost catching a shin, but Richard was too quick.

The pagan king was a wolf.

But Richard was a lion.

Be yourself.

The next time Wulfhere lunged toward him Richard changed, not dancing away from the blade but lunging over it. He slipped past the sword that was thrust toward his heart. He used his own arm to trap Wulfhere's against his body. The pagan king's eyes went wide in surprise, but he immediately swung the axe up, looking to bury it in his enemy's skull.

Richard leaned back, pulling Wulfhere off balance. Before he could recover, Richard had the edge of his sword pressed against his throat.

"Yield," he growled.

"Never."

"I am a king of mercy."

"I am not." Wulfhere spat in his eyes. "I will come for you. I will hunt you. I will track every person you love or loves you, and I will destroy them." The man sought death.

"I believe you," Richard said softly.

Wulfhere's head came free of his body before Richard drew half the sword length through his throat.

CHAPTER TWENTY-SEVEN

Every man among them was exhausted—practically dead on his feet—yet all were happy to march if it meant getting away from the place of so much misery and loss. They had taken what horses they could from the stables, but there were still many who had to walk.

"I think we need to stop and make camp, rest a while. Eat, sleep," Robin said. They were about five miles from the castle and more and more were staggering. Many were held up by comrades who were in nearly as bad a shape.

He didn't like it. Every bone in his body urged him to get back to England before things got even worse there. He worried for his friends and particularly for Marian.

"That would be wise," King Richard agreed. "Halt! Set up camp, as well as possible," he called out. "Eat and rest as much as you can. We have a hard road ahead of us, and we will resume in the morning."

Nearly a third of the men toppled to the ground, most falling instead of simply trying to sit. A chorus of weary groans rose all around.

"We have no food to give them," Robin noted.

"Actually, thanks to Old Soldier we do," Philemon said. "As we prepared for you to enter the castle, he acquired a stash of food. It's about a mile from here. We left it fairly well hidden with a wagon. We can take a horse and go to bring it back."

"I should have known," Robin said wryly, then he quickly added, "I'll go." Though his father stood straight as an arrow, there was an unfortunate pallor to his face.

"I'll go with him, to show him the way," Old Soldier said. Philemon looked as if he wanted to object, and Robin put a hand on his shoulder.

"The men need you here to get them organized," he said firmly. "Set up a rudimentary camp. We'll be back quickly, and we don't need to be mobbed for the food."

His father acquiesced with a nod. "Very well."

"Good." Robin grabbed a horse and mounted while Old Soldier did the same. As they turned and prepared to leave, there was a shout.

"Robin," his father called.

"Yes?"

"Thank you."

Robin smiled. "You're welcome," he said. He turned and headed out after Old Soldier, even as he tried to remember the last time his father had thanked him for anything.

Once clear of the men and the other horses, Old Soldier kicked his mount into a gallop and Robin followed suit. Before an hour was up, they reached the place where Old Soldier had hidden the wagon. It was loaded down with food—enough provisions for at least one meal.

"Where on earth did you find all this?" Robin asked.

Old Soldier shrugged. "Where there's a castle there has to be farmers and crops nearby to help feed the lord and his men. It wasn't difficult to find and the man who worked the land wasn't difficult to persuade."

"We're going to have to find more soon," Robin said.

"It's a pity we couldn't take any of the food from the castle," Old Soldier responded.

"Indeed," Robin agreed, "but we couldn't trust anything they might give us—that they weren't drugged or poisoned. As it is, we were fortunate to… acquire some blankets and clothing. The season is cold."

"We should be able to pick up a couple more wagons of food along the way," the older man said. "We need to be traveling light and fast, though." He slid off his horse and began the work of hitching the animal to the wagon. Robin dismounted and moved to help him.

"Thank you for everything you've done," he said. Old Soldier turned and looked at him with a comically puzzled expression.

"In truth, I should be thanking you," he replied, "for stepping up, leading as you have. There are always battles to fight, but none ever more worthy than this. Every soldier needs a lord who understands what he's up against."

A lord, Robin mused. It was a strange thought.

"We need to move fast," he said, "but the men need rest and good food more than anything. We can't show up in England with them in such rough shape. They'll be slaughtered."

"That's been weighing on my mind, too," Old Soldier answered thoughtfully. "We're no good to the lady Marian if our army is a shambles."

"What do you think we should do?"

The old man shrugged. "I don't know. I'm hoping that you'll think of something."

Robin sighed. "I'll do my best," he answered, "but if you have any ideas, don't keep them to yourself."

"I never do." With his horse hitched to the wagon, Old Soldier climbed into the seat and picked up the reins. "Let's get back. They'll be wanting this food, and the barrel of ale I managed to get hold of," he said, a twinkle in his eye at the last.

Robin laughed. "Even the king will thank you for that."

"He should. A little good cheer will go a long way. The ale will also help them sleep faster and deeper, as well, especially on the rough ground."

Robin chuckled. "Clever."

"I've done this once or twice." Old Soldier grinned and slapped the reins along the horse's back to get him moving.

As they rolled into camp, Robin was surprised to find his father had managed to organize the men, and quickly. A peat fire was built and burning. Half the men were sitting around it, while the other half were curled up on the ground a short distance away, already asleep. They were wrapped in cloaks and horses' blankets.

The horses had been stripped of bridles and saddles and were already hobbled and munching grass a short way away.

"Figured we'd eat in shifts," Philemon said. "This lot were the ones capable of taking care of the horses and the fire."

"Don't be surprised if the others suddenly wake," Robin said, "when they hear what Old Soldier's brought them." He took his mount and settled it in with the others, then did the same for the horse that had pulled the wagon. The men made quick work of unloading the wagon and soon were eating. To Robin's surprise they drank sparingly of the ale.

Some of the sleepers did stir, rose, and joined them. When they had eaten, most of the men turned in. Those who could stayed awake to stand guard. It was understood that in a few hours they would wake the rest so they could eat.

As the sound of snoring rose up around the camp Robin finally sat down by the fire with his own sack of food. He was joined by his father, Old Soldier, Much, and King Richard.

"You all did good work," King Richard said.

"It was just our duty, sire," Old Soldier said.

"No, what you did was far more than that." King Richard clapped Much on the shoulder. "And this one is already legend among the men. Word spread about his bravery while you two were retrieving the food."

Much blushed. "I didn't do anything."

King Richard laughed softly. "You did everything, son. You

showed as much courage as I've ever known. You stood your ground and fought like a young lion. You may be the strongest man in England."

"No," Much said, blushing harder. Robin could tell that the praise pleased him. "That would be Little John. He was the strongest man in England."

"I've heard of him," King Richard said.

"He was killed in the fighting," Old Soldier said.

"I'm sorry to hear that," King Richard said. "But then, I think his passing allows you to claim the title, young man. And I have no doubt that he would be proud."

"Thank you," Much said, and Robin smiled. The miller's son deserved every drop of praise he got and more.

"And since you defeated death itself, your legend will only grow, you mark my words," King Richard said. Then he looked around. "All your legends will grow for what you have accomplished here today." He focused in on Robin. "And for what you have done back home."

Robin lifted a cup of the ale. "I've only done what is necessary."

"That's not what I've been told," King Richard said, glancing at Much. "I hear you've done extraordinary things, stepped up to lead the people, even taken on the mantle of outlaw in order to do it."

"That wasn't exactly my idea," Robin said, laughing, "but I warmed to the idea, then happily took part in it. You can thank several others for concocting the scheme, including Marian."

"Marian." King Richard's face darkened. "I wish I had not left her defenseless in such a nest of vipers. How... is she alright?"

"Last I saw her she was well," Robin said. "She's leading the others back in Sherwood."

"In Sherwood?" the king asked, startled. "She's living there now?"

"All who oppose the Sheriff have been forced to flee to Sherwood for safety," Robin said carefully. He glanced at his father, who nodded slightly.

"Yet you're certain she is well?" Richard asked anxiously.

Robin felt his chest tighten slightly. He nodded.

"She was the last person I saw before we set off to find you."

Philemon cleared his throat.

Robin felt himself flush. "Although, there is something I should tell you concerning her," he said, feeling suddenly awkward.

"What it is?" King Richard asked sharply.

"She and I were married the night before I left."

"Married?"

"Yes, sire."

"You married my niece... without my permission?"

Robin squirmed slightly. "I would not have taken such liberties, sire, but Marian... insisted. It's impossible to deny her, when she sets her mind." He paused, then continued. "We've lost so many friends, and she said that we couldn't be sure we'd ever see each other again in this life." He lowered his head. "I'm sorry."

"Marian insisted that the two of you get married?"

"Yes," Robin said, waiting for the king's wrath to fall upon him.

Suddenly Richard roared with laughter and slapped his leg.

"I knew she liked you!" he burst out.

Robin stared at him in surprise. Richard just turned toward Philemon with a grin.

"How about those two?" he said. "All our efforts at matchmaking, and the two of them took care of things themselves."

"I have to admit to being quite pleased at the outcome," Philemon said with a faint smile.

"I couldn't be happier," Richard said. "I've always wanted her to find the man she wanted, to choose for herself. I just thought she would have told me, before she went ahead and married him."

"I'm sorry—"

Richard cut Robin off. "No need to apologize... nephew."

That took Robin by surprise. He felt strange at the familiarity between him and the king. He opened his mouth to speak and found that he had no words.

"Wipe that look away, lad," Richard said. "Would you prefer I call you *Prince* Robin?"

"Um," Robin said. "No."

"I thought not, you wild scoundrel."

Finally Robin started to grin. Richard turned to Philemon.

"And you, old friend, it seems we're relatives after all."

"Looks as though," Philemon said.

Richard held up his cup. "May you and Marian live a long, happy life together."

The others raised their cups in toast, and then they all drank. Despite the circumstances and the uncertainty of the future, Robin couldn't help but feel a warm glow.

Marian woke with the dawn. She'd spent a long night comforting Chastity and praying for Alan, but had finally managed to get some sleep.

The camp was quiet. Only a few people were up. Jansa was already busy making breakfast, and she bobbed her head to Marian as they passed. Marian had already chewed some of the mint and her stomach, though feeling unsettled, didn't seem like it was going to rebel.

Still she slipped into the forest, breathing in the scents all around her, and tried to let the cold air clear the cobwebs from her mind. Once among the trees, however, she thought they seemed to be anticipating... something. Feeling the need to remain close, she didn't venture as far from camp as she normally would. Instead, she sat down at the base of a tree and tried to organize her thoughts, but they proved elusive.

A bird perched on a branch above her, and for a moment she lost herself in its song.

Deep down Marian knew that Robin was alive, and that gave her a sense of hope. They had to be ready to take the fight to the Sheriff when her husband returned with King Richard. She had to believe that *both* were alive, and coming home with the king's army. They had to have the strength to defeat their enemies.

Henry and his own army posed a threat she could grasp, but she still struggled to figure out how to defeat the Sheriff and his demons. If only the Cardinal still lived, to suggest some religious ritual they could use. Alan might know, and if he survived she would ask him.

Barring that, though, she was going to have to consult the fey. She found the thought disagreeable, however. Worried that it might raise more doubts among the elementals, about her fitness to lead. Nevertheless, it might prove necessary.

She sighed and closed her eyes, almost wishing that she could return to her childhood, when life had been far less complicated. It took her a few moments to realize that the bird above her had stopped singing. She glanced up. The bird was still there but it had gone completely still.

Suddenly she realized that she couldn't hear any of the creatures of the forest. They were all quiet, listening.

That wasn't good.

Marian scrambled to her feet, the hair prickling on her arms. That sense of anticipation she'd felt earlier was swiftly changing. No longer was there something coming. Something was happening right now. She placed her hand against the trunk of the tree and felt a tension, a thrumming *energy* moving through it.

Near her the brush parted unexpectedly and she nearly jumped. The King of the Forest stood there, with his enormous rack of antlers that seemed too large to be held up by his noble neck. He stared at her intently.

"What's wrong?" she found herself asking.

The stag turned to look over his shoulder, as if indicating that he wanted her to follow. She did so hastily. He moved at a steady pace and she followed at his flank. Minutes later he stopped near the base of a large tree. He bowed his head, pointing with his antlers.

There she saw Audric, sitting, blood covering his shirt. She dropped down beside him.

"What happened?" she asked the boy.

"I was going to sneak into town. At the edge of the forest I found soldiers. They were entering the forest. They saw me and shot me with an arrow. I ran and then I fell and I woke up again here. I don't know where the camp is."

"What were you doing sneaking into town?" Marian asked despairingly.

"It... It doesn't matter," Audric said. "They're coming. They'll kill everyone. My brother, Haylan."

"No, you've warned us, and we will be alright."

She pulled aside his blood-soaked shirt. The shaft of the arrow had broken off and it was still lodged in his chest, close to his heart. She sucked in her breath as she realized the wound was mortal. There was nothing she could do for the boy... but there was still much he could do for her.

"Audric," she said, struggling to keep her voice steady. "I need you to tell me about these soldiers, what they were wearing, where they were, how they were armed, how many of them there you saw."

"It was an hour and a half from camp, or more." The boy coughed up blood which dribbled down his chin. "They were well-dressed and they weren't the Sheriff's men."

Henry's army, Marian thought to herself.

Audric began to fade. His eyes were becoming glassy.

"Audric, how many?" she asked, gripping his shoulders.

He looked up at her with eyes that were losing their focus. He was looking at something past her. A small frown tugged at his lips.

"How many?" she asked again.

"Hundreds."

CHAPTER TWENTY-EIGHT

As Audric closed his eyes for the last time, Marian stood up, heart pounding in her chest. She turned to the stag.

"You brought him from there?" The beast nodded its head, intelligent eyes staring intently at her, and she understood all too well the question in them.

What will you do?

There was a sound above. She looked up and saw a large black bird sitting on the tree, watching her just as closely. She whistled and held out her arm. It came down with a flutter of wings and landed on her wrist.

"I need you to gather the fey," she said. "Bring them to me—where the invaders are." The bird chirped once then took wing, soaring quickly away. Marian turned back to the stag.

"Take me there," she said.

The stag inclined his head again. She moved over to place her hand on his back. He knelt and she climbed up, then settled herself. He rose to his feet and was off, hooves flying as he bounded through the woods.

Marian leaned low across his withers and clung to him tightly. His gait was nothing like that of a horse. She both thrilled to it and feared that one of his sharp turns would send her flying. As she rode she tried to think what she would do when she found

Henry's soldiers. The men and women back at camp weren't prepared for a fight—not on that scale. Not right now.

She hoped the fey would heed her summons. Sherwood was known to be haunted. Everyone knew that. Rumors had spread far and wide over the years. Hopefully some of Henry's soldiers had heard those rumors, as well, and their fellows were superstitious men.

This couldn't come to an all-out battle.

Not now. Not here.

The stag leaped a fallen tree and it was all Marian could do to hang on. The wind whipped her hair all around, and she couldn't deny how alive she felt in that moment. She thought of Champion. He'd been sleeping in the tent still when she rose. He'd look for her, but hopefully she'd make it back before he tried to track her this far. The others had become used to her being off by herself for stretches at a time. Even Tuck. She didn't know how long it would take before they started to worry.

Finally the stag slowed. His movements were no less graceful and there was no sense of fatigue. Knowing they must be close to where the soldiers had entered in the forest, she felt the pounding of her heart. The animal came to a stop and she slid off his back, legs shaky as she touched the ground.

Marian braced herself against it for a moment while she got her balance back. The stag pawed at the ground and then pointed toward the right. She moved quietly in that direction. Seconds later there came the sound of men talking. Whoever they were they weren't interested in keeping quiet.

Marian smiled slowly. That could work in her favor.

Robin was dreaming. He knew he was, but at the same time he was loathe to wake up, because he was dreaming about Marian.

She was in the forest, walking, communing with it as he had so many times. Then the stag appeared to her, startling her. A minute later she was on its back, racing through the forest. Away from danger? No! Toward it. There were soldiers—a great many of them, tromping through the trees. They were armed and looking for anyone they could find to kill.

In his dream the raven swooped down, until all he could see were its eyes boring into his own. He woke up with a gasp and sat up.

It wasn't yet nightfall. The second wave of men were just finishing up eating. Robin rose swiftly, then found his father and King Richard talking quietly over by the horses. They looked up at him as he joined them.

"You should have slept more," his father said with a frown.

"And you both should have been asleep already," Robin countered.

"We will, soon," King Richard said. "We've been discussing. The three of us are all that's left of the noblemen who came here. All the others were killed, decapitated," he said with a bitter edge to his voice. "We lost a lot of good men."

"Yes, and we've kept a lot, too." Robin gestured to the soldiers around them.

"True," Richard admitted, nodding.

"There's something else," Robin's father said. "What is it?"

Robin took a breath. "I had a dream, but it was more than that. I think Henry is sending his army into Sherwood. I need to get there faster to help defend her, everyone."

"We can push faster, start marching in another hour or so," King Richard said. "It will be night, but we can continue."

"No, I need to move a lot faster than we can move this army," Robin said. "Also, when the army gets there they need to be ready to fight. They can't be dead on their feet."

"You want to go alone?" Philemon asked. "That's suicide." His features twisted in worry.

"I've done more lunatic things in the last year," Robin said grimly. "I'm afraid if I don't go now, that it will be too late when the rest of you do arrive."

King Richard nodded his head. "I've learned to put a lot

more stock than I once did in dreams and visions. Go with our blessings. If you want, take someone with you."

"No, I'll travel faster alone. I will take a horse, though."

"Take some food, as well, so you can limit your stops," his father suggested.

"Thank you," Robin said. "Thank you, both." He turned aside and quickly chose his horse. The gray was built for speed and had incredible endurance. He bridled the animal and then turned just as his father put the saddle on the creature's back. When he was finished cinching it down Philemon turned, his face working with emotion.

"God speed, son," he said roughly, before pulling Robin into an embrace. He hugged his father back then pulled away.

"I have to go," he said.

"I know. We'll come after as fast as we can," his father said. "Be careful, use the Roman roads as much as you can without being noticed. I'll see you in England."

"In England," Robin echoed as he swung up on the back of the horse. He gave his father a parting nod then kicked his heels into the animal's side and sent him galloping down the road. In moments the camp was lost to sight behind him, but he focused on the path ahead.

Hold on, Marian, I'm coming.

Marian peered through the trees, and she saw the rows of soldiers trying to walk into the forest. They were forced to break up their orderly rows, though, because of the terrain. There was a lot of grumbling because of it. The majority were on foot, although there were at least a dozen horses that she saw.

"I'm telling you, I shot an outlaw," one man was saying to those nearby.

Another snorted derisively. "You shot a deer, and it got away from you anyway."

Her blood boiled as she realized she was looking at Audric's killer. Balling her hands into fists she forced herself to stand stock still, letting her eyes drift over some of the other soldiers trooping along. Some were attentive, some were slogging along mindlessly. She smiled wickedly as she noticed that quite a few looked nervous.

Slipping silently back into the forest, she began to form a plan. It would require help for her to execute it. The stag was waiting where she had left him, and she retreated another hundred feet farther back from where the soldiers were. He followed her, watching with his large eyes, studying her, sizing her up.

"We will drive them off, but we need help," she told him softly.

"Then it's a good thing I'm here."

Suppressing a cry, Marian spun around and saw that it was the fey girl from the river challenge. She heaved a deep breath upon seeing the girl.

"Thank you for coming."

"You called." The girl shrugged. "Where else would I be?" Before Marian could answer the girl continued. "Oh, and I brought someone who was looking for you." She stepped to the side and Champion bounded forward.

Marian was glad to see the fox, but she worried. She didn't want to risk him getting hurt.

"Nothing could have stopped him from coming," the girl said. "I just made sure he got here in time."

"Thank you," Marian said as she picked up the creature and buried her face in his fur. After a few moments she put him back down.

"So, what is your plan?" the girl asked.

Marian hesitated. "We should wait for more to arrive, so I can explain it all at once."

"No others are coming... yet," the girl said.

"What? What do you mean?" Marian asked, her heart sinking. What they needed to do could not be accomplished by just the four of them.

"You are to tell me," the girl explained. "I will tell them. If they agree it is a good plan then they will help."

"We can't do this by ourselves."

"And we won't. I understand you. I trust that your plan is good."

"Okay." Marian nodded slowly, realizing it was the best she was going to get. "These soldiers aren't from here, but many of them have heard the legends of Sherwood."

"Which ones?" the girl asked curiously.

"That it's haunted."

"Is that what they say?"

"Yes," Marian answered, and she began to be irritated. She calmed herself. The girl was a fey of Sherwood. She didn't consort with humans, generally speaking, so as strange as it seemed, she wouldn't necessarily know what the humans outside the forest said about it.

"Many humans are afraid of the forest," she said. "They believe that ghosts live here."

"We live here," the girl said.

"Yes, and some believe in the fey and some don't, but they all believe in ghosts. And they're terrified of them."

The girl got a wicked grin on her face. "We can play ghosts."

"That's exactly what I was thinking," Marian said, "and I think you'd be *especially* good at scaring them." She added her own smile.

"Of course I will be." The girl's grin grew even more. "I will go and tell the others." She turned away with a skip in her step. Seconds later she had disappeared into the forest. Marian stood there, waiting, hoping, though she wasn't sure what she should be expecting.

A minute passed, then another. She had no idea how far away the other fey were gathering. She felt frustration building inside of her. She should have stressed the importance of time and wasn't certain the fey even knew the concept. They needed to do this now, though, before the soldiers made it much farther into the woods.

Maybe I'm going to have to do this by myself.

She turned and found the stag blocking her path. He shook

his antlered head, as though to tell her to turn back.

"Someone has to," she told him. "If I have to do it alone, I will give it all I have."

"Fortunately, you don't have to do it all alone." A voice that was now familiar piped up behind her. Marian spun in surprise.

"Do you always like to sneak up on people?"

"It's not my fault people turn away just as I'm approaching."

Marian very much doubted that was the case, but she held her tongue.

"They have decided that your plan is a good one."

"Wonderful," Marian said. "When can they start?"

"Oh, they've already started," she said. The girl cocked her head to the side.

"Oh!" Marian said. She'd thought there would be more planning.

"I brought this for you, so you can watch if you want, and yet still just be a ghost to them." The girl handed Marian a light gray bundle. She took it and shook it out. The bundle turned out to be a cloak, though it was tattered and had material that fluttered all about it in varying shades of gray. It looked like death to her, though she couldn't have said just how.

Then she smiled as she realized how she would look when wearing it.

"Thank you," she said as she slung it around her shoulders. The material draped behind her, giving her a flowing look. The hood was oversized so that her face would be lost within its darker folds.

"There, you're a ghost now, too," the girl said somewhat too gleefully. "Don't you feel better?"

"This should fool them beautifully," Marian said. She didn't bother to tell her that she didn't actually want to *be* a ghost.

"You just need one more thing," the girl said.

"What's that?" Marian asked.

The girl leaned down and stroked her hand across Champion's back. Beneath her touch his fur turned a silvery gray that was almost translucent. Marian stared in shock as the girl lifted her hand, but the effect continued to ripple through Champion's coat.

"Don't worry, it will only last a night and a day, and then he'll be his normal color again," the girl said. "Until then only ghosts should be seen walking with one another."

Marian glanced down again at Champion and then looked at the cloak she was wearing. She pulled it closer around herself and lifted the hood.

"You are so right," she said.

"Excellent, now come with me," the girl said with impish glee. "It's time we show these men just how haunted Sherwood is."

CHAPTER TWENTY-NINE

Marian paused behind a tree with the girl fey. Champion stood with his nose pressed against Marian's leg, staying as close to her as possible.

"They're good and scared already," the girl whispered to her. "They've been hearing noises, seeing things move that aren't there when they look at them straight on. It's only going to take one or two good scares to send them running," she said confidently.

The talking had died down. They still could hear the sounds of the army moving, but it was just the noise of feet and hooves on leaves and twigs, the shuffling of a great many bodies through the trees and brush and snow.

Marian cautiously peered through the underbrush. The men in front looked nervously around, eyes wide as if expecting anything. Every one of them had a hand on a weapon, scared but prepared to strike out at whatever came into their sight. It wasn't the right time or place for her to make a sudden appearance.

She gritted her teeth in frustration. The girl drew her back a couple of steps and whispered.

"How brave are you?"

Marian stared. "As brave as I need to be."

The girl nodded. "Then watch, and choose your moment."

Marian nodded back, and returned to her observation spot. A

break appeared in the ranks—a decided gap between the front half of the men and the back half. It looked to be at least thirty feet.

Glancing across from where she was, she saw a very large tree. Behind it there was a lot of thick brush. It would be easy to get lost in there if she had to.

She looked again at the second group of men. They seemed tired and a bit nervous, but not nearly to the extent that the first group had been. Likely the fey had been harrying them less. Their swords were still sheathed, their bows still slung on their backs.

Marian made up her mind.

She waited until the last men in the first group had passed. Then she stepped out behind them, moving directly across the path of the second group. She walked as smoothly as she could, attempting to glide. The fabric billowed around her, trailing wisps of it and swaying as she moved. Champion walked at her side, looking like a ghost himself.

She stared straight ahead but heard gasps going up. She would have to move fast before the group in front realized what was happening and turned. When the moment was right she twisted her head toward the approaching men.

I should say something, she realized.

Then, suddenly, from all around her a hundred voices whispered.

"You should not be here."

"Ghost!" one of the men shrieked at the top of his lungs before turning and plunging into the soldiers behind him, knocking several of them over. Marian and Champion made it to the safety of the large tree and hid behind it to watch.

Suddenly it was pandemonium as men began to scream and run. The group in front turned and arrows went flying through the air, only to find homes in the chests and backs of the soldiers in the second wave. A sudden keening sound went up from the forest all around, a hundred voices rising in unison.

The men in the front group broke, most of them running back the way they'd come, a few running deeper into the forest. One of the fey that Marian did not recognize, a large creature with nearly albino skin, ran in front of those, causing them to turn back.

Soldiers collided with one another and went down in piles on the ground, shouting and trying to pummel each other in their attempts to escape. The smell of blood filled the air as those who had been shot with arrows collapsed on the ground, and others began bleeding from broken noses and bloody mouths. It was absolute chaos.

The few who were riding horses urged their frightened animals away from the confusion. The mounts, succumbing to blind panic, trampled several of the soldiers who had already fallen and knocked still others down.

Those men who could run followed their leaders back the way they'd come. Those who couldn't dragged themselves along the ground in an effort to escape the horrors that had descended upon them. They lashed out at anything that got close, their terror rendering them unable to distinguish between friend and foe.

Within moments all that was left were the dead and those who had been too badly injured to get away. Suddenly, from out of the forest, fey of all types descended with high-pitched shouts that literally hurt her ears, so intense were they. She was paralyzed as they ripped apart the men who were still alive, until not one was left.

Then silence descended upon the forest, eerie and final, like the grave.

Marian just gaped at the aftermath. There were at least sixty men dead, maybe more. The carnage was awesome. Anyone who happened upon it would never be able to tell exactly what had happened there.

Not that any of the soldiers who had fled would ever be stepping foot in the forest again. She was quite certain of that. A fierce sort of joy burned in her for a moment. Sherwood was England, wild, untamed, strong. It would survive and crush her enemies beneath its heel.

And so will I, Marian vowed, as her thoughts turned to the

Sheriff and her cousin, Henry. They were the ones who had declared war, not her. Yet she was the one who was going to finish it.

The girl fey appeared at her side.

"You did well."

"Thank you," Marian said.

"The bloodshed, it does not bother you?" the girl asked sharply, her eyes probing. Marian shook her head slowly.

"The moment they stepped foot in Sherwood, violating the sanctity of this place, their lives were forfeit."

"Good," the girl smiled. "You are becoming one of us."

"One of us."

The words echoed in her mind, and slowly Marian smiled back.

Glynna woke with a cry of anguish. It was before dawn, and she shivered in her bed. Normally that time, when all was darkest, was her favorite. This morning, though, the blackness around her just served as a backdrop for silvery images that seemed to explode all around, her dreams made manifest in horrific fashion.

Ships were sailing, barreling down toward her on the tides of darkness. In her dreams those tides had been blood, not water, but the silver images that traced in the air around her showed no color. At the bow of the first ship stood a great lion, his mane billowing in the breeze, his teeth bared in anger and his paw raised as though ready to strike. Next to him was a tiger whose eyes burned into her soul. In her dream those eyes had been the eyes of Philemon, Lord of Longstride. There were others with them, so many others.

Most took the form of starving wolves.

The boats circled around her, an invisible tide drawing them closer and closer. They would reach her before she knew it. She screamed and shut her eyes to try and block out the visions, but they etched themselves into her eyelids so the silvery lines kept swirling.

"It can't be true!" she wailed, fear making her entire body shake.

King Richard and her husband were coming home.

She slithered from the bed, keeping her eyes tightly closed. She pulled a cloak about her, not daring to try and call the shadows around her. All she wanted was to find her love and warn him of what she'd seen.

Once she had left their room she opened her eyes a slit. She was relieved to see only the torchlit hallway, the flames dancing on stone. She began to walk, gaining confidence, leaving behind the dreams that had disturbed her. She should have known better than to worry. Her love could handle whatever and whomever came their way.

Suddenly she caught motion out of the corner of her eye. She turned her head to the left. The fire from the torch nearest her seemed to leap from its place and dash itself against the walls. It exploded against the stone in a shower of sparks, but then suddenly fire seemed to trace its way along the stones, running in rivulets.

She stopped walking and stared in fascination, wondering what it was that she was witnessing. The fire continued to run and spread. It swirled and then began to take on form. Her stomach clenched as she suddenly made out the image of a ship, inscribed in fire on the stone. It seemed to approach, growing larger and larger until she could see every part of it clear. There at the bow was the lion, the tiger beside him. Behind them the pack of wolves gathered.

More ships began to form behind the first.

The lion opened his jaws in a silent, fiery roar and the tiger bared its teeth. She screamed and turned away. There, ahead of her, though, the flames from all the torches leaped to the walls as well, and began forming the same scene, over and over.

Glynna ran down the hall, trying not to look, her heart pounding within her. What kind of magic was this that kept showing her the same image, even while she was awake? She needed to be away from it. Fear roiled through her. It was an emotion that she thought she had forgotten, from the moment she'd laid eyes on her lover.

She was sure he could drive it from her now.

Dropping her eyes to the ground, she refused to look at the walls. Suddenly fire raced down and traced lines in the stone beneath her, making it look as though it were waves on the sea. Her foot landed on one of the waves and she screamed as her flesh sizzled at the contact.

Running faster, leaping and twisting and trying to avoid the flames that reached out for her, she made it at last into the great hall and came to a stop. Even through her fear the thought came to her that it would be wrong for anyone to observe her in such a state of terror. She was the Sheriff's woman.

She must appear in control. Nothing could defeat him.

That had been her belief when she went to bed the night before. She would believe it again. Until then she could not let anyone else doubt it, particularly that fool Henry. Her footsteps bent toward the throne room. Her love often went there to think and plan. As she neared the doorway, she heard angry voices and realized he was not alone.

Glynna composed herself, threw her shoulders back, and fixed a smile on her face. Then she walked inside. Her love was there, along with Henry and a couple of other men, both of them soldiers. She walked closer, putting sway into her motion. She found that it seemed to have a hypnotic effect on men.

"Ghosts?" Henry said. "*Ghosts* killed nearly a hundred of my men?"

"Yes," the soldier said.

"You fool," the noble replied. "No doubt it was a bunch of peasants running around shouting 'boo.' Your men are *cowards*."

"With all due respect, sire, it wasn't," the man said. "I saw one of them... it wasn't human." He spoke in strong, confident tones, and didn't seem the sort who would be given to exaggeration or hysteria. Whatever had occurred, he was convinced of what he'd seen.

The fey, she realized.

The fey had taken to defending the forest. She could tell

by the look on her lover's face that he had come to the same conclusion—and it didn't make him happy.

"And what about you?" Henry demanded, turning to the other soldier.

"We found a series of caves," the man reported. "There was gold there, some of the shipment that was taken. There was also evidence that someone is living in there. We found food and water."

"But no people?" Henry spit out.

"No, but it's possible they were there and we just couldn't find them. The caves are extensive, and without knowing them it would be too easy to become lost."

Henry looked like he was about to explode. A blood vessel throbbed redly in his forehead, making him look quite ridiculous.

Her love, on the other hand, was just as furious, but he kept his demeanor calm, controlled.

That's why he's in charge.

She glided to a stop a couple of feet away from him. He turned his head slightly in her direction and nodded.

"You need to go back in those caves," Henry said, almost shouting. "And into that forest, to find whoever is in there!"

"Actually, you need to do the opposite," Glynna said.

Everyone turned to look at her.

"Instead of chasing them into their holes, you need to lure them out. If you can't find them in the caves, and you can't get to them in the forest, then you need to find a way to make them come to us."

"I'll burn the forest down to the ground," Henry snarled. "That should settle this once and for all."

The Sheriff turned and gave him a condescending look.

"With the snow on the ground and on the trees, how easy do you think that will be to accomplish? We also know that there is magic protecting the forest, and we can't use magic of our own on it."

Glynna smiled at Henry and batted her eyelashes. The man was an idiot, but he would come to see the wisdom of her plan.

And if he didn't, they could kill him like they'd killed John.

The Sheriff turned back to her. "What exactly did you have in mind, my love?" he asked, his voice a soft purr.

"A grand spectacle, an archery tournament, a feast, and to top it all off, an execution."

"Who will we execute?" Henry interrupted.

Glynna stared at him. "I'm sure we can think of someone," she said frostily.

The Sheriff clucked at her. "You think they might come out to save those who are to be executed?"

"Yes."

"They'll surely know it's a trap," Henry scoffed, "and not risk their necks."

Glynna didn't even bother looking at him this time. Instead she looked at her love and smiled, just for him.

"Of course they will, but theirs will be some of the necks on the block. We'll catch the Hood once and for all—at the archery tournament."

"What makes you think he'll risk it?" Henry sputtered. "I mean, you think the man's ego is so large that it would outweigh his sense of self-preservation?"

"No. I think he'll enter because we have something he wants," she said. "Something he needs."

"And what exactly would that be?"

Glynna turned and looked at the wall. Hanging on it was a hunk of rotting flesh that had once been part of the chest of Guy of Gisbourne. And, sticking out of it, unable to be released by any force or magic that they had employed, was something she knew the Hood would want very much.

She turned back to her love and he smiled at her.

"The black arrow, of course."

Henry glanced at it, a look of disgust forming on his face.

"And when he comes for the arrow, we'll be ready for him," her love purred.

We both will, she vowed silently. The vestiges of the nightmare still clung to her, but an idea was beginning to take hold. Her love's soldiers were monstrous, terrible in battle, and they had only one weakness in that they were vulnerable during the day and resurrected only at night. In her mind she was conceiving a spell so great, so terrible, that it would solve that problem once and for all.

And how much more would her dark lord love her then?

CHAPTER THIRTY

Audric's ceremony was brief but moving. His younger brother Haylan was devastated, and his grief was made worse by the uncertainty of Alan's fate. The boy had grown very attached to the bard and had been learning much from him. Now Alan was the last person he had left in the world.

Marian had grown weary of funerals and wanted them to stop. She glanced over at Jansa and her new husband. At least there were a few bright spots. It seemed as if Friar Tuck was starting to perform as many weddings as funerals.

She had returned to camp with the body of the boy after the fey had confirmed that all the soldiers had fled Sherwood. It was only a matter of time before they'd be back, though, and she wondered if men had also been sent to the caves where they had hidden some of the gold from the latest robbery. If so, she hoped that they became lost in the tunnels, unable to find their way back out.

Closing her eyes, she felt herself becoming colder, more indifferent to the deaths of others. Many of those men were just following orders, unaware that Henry had thrown in his lot with the devil. They needed to find a way to bring some of those men over, let them see the truth of what type of war was being waged. But how?

She'd have to talk with Friar Tuck about it later that afternoon. She wished Alan was not ill, for she could use his counsel, as well. Most of all she wished her husband was there.

Robin, I need you.

Her hand drifted to her stomach. Marian was convinced now that Jansa was right. She could feel it herself. There was life growing within her. She smiled as she thought of how Robin would react when she told him he was going to be a father.

Looking down, she saw that Champion was still the silver gray color the fey girl had turned him. He looked up at her and leaned against her leg, and she found the contact comforting.

When the funeral was over Marian retired to her tent, exhausted and needing to rest a little. Chastity joined her there.

"Is there anything I can do for you... Marian?" her friend asked, still hesitating a bit on saying her name.

"Not unless you can think of a way we can convince Henry's soldiers that they're fighting on the wrong side and make them understand that this is a battle between good and evil."

Chastity frowned. "I will give it some thought."

"I would appreciate it, because nothing is coming to my mind."

"That's because you've got too much weighing upon you."

"No more than usual."

"That's not true, not with a baby coming and all."

Marian stared at her. "How did you know?"

Chastity grinned. "I'm pretty sure the whole camp knows. Everyone's just waiting for you to confirm it."

"Did Jansa or Esther say something about my morning sickness?"

Chastity laughed. "No, but that would confirm it."

"Then how does everyone know?"

"Because you're glowing, Marian. It has nothing to do with the torc you're wearing, either. You're glowing like women glow when they're with child. And, it's not like you're a maid anymore," Chastity said with a wink.

"No, that's true." Marian blushed fiercely.

Chastity touched her arm. "You worry about getting some rest and taking care of yourself. Let me figure out how to turn Henry's men to our side."

"Very well," Marian agreed.

Chastity left and Marian marveled at how happy she seemed that Marian was going to have a child. She thought about what her friend had said, about the entire camp waiting for her to confirm it. Maybe everyone was so eager for another bit of good news to hold onto. Perhaps she *should* tell them.

Not today, though, she decided. Today they would remember and honor Audric.

Tomorrow will be time enough.

Chastity had an idea, but it would require leaving Sherwood to do a little reconnaissance. If she was right, though, it would be worth the risk. She left Marian, briefly told Friar Tuck where she was going in case Marian asked for her in her absence, and then donned a cloak and left the safety of the camp.

She traveled swiftly through the forest, eager to get to her first destination. A lot of men made up Henry's army, and they would need to be housed and fed. There wasn't room at the castle for all of them, so it was possible they were set up in an encampment outside the walls. However, if Henry was intent on staying, it was equally possible that some of the neighboring homes were being used. They weren't at Locksley castle, but they might be at the homes of other nobles.

The nobles who had signed fealty to John still seemed to be in thrall, perhaps to the Sheriff. For whatever reason, they put up no resistance, and this made their homes the most likely places to find the soldiers. They would be being fed and tended to by frightened wives, children, and servants. People who knew what was happening in Nottingham.

They were the ones who could spread word to the soldiers.

A cousin of hers worked for Lord Montjoy as a cook. At least, she had last Chastity knew. She'd have to find out if that was still the case. Sarah had always been a smart woman. If she was there and alive, Chastity was sure she could make her see reason.

It was early morning when Marian awoke abruptly from a nightmare. Fortunately it slipped back into the mists from whence it had come, and quickly so she didn't have to relive it. She was pretty sure it had something to do with Robin, but that was all she could remember.

She rose quietly, knowing she'd get no more rest, and walked through the camp. Only the few sentries were awake, and they nodded as she passed. Leaving the perimeter she moved into the forest, and a moment later Champion joined her.

Things were different, and she felt unsettled—more than she usually did these days. It was as if the consequences for their rout of the soldiers were about to come crashing down on them. She tried to tell herself she was just being morose, affected by the nightmare and the funeral for Audric. Something deep inside, though, told her that wasn't the case.

Change is coming.

The words seemed to whisper in her mind, rattling around and around. Marian knew that change could be a cataclysmic thing, but it wasn't always bad. She struggled to get a sense of *what* was coming, but aside from her own dark thoughts there was nothing else. If change was coming, perhaps it was up to them to take advantage of it and make sure it worked out to their favor.

She found her favorite log, from which she often contemplated the forest around her. This morning, though, she was interested only in contemplating what she was feeling inside. Champion jumped up to sit beside her. Usually this early in the morning he was off hunting breakfast. Now, though, he curled up tightly next to her as though offering his support, his comfort.

Dropping a hand down, she ran it through his fur, once again its natural red color. She bowed her head and began to pray, asking God to show her the path, the way to victory. They needed to defeat the Sheriff and his minions. They needed to preserve England and stop the spread of evil.

She prayed, begging God for a sign. Promising to do whatever it took. She just needed to know what to do next. As she prayed she began to weep, missing the friendship and the counsel of the cardinal. At that moment she was reminded how lost she had felt the last few weeks.

"I just need a sign," she whispered out loud, the words wrenched from her. "Show me what I must do to defeat the Sheriff."

She didn't know how long she sat there and prayed. When she was finished, though, she felt as if a kind of peace had descended on her. Change *was* coming, and God would help her seize the opportunities coming her way.

It had to be well past breakfast given how hungry she felt, so she stood and headed back to camp. Champion trotted beside her, still showing no interest in catching his own meal. Maybe he sensed the same thing she did and wanted to keep close.

When she stepped foot into the clearing she knew that something had happened. There was an electricity in the air. People talked excitedly with one another. Eager to discern the cause, she found Chastity and Friar Tuck. They were speaking together next to Alan's bed. The bard was awake and clear-eyed, which brought Marian no end of relief.

"I'm glad to see you awake," she said to him.

He nodded and gave her a faint smile.

She turned to Chastity, who looked like she was about to burst.

"What's going on?"

"Yesterday you asked me to find a way to let Henry's army know the truth of what's happening here. Well, I figured that some of them would be billeted in other homes, because of the numbers. I went to see if I was right—and I was. There are fifty of them staying on Montjoy land. My cousin is a cook there. She agreed to help spread the word. I was planning on going to see if I could recruit some other people at other homes. A message came this morning, though, and I thought I should bring it right away." Chastity handed over a parchment.

Marian quickly read it, and her heart skipped a beat.

"It came this morning?"

"Yes, milady," Chastity said, slipping in her excitement.

"Have you read this?" she asked Friar Tuck.

He nodded.

Marian took a deep breath and looked it over again. The Sheriff and Henry were declaring a festival, complete with a feast, an archery competition, and a public execution. The winner of the competition would win a magic black arrow—one that had been used to kill a monster.

"This is it," Marian said, tears stinging her eyes. She had asked God for a sign and He had provided. This was the opportunity they could seize. Her heart began to pound as she looked at the parchment again. The festival was happening in five days.

Change is coming. And with the black arrow, they could make sure that the change benefited them.

"We have to go," Marian said. "We need to get that arrow."

"You know the truth of this?" Friar Tuck asked stubbornly. "It is only being done to flush us out."

"I know, but we can't pass up the opportunity."

"We don't have an archer with enough skill to win."

"I can win," she said, folding her arms across her chest.

"Yes, she can," Chastity said indignantly. "Marian's as good as any man with a bow."

"We can't risk you," Tuck protested.

"There's no one else to go, and it is worth the risk," Marian insisted.

Friar Tuck rolled his eyes. "Look, Alan, you agree with me, don't you? That risking her life is too much?"

They all turned to look at the bard. He shook his head slowly.

"How can you *not* agree with me?" Friar Tuck asked angrily.

Alan didn't even bother trying to get out his pen and parchment. He just glared, and Marian spoke up.

"It is because we are coming to the end," she said firmly. "If we allow the Sheriff to continue any longer, to amass anymore power, then all is lost," Marian added. "And, if it's true that he has the arrow, we need to get it back. It's the only thing that we know can kill him."

"Robin couldn't retrieve it from the body of that monster," Tuck said. "How do you think they managed it?"

"I don't know, but the body of the monster has been in their possession for weeks," Marian said stubbornly. "Who knows what they could have done in that time. Maybe they just cut it out of him." In her heart she knew she was right.

"What if you don't win?" Friar Tuck asked.

Marian smiled. "Then we steal the arrow."

"It might be a ruse. They might not even have the arrow there."

That was true, she had to concede. She couldn't explain it, though, but she felt the hand of God at work. She was sure that their enemies had the arrow, and she was sure that it would be on display.

"Even if it's not, you know we have to be there to stop the hanging," she said quietly.

"We don't even know who they're hanging. It might be that *we're* the ones they intend to execute, and by showing up we're giving them everything they want." Friar Tuck was running out of arguments, however. He heaved a sigh.

Marian reached out and put a hand on his arm.

"Old friend, I know this seems like an incredible risk, foolish to even attempt. I can't explain what I'm feeling. I just know that this is our chance to end it. I don't know how it will all play out. We haven't the numbers to fight them." She peered at him. Both of their faces were awash with emotion. "This is it, and if we let this moment pass all will be lost."

"Then God save us all," Friar Tuck said slowly.

"God protect us all." Chastity nodded. "Right, you get ready for the festival. I'll go see how many others might have the ears of the soldiers. The more we try to turn, the better our chances."

"I'll get the men ready, make sure we have all the weapons we can carry," Friar Tuck said. "And I'll try to find disguises for us."

"Us?" Marian asked.

"You don't think you're going in there alone, do you?" Tuck asked. "No, if this is it, then all of us go."

"All of us go," she echoed in a whisper. Marian nodded slowly, turned, and surveyed the camp. "God be with us."

CHAPTER THIRTY-ONE

Chastity didn't know how far she'd walked in the last two days but she was convinced it had been more than she'd ever walked in her life. She'd visited five manors where Henry's soldiers were staying and had been fortunate enough to find a sympathetic ear in each place.

She had one last place to visit before returning to Sherwood—a place she thought would have been torn down after Will confessed to being the Hood. His father, though, had been the first to pledge fealty to John, so they had spared the manor.

Her chest constricted as she approached. She loved him still and every night prayed that God would let her join him one day in heaven. Tears burned in her eyes, and she dashed them away.

She had met the cook once, a frightful old hag of a woman, and didn't fancy trading words with her. There had to be a servant who would help, though—someone who would want to avenge Will Scarlett.

Nevertheless, she approached the manor cautiously. Will's family were still nobility, if somewhat lesser than the Longstrides to whom they were kin. In the garden by the kitchen door she spotted a young servant girl, probably only a year younger than Chastity herself, and pretty enough to turn any soldier's head. Most likely the girl could convince a lot of men of anything she chose.

Chastity hailed her and the girl straightened, a look of trepidation on her face.

"Who are you?" she asked when Chastity drew near.

Chastity took a deep breath. "I was friend to Will Scarlett."

The girl paled. "Then you're not welcome here," she said. "You should go."

"Is this not his home?"

"It was, until he got himself mixed up and killed."

Chastity stepped closer and dropped her voice. "He fought to free all of us from the evil that has seized the land since King Richard set sail. There are those of us willing to carry on. I'm looking for someone—"

"You'll find no one here willing to fight, or risk their life."

Chastity forced herself not to hit the other girl, but loathed her cowardice. "I'm not asking for fighters. I'm asking that the good soldiers who have come here be told the truth of what they're being asked to do," she said, keeping her voice low. "So they know they are fighting against God, are given a chance to reconsider."

If possible, the girl turned even more pale. "I won't be talking to any of those men."

"Are you afraid of them?" Chastity asked. "Has any of them harmed you, or anyone else here?"

"Not yet, thank God," the girl replied, "but I'll not give them any cause to."

Chastity nodded but continued to try. "I'm just asking you to plant a seed," she said. "To speak truth."

"Truth puts you at the end of a hangman's noose."

Before anything more could be said, the cook came storming out of the kitchen.

"We've all had enough trouble rained down on our heads because that whelp chose to mix with the wrong sorts and got himself killed," she said loudly. "If you know what's good for you, you'll leave right now before I send for the Sheriff."

Rage tore through Chastity. With every bone in her body she wanted to strike both the women who stood in front of her.

"Will was a hero and you owe him *everything*," she whispered fiercely before forcing herself to turn away. It would gain her nothing to get into a fight right now. All it would do was draw unwanted attention.

As she walked away she took a deep breath, reminding herself that they were afraid. She had seen it in their eyes. Even if they *had* cared there was no way they'd act, for fear of retribution. She shouldn't blame them—yet she did. Will had died for the likes of them, and they didn't deserve his sacrifice.

She made it to the road and paused for a moment. There was nowhere left to go. At least, nowhere safe. It was time to return to Sherwood, even if her failure here galled her bitterly. She just prayed that the men on this land wouldn't be the difference between winning and losing.

There was a light step behind her and she spun, fearing that she hadn't left fast enough. An older woman stood there, her face lined with grief. Chastity had never seen her at the castle before, but her features were familiar nonetheless. The woman stared at her through haunted eyes.

"Are you... is your name Chastity?" she asked.

"Yes," Chastity answered cautiously.

"I received a letter just a couple of days before... it was from my boy," she said, and tears began to sparkle in her eyes. "It said that things were becoming worse, dangerous. He told me that if something should happen to him, that I should welcome a girl named Chastity into my home. I waited, but you did not come and I was beginning to fear..." She stopped, her lips trembling for a moment and then continued. "I am Will's mother, Mary. Are you the Chastity that he loved?"

"Yes," Chastity whispered.

Will's mother threw her arms around her and held her close as they both sobbed. Anguish tore through her anew, but also a sense of what could only be called joy. He had truly loved her. Any doubt she'd had fled in an instant.

After a while Mary pulled away and with her hands she wiped

the tears from Chastity's cheeks, then her own.

"You are as lovely as he said you were," she told her with a smile. "When this madness is over I will welcome you into my home as the widow of my son."

"My lady, we were not married."

"No, but if he lived you would have been."

Fresh tears rolled down Chastity's cheeks. "I'm not a noble born."

"But you are noble wed," Mary insisted. "And that makes you a noble. None will ever know from me that it's not true," she added with a hint of a smile. "For now, though, I fear it is not safe for you here."

"Thank you," Chastity said, marveling in the love she felt. "Your son was an amazing man."

Mary bit her lip and glanced over her shoulder. "I want nothing more than to sit all day with you and tell stories of him, and learn everything about you. We don't have that much time, though. What is it you need from me?"

Chastity took a deep breath. Asking a servant to help was one thing, asking Will's mother was quite another.

"I came seeking help. We believe that many of the soldiers under Henry's command might be God-fearing men who would think twice if they knew the hellspawn nature of the Sheriff, and that they were fighting against God."

Mary nodded. "You need someone who can open their eyes to the truth."

"Yes. I tried talking to the cook and a servant girl, but—"

Mary held up a hand. "Leave it to me. I will make them see the truth. I have lost everything to the evil that has taken our land. If I cannot sway them, then no one can."

"I don't want you to risk yourself."

"My son risked everything for this land and its people." Mary shook her head. "If I honor him, how can I do any less?"

Chastity hugged her again and Mary pressed a cheek to hers. "We will see each other again," Mary assured her. "Now that

I've found my daughter, I will not lightly let go."

"Thank you... Mother," Chastity said, the endearment coming out of her more easily than she could have dreamed. Mary pulled away and kissed her forehead.

"Now go, quickly."

"We need the men turned in three days' time."

"It will be done," Mary said, resolve etched on her face.

Chastity nodded, words failing her. Mary turned and headed back to the manor. Chastity stood a moment, then turned and headed swiftly toward the safety of Sherwood. Over and over as she headed down the road she replayed all Mary's words to her. They filled her with a warm glow. Her own mother had died when she was young and it would be nice to have someone to care for her in that way that she could care for back.

Tears stung her eyes as she kept walking, so preoccupied that when a shadow darted across the path in front of her it took her a moment to realize what she had just seen. She stumbled to a halt and her heart began to pound. Sweat began to pour off of her and her stomach twisted in knots. She yanked the dagger out of her bodice and stood, the bare blade in her hand. Her breath came in short, frightened gasps. She twisted her head from side to side, trying to see where it had gone.

It was one of the Sheriff's pets. That it had to be was proved by the sickness that threatened to overwhelm her.

"God protect and defend me," the words bubbled out of her.

She took a step forward, waiting for the thing to lunge at her from someplace. The forest was close. Those things could hide in the bushes and shrubs that lined the road, but they couldn't enter the forest proper.

I can't die. Not after everything that's happened. Not like this, she thought.

She took another step, trying to measure the distance to Sherwood. It was too far. Even if she ran her fastest the creature would be on her before she'd made half the distance. She tried to swallow down the terror. Sweat rolled into her eyes, stinging them and momentarily blinding her. She blinked it away, took another step, then shrieked as something black and monstrous hurled itself at her from the brush at the side of the road.

Swinging her knife, she stabbed only fur even as pain exploded in her calf and she fell, the bottom of her dress shredded and blood seeping from deep scratch marks on her leg. The thing disappeared again.

Chastity forced herself up onto her feet. Before she could move the creature seemed to flow out onto the path ahead of her, its movements fluid, then it turned solid as it formed itself into something covered in fur and bristling with teeth. It stood between her and the forest, and opened its mouth in a silent snarl.

A sudden, piercing howl rose up from nearby and four streaks of gray flashed out of the forest, heading straight for them. Chastity gaped in shock as four wolves, lean from hunger, fell upon the Sheriff's monstrous pet. It snapped in surprise as it turned to face its attackers.

Chastity seized the opportunity and ran toward the trees. She could hear growls and hissing sounds behind her as the wolves battled the monster. Her leg throbbed and blood rolled down it, but she kept running. As soon as she made it to safety she stopped and leaned against a trunk to catch her breath.

Then she turned and looked back. One wolf was down. The other three looked to be tearing the Sheriff's hideous creature from limb to limb. A feeling of fierce joy surged through her as she watched them destroy it. Turning again, she began to make her way back to camp. She had to tell Marian everything that had happened.

They had more allies than they had thought.

CHAPTER THIRTY-TWO

Marian closed the ancient book, sighed, and leaned her head back against the hollow tree. She had prayed that something in its pages would help her in the coming battle, but there was nothing. All she had found were warnings, specifically about the dark power that could be wielded by a demon-human offspring.

Glynna's child. Marian knew in her heart that the prophecies were about that creature. The more she read, the more she understood that no matter what happened to her, or any of the rest of them, the demon child had to be destroyed before he brought about the end of the world.

Tears of frustration slid down her cheeks. She wished that Robin was there. She needed his strength at that moment, more than she could say. She had asked God a hundred times why they had to be embroiled in this battle. He had never answered her.

All around her she could feel an increase in the energy of the creatures of the forest. They were becoming more active and could sense the trouble coming as well as she. They were unsettled, fearful, even angry. She had never dreamed that they understood as much as they did, and that their emotions so closely mirrored those of humans. Something new was stirring now. She felt the restlessness deep within her. It was time to get back to camp. Something was about to happen.

She just wished she knew what it was.

So she carefully replaced the book in its hiding place. It might not offer any answers for her now, but there were still many trials ahead—things that the book addressed. If they didn't stop the bastard child, then the dark prophecies would come true.

Friar Tuck was on edge. It was more than just the impending battle, which he prayed wouldn't see them all dead and England lost forever. It was more than his fears over Alan's condition.

For the last couple of days he had felt a sense of evil in the camp, and he had been unable to pinpoint the source. He had performed every ritual he knew to banish dark things, but to no avail. After prayer and hateful fasting he had come to the belief that there was a traitor in their midst.

At first he thought one of their own might have been cursed or poisoned, like he had been when they had been attacked at the port. It didn't feel like that, though, and no one behaved in a manner different from before.

This threat was something new, he was sure of it. Ever since his own experience, he had become more sensitive to the presence of evil. Had it not been for that, he probably wouldn't have realized anything was wrong. Miraculously God had taken something meant for evil and turned it toward good.

A dozen new people had come to them over the last couple of weeks, most of them servants from the Locksley household. From what they revealed, when their master was killed the steward had given them each money and told them to flee. They had, but many had no idea where to go. It was hard these days to flee the reach of the Sheriff.

Tuck located the newcomers, one by one, and surreptitiously managed to sprinkle a precious bit of holy water on them. None had reacted, which ruled out possessions and spells. As a result the person he sought had to be, at the core, evil in and of itself.

He hadn't shared his concerns with the lady Marian. She had

busied herself practicing for the archery tournament, and she was quite good. Good enough perhaps to win the arrow. He just hoped the disguise he had prepared for her would be equally effective. He was loathe to reveal it, though, before he had found the traitor.

So he walked the camp, trying to find each of the newcomers.

Turn around.

He blinked, not sure if he'd heard a voice, or if the words were in his head. He turned and he found Haylan sitting by himself on a blanket. His heart went out to the boy who had lost so much, and he gave a heavy sigh. Finding the traitor would have to wait a few more minutes. He headed over and eased himself down onto the blanket.

"How are you?" he asked.

Haylan looked up, tears sparkling in his eyes.

"I'm angry," he said.

Friar Tuck nodded. "When we lose someone we care about, it's natural to be angry at some point. Angry that it happened, angry at the person who is gone, even angry at God. It's all right, Haylan. It will pass."

"I'm not angry at God or Audric."

"Then who are you angry at?" Tuck asked.

"Ean."

"Ean?" Tuck said. "Your brother's friend?"

"Yes."

"Why are you angry with him?"

"If it wasn't for him being so stupid, Audric wouldn't have gotten killed."

"How so?" Tuck asked.

"Ean and Audric got into a disagreement. Ean said that there was no such thing as fey, and Audric told him there was. Ean demanded that he prove it. Audric told him about some little purple flowers where the fey are supposed to live. He said he could catch one. Ean said he'd give him gold if he brought him one." Haylan paused and clenched his jaw. "So, Audric went off to catch a fey for Ean, and he got killed instead."

Friar Tuck licked his lips, which suddenly felt very dry.

"Let me get this right," he said, his voice a bit hoarse. "Audric went to look for fey the day he was killed?"

The boy nodded.

"And he did so because Ean promised to give him gold?"

Haylan nodded again.

"How did Audric know Ean could keep his promise?" Friar Tuck asked.

Haylan hesitated. "It's a secret," he said. "Audric wasn't supposed to tell, and he made me promise not to tell anyone else."

The back of Friar Tuck's neck began to itch. "Listen very carefully to me, Haylan. If Ean had something to do with Audric getting killed, and was after the fey, you need to tell me. It's important."

Still the boy hesitated. Friar Tuck sucked in his breath.

"Confession isn't breaking a promise," he told the boy.

Haylan thought about it for a moment and then arrived at a decision. "Ean says he can do magic," he blurted out.

"Did he ever show Audric any of his magic?" Friar Tuck tried to remain still and keep his voice calm.

"No."

Tuck needed to think. It might just have been one boy bragging to another, trying to impress or influence him or even just make friends. Children sometimes made up things, even dangerous, outrageous things. It didn't necessarily mean anything.

"But I saw him doing magic, when he didn't know anyone was watching."

Friar Tuck was frightened. He had never had to face a magic user by himself before. He didn't particularly want to do so now, but he refused to put either Marian or Will in harm's way, nor would he risk the life of any other innocent.

He wished the cardinal was there. He prepared himself by

kneeling in prayer for nearly an hour, girding himself for the battle to come. He had a dagger up his sleeve, and he'd sprinkled it with holy water just to be on the safe side.

At last he rose. The time had come. To delay anymore risked too much. He walked around the clearing until he found Ean. Finding the boy, he forced a smile onto his face.

"Hello, Ean."

"Good day, Friar," the boy said hesitantly.

"Settling in alright are you?"

"Yes."

"Good," Tuck continued. "You've been here long enough it's time you started taking a sentry shift. Don't worry, though, it's not too hard. A lot of standing around staring and trying not to act too bored. Let me walk you around and show you all the things you'll be looking for."

"Okay," Ean said. He still looked hesitant.

Friar Tuck put a hand on his shoulder, and Ean flinched at the contact. A wave of nausea rolled through the monk, but he refused to give any sign. Casually moving his hand, he pointed toward the one side of the clearing.

"Let's start over there," he said. In the distance he could hear Alan starting to play his harp. It was a haunting melody that pulled at him. It was distracting, but he was grateful that his friend was feeling well enough to play. They moved out of earshot of anyone in the camp, and Ean turned to him.

"What are we looking for when we stand sentry?"

"Mostly we're keeping watch for strangers coming our way," Tuck replied. "Oft times they're folks needing help, like everyone here. We wouldn't want soldiers or the Sheriff's men surprising us, though."

"That would be... bad," Ean said as though struggling to complete his thought.

"Yes, it would. Ordinarily it's best to stand at the edge of the clearing, although I've found it can be quite helpful to stand just inside the trees themselves. One hears and sees things a bit differently there," Tuck said, watching the boy's reaction.

"Like what?" Ean asked quickly.

"Like ghosts," Tuck said as they stepped into the trees.

Ean looked at him sharply. "You believe in ghosts?"

"Yes, ghosts, fey, all of it."

"Have you ever seen any?"

"Ghosts? One or two." They were out of sight of the clearing. Tuck's mouth was going dry. He didn't want anyone to witness what was about to happen. On the other hand, if he ended up in trouble, there was none that could see to help him. He was on his own.

He moved his arm and the hilt of the dagger slid into his palm.

"What about fey?" Ean asked intently.

"Fey? I know they're here."

"Yes, but have you seen one?" There was an intensity to the boy's questioning. It would be good to know the reason behind it.

"Why are you so interested in the fey?" he asked. "Most folks would prefer not to think of them and to leave well enough alone."

"My father saw one once," Ean said. "He told me about it. I've always wanted to see one ever since." He was lying. Tuck could read it in the boy's face. He might be evil, but a practiced liar he wasn't. They could still hear the music from Alan's harp. It seemed to rise in volume and made a buzzing sound in the air around them.

Ean narrowed his eyes. "What is the bard doing?"

Friar Tuck stared. "I think the better question is what are you doing?"

A knife suddenly flashed in Ean's hand, and he slashed out with it. Tuck gave a shout and lunged to the side, producing his own weapon. A thick liquid dripped off the boy's knife and the friar's heart skipped a beat as he realized it was likely poisoned.

"Tell me where I can catch a fey," Ean hissed, his face contorting in a snarl.

"Why do you want one so badly?"

"Their life force protects this land."

"And the Sheriff intends to do what, use one in a ritual to help destroy us all?" Tuck guessed. "What will he do to you if you can't get him one?"

He stalled as he tried to find an opening. The boy hunched over, making a smaller target of himself. Tuck meanwhile was painfully aware of what a large target he presented. He had expected the boy to lash out at him with magic, not a blade. Otherwise he would have brought a sword with him instead of a dagger.

Better to have struck while we were walking, before he knew what was coming, he lectured himself. It was too late for that, though. At least he knew what the boy's purpose was. Hopefully he would live to share that knowledge.

He feinted but it didn't work. The boy kept eyes fixed on him.

He knows that he has the advantage, because all he has to do is scratch me. Tuck began to sweat, and it rolled down his forehead, stinging his eyes. He was going to die soon if he couldn't cause the boy to make a mistake.

"You'll never get your hands on a fey," he said. "Even if you escape here, you'll never be able to find one by yourself."

"By myself? Who can show me?"

Tuck smiled. "Several here can, but they're not going to."

"Who? The bard?"

Tuck just laughed.

"The princess?"

Tuck forced himself to laugh some more.

"Who?" Ean demanded, becoming agitated.

"It turns out you asked the wrong brother," Tuck said gleefully.

"What?" Ean stared at him in shock. His blade lowered slightly. Just as Friar Tuck was about to lunge forward, he saw a flash of movement behind his opponent.

"Yup, you asked the wrong person."

A long, slender green hand snaked out of the brush, grabbed the boy's wrist, twisted it and plunged the knife into Ean's stomach. The boy shrieked and fell to his knees. The fey who had slain him danced around into his line of sight.

"I heard you were looking to catch a fey," the creature said, wicked teeth bared in a snarl. "Perhaps you should have been more careful."

Ean's skin changed to a mottled gray, and then he fell backward, dead. Friar Tuck stood there, trembling as the fight left his body. The fey turned large eyes on him.

"We have heard the call."

"The call?" He struggled to understand.

A girl creature covered in pink came out of the woods next. "Yes, your minstrel has played the song. It has been heard. He has called us to war."

The song that Alan was playing. He had been calling the fey. In doing so he had saved Tuck's life.

"Thank you," he said, then he turned and ran.

The last notes of the song still drifted on the air when he reached Alan's side. The bard's eyes were dazed. Haylan sat beside him. The girl fey appeared at Tuck's side, knelt down, and touched Alan's cheek.

"He has given his life for the song," she said.

"What?" Friar Tuck demanded, praying he had not heard her correctly.

She glanced up at him. "To play the songs of the fey, it takes more from a bard than knowing the notes to play. It takes a part of him, heart and soul, to give the notes the proper weight, to make them dance, to make them heard. He was dying, and with what he had left he has saved you by calling us."

Friar Tuck spun. "Alan, no," he said, falling to his knees in anguish. "Alan, no—I didn't want you to die." Haylan remained quiet by the bard's side.

"He knows," the fey said. "He also knew this was the only way. He says not to blame yourself. He dreamed of this day many months ago, saw the end at the start. He knew the why and the how, but not the when."

Alan blinked up at him as if to say it was true. With great

effort he turned his head a fraction of an inch toward Haylan. He stretched out his hand slowly and pressed his harp into the boy's arms.

"To you, young one, he is leaving his greatest treasure," the fey continued. "I have promised him that we will complete your training, teach you the songs he could not."

Haylan nodded, clutching the harp as the tears rolled down his cheeks. Alan turned his head back toward Friar Tuck, and his eyelids flickered. A smile found his face.

"He wants you to know that of all the people he has known his whole life, you are his favorite," the girl said.

Tuck reached out and grasped his friend's hand.

"You are my favorite, too," he told him.

"He cannot hear you any longer, but I have told him." She closed Alan's eyes and then a moment later pulled her hand from his face. A shudder passed over his lean frame.

"He is gone."

Tuck began to weep bitterly.

Marian ran up just then, flanked by several others.

"What is happening?" Jansa gasped, staring at the fey. The girl rose and turned to Marian. She bowed to her.

"Marian, Queen of the Fey, your bard has called. Your army has arrived." She turned and swept her hand toward the tree line as out of it stepped hundreds of creatures, the likes of which no human had ever seen.

CHAPTER THIRTY-THREE

The day dawned cold and bright. Marian could see her breath in the air as she rode toward the castle on an old nag of a horse laden down with pots and assorted tools for metal work. Her pants were very comfortable and it felt good to be astride a horse, even if it was one as disreputable looking as the bay she was riding.

After she had donned the costume and smeared her face with grime, Chastity had declared that no one would recognize her as a woman, let alone the princess Marian. That was good. Friar Tuck had lived up to his end of the bargain. Now if she could win the black arrow, she'd have lived up to hers.

They still didn't know who the Sheriff planned to hang, furthering the suspicions that he was hoping to catch the Hood and his supporters at the gathering. There was nothing she could do about that, though. She just had to trust that God was on their side, and her army would be enough.

On the road she was joined by others heading to the festival. It was good that she arrive amidst others unknown to her. She planned on speaking only when absolutely necessary.

Many of her allies had departed the day before, to be in place for whatever was to come. Friar Tuck had dressed like a peasant. It was the only time she'd ever seen him in something other than his robes. Even when masquerading as the Hood he'd worn them beneath the cloak. He looked ridiculous trying to adjust to his breeches.

Haylan clung to him, pretending to be his son. Chastity had left as well, making a final round of the manors. No one was left behind. They didn't want to risk the camp being discovered while the fighters were away.

Nor could they spare a single man, woman, or child. When the fighting came, all had the right to fight for their lives. Remembering the expressions she'd seen on their faces, she felt confident that they would.

Thomas had taken charge of two wagons carrying the parts of the trebuchet he'd managed to construct. It hadn't yet been fully tested, but there was nothing to be done about that. They'd run out of time.

When the castle finally came into sight she felt a swell of emotion in her breast. So much had changed since she had fled it. Even if they were victorious today, it might never truly be her home again.

The ground to the left of the keep had been set up as the festival area. There she surrendered her horse to one of the stable boys who was caring for the beasts and presented herself to the man in charge of the games.

"Here for the archery tournament?" he asked, looking her over and taking into account the bow slung around her slender shoulders.

She nodded.

"You actually know how to use that thing?" he asked.

"Want me to plant some feathers in your chest to prove it?" She kept her voice hoarse. He rolled his eyes and wrote something down on a parchment.

"Contest starts at noon." He pointed to a section of grass where targets were already set out. She nodded and turned to go.

Walking along, she watched the people around her, seeing if she could spy any friends in the crowd. She couldn't, and it was probably a good thing. If she couldn't find them, then neither were their enemies likely to do so.

Her stomach did a flip and she panicked for a moment, thinking that it might be the morning sickness rearing its ugly head. It settled within a couple of moments, though, and she realized that it must have been nerves.

As she walked she carefully surveyed the lay of the land, marking where everything was so that she could navigate her way through it all quickly, if the need arose. A stand had been built from which the Sheriff and Henry and their select others would be watching the proceedings. Most likely it was there the black arrow would be kept. At the start of the tournament they would display it as the prize the archers sought.

If they didn't, then she'd have to assume Friar Tuck had been right—that they didn't have it at all, or were keeping it safely hidden away. She'd cross that bridge when she came to it, though.

Friar Tuck was still raw with grief, and the chafing from his disguise did nothing to improve his mood. Still, he had his duty and performed it, walking through the festival, keeping a sharp eye out for anything that might be useful. He wished they could have planted weapons in various locations, but they hadn't been able to plan that out properly. As it was each man of Sherwood was responsible for carrying in as many weapons as he could, and doing so discretely.

Tuck himself was carrying a short sword and four daggers. The boy at his side was carrying three.

"Do you think the… tinker will win?" Haylan asked.

"I hope so," Tuck said. "At least I think I do." Truth be told he wasn't sure that the winner wasn't going to have his head instantly parted from his neck, just for good measure. Now that the Sheriff knew the Hood was alive—or at least that his followers were carrying on in his stead—it would make sense for him to kill the best archer in the competition instantly.

He glanced at the sky. It was getting close to noon.

"Let's go get a good place to stand and watch," he said.

Haylan nodded and grabbed his hand. Friar Tuck squeezed it, wishing he had words of comfort for both of them.

A crier announced the beginning of the tournament and Marian stepped up to take her place among the men. It looked as if there were only about a dozen competitors. A magical black arrow wasn't quite the enticement as the gold that tournaments usually offered. Some likely stayed away just because they didn't want to be on the Sheriff's radar. She couldn't blame them.

The competitors were mostly peasants and farmers, from the looks of them. There were also three members of Henry's army. Noticeably absent were any of the Sheriff's dog soldiers, nor could any be seen on the grounds—although she was sure they were around in great numbers. The low number of entrants made her nervous, as each one would face greater scrutiny.

The Sheriff, Glynna, and Henry were introduced, and all took seats on the platform to watch. Glynna was carrying a pillow with something on it. She craned her head, trying to see. Before she could tell what it was, however, the Sheriff stood and all eyes turned to him.

"Thank you for coming to today's... festivities," he said in his oily voice. Just hearing him gave Marian a visceral reaction which she struggled not to show. Still she watched intently, hoping to see the black arrow.

"As eager as we are to proceed with the hangings," he said with dark humor, "first we shall have a bit of competition. This is the prize these fine archers are shooting to win." He reached over and picked up the pillow Glynna was holding. He hoisted it aloft and Marian sucked in her breath. On it was indeed the black arrow still lodged in a chunk of the monster's decaying flesh.

"It's a magical black arrow, used not long ago to bring down Guy of Gisbourne," he said. "A rare prize indeed. And truly priceless." At his words Marian hazarded a glance at the other archers, wondering if any of them had any idea about the shaft's significance.

"We begin with twelve contestants, from the look of it," the Sheriff continued. "After the first round, half will be eliminated, leaving six. After the second round another half will be eliminated, leaving three. The final three will shoot for the prize." He handed the pillow back to Glynna and stared back out at the gathered archers. "To make things even more interesting," he said directly to the archers, "and to make certain you are trying your best, allow me to explain what it means to be 'eliminated.'"

A sudden sick feeling seized Marian.

"The losers," the Sheriff continued, "as in the first nine to be eliminated, will be hanged this afternoon." He paused for effect, then added, "Best of luck to you all."

The contestants all looked stunned. Two men immediately turned and tried to escape. The Sheriff's dog soldiers appeared seemingly from nowhere and grabbed both of them, returning them to their positions and holding swords to their backs. The message was clear. Anyone who lost would die later. Anyone who refused to compete would die now. Even Henry's men looked disconcerted, glancing toward their liege, who only nodded. They looked away again, and all wore expressions of grim determination.

Marian's heart was in her throat. There was no alternative plan that would enable them to steal the black arrow. She had no choice—she needed to win. Her life, the life of her unborn child, and the future of England might well depend on it.

"Archers to your marks," the crier shouted. "The targets are currently set at twenty-five paces. Each man will be given three arrows for this first round. The best arrow will be counted." He raised his arm. "Ready first arrows!"

Marian unslung her bow from her shoulders, pulled an arrow out of her quiver, and notched it. Her heart pounded in her chest as she sighted down the length of it.

"Steady!" the crier called. "Let fly!"

Marian let fly. Out of the corner of her eye she saw the arrow of one of her opponents go completely wild. Her own shaft flew true and made it to the second smallest ring, just short of a bullseye. Not bad considering the sudden nerves she was experiencing. Still, she could do better. She *had to* do better.

"Archers, ready second arrows!"

She pulled her next one from her quiver, notched it, and worked to still her breathing. With the first arrow she hadn't had it under control, not enough.

"Steady… let fly!"

She loosed her second arrow. It hit between her first arrow and the bullseye. Better, but still not where it needed to be. She was settling down, though, she could feel it. Her mind was calming, clarifying. The world around her fell away until there was only her, and the target.

"Archers, ready third arrows!"

As she pulled the third shaft from her quiver, she could hear the man next to her begin to sob and was forced to push the sound from her mind. She focused on the bullseye. In her mind she saw the arrow flying to it. She notched the arrow, took a breath, held it.

"Ready!" the crier called. "Let fly!"

Marian's arrow flew straight and true, striking home in the bullseye. No cheering greeted such a feat, as would normally be customary. When she straightened and turned, the crowd was silent, watching in spellbound horror all.

The man next to her had missed completely with one of his arrows. The other two had hit the outermost edges of the target. Tears streamed down his face. She bit her lip and focused on the pain of it to keep herself from crying for him. Further down the line, only two others looked to have done well enough to remain. That was small comfort, though, since she would still need to remain in the top three after the next round.

Screaming rose from voices in the audience, and wailing as the crier announced the round's winners and the Sheriff's soldiers marched forward. The two who had tried to run were the first led off. The man standing next to her went third, and three other contestants were also led away, all of them looking stunned and helpless. None resisted, however.

She wanted to yell to them to fight, but it would only get them killed immediately, when she had no chance of helping them. Better to delay their sentence by even an hour, to give the rebels time to maneuver. That left Marian, two farmers, and Henry's three soldiers still in it. She drew a steadying breath.

You can do this, she told herself.

She didn't look at the crowd, from which there came only stunned silence, while a few of the spectators wept openly. She couldn't risk seeing someone she knew, as it might break her concentration.

Six of the targets were moved and she shifted over, taking the spot of the man who had stood weeping beside her. Marian found herself standing next to a farmer, who looked composed despite his ashen complexion. On the other side of him was one of Henry's soldiers, a man with thick gray hair, a deeply tanned face, and a scraggly gray beard. He'd done well in the first round, and had a determined look to him.

"Archers! The targets are now set at fifty paces," the crier called. "You will have two arrows in this round. Ready your first arrow!"

Marian pulled the shaft. She notched it, sighted, and then checked her breathing. In… out. In… out. In. Hold it.

"Steady! Let fly!"

The arrow sailed straight and true. It hit the bullseye, and she let out the breath she'd been holding. Her second shot couldn't get any better than that. It had to be enough to get her into the finals.

"Archers, ready second arrows!" Marian pulled the arrow loose from its quiver.

"Good luck to you," the man next to her whispered. She glanced quickly at him. There was something in his eyes that made her pause. He knew he was done, yet there was a light in his eyes that burned intently. She couldn't look away as he notched his second arrow.

"Steady!"

Marian quickly turned her attention back to her target. She notched her arrow just as the crier shouted.

"Let fly!"

Her arrow sped away. It wouldn't be a bullseye, but suddenly that was the least of her concerns. The man next to her spun on his heel with a shout.

"Death to demons!" he shouted as he let his arrow fly straight at the Sheriff.

It struck his target directly in the chest, forcing him back. There were shouts from some—including Henry—but the Sheriff calmly pulled out the shaft and snapped it in half. He shook his head at the archer.

"Not the best use of your arrow," he called.

Murmurs and gasps came from all around them as she stood, heart pounding. Before that moment, not all of these people had seen for themselves the Sheriff's true nature. Now they had—including Henry and his soldiers. While the king didn't seem as surprised as she might have expected, the soldiers were another matter. All three of the ones in the competition stared openly, then glanced uneasily at one another.

"Long live King Richard!" the farmer shouted as a dog soldier walked up behind him. Marian braced herself, waiting for him to be beheaded. Instead, the soldier knocked him unconscious and hauled him off the field.

Soldiers then came for the other farmer and dragged him off. Some of the Sheriff's men moved toward one of Henry's soldiers, a young fellow who gaped in shock. When the Sheriff's men laid hold of him he turned to fight, and they promptly knocked him out with a sword pummel to the head.

It took a few moments for the clamor to die down. Marian and the two remaining soldiers shifted again, so the one with the scraggly beard stood next to her. On his other side was a large man with a commanding presence. This had to be a commander in the invading forces. He turned to stare at both of them, and she kept her gaze averted so he couldn't get a good look at her.

"I don't like this one bit," he said, softly enough that only they could hear. She knew then that she had to seize the chance while she could. She made sure to whisper and continued to make her voice sound hoarse.

"The Sheriff is an archdemon," she muttered. "He was summoned from hell by Prince John, then killed the prince to seize power. His reign means doom for us all." The man stood for a moment without making a reply, then he glanced back at the Sheriff.

"I'd heard the rumors, but until now..."

"He kills all who speak up," Marian pressed. "Who but a monster kills the losers of a tournament?" They were running out of time. The targets were nearly moved into their new positions. She had to make him understand.

The other man was listening, as well, but had his face slightly turned away so she couldn't tell if she was reaching him. It didn't matter, though. If she could persuade one of the commanders, that was an effort better spent.

The Sheriff rose and clapped his hands together, the loud *crack* of his gauntlets echoing louder than it should have. When all attention was back on him, he spoke in a loud, clear voice that nevertheless made her skin crawl.

"We must congratulate our three noble finalists," he said. "It will be truly exciting to witness your displays of skill in this final round, and discover to whom the lady Glynna will grant the coveted arrow." As the Sheriff spoke, Marian found herself glaring at the woman and forced herself to look away.

"Good luck, to all of us," the commander said, sincerity in his voice.

"Luck," Marian and the other man echoed together.

"Archers! To your positions!" the crier said as the Sheriff resumed his seat. "The targets have been moved to one hundred paces. You will each get one arrow. Good luck."

Marian took up her position and drew her arrow. She notched it and tried to shut out the rest of the world again as she stared down the shaft at the target. She adjusted slightly for the increased distance, breathed in and out, finally breathing in and holding it.

"Steady!" the crier called. "Let fly!"

The arrow left her fingers like silk and she watched it speed toward her target. It struck dead center and she gasped. A perfect shot.

Looking to her side, she froze. The soldier next to her had hit his target dead center, as well. The commander's arrow had landed on the line straddling the bullseye and the next ring. It was a brilliant shot… but not a winner.

"I know when I'm bested," he said. He backed away, applauding them both. Then he turned and bowed to the platform. "My liege, I know when I have been beaten. I yield the ground to these two."

Marian held her breath, wondering what would happen to him. She saw Henry lean over and whisper something to the Sheriff, who nodded. Henry stood and lifted a goblet.

"Well done, Jerome," he called out. "You have earned a seat of honor at the feast tonight. You may take your leave now."

"Thank you, my liege," Jerome said, bowing again before melting into the crowd. Marian understood all too well the whispered words Henry had shared with the Sheriff. He knew Jerome personally. Since the commander had come with him, he could not be one of the rebels they were looking for.

That left only Marian and the soldier standing next to her. Did Henry know him, as well? She pushed the thought to the back of her mind as the crier went and inspected both targets. He came back.

"My lieges," he said loudly, "both arrows have flown as true as they could. It is a tie. With your permission, I will offer an additional round." Henry and the Sheriff both nodded. The crier turned and signaled, and one of the targets was removed.

"Archers," he called. "For this last round, the target is set at one hundred and fifty paces. You will each be given one arrow, and you will fire at the same target."

The man beside her nodded. "I will let the tinker go first."

"Very well," the crier said. Marian wasn't sure if going first was a blessing or not. At least she wouldn't be distracted by the other arrow, sticking in the target.

The target was moved and the crier gave a satisfied nod.

"Archer, take your position!" he said. "Let fly at will."

Marian stepped up, pulled the arrow from her quiver, and examined it for a moment. She didn't like the feel of it. She replaced it and pulled another one out. Satisfied, she notched it, took a steadying breath, then sighted down the shaft. She could feel the tension of the string between her thumb and fingers and adjusted for distance. She had never fired at something so far, but she worked it out in her mind.

Then she focused on her breathing.

In... Out. In...

Hold.

She let go and the arrow sped away. It rose slightly and then sank. Her legs nearly gave way beneath her when her arrow hit the target.

It was dead center.

She turned and stepped out of the way, feeling dizzy. One way or another this would be over soon.

The other archer strode forward. He took an arrow from his quiver and she watched him as he notched his arrow. He turned and looked at her.

"It's time to end this charade, don't you think?" he asked in a husky voice.

She didn't know how to respond. He turned back toward the target, brought up his bow and seemed to pull and then release in one fluid motion. She stared in shock. It was the first time she'd been able to watch him shoot and it was remarkable. She hadn't even seen him sighting. It was as if he just knew where to shoot.

She twisted her head just in time to see his arrow land.

It split hers in half.

Marian gaped. She wouldn't have believed it if she hadn't seen it with her own eyes. She turned back to find him staring intently at her. He hadn't even seen his arrow land, she realized.

He smiled at her and suddenly she saw him, really saw him. She saw past the gray hair and the scraggly beard and the soldier's uniform. And what she saw shocked her more than she could have imagined.

She saw her husband.

CHAPTER THIRTY-FOUR

Robin couldn't help but smile at the look on Marian's face. He knew she hadn't recognized him at the start, even though he had seen right through her disguise, clever as it was. She blinked at him in shock, tears filling her eyes, and started to move toward him.

As much as it pained him, he took a step back and cleared his throat.

"It was an excellent contest, tinker," he said loudly.

She stopped, shook herself slightly, and then nodded. He gave her a wink and then steeled himself for what was coming next.

"The soldier wins!" the crier announced.

"Time to collect my prize," he said, putting swagger in his voice. There were a few weak cheers from an audience that was still traumatized by the brutality of the contest.

Robin had arrived back in England just in time to learn of the tournament. He'd barely had enough time to find and overpower a guard whose uniform he could steal. Knowing that the black arrow was the prize, he'd assumed one of his would enter the contest in an attempt to win it. He also knew that it had to be a trap.

The black arrow was real, though. He had recognized it the moment the Sheriff held the pillow aloft—felt it calling to him, throbbing in the mark it had given him. He still didn't know why he hadn't been able to pull it from the body of Guy of Gisbourne, but he was gratified to see that no one else had been able to do so, either.

He noticed the Sheriff took pains not to touch the shaft.

Robin held his bow in his left hand, down at his side. He was ready to use it again in an instant, if he had to. The crier led him up to the platform from which Henry, the Sheriff, and Robin's mother watched intently. The commander, Jerome, stood to the right of the platform and gave him a respectful nod.

Before the tournament started, Robin spent a few minutes talking with him, hoping it might stand him in good stead. The man seemed decent, reasonable, and the Sheriff's cruelty had surprised and upset him profoundly.

Henry leaned forward on his chair, scrutinizing Robin closely. He whispered something to the Sheriff, then when Robin stopped in front of them, he turned back.

"Soldier, I admit I don't know you," Henry said.

Robin sucked in his breath. Before he could say anything Jerome stepped forward.

"Sire, please allow me to present one of your finest soldiers, Reginald," the commander said. "It's no surprise that he won today. He's consistently been the most outstanding archer in his regiment, as long as I've known him."

Robin bowed deeply to hide his surprise. When he straightened up it was with a regained composure, and he kept his eyes fixed on Henry as one of that man's soldiers would be expected to do. The Sheriff and his mother remained in his peripheral vision. Henry nodded, seeming to be convinced.

He said something under his breath to the Sheriff.

"We congratulate you on your victory," the man in black said. "Before we present your reward, let us also speak with your admirable opponent."

Robin tensed, though he managed to keep calm. He had hoped Marian would be able to melt back into the crowd, untouched by whatever was coming next. That had been a fool's hope, though. Since the Sheriff was looking for the Hood, now that Jerome had vouched for him, the tinker was the next logical choice.

And, in a way, they would be right. Without Marian, there would be no Hood. He couldn't let them take her captive, though, not even for a moment. His hand tightened on his bow and he measured the distance to the black arrow. Its point was still buried in a chunk of rotting flesh. He'd have to dislodge that.

There was motion to one side and he turned his head slightly as Marian joined him, then gritted his teeth. One of the Sheriff's demon soldiers stood at her back.

"I commend you both on such a fine display of marksmanship," the Sheriff said. He stood, a half sneer on his face. "I've never seen the equal."

They both bowed their heads in acknowledgment. Out of the corner of his eye Robin saw more demon soldiers moving into place. He had no idea where Friar Tuck, Alan, or any of the rest of them were or what the plan was should this happen. He could see a lot of soldiers, though—enough to make it nearly impossible for them to escape, even if the whole camp had been present.

If Henry's soldiers decided to join the fray, then God help them all. He needed to do something unexpected, a distraction.

"Hit me," he whispered.

Marian bobbed her head slightly.

He raised his chin. "My lord, thank you for the praise, but truth be told, this scum never stood a chance of winning against me," he announced. "He should go on his way before he embarrasses himself any further." Robin moved in front of her and sneered.

Instantly she hit him in the jaw, harder than he would have guessed, and he staggered back into the platform. There was a shout of alarm from Henry. Robin twisted and snatched the black arrow off the pillow before his mother could react.

"Thank you for the prize," he said before spinning back toward Marian. Already soldiers were closing in on her. "For

God and King Richard!" Robin shouted, holding the black arrow high.

The soldiers froze, looking to the Sheriff for orders.

"We call on each soldier here to join us and fight the demons who seek to take over this land!" Marian shouted. When she stopped, there was dead silence.

Then pandemonium broke out.

"God and King Richard!" All around them voices rose up. Everywhere he looked men and women—some of them alarmingly young—tossed off cloaks and drew weapons. Henry's men still hesitated, but the dog soldiers moved toward the rebels, and he feared the bloodshed that would come.

Then, he froze, and saw something he had never dreamed he'd see.

The Guardian, the one from whom he'd taken the black arrow, came striding forward from the back of the crowd, cutting down demon soldiers with his sword. Their blood smoked on his blade. Behind him came fey of every size and color, some armed with weapons, others baring claw and tooth.

Marian grabbed Robin's hand and pulled him from the platform. Around them their men and the fey swarmed the Sheriff's demon soldiers. They needed to get to safety.

"The Sheriff!" He pulled back. "I have to kill him!"

"Later," she snapped. "Where are King Richard and his men?"

"Likely a couple of days behind me. We rescued him and I came on ahead as fast as I could," Robin said. Marian cursed but kept pulling him along. They reached a patch of grass that was away from the fighting and she turned and kissed him hard.

"We've got this," she said pulling away. "And you've got the arrow."

Robin placed the rotting flesh on the ground, took hold of the arrow, put his boot on the flesh, and strained to pull the arrow free.

Nothing.

"Why won't it release?" he asked, desperation in his voice.

Marian turned to look back at the fighters. For the most part Henry's soldiers stood and stared. Soon Henry would order them to fight, however, and the tide might turn. She turned back to Robin.

"I don't know," she said. "Maybe it *chooses* when to release."

"Perhaps. It chose when to be used," Robin panted, "but this is absurd. Without the arrow we can't kill the Sheriff." He pulled again.

"Maybe one of the fey has a weapon that could do it."

"I pray you're right, but we can't leave this to chance," he said.

She looked back at the fighting, which was furious. Her skin felt like it was crawling, and she felt as if she vibrated with a fierce intensity. This was the final fight. She knew it. She needed to be out there, taking part in it.

"Robin, there's something I need to tell you," she said, her hand going to her stomach.

"What?" he asked, stopping to look at her.

She opened her mouth to speak, then stopped.

"I'll tell you after it's over," she said. "After we've killed the Sheriff."

Nodding, he struggled with the arrow, then glanced up.

"The guardian," he said. "I saw the guardian of the arrow—the one I had to fight for it. Maybe he can tell us how to make it release."

"Then find him quickly, my love."

He bent down and kissed her, and then he was off again, lost in the swirl of battle. She felt a moment of fear, terror that she would never again see him alive. She couldn't think about that now, though. There was too much at stake. This was bigger than both of them.

"God be with him," she whispered. Then she pulled her sword from its scabbard and headed back to the fray.

* * *

Friar Tuck didn't know the man who'd won the tournament, but he seemed to be on their side. He and Haylan had been as far away from the Sheriff's platform as they could be, while still having a clear view of the archers. They stood back to back now, slashing at any of the Sheriff's men who came close to them.

The boy was brave, braver than Tuck would have been at his age. Then again the desperation could do that.

"Friar Tuck, look!" the boy shouted suddenly.

King Henry was on his feet shouting. Several of his soldiers had joined in the battle, slashing and hacking at the fey and Tuck's friends. Not all the soldiers were joining the fight, though, and his heart lifted a bit. Maybe their strategy had worked. He hoped so—they needed every man they could get on their side. Barring that, they at least needed fewer opponents.

As it was, many of the Sheriff's men were already down. Darkness wouldn't come for hours, so they wouldn't be resurrecting any time soon. If they could end this before the sun set, they had a chance.

"We might just win this thing," he said. Suddenly there was a sound—a new roar that swept over the crowd. He turned back and his heart sank within him. From behind the castle new figures emerged. It was more of the Sheriff's dog soldiers.

They kept coming in wave after wave.

"Dear God, spare us all," he breathed.

There were hundreds of them—or more.

CHAPTER THIRTY-FIVE

Marian did her best to hold her own. There was a mighty cracking sound and out of the corner of her eye she saw a massive boulder flying through the air. Thomas's trebuchet had sent it flying. She turned and saw it smash into a wave of the demon soldiers, crushing at least a dozen of them. Those behind ran around their fallen comrades as if it were nothing.

At the back of the fresh wave of the Sheriff's demons came those nobles who had sworn fealty to John, moving as if sleepwalking. They were fighting, though, which presented a new problem—they were going to get themselves killed.

Quickly that became the least of her problems.

They were losing, Marian realized, even though about a third of Henry's forces were fighting for them. She had to increase that number, so she found the body of one of the demon soldiers and set to work pulling off its helm, then cutting off its head.

The thing was grotesque, yet she picked it up by its hair and battled her way toward the platform where Henry stood alone, abandoned by the Sheriff and Glynna. Dozens of his men had closed ranks in front of him, guarding him from the onslaught, and that left him nowhere to go to escape.

I will never reach him, she thought with despair.

Suddenly Marian realized that she was being protected. Every time she was slow to lift a sword, or found someone rushing her too quickly to parry, one of the fey stepped in. With this realization, she felt new resolve. She just wished she could ask them to protect Robin, too.

After what seemed like far too long, she reached the area where Henry's men were clustered to protect him.

"Listen to me!" she shouted, but her voice didn't carry far enough over the din. Only two or three of the soldiers reacted at all. She'd never be able to reach them all, and certainly not Henry.

"What do you need?" She jumped at the voice and looked down at a short fey about half her size. His voice was surprisingly deep.

"I need them to hear me," she said.

"SILENCE!" he shouted. "ATTEND THE QUEEN!"

Marian cringed, and had she been able she would have thrown her hands over her ears. His voice boomed so loudly that it *hurt*. It also cut through all the sounds of battle and startled everyone close by so much that they ceased fighting and turned to look. An eerie silence settled so that the fighting that continued seemed far away.

She pulled off her hood and yanked down her braided hair.

"I am the Lady Marian," she called as loudly as she could. "Niece of King Richard, Queen of the Fey, protector of this land." She turned directly toward Henry. "Cousin, you and your soldiers need to know what the Sheriff truly is, and what you are fighting for!"

She held aloft the grotesque head. Gasps rose all around.

"The Sheriff is a demon who was in league with the sorcerer John," she said. "Together they planned to bring about hell on earth, starting with England. This is a fight against *evil*. Witness what his soldiers are, beneath their masks." She shook the head, sending a spray of dark blood. "Good Christian men of England, you must stand with us!"

Many of Henry's soldiers crossed themselves. They turned to look at their liege, who rose from his seat. He was pale and shaking, and she knew she had backed him into a corner.

He knew, she realized. *But he cannot continue without the loyalty of his men.*

Henry stood there for a moment, beginning to shake. She couldn't determine if it was from rage or fear. At last he lifted his hand.

"We stand with England," he called out as steadily as he could. "Together we will drive back these fiends from hell, who would destroy us!"

A cheer rose up, from many voices.

"Come on then, men, let's fight!" Jerome shouted, suddenly appearing from somewhere to Marian's left. Wherever they stood, Henry's soldiers turned from their rebel opponents and set upon the Sheriff's demon soldiers.

Marian dropped the head she was holding, grateful to be rid of it, and turned to thank the fey who had helped her, but he had already disappeared back into the crowd.

Robin carried the black arrow in his left hand while he hacked through the wave of enemies with the sword in his right. Every time he caught sight of the Guardian he would lose him again just a moment later, when a new soldier launched an attack.

He twisted around, scanning as far as he could see. A short distance away a man dressed in peasant clothes was knocked down by one of the demon soldiers. Robin rushed forward with a shout and ran the creature through. Looking down, he was surprised to see Friar Tuck, and offered his hand to help the man up.

"I almost didn't recognize you without your robes."

Tuck glanced at him sharply, and then his eyes opened wide.

"Robin!" he cried. Throwing out his arms he hugged him fiercely, and then let him go quickly. "The king?"

Robin shook his head. "On his way, but not yet here."

"Praise God he's alive." Friar Tuck looked torn between relief and despair.

"Praise God," Robin agreed, then he asked, "Where's Alan? Is he in disguise as well?"

Friar Tuck looked stricken and slowly shook his head.

"I'm sorry," Robin said. There was a sudden motion to the side, and he turned in time to slash an attacker, then run it through. He pulled free his sword.

"We got Chastity back," the friar said, "and she rescued the missing children."

"Good news indeed," Robin said. "We must take our victories wherever we can." He turned to go. "Stay safe, good friend."

With that he plunged back into the fray, searching again for the elusive Guardian. It took what seemed an eternity but he finally spotted the fey and made his way toward him, determined not to lose track of him this time.

At the first sign of trouble the Sheriff and Glynna slipped away, returning swiftly to the castle where their son was. Between his demons and the soldiers who remained loyal to Henry, there was no way their enemies could prevail. Nevertheless, he would take no chances.

When they reached the castle he made straight for their son, to reassure himself of the child's safety. All was not lost as long as they lived. If any of the rebels had dared harm his scion, they would plead for a death that would be long in coming.

Entering their chambers, they found the child and its nurse, safe and sound. Instead of doting over her offspring, however, Glynna made a detour to a trunk in the corner of the room. She threw it open and fell to her knees, pulling items out.

"What are you doing?" he asked sharply.

"I need to help, cast a spell."

"It will soon be over," he growled. "Even if Henry can't control all of his men, our soldiers are more than enough to take care of the intruders—even the fey. Henry himself is expendable—I only tolerated him this far because I thought I was going to need his men to enter Sherwood. Since the outlaws have so kindly come to us, though, he is no longer an asset."

"I don't think the battle is going to fare as well as you think." Glynna's voice was tense.

"You're worried about your dream?"

"It wasn't just a dream," she said, hands balled into fists. He had seen many sides to her, but he'd never seen her frightened this way. He worried that it might make her... unpredictable.

"What are you planning?" he asked.

"I've been working on a spell that will bring night early, in order to resurrect any of your soldiers that have already fallen."

He stared at her intently. "You can do that?"

"Yes, but I need some time to prepare the ritual."

"Do you require anything from me?"

"Yes," she said, looking up at him. "The final ingredient is a heart of pure darkness. Find me one of your little followers. Those charlatans you call magicians."

"Which one?" he asked.

"The darker the heart the longer the spell will last."

He nodded and left her to her preparations.

They languished in a large chamber with walls of stone. There were benches and sleeping arrangements—certainly more comfortable than the other cells. Nevertheless, this was a dungeon, cold and damp. For their failures, the Sheriff had put them here—for how long, none of them knew.

The sounds of fighting came through the window, but it was high in the wall and offered no view of the outside. Judging from the intensity, however, this was far more than a skirmish. And there was magic in the air—the fey were close.

Suddenly the Sheriff came out of the shadows, striding into their midst and causing even more of a stir than usual. The air seemed thick around him.

* * *

As soon as he stepped from the darkness he could tell that they'd been plotting to betray him. It mattered not. After today they all would have outlived their usefulness. But one could still be of great value.

"One of you will be free of this prison today," he announced. "But only one who is willing to plumb the depths of darkness."

There, he thought. *That should bait the hook.*

Yet they hesitated, for they knew it wasn't always the best thing to have his attention focused on an individual. Then Sera, the ancient witch, raised a bony finger and pointed it at the Mad Monk.

"Truly he has the darkest heart among us."

"You speak truly," the Sheriff replied, striding over and laying a hand on her shoulder. "And in doing so, you reveal your own worth." With that he snapped her neck, and she sank to the stone floor without a sound. He turned to the Mad Monk.

"Come with me," he said as he moved toward the door. "We have work to do."

"Where are we going, my lord?" the man asked, yet he followed.

"To attempt the unthinkable," the man in black replied. "You've always wanted to capture an angel, let's see if we can't make that happen."

An insane light flickered in the monk's eyes.

At the door the Sheriff turned. "As for the rest of you... know the price of failure." He snapped his fingers, and winding tendrils of darkness flared up around them. Some screeched, but as they opened their mouths the darkness wound down inside of them, until all that could be heard was gurgling and the writhing of their bodies.

The Mad Monk gaped in shock as his master pushed him out the door. Before they could make their way up the stairs, however, one of his servants came scurrying up to him and dropped to his knees.

"What is it?" the Sheriff snapped.

"My Lord, the commander of your forces has sent me," the man answered without looking up. "The tide of battle is beginning to turn. There are many dead among your enemies, but too many of your soldiers have fallen. They need more..."

"You shall have more, and shortly," he said. "Now go, and report again if anything changes." The man rose and scurried off, and the Sheriff pushed the Mad Monk up the stairs. There still were many hours until nightfall...

He growled beneath his breath. The black arrow was in the hands of his enemies. If they knew how to release it from its pulpy burden, it could mean the end of him. Glynna was right. They needed to do the spell, resurrect those who had already fallen, and overwhelm their enemy.

They needed to do it quickly.

At last he ushered the Mad Monk back to the chamber where he had left Glynna and their son. She was working over a mixture which reeked of death and decay. He didn't ask what was in it, but the stench gave some clues as to the ingredients.

"How go the preparations, my love?" he asked.

"They are complete," she replied. "All we need now is the last ingredient."

"That's it?"

"Yes," she said. Then she looked up and scowled. "This? This is the best you could find me?"

"I will serve to the best of my ability," the monk said, his eyes flashing. "You only need to instruct me, and your will shall be done." As he spoke, the Sheriff pulled a dagger from his sleeve and plunged it into the Mad Monk's chest. He gaped at it, yet somehow he didn't seem surprised.

"One works with what they have," the Sheriff said. Moving quickly, he cut into the man's chest. Blood sprayed as he wrestled with the body, until finally it fell to the ground. Lifting the heart, he walked over to Glynna. When he held it above the smoking mixture, it began to turn black in parts, gray in others. The mixture hissed where blood dripped into it.

"It won't suffice," Glynna said, and she scowled. "He was insane, but he wasn't a true adherent to the darkness. None of them were, and that is why they failed. You need the life force of someone who is pure evil."

He set the heart down on the ground. "You're right, of course. You always are," he purred. As he did, a frightened expression appeared on Glynna's face, and she looked to her child.

"You can't," she said. "You wouldn't..."

"No, I wouldn't." With that he took the dagger and plunged it into her breast. Her eyes went wide, but she didn't give him a look of surprise, nor of hate, but rather one that mixed ecstasy, and love.

"For you and our son," she whispered.

"Your sacrifice is the finest there could be," he assured her, as he bent and kissed her. Then he cut out her heart. It came free more easily, and her body fell backward onto the floor. He held the heart above the cauldron.

It turned the deepest, coal black. With a smile he dropped the heart into the cauldron, and immediately power began to crackle in the air as the darkest smoke spewed forth.

Robin felled another enemy, spun, and came face-to-face with the Guardian. The big creature nodded in recognition, and his eyes were drawn to the arrow.

"You still wield it."

"I could wield it a lot better if I could find a way to remove it from things it's killed," Robin said, hoisting it aloft.

The Guardian blocked the blade of a soldier who rushed them, then slit the man's throat.

"The arrow has a will of its own."

"I've noticed."

"It won't let itself be drawn in futility."

"That explains little... but how do I pull it free?"

"You don't pull it free. If it has buried itself, you must burn it free."

Robin cut down another attacker.

"You couldn't have told me this before?"

"You were in a hurry." Robin glared at the man, who finally shook his head. "And I thought it would find its way back to the forest long before this."

"Well, thank you for the help," Robin said sarcastically.

The man dipped his head. "You now know what I know."

"Somehow, I doubt that," Robin grunted as he parried another attack.

"What else do you wish?"

"Well, at the moment, the location of the nearest fire."

"We'll all know that," the Guardian said, "and shortly." His eyes widened suddenly as he stared past Robin. There, spreading out from the castle, was a thick veil of billowing darkness that blotted out the sky and soon would block the sun. Robin spun, staring in horror at the dead demon soldiers around them.

"What is it?" the Guardian asked.

"They're all going to come back to life," Robin said hoarsely. "We'll be overrun. Given the numbers of those we've cut down, we'll all be dead within the hour."

CHAPTER THIRTY-SIX

Friar Tuck stared in horror as darkness spread from the castle and rapidly covered the sky. It was magic. It had to be. He looked around at the bodies of the Sheriff's men. They'd be rising again.

Heaven help us all.

There was no victory to be had here. There was only death. The battle was over where they stood—at least for the moment. He feared that moment would be very brief. Glancing down at Haylan, he was struck by the thought that he would watch the boy die, and it was too much for him. He couldn't do this, not any longer.

"We're not soldiers," he muttered. "We shouldn't die here." He grabbed Haylan's hand and began to drag him away from the battlefield, trying to get clear of it. Yet everywhere he turned there was a sea of bodies.

There was no way to escape, not before the monsters started rising. Nearby he saw the fingers on one twitch and he jerked the boy away. The sword slipped out of his blood-soaked hand and fell to the ground as terror seized his heart.

Haylan looked up at him, and in those eyes there was wisdom beyond his years. He suddenly reminded Tuck so much of Alan that he let out an involuntary sob.

"Every man should do that which he is born to do."

Tuck blinked at him, taking in the child's words. They were so simple yet so profound.

Out of the mouths of babes.

Tuck fell to his knees there on the bloodstained earth and began to pray as he had never prayed in his life. Beside him Haylan pulled the harp out of his cloak and began to play, a song of hope and faith while surrounded by despair and loss.

The darkness rolled over them, blotting out the sun. Out of the corner of his eyes Tuck could see more of the fallen demons starting to move. Around him he heard shouts of terror from Henry's soldiers and their own men. A few high-pitched cries rang out as well that could only have come from fey.

The demon fighters would now outnumber them all, two or three to one.

Through his roiling thoughts he kept up a steady torrent of prayer to God. Only a miracle could save them now. Yet all around him he heard the sounds of battle beginning anew, and he could feel the defeat that hung heavy in the air.

It couldn't end this way, it couldn't.

Look up.

The voice spoke in his mind, and he did. There in the dark shone a light. It was distant at first, but it grew nearer. It wasn't in the sky but was hovering just above the ground, becoming brighter and brighter still, then separating into different shafts of light, distinct from one another. He stared, wondering if a group of angels had come to rescue them.

"It's King Richard!"

Much charged behind the king, wielding one of the glowing swords. This was a darkness that couldn't defeat him, and he ran as fast as he could, eager to destroy the Sheriff's demons.

"For God and King Richard!" Old Soldier shouted beside him.

The shout was taken up all around, and Much joined his voice to theirs, these soldiers of the king. He was one of them now, at least for this battle. If only his father could have lived to see him.

Ahead of them the demon soldiers formed up, preparing to meet the charge. The king's men broke upon them like a wave. Much slashed at each of the monsters, insane with the joy of knowing that whatever monster he so much as cut, he killed. He hit as many as he could, knowing that many of the men coming behind him didn't have the specially blessed swords, and so did not have the same advantage.

All around them the smell of sulfur rose up, mixing with screams of agony as demon after demon was sent back to hell. Satisfaction roared through Much as the creatures actually winked out of existence time and time again at the touch of his blade.

Robin raced for the castle, from which the darkness was coming. That was where the Sheriff would be, but there were a lot of opponents—living and reviving—between him and his destination. He had to stop him once and for all, or this wouldn't be the end of it.

When he finally skidded into the main hall of the castle he was surprised to find it empty. There was a dark haze on the staircase, and he knew where he had to go. Making his way to the nearest torch, he thrust the front end of the black arrow into it. The flesh on it sizzled and smoked and finally caught fire. Robin held it there until the shaft was free.

Holding up the arrow, he marveled that the fire had caused it no harm. The Guardian had been right. Now he knew another of the weapon's secrets.

Spinning he made his way to the staircase and bounded upward, taking the stairs two at a time. Plunging into the billowing darkness, he covered his mouth and nose with his arm and sprinted down a hallway, winding through the corridors until he came to a bedchamber he knew all too well.

He burst into the room and found the body of a man in gray

monk's robes. Peering past him he saw a smoking cauldron set near the window, spewing its dark poisonous night out into the sky. Next to the cauldron was the body of a woman. By the twisting of his stomach he knew without seeing her face that it was his mother. It was her spell, and by the looks of it she had given her life for it.

He scowled and twisted his head, looking for a sign of the Sheriff. Suddenly his enemy seemed to materialize out of the shadows. He swung a wicked looking dagger and Robin barely thrust his arm upward in time to block it. The Sheriff kicked out and swept Robin's legs from under him. He landed hard enough to knock the wind out of him, but held onto the arrow. The man in black had something in his other arm that he was clutching to his chest.

Robin looked up, expecting him to attack again.

Instead the Sheriff bolted from the room.

With an oath Robin made it back to his feet and gave chase. He heard the Sheriff running down the stairs and followed, clattering down and leaping the last few. He made it to the great hall just in time to see his father and King Richard burst through the front door with glowing swords held high.

Something dark covered in fur seemed to leap off the Sheriff and charged at the two men, fangs bared. With a shout of surprise Philemon shoved Richard out of the way of the creature, twisted, and managed to thrust his blade through its neck. It let out an unearthly scream before turning to ash.

The Sheriff drew his own sword and attacked them with wild ferocity. Robin had never seen someone move a sword so fast. He hung back, waiting for an opportunity. It only took a moment, though, to realize that the Sheriff was besting them both.

He twisted and Robin finally got a good look at what he was holding—it was a child, the spawn of the Sheriff and Robin's mother. His skin crawled at the realization of the unholy thing. It also explained why the Sheriff was fighting even more fiercely than would be expected. He was protecting what was his.

There was a terrifyingly rapid flurry of blows, and Robin's father went down on his knees. Before the Sheriff could finish him, though, King Richard stepped in. Once again the Sheriff's resolve gave him the upper hand, and before long the king began backing away.

Robin moved to step in, hefting a sword in one hand and the arrow in the other. As he took the first steps, though, there was a clatter of boots coming from the direction of the kitchens.

"My love!" Marian screamed.

She threw a bow through the air. Robin dropped his sword with a clatter and grabbed it. He notched the black arrow, turned and fired.

The arrow sped straight and true and punched through both the Sheriff and his child. The man in black gave a hideous roar, then crashed to the floor. King Richard stepped in, lifted his sword and brought it down. The bodies disintegrated instantly, sending forth a foul stench and leaving a pile of ash on the floor.

The black arrow fell onto the pile along with something circular, made of metal. Robin blinked in shock as he recognized the iron torc, the mate to the one Marian wore.

There was no time for celebration, and Marian dashed toward the door. There were more enemies to kill. As she bolted through the entrance, she froze. Everywhere she could see, the surviving demon soldiers were collapsing. Once again the ground was a sea of the dead.

It had been the Sheriff's will that gave them life.

All around the crusaders continued to hack at the creatures, as if to make certain they wouldn't again rise.

She saw one of the nobles who had been trapped under the fealty oath. He had fallen to his knees and looked to be waking as if from a terrifying dream. More could be seen, some collapsing to the ground, others standing there weeping openly. Marian hoped they had no memory of what had occurred—what they had done—but she feared that was not the case.

They would live with the horror the rest of their lives.

What was left of Henry's army was rallying to Jerome. He spotted her and gave her a salute, then nodded toward the platform. There was a body there, and Marian surmised that Henry had met his fate—at the hands of whose blade she didn't know or much care.

Now that the spell had ended, the blackness began to dissipate. Dark haze gave way to blue sky and normal white clouds. The pervading fear gave way, though for the moment it was replaced by a sort of numbness.

It was over. Silence began to settle over the battlefield. Slowly the tension began to leave her body. They had worked so hard and long for this, that it was hard to believe that they had truly won.

The girl fey with the pink flowers approached Marian. All around them the creatures who had survived were picking up those who were injured or dead. Tears came to Marian's eyes.

"Will you be able to rebuild your numbers?" she asked.

The girl shook her head. "Every generation, fewer have been born, and none of late," she said softly. "One day we will all be gone, I fear. But today we were happy to serve. You led us against the darkness, and we prevailed."

Her answer tugged at Marian's heart.

"Thank you," she said.

"Queen Marian, your home is in Sherwood," the girl said. "You may call upon any of us any time you have need." Then she bowed and turned to go. She hesitated and then turned back, her large eyes open wide. "I'm very glad you did not drown in the river, or get eaten by the monster," she said.

"So am I," Marian said with a smile.

With that the girl was off. The fey took their leave all at once, slipping away quickly and quietly. Even Marian had a hard time tracking their going. She did notice, though, that when none were left in sight, she felt a bit hollow for it.

* * *

Much was sad to see the fey go. He had been awed to watch them. Maybe he would see them again someday. But he knew there was a lot that had to be done, before such a day could come.

The thought made him blink, wondering what he was going to do next. He was no longer the miller's son, since there was no miller. Nor was he an outcast hiding in the forest. Maybe he'd become the *new* miller. The thought seemed strange to him, but didn't sit quite right. His father was the miller, not him.

He frowned and then put the thought aside. There would be time to think about it, and he had friends to help him figure out where they all went from here.

They set fire to the tapestries John had brought into the castle. As they burned Marian could hear the unearthly screaming, and it sent chills up her spine.

"We'll need Friar Tuck to bless this place, drive away all the darkness," she told Chastity.

"It might take more than just him," Chastity said with a shiver. "There's one thing we can do to help, though."

"What's that?"

"Tapestries we managed to save, when John moved in, are still safe."

Marian closed her eyes and gave a little sigh of relief. "Praise God for small miracles."

"That was no *small* miracle, princess," Chastity said.

"True."

"Have you had a chance to tell your husband the good news yet?"

"No," Marian admitted.

"Niece!" King Richard strode into the room.

"Excuse me," she said to Chastity before hurrying over to embrace her uncle. He looked down at her with unbridled affection.

"You've become a woman in such a short time," he said. Then the smile left his face, and he looked stern. "I also understand that you took Robin to husband."

"Oh, he told you," she said, blushing.

"He did," the king replied, and the smile reappeared. "I'm so glad you found love."

"Thank you, Uncle."

He nodded. "Now, come with me, we have much to do."

CHAPTER THIRTY-SEVEN

It was late that evening when everyone was finally gathered in the great hall. King Richard sat on the throne, and Robin couldn't be happier. Part of him still struggled with believing that it was real.

After he'd left their company, the King and his father had realized they could use the swords to heal the injuries sustained by the men. They chose those who would most benefit, and the combination of magic, sleep, and food had restored them to the point that they could travel far faster than anticipated.

Robin had needed three days to locate a small boat and slip across the channel unnoticed. Even then he had landed in rough terrain and made his way to Nottingham. By contrast Richard's forces had acquired a couple of large ships and sailed into the harbor, quickly overpowering the few soldiers who were stationed there. Since they hadn't expected an assault of such magnitude, most of the guard had been recalled by the Sheriff to kill the Hood and his sympathizers.

With a mood that was a combination of somber and celebratory, King Richard was speaking, vowing a return to the light and restoration for all that had been lost. Some of the lords were present, though many still suffered from the knowledge of what they had done—what had been taken from them.

Robin was half-listening, but mostly he stared at Marian, who stood next to the king. She had found a moment to change out of her tinker's disguise and into a simple dress of forest green. It suited her. Other than that she had been at the king's side since battle's end.

She should be, he mused. It was her place as his niece and heir. Still, he longed to have her by his side so he could touch her hand, feel her close. They had so many things they needed to say to each other.

"Robin Longstride, step forward," King Richard said.

Startled, Robin walked to the front and stood in front of the king, who looked him up and down. The expression on his face was difficult to read.

"Robin, you have been accused of a great many serious crimes including robbery, insurrection, and murder." His expression was stern, as if he was unhappy with what he was going to have to do.

Robin glanced uneasily at Marian.

"As if that wasn't enough, you had the unmitigated gall to marry my niece without the leave of your king. What exactly do you have to say for yourself?"

"I did what in my mind was right," Robin said.

"Did you indeed?" The corners of Richard's mouth twitched up.

"Aye, sire, and I'd do them all again."

"I'm glad to hear it." The king's expression softened, though there was still a serious aspect to it. "England needs more men with your courage. Take a knee."

Blinking, he knelt before the king. Richard pulled out his sword and tapped Robin first on one shoulder and then the other.

"I Richard, King of England, declare you Sir Robin, Lord of Locksley and heir to the lands and title of Longstride. You may rise, Lord Robin."

Robin stood. "I don't understand, sire."

King Richard smiled. "I have made you the acting Lord of

Locksley, and upon your father's death the lands of Locksley and Longstride will once more be united, under you. Now, I know you had no love for the previous Lord of Locksley, but try not to hate the name too much, since it's now yours."

Robin frowned as he wrestled with the notion. Then he gave a smirk.

"I will endeavor not to, sire."

"In addition I declare that you and Lady Marian of Locksley are hereafter the official guardians and protectors of Sherwood. You may consider that a wedding present," he added with a wink.

"Thank you, sire," Marian said with a twinkle in her eye as she stepped forward to join her husband.

The king picked up something from a table beside him and handed it to Robin. "You'll be needing this." It was the iron torc he had received in the heart of Sherwood.

"Sire, that belongs to you," he protested.

"It belongs to the man who is wed to the Lady of the Forest." He raised an eyebrow. "That is you, isn't it?"

"Yes, sire," Robin said, accepting the torc. Then Marian took it out of his hand and put it around his throat. For just a moment he thought he heard singing coming from the metal. Marian smiled at him, eyes glowing softly. Finished, she turned back to the king.

"It's my understanding that congratulations are in order for something else as well," the king said, and Robin glanced at Marian, wondering what he was talking about.

She blushed. "I'm sorry, I wanted to tell you myself."

He still didn't understand.

"You're going to be a father," Richard boomed. "And I'm going to be a great-uncle!"

"What?" Robin turned to Marian, who smiled at him.

She nodded. "Surprise."

Without warning he wrapped his arms around her and held her tight as he struggled to take it in. A moment passed, and he remembered where they were. He let go of her, and they both turned and bowed to the king before stepping to the side, where Robin's father was quick to embrace them both.

Richard spoke again. "Now, we have lost other nobles, including Lord Minter, Lord Staunton, and their families. We will need to find men of exceptional character, strength, and loyalty to take their place." Eyes flicked around the room as many wondered who the king was talking about.

Robin smiled. He had an idea.

"First, I call upon Much, the miller's son," King Richard said.

Blood draining from his face, Much hastened forward, his look of bewilderment making Robin grin twice as hard. The young man practically fell to his knees, and King Richard knighted him. When he arose the look of shock on his face was wonderful.

"I don't deserve this honor," Much finally managed to say.

"On the contrary, I can think of none who deserve it more," King Richard reassured him.

"Don't worry, Lord Much," Old Soldier said from close by. "I'll help you run things until you get your feet." Still wearing a look of shock, Much moved back to stand next to him.

"That might be a little difficult," King Richard said with barely concealed humor. "Given that you are going to be busy running your own lands."

"Sire?" Old Soldier asked with a puzzled frown.

"You heard me, you old scoundrel. Come forward."

Obeying his king, Old Soldier went to stand before him, the frown replaced by a look of anxiety. "It's not necessary, your Majesty," he said. "Really..."

King Richard laughed. "You have the gall to offer me advice without my asking? Only a lord would take such liberties. Are you sure I haven't knighted you already?"

Old Soldier flushed.

"Take a knee, old friend."

The man sank slowly down and Robin stood a little straighter, eager to hear what his name really was, after all these years. All around him many did the same as Richard spoke again.

"—and in light of the fact that you have forsaken all other names, I shall give you a new one," he said. "Rise, Lord Stalwart."

Robin let out a little grunt of disappointment. Hearing it, Philemon clapped him on the back.

"Don't worry. I don't know it either," he said with uncommon warmth in his voice. "Then again I'm learning that it's not who a man started out as, but who he ended up that matters."

"Stalwart is a good name for him," Robin said.

"I'll bet you ten gold coins he refuses to let anyone call him that."

Robin snorted. "I don't have ten coins to bet."

"Sure you do, Lord Locksley." Philemon laughed softly, and Robin winced.

"That's going to take some getting used to."

"A lot of things are," Philemon said, glancing at Marian. This time Robin flushed. He didn't even know how to be a proper husband, and now he was going to be a father.

A father… As if reading his mind Marian leaned over.

"Don't worry, you'll figure it out," she whispered. "You always do."

"Thomas!" King Richard boomed.

Robin looked around. One of the men from the forest stepped forward hesitantly to face his king.

"I understand that you are responsible for creating that new trebuchet," the king said.

Thomas nodded. "It was Lady Marian's design, and I did what I could. I'm sorry, your majesty, that I was only able to get one stone out of it. It needs a lot more work on my part."

"And it deserves it. We have need of a weapon such as that. I'm putting you in charge of perfecting the design and producing more, both for use here at home and abroad. You will have whatever men and tools you need to accomplish this."

Thomas bowed low. "Thank you," he breathed. He then turned and hurried back into the crowd.

It was one of the strangest nights of his life, Robin mused.

Outside of the castle, the dead lay all around. Friar Tuck had given last rights to many of them, prayed over those who were already gone, then joined the group in the great hall. A young boy from the camp was with him. Chastity was there, as well, and a furor arose when the stolen children were reunited with what was left of their families. It quickly became subdued, though, when it became apparent how many had not survived.

Robin felt restless. Life at court had never been something for which he cared, and in light of everything that had happened, he was more eager than usual to retire for the evening. He kept glancing at Marian, noticing that she was stealing glances at him, too. They were thinking the same thing, yet they couldn't take their leave until the king allowed it.

Servants filed in and a makeshift feast was set up as even more people arrived, noble and peasant alike. They ate what food was there and relished the victory of being alive. The relief that filled the room was palpable.

Robin, however, worried about the future. There was much to do, and the king was still needed in Jerusalem. Now that he understood the gravity of the battle being waged for the soul of the world, he understood the need to go. When Richard left again, though, Robin knew it would fall to him and Marian to keep England safe. It was a daunting task.

"Something wrong, son?" his father asked him.

Robin forced a smile. "Just contemplating my... responsibilities."

"At the moment, your most pressing one is to your bride," Philemon said. "No one here would begrudge you departing for the evening." For once, Robin found himself agreeing with the older man. He rose, approached King Richard, and bowed.

"Milord, may I have your leave to retire?"

King Richard inclined his head. "Lord Robin, I will see you again in a fortnight, when we will discuss the future in depth." His eyes flicked to Marian. "Until then, leave this table with my blessing. Both of you."

Marian blushed but was quick to stand. She moved to Robin. Together they exited the great hall and then stood for a moment outside. Robin's eyes flicked toward the staircase.

"What's wrong?" Marian asked.

Robin turned to her. "Your home has always been here. My home has burned down. I've been named Lord of Locksley, so I will need to move to that castle at some point."

Marian shuddered. "From what Chastity has said, you're going to want Friar Tuck to bless it before you do."

"He's going to be busy blessing this place," Robin muttered. The darkness still lingered in the corners of the castle. He couldn't help but wonder if it would ever truly be gone, after all that had happened here.

"Robin," Marian said, reaching out to take his hand. "Let's go home."

"I don't know where that is," he confessed.

"Sherwood," she said with a smile. "Always."

ACKNOWLEDGMENTS

Thank you to my husband, Scott, you are my hero and you always will be. Thank you to James for being part of this crazy journey with me, and for just smiling when I make all the jokes about writing Robin Hood with a man named Tuck. Thank you to Steve Saffel for his diligence and care as an editor. Thank you to my agent, Howard Morhaim, for all that he does. Lastly, thank you to all our readers who have become our Merry Men.

—DV

Thank you to my co-writer Debbie and the super editor Steve. Y'all rock.

The Titan crew for making our words a real book.

Thank you readers for your curiosity and courage. You make the magick.

—JRT

ABOUT THE AUTHORS

Debbie Viguié is the *New York Times* bestselling author of more than four dozen novels including the *Wicked* series co-authored with Nancy Holder. In addition to her epic dark fantasy work Debbie also writes thrillers including *The Psalm 23 Mysteries,* the *Kiss* trilogy, and the *Witch Hunt* trilogy. Debbie plays Claire on the audio drama, *Doctor Geek's Laboratory.* When she isn't busy writing or acting Debbie enjoys spending time with her husband, Scott, visiting theme parks. They live in Florida with their cat, Schrödinger.

James R. Tuck lives and writes in Atlanta. He loves the blues and used to throw people out of bars for money.

CHAOS QUEEN: DUSKFALL

Stuck with arrows and close to death, a man is pulled from the icy waters of the Gulf of Nahl. Winter, a seemingly quiet young fisherman's daughter, harbors a secret addiction that threatens to destroy her. A young priestess, Cinzia, must face a long journey home to protect her church from rebellion. A rebellion sparked by her sister.

Three characters on different paths will be brought together by fate on one thrilling and perilous adventure.

"*Duskfall* is a delicious mix of Jason Bourne, dark fantasy, and horror. Husberg has written the kind of debut that has me thrilled for the future of Fantasy." Steve Diamond from Elitist Book Reviews, and author of *Residue*

"A fascinating mystery that slowly unfolds, cultures and religions in conflict. Enjoy." Melinda Snodgrass, author of *The Edge of Ruin*